34 x 1/06 4/06
36 x 8/09   4/10

Last Copy

SWEETWATER FEVER

Books by Robert H. Adleman

The Devil's Brigade
(with Col. George Walton)

Rome Fell Today
(with Col. George Walton)

The Champagne Campaign
(with Col. George Walton)

The Bloody Benders

Baker

Annie Dean

The Black Box

What's Really Involved in Writing and
Selling Your Book

Alias Big Cherry

SWEETWATER FEVER

Robert H. Adleman

MᴄGʀᴀᴡ-Hɪʟʟ Bᴏᴏᴋ Cᴏᴍᴘᴀɴʏ
New York • St. Louis • San Francisco
Toronto • Hamburg • Mexico

1 2 3 4 5 6 7 8 9 D O C D O C 8 7 6 5 4

ISBN 0-07-000354-8

LIBRARY OF CONGRESS CATALOGING IN PUBLICATION DATA
Adleman, Robert H., 1919–
Sweetwater fever.
1. Oregon—History—To 1859—Fiction.   I. Title.
PS3551.D57S9 1984   813'.54   83-22263
ISBN 0-07-000354-8

For George Edelman

The primary characters in this book are fictional, but most of the others, as well as a majority of the scenes appearing within these pages, are based upon actual people, places and events. Jacksonville, Oregon, is real. It began as a gold mining camp in 1852 and endures today as a small place of quiet beauty.

Prologue

WHENEVER THE HUNGER for the past becomes too great to withstand, I return to a very small town in Oregon named Jacksonville. I go there to sit again in the kitchen of Mrs. Phoebe Hume who—I swear it—occasionally calls me "young man" as she bakes another of those golden-crusted blackberry pies for me and watches while I eat every mouthful and drink all of the beaker of cold milk that has forever been that treat's indivisible companion.

I eat this pie and drink this milk because subsequent gas, sour stomach, and flatulence are reasonable exchanges for a visit with Phoebe Hume and once again, as we talk, to become young with her son, Sam, and with Tony Johnstone and Chung Lin.

Those days are yellowing at the edges for me and too covered with dust for comfortable recollection, but they've always remained fresh for her. "Why don't you do it, Collie?" she once urged. "Why don't you write down what it was like?"

I shrugged but she persisted, "Write down the story. It's your duty, Collis Gibbs," really addressing her own wistfulness for those days. "You promised Anthony and Chung Lin, and you're the one that knows everything they did. Every one of them. They told you things they didn't tell to themselves."

"That's not so," I protested. "Nobody was more close-mouthed than your Sam, unless maybe it was Tony. As for Chung Lin, he couldn't ever have told the truth about anything unless he thought you were convinced he was lying."

"Even when they didn't tell you, they told you because you were watching them. You never bother to hear what people say, anyway. You're always too busy listening to how they say it."

I laughed. "How about you? What ever gets past you, Mrs. Hume?"

"Thank the Lord I wasn't there when most of the devilment was going on."

"But you knew about it."

"I didn't know the half of it, nor do I want to. The story's not for my benefit, Collis Gibbs."

She meant the others. She meant—oh, what the hell difference does it make whom she meant? In the same motion as I turned from her to stare out the window, the dust was blown off the memories and the town became once again as brawling, lusty, totally alive and vital as it was in—dear God, was it really so far past as 1853 that Sam and I were eighteen?

Let's see, now, Chung Lin was a whole year younger, but there had always been an old man in the head of that heathen.

And Tony Johnstone hadn't burnt out as yet, although at nineteen he was already cynical, methodical, and English enough to warrant our belief that his urine was mostly iced water.

Phoebe called me back for a moment. "Boy, what are you staring like that for?"

"I'm thinking, Mrs. Hume."

"That's what you did best."

"Thinking?"

"Staring off into space. Collis Gibbs, you come back to see me not more than once every other year, and then you sit here spending most of your time moping out that window."

She's right. I've stopped following the train of her brisk patter. This time I've been watching the tranquil street being repeopled with the familiar mob of loafers, gamblers, and whores that filled it on the day when the three of us—her son, Tony, and I—walked among them while they tried to decide where to hang the Indian boy named Billy Tell.

1

NORMALLY, the three blocks of our main thoroughfare, California Street, were knotted by groups of men passing and repassing each other, talking, swearing, bawling out price offers to an occasional covey of whores and whooping with laughter as if the doxies sailing by in disdain were the funniest things they'd ever seen. Just about every other manjack of them had bedded down the girls yesterday, that morning, the night before or whenever—so there weren't many mysteries remaining between the prostitutes and the men of the town. The business sense of most of the madams dictated that no whore ever recognized one of her customers on the street, so tempting the girls to break that rule was a morning's sport.

On this special morning in May it was as if somebody had picked up the north corner of California Street and shook all the inhabitants down into the other end. Even the thimble riggers—they were the French monte dealers and string-game tricksters—had quit their stands in order to offer their say about where to hang Billy Tell.

Odd. It took several moments for that teeming street to come into focus for me, but the voices of the corner gamblers came back immediately. Even now I hear the urging cries: "Six ounces, gentlemen, that no one can tell where the little joker is!" or, "Bet on the jack! The jack's the winning card. Three ounces no man can turn up the jack!"

Today, the gamblers had found a more interesting game. Prudence kept them from offering their opinions too loudly, because they knew damned right well that the crowd pushing and shoving around the boy marked as the day's main entertainment would have hung them as cheerfully as they would any Indian.

The rope was already around the boy's neck, and every so often someone would yank it in another direction, depending on where they wanted the grisly event to take place. Even the foreigners in the crowd (God knows we had enough Kanakas, Chileans, Mexicans, those physically filthy Australians and the like among us) weren't shy about wanting to kill this boy in order to make the West safe for their families, if they ever got around to having any.

"What's it all about?" I asked a one-legged old sourdough who'd been hopping around in the mob, trying to keep his balance and looking for all the world like a bottle bobbing in the sea.

"It's a goddamn spy!" he yelled into my face, whiskey breath hitting me full square. "The sneaky son of a bitch comes wandering in lookin over everything we got, and somebody knowed him from afore as a thievin rapin son of a bitch, and we catched him just afore he could get back to fetch the rest of his goddamn Siwashes after us tonight!"

I backed off, wanting as much to get away from the hate in his face as to be out of the vicinity of his breath. Then, pushing through the mob that was so intent on its purpose that not one took his eyes off the captive long enough to curse or even notice me, I elbowed my way in the search for my friends.

I was sure they'd be there, although ordinarily neither Tony nor Sam would have been drawn to this kind of unpleasantness. Sam was a loner under any circumstances, and as for Tony, well, that snotty Englishman couldn't have cared less if the entire citizenry of Jacksonville had marched stark naked, two by two, over to Sterling Creek and jumped in.

But not today. Every single soul in the place was out and milling around. We had been under so much fear of the Indians that anything to do with them had set the community's nerves to twanging like a Jew's harp. The loafers and drunks were the ones shoving around in California Street, but the merchants and the family men were silently supporting them from the planked sidewalks—their women looking out from inside the stores and most of their kids perched up on the roofs of the one-story buildings that flanked our street.

I even caught a glimpse of Chung Lin standing on one of the corners about one hundred feet away, and that was a real testament. Our Chinese ordinarily kept as far away as possible from whatever was going on in the town because there wasn't a one of them that hadn't learned that whenever any of the farmers or miners were drunk enough to be up and doing, then the nearest slant-eye was due to catch hell one way or another.

But there was Chung Lin, hands clasped behind his back in a way that meant he was interested but wasn't about to come a step nearer. We'd been friends for too long for me not to be able to understand him occasionally. Even at this distance I could see by the way he stood that he was playing a mind game figuring out which way the hanging would go. If I had been alongside of him, he would have laid me the odds against whatever my own choice might have been.

"Do you see him?" a voice said in my ear. No yell this time, just the unruffled tones that are generally produced by centuries of being left unbothered by even the few people in the English countryside with enough importance to come visiting your family. I turned, my face almost brushing Tony Johnstone's sandy-haired head.

"Tommy?" I asked. "He's way back over there."

"You sod," he answered, meaning he referred to Sam and wasn't concerned about Chung Lin, whom Sam Hume had nicknamed "Tommy" at their first meeting.

The noise of the cursing and laughing and threats and some snatches of a patriotic appeal to get on with the hanging was blending into a din that made further conversation between us almost impossible. So we kept quiet and waited and watched and every so often were jostled together or apart by the crowd swirling forward to get closer to the tight circle of the Indian boy and his proud captors.

Sam spotted us long before we saw him towering head and shoulders above the people he was ploughing through as he headed for us.

Let me tell you something right here and now about Sam Hume. There were few women in our town, even the righteous biddies who made a point of letting you know they'd faint at the thought of flashing an ankle, that didn't consider him the handsomest damned thing ever, and this began when he was not much more than a boy. I'd see it in their faces, read it in their eyes when he'd walk by or come into a room, even the church. Once, I swear it, I watched a film of perspiration begin to glisten on the brow of the leading singer in our choir, Mrs. Cook, every time she glanced in our direction.

Sam Hume was rarely stupid, so he came early to know about the way his big body and his face that looked as though it were carved out of granite affected the females, but it never really mattered one way or another to him. I can't ever recall seeing him preen or prink or doubt about what kind of clothes he was wearing.

Now that I think of it, I guess he didn't have to.

He generally displayed little enough emotion, but he looked grimmer than ever on the day of Billy Tell's hanging. His first words after he reached us showed that he had the same feelings as we did about the sorry thing that was going on. "Like a bunch of coyotes around a stray calf," was all he said, but his face made it clear that he'd be willing to try and stop it if given half the chance.

Just then the voice of the crowd began to take on a businesslike tone, rising and falling in response to the single voice that seemed to be coming from up front. At first we couldn't make out the message, but its meaning was clear because it was a screed preaching hate, and every time it paused there was an answering rumble of agreement from the rest of the flock.

Finally, we understood why the words of this cursed choir leader were so hard to decipher; they were loaded with the accent of some other language, and it took almost another minute to identify it as French. Both Sam and Tony nodded an amen when I exploded, "That son of a bitch! It's Boudreau!"

By now he was damned near screaming that the Indian boy be hung without any more delay. The words came spurting and tumbling out of him, his spleen complicating his English with even more effect than usual. But there was never an instant's cloud around what he wanted: *Hang the Indian varmint now and without any more palaver!*

"Old Henri's really gonna get it done, isn't he?" said Sam.

Tony asked, "How long do you think, Sam?"

"Not more'n fifteen minutes. Maybe even five and they'll be ready to play out the rope."

"Would this be the time to remind them that Henri used to have an Indian wife?"

"Wouldn't do no good," said Sam. "In the mood they're in they'd want to do it even more just to show that they're with him. Most of them know it in their minds anyway, and it's their way of telling him they want to kill that Indian just as bad as he does."

"Sam, we've got to do something!" It was Elva calling out as she pushed her way toward us, the horror in her voice adding a shrillness that cut through every noise in the crowd except the sound of her father, Henri Boudreau.

She ran the remaining few steps to where we stood but addressed herself only to Sam. "Please, please do something. Pa doesn't know what he's saying! You know he doesn't mean it! Please, Sam." Then, turning to Tony and me, she added, "If he does this thing. . ." leaving unvoiced whatever it was that this murder would add to the awful weight that had never left Henri ever since it had been piled on him last year back in Fort Laramie. Anyone who looked in Boudreau's eyes saw the burden.

Elva's hysteria was growing in pace with the crowd's but, like a fool, all that reached me at that moment was being hurt because she had instinctively turned first to Sam, just as she always had from the day she and her father had come here seven months ago.

"I know what we'll do," I said.

There was no doubt in any of the three as they looked at me, only hope. Sam might be the strongest among us, but even he never questioned any plan that I was serious about. All he or Tony and, every so often, Tommy, ever needed to get going was that I was certain something was going to work.

"There's no use trying to do anything here," I told them. "We couldn't make our voices heard, let alone cut down the pitch that Henri's worked them up into. So we need a diversion."

I said those words quietly and businesslike, but I was really enjoying the drama of the setting and their reactions. Sam's face, as always, impassive; Elva, looking at me in a way that was a prayer; while Tony, quickly catching a glimmer of where I was heading, began to nod with that quiet smile of his.

Their attention deepened my grasp on the plan I was putting together. I tend to become cold-headed in an emergency, which is one of the few things that puzzles Tony. He feels the trait doesn't tie in to the rest of me.

"You know that pile of garbage behind Lohmeyer's saloon?" That was rhetorical, of course, because every building along California Street had trash heaped somewhere out back. "Sam, you and Tony slip around and set it on fire. Everybody'll think Lohmeyer's is burning down. Then I'll yell out, 'Get the fire before it spreads,' and while they're making up their minds which way to scatter, the Indian boy can run off."

"It'll work," said Sam without any hesitation, "only let me do the yelling out here. Might be I can do somethin to help the kid get away better."

It took a fraction of a second for me to shake my way through another stab of jealousy before I realized Sam wasn't just showing off for Elva. He had volunteered for the point man's job because if the crowd's attention ever wavered, anyone seen tampering with their captive was in for some real trouble. If that happened, he was the one of us best equipped to handle it.

As I say, all of this took but a flash to get through my head, which is what it had to be; we were running out of the time to do anything but let the crowd take the course on which it was set.

Tony saw it, too. Steering me by the elbow he said, "Let's go, Collis."

No one, not even the kids roosting up on the roof, noticed us running off behind the row of stores, and no sooner had we gotten to Lohmeyer's than Tony had a lucifer out and a fire going. We fanned it until we had a strong flame, and then we dumped some of the garbage lying in heaps around us into it. This gave us a good smolder, so then I ran over and opened the back door of the saloon and the smoke began drifting through the place, toward the front door, which was naturally open.

Tony helped me fan smoke into the saloon, and although we couldn't hear Sam yell out, the new tone in the crowd's rumble told us they had noticed that Lohmeyer's was on fire. I suppose the fact that Lohmeyer had the cheapest whiskey prices in town added a note of anxiety to the noise. Of course, I may be only fooling myself about remembering this added dimension.

It worked without a hitch. Later, Elva told us, "They all turned to watch the smoke coming out, and Sam just stepped up natural to the boy and talked into his ear. I was lookin close and there wasn't one person in the crowd that seen what he did.

"Then, when the crowd pushed out towards Lohmeyer's place, the Indian boy, who all this time had been standin there like he didn't understand nor care about what was goin on, he took off as fast as the wind, no one missin him until after he had streaked out California Street and was headin towards the north hills and trees, and by then it was too late for even a man on a horse who knows how to get through manzanita bushes to ketch up.

"That Sam! When he stepped up to the boy he was as steady as if he was just asking for a drink of water. Do you know, Collie, if anyone had seen him do that, they'd a made a madrone blossom out of him instead of Billy Tell?"

Then she hurried away to overtake her father who was walking away alone, now that the crowd was dispersing to get back to whatever they had been doing before Richard Mulligan, who had first collared the boy, started the thing that he was probably a spy. She didn't say anything more to us, but we understood she wanted to be with Henri before he went to pieces.

That left Sam, Tony, and me standing there, too excited by what we had pulled off, not to want to go on about it to each other, but knowing it would have been curtains to let anyone overhear us discussing it. So, after a while, I suggested that we go up to the cabin on Marguey's High, and they didn't find it necessary to even nod agreement before they turned and we all began heading in the same direction that the Indian had gone.

2

ALTHOUGH she doesn't figure overmuch in the story of how and why Tony Johnstone, Chung Lin, Sam, and myself became men, I should dwell a bit upon Mrs. Phoebe Hume, who was the source for Sam's hard-headedness. In those days we never saw much sentiment in her, except where her husband, Edward, was concerned, but she was the one who insisted on whatever civility there was in our lives. Even if we four had not been knit together by circumstance, Mrs. Hume would have been enough reason for the brotherhood among us.

Once, during a trip back to Jacksonville—I think for her ninetieth birthday—I heard for the first time of how the Humes came to Oregon. In order to make some point or another, she had mentioned her dead husband's name and then, uncharacteristically, fell silent. I waited, realizing that an important part of her life was being reeled off within her. After a bit, she added, "He was a good man. Mr. Hume (even in bed that tall, glowering man would not have encouraged familiarity) may have missed reaping some of this world's goods, but, boy, you just name me one miner that kept enough money to leave his family well off. Not a one of them! They found the nuggets and the dust they came here to search for, but it all ended up in somebody else's britches. Name me just one that left anything to pass on!"

Since I was then once again a boy (of seventy-two), I obediently gave the argument expected of me: "Well, there was Mr. Witham . . ."

"Hah, Witham! When did he ever pick up a shovel or a rocking pan?"

"They say he did before he became a banker."

"Who says? Only his daughter when she's talking to the historical society, that's who. Jabez Witham did his best mining when he dug into the pockets of men like Mr. Hume." She sniffed and was silent again, remembering the days with her husband, dead these many years but, as always where he was concerned, only briefly gone.

After a lond pause she stared at me full in the face. "Ah, Collis," she said in a way that made it clear that it wasn't me she was seeing but was looking to the far side of that chasm whose floor was littered with the spent years. I sat back because this was what I had come hoping to hear. The early years. The years that never existed for us in our youth because that had been a time when we never questioned that our parents had been born old and the future was just another irrelevant element in each day of the present.

"Gracious," she said, now seeing that far side in very sharp focus, "gold had put the fever in just about everybody's head. There wasn't a soul back East who didn't dream of becoming rich as Croesus after reading about the way they were scooping gold nuggets up off the streets in California.

"That's where we started for, you know. We had no idea of coming to Oregon. It was 1852. March—no, it was February. February in 1852 we left home for California and which is how we kept headed until May when we reached old Fort Hall in Idaho. That's where you can fork off for Oregon, which was the furtherest place from our minds until we heard the stories about those enormous gold strikes being made in the Rogue Valley.

"I remember the names of the first lucky men. It was Mr. Cluggage and Mr. Poole who the Shasta newspaper said were averaging seventy ounces of gold a day right here in Jacksonville. Right then and there Mr. Hume decided it was going to be Oregon for us because it was plain that Oregon was bound to be less crowded and was probably even richer than where we had been heading until then. So that was the branch of the road we took, with half of our wagon train choosing to go with us because they reasoned it out just like Mr. Hume.

"Those days are still so clear that they just come tumbling in on me. I swear, I can't remember where I laid my thimble down this morning, but I never forget a single day of that trip.

"Anyway, we came from upstate Ohio, you know. A little town named Dicksville that no one ever heard of, and I doubt if it's even still there. Mr. Hume, he was the son of our preacher, and my folks were farmers so we started farming too after we were married, but it never seemed to work out for us as well as it had for my folks. Not that Mr. Hume wasn't a good farmer! He was alongside the best of them, but it just seemed that he was like a magnet to draw every bit of bad luck that ever hit our county. If the hailstones fell, it was mostly on our crops. When summer got hot enough to begin drying up the wells, ours was always the first to go. Things like that were always happening no matter how hard my husband tried.

"Mother and Father weren't too understanding about it, either. They had never wanted me to marry Mr. Hume in the first place. I mean, they sent me to school to be a teacher, and no sooner than I had my certificate—I was seventeen then—I met Mr. Hume and that was that, as much as Father tried to reason with me. I knew as soon as I came back from school and saw how that preacher's gangly son had turned into a big, handsome man; he was the one I was going to marry, no matter what. He felt the same way, although he was never the kind to talk about it overmuch.

"Anyway, after we married there wasn't one year out of three that the crops were enough to support us. I had to go to teaching, and that was something else my folks held against my husband.

"So when we heard how easy it was to get rich out West, we decided that's where we would go. I can still remember what Mr. Greeley wrote in the copy of his newspaper that my husband brought home for me to read. It said (and here Phoebe Hume's voice took on a sing-song quality, making it clear that the words had been memorized as a litany): *It is a golden chain by which Hope is drawing her thousands of disciples to the new El Dorado, where fortune lies abroad upon the surface of the earth as plentiful as the mud in our streets. The only machinery necessary in the new gold mines of California is a stout pair of arms, a shovel, and a tin pan.*"

What a preposterous horse's ass that Horace Greeley had been! But if I had made the mistake of asking her if she had ever regretted their blind banking on those pompous phrases, she would undoubtedly have answered, "Why, of course not! Mr. Hume found the gold, didn't he?"

Understand now, I'm not faulting the Humes for their unquestioning reliance upon the advice of that little word-monger. He was simply echoing what every journal of that time solemnly proclaimed on an almost daily basis: Wealth beyond count was available to every emigrant to the West, and the only forseeable problem was that this easy gold's weight was so great that only the stoutest backs could carry enough to make a man a millionaire. Need I add that the price of mules probably escalated sharply during this period?

"With the money they loaned us," she continued, "we went by rail to Saint Louis, where we bought passage on the river steamer *Empire State*, and that took us to Saint Joseph, which was one of the chief jumping-off places for the Gold Rush.

"We stayed for two weeks while we bought all the supplies for the journey. We bought mules and oxen and a wagon which wasn't one of those big prairie schooners you see in the pictures, just a good high-axled farm wagon that could ford streams without foundering. And, of course, the hardware like guns and nails and everything else they told us we would need. But not one thing extra. Mr. Hume was too smart a man to load us down with the fripperies that most people thought they had to have.

"One family I knew of actually brought along a harp so they'd have music around the campfires. I'll bet that was one of the first things they got rid of as soon as they started getting out and pushing their wagon over the Rocky Mountains. There were others who carried with them every single stick of family furniture plus all the heirlooms that had come down to them from their folks. Some even added to their load with fancy gold-mining dredges and extra-big shovels and all the other junk the profiteering buzzards along the way had convinced them to buy.

"All of it had to go! There was no way to make that trip carrying excess baggage. As soon as the trail got hard, at almost every bend along the road you'd see the leavings of all the mistakes the wagon trains before us had made. The countryside was littered with feather beds, cook stoves, chairs, tables, bedsteads, and I don't know what else.

"It was such a sin, because most things were in such good condition. I wanted to scavenge some pieces for ourselves, but Mr. Hume rightly pointed out that they shouldn't be seen as temptations but ought to be lessons on how to lighten our own load. So we passed them by, but I couldn't stop thinking about the grievings that the women before us must have had when it came time to part with the treasures that had probably been in their families for generations. Now they were all rotting among the lava rocks by the side of some trail with only the coyotes and rabbits to appreciate them."

She drew in a deep breath and was silent for a moment, freshly reexperiencing the emotional and physical hurts of all the women who had followed their husbands' dreams on that rocking, jarring trip across the country. Then she went on. "Most of the time after we were really out there on the prairies we used buffalo chips for fuel. Getting the fire going was generally the job of the boys in the family. They'd dig a shallow trench in the direction of the prevailing wind and heap the trough as full as they could of all the dung they collected. Yes, dung. It doesn't sound so pretty now, but those buffalo droppings were as much a help to us cooks as our sunbonnets were during the day.

"Chips burn with a very small flame that won't give much heat, but it's passable for cooking, so we learned to be grateful for it because wood turned out to be a mighty precious commodity on some of the legs of the trail. Sometimes we'd find a clump of driftwood along a stream bank and we'd carry it for miles next day, just to be sure we had a little warmth the next night.

"But it really wasn't near as grim as it sounds now. We had nice times, too. Maybe some of the best times I ever had. Whenever people get to telling how much of a struggle it was to get here, they're mostly trying to impress you with how strong they were. They're glossing over the feeling of how close you felt to the others in the train, how much you depended on them, and they on you, and the good feeling that came out of it that you remembered all of your life.

"Like whenever wood was a mite more plentiful than scarce, we'd have a campfire and sit around it and sing such songs as 'Fanny Gray' that was about the pain of a man whose wife had died, and all of us would get tears in our eyes no matter how many times we'd sung it. Sometimes we'd spend the whole night before bed singing hymns, and even those who didn't believe were comforted."

She was silent for a moment and then fell to busying herself cracking eggs. Her face said she was going back beyond old songs sung around the campfire or even a road marked by abandoned and splintered clothes chests and rusting iron skillets and the ivory keys of jettisoned spinets grinning up at the sun. She was remembering the graves beside the trail, too.

I was generally the best among the boys when it came to starting her off on her recollections of the trek west, but there wasn't anything I could do to shake the sadness that came over her then. So that was the end of our talk that day. The rest of the story came out in later visits and, piecing it together, the way she said it happened was this:

At that time, Fort Laramie in southeastern Wyoming was the trail's first way station where the emigrants paused to replenish their supplies and pick up the latest news of whatever lay ahead. When the Humes' train reached there in 1852, a redheaded French ex-trapper named Boudreau was in charge of its store, and he and his squaw wife and children made the party welcome, selling them their needs at a fair price, which, although they were still too green to appreciate it, was a departure from the usual practice of most trading-post managers.

He also did his best to keep away from them the Indians who hung around the post. Most of these redmen were enthusiastic beggars who weren't at all above asking for any of the emigrants' possessions that struck their fancy and turning sullen when their preposterous pleas were refused. Some of the few who didn't beg tried to ingratiate themselves with the travelers by offering small gifts and showing friendly interest in the various family groups. Later the travelers realized that these Indians had been much more interested in gauging the battle capacity of the train's menfolk and the number and quality of guns they carried.

After replenishing its stores, the wagon train again took to the trail. The morning following the first day's journey, two half-naked and unarmed Indians appeared, showing by signs that they were hungry. Acting on the advice of Mike Coffey, the wagon master hired for the trip, the savages were given provisions and sent off. As they rode away, Coffey squinted and said, "Them critters was here to spy on us. They wanted to see how ready we mought be to fight."

He was right. The attack began without warning in the late afternoon as they halted to make camp. Two arrows whizzed in out of the dusk, one of them lodging in the shoulder of the mother of the family settling next to the Humes.

However, due to Coffey's estimate, they were prepared for a fight. Taking positions while remaining silent, the defenders held their fire until they made out all the forms in the raiding party, almost twenty savages. Then Coffey sang out, "All right boys, leave 'em have it!" and each man fired whatever he had. Three raiders were killed. The others ran, screaming gibberish that Coffey described later as meaning, *Let us go! These Americans make bad medicine!*

This translation was probably Coffey's reminder of his value to his charges. Wagon masters' fees in those days were often set by the size of their reputations.

Brief as it was, the battle left weakness in its wake. The men were pleased by the answer to the secret fear they all shared of failing to protect their families from an enemy that had been painted back home as ferocious beyond belief, but, even so, the immediate aftermath left them with a trembling and depleting realization of how close they had come to having their lives and dreams destroyed.

As for the women, in the first moments between sighting the Indians and their subsequent rout, many of them had thoughts of rape, mutilation, and slavery. This was a forgivable reaction since these were staples of the Indian stories that almost every eastern magazine printed and of every whispered discussion they had held with their friends before starting out.

Their men had saved them from this fate, but it was too soon for gratitude. Now was the time for the tearful embrace of their beloved defenders. Recognition and praise would follow and, inevitably, after that the boredom with their men's stretching-out of the stories of their heroism.

It took until after supper had been cooked and eaten at the campfires for the euphoria to emerge fullblown. The men looked gravely at each other and began the recitation of their recollections and anecdotes. They solemnly agreed to everyone else's bravery, and even when three men claimed to have shot the same Indian, there was no dispute. If Ethan and Henry and Jacob all said they had been the marksman, then that was the case.

The women were content to cook and serve and regard their heroes with an approval approaching awe. Who would have ever dreamed that their own familiar failures and malcontents could have grown so tall within a single afternoon?

Mike Coffey, joining the moment's mood, distributed approving nods, occasional claps on the back, and kept to himself the knowledge that a physical letdown would soon be demanding payment for the day's excitement and that the band of savages was still out there waiting for the early hours to attack again. While dealing out his broadest smiles, he privately wondered how his cocky charges were going to accept his verdict that guard duty was going to keep most of them up for the rest of the night. He knew of too many trains where the paid captain or guide had been outvoted by the rest of the company who, after they took destiny into their own hands, learned to live with deprivation and, often, bitter tragedy. *There's nobody deafer'n a man who just won his first fight,* thought Coffey, resolving to leave the train and head back to Fort Laramie if his cautions were ignored.

But the appearance of Henri Boudreau at one of the campfires resolved his dilemma.

At first, the Frenchman's wild look sent some of the men grabbing for their rifles and pepperbox six shooters, but after he was recognized as the fort's storekeeper, he was made welcome. And since they were still so full of their victory that they saw him only as a new audience, they began to describe the afternoon's exploits all over again.

However, Phoebe Hume sensed something else in the man who was wolfing down the food offered him. "What brings you here, Mr. Boudreau?" she asked. "I mean, you're welcome, Lord knows, but is there some trouble?"

Putting down his pannikin as if it had suddenly become alien to him, he stared at Mike Coffey. "I have the trouble."

Not understanding that Coffey's somber silence was an answer in itself, she went on, "Can we help?"

"I don't know." Continuing to study Coffey, he added, "The Indians you all tell me about. They were from the fort?"

The wagon master answered, "I think so. I think I rekkanized one. A tall ugly breed with half an ear."

Boudreau nodded slowly in recognition. "Very bad. You could not have seen if it was the whole party?"

"If you mean was there any more of them, there's no way I could tell. It was just a bunch of them lookin for whatever we got with us. But we ain't so far from Laramie that they couldn't have rode out light, fixin on either goin back after they'd done with us or maybe to keep on to wherever they got a camp, maybe around South Pass."

When the Frenchman remained silent, Coffey continued, "They got somethin of your 'n, Boudreau?"

"My daughter Elva. She has been missing since they go, I think yesterday morning."

"What does your woman say?"

"She says they took the child."

Remembering that Boudreau's wife was a squaw, Phoebe Hume asked, "Wouldn't they respect her?"

The trader simply faced her in answer. She wondered if any of the others clustering around saw the tears in the man's eyes.

Coffey took over. "Henri, I don't know what to tell you 'cept I reckon they ain't too far away. I'm thinkin, in fact, that they're gonna be back at us again tonight. I don't know where they're nestin, so it'd be kind of green to go roustin out after them in the dark. The best we can do is to be ready and when they come get as many of 'em as possible. Maybe we can get all if we fight as good as we did this afternoon.

"Then," he continued after seeing the men of the train nod agreement in recognition of the need that they all remain on guard that night, "in the morning we can fan out after whatever brutes are left or wherever their camp is. Meaning no disrespect, Henri," indicating that he had not lost sight of the fact that the trader's wife was also an Indian.

When there was still no evidence of dissent, he concluded, "All right, then. Let's all head back to our wagons, get the womenfolk secure, and in the meantime I'll be working out the guard details. How about you, Henri, you'll take one of the watches?" He asked it gently because he was aware that the man had been riding two days without food or rest in the effort to catch up with them.

Phoebe Hume, ignoring that this wasn't women's business, added, "Mr. Boudreau, I know you'd rather take out again after those people, but Captain Coffey is right. You won't find anything riding around in the dark tonight, and tomorrow morning every one of our men will be proud to go with you." She looked to her husband, who had been standing by.

Scowling in answer, he walked over to the Frenchman and said in his low, grumbling tones, "The woman's talking sense. We'll either get them tonight when they come after us or we'll go out for them as soon as daybreak."

After those in the front row saw Coffey's grave wink of approval, the word spread back through the rest of the group, and there was no argument as they dispersed to begin their preparations for the night. Calling after them, Coffey warned, "We need every point around the camp covered. That mought mean some womenfolk as well as the men and the boys."

It wasn't until another half hour had passed that Sam Hume's absence was discovered. The elder Hume became aware of it only when his wife came over to where he sat cleaning his shotgun and said, softly, "Samuel's gone."

His judgment was harsh. "The boy ducked out?"

Panic showed through her flare of anger. "You've no right to say that! He's just not to be found! No one's seen him. Something's happened to the boy, Edward!" Her use of his forename told the man that only mortal conviction could bring his wife to speak so sharply to him.

She went on in quiet urgent tones. "I don't even know if he was here when Mr. Boudreau rode in. You must do something, Edward!"

They went together to every campfire, but even the boy's few friends had no suggestions as to where Sam might be. The younger brother of one of them offered, "I don't know, Miz Hume, maybe he got hit by one of the stray arrows in the fight this afternoon and didn't want to say nothin to nobody, and he went off by hisself. Sam's like that, ain't he?"

"He is not!" she said, but in the back of her mind the thought began to grow that her son *might* have acted in this manner. He was a loner, rarely sharing his fears or even his triumphs with others. The fear gained strength. *If Sam had been hurt in some way when the Indians attacked, maybe he was out there somewhere by himself!*

Growing conviction was becoming a wild certainty until her husband growled, "I saw him looking at me after the fight was over, and the only thing bothering him was that he didn't get into it." To the youngster, he added, "You danged little fool. You're guessing and talking to make yourself important."

The boy dodged as if Hume were going to hit him and ran back to his family's campfire. Hume turned once again to his wife, but she had gone, heading for their wagon.

Following and overtaking her, he said nothing until they reached their own campfire, the meat in the unattended pot scorched by now. "I'll cook up some more," she said dully, "but it'll be too late for the bread."

"Never mind." He took some jerky from one of the saddle pouches and began to chew on it, staring into the embers.

The two of them sat by the dying fire, waiting for Coffey to call him to guard duty, waiting for someone to come over and say that they had seen their son. But they weren't waiting for the son to arrive. They had already accepted that the time for that to happen had passed.

Wondering why they were here on this lonely trail, each searched for a way to tell the other in the morning that it was pointless to go on, that there was nothing in the gold fields worth what they had lost. The sounds of other campfires surrounded them but never reached into their own. It was as if they were isolated and already no longer a part of this train's community. The loneliness of each was shared only when Phoebe Hume reached out and took her husband's hand in hers.

They sat this way until Mike Coffey strode up. Seeing him, Edward Hume reached for his gun, mechanically preparing to take his place in the guard.

And then his loneliness was breached when he heard his wife scream, "Oh, Edward, Edward, he's got Sammy with him!"

"That's right, Miz Hume," said Coffey, grinning broadly. "Here's the scoundrel. But afore you give him what-for the way he deserves, better hear out what he's been up to."

As she ran to her son, arms outstretched, Henri Boudreau stepped out of the dark. His face held excitement and hope instead of the desperation that had been there before. "He found her. He tracked down where the Indians are with Elva."

Edward looked from face to face and then at his son. Finally understanding, he said, "Boy, you went off without telling us."

"You'd a stopped me, Pa. And I figured I could do it." Then, aware of the hysteria in his mother's tight embrace, he added, "Ah, Ma. I'm sorry. I figured they'd be close enough that I'd be back before anybody could a said somethin." He looked back to see if his father's disapproval had been softened by the smiles on the faces of Coffey and Boudreau.

Hume probably wanted to reach out to his son, perhaps tousle his hair, certainly not to put his arm around his shoulder but at least slap him on the back, but at this moment of pride and overwhelming relief, the best he managed was, "We'll see. Get on with tellin about it."

In reply, Sam might have said, *It wasn't that much,* like any other seventeen-year-old boy expecting praise but, instead, told the story as clearly and quickly as possible.

In later years, a cowhand observed, "Sam Hume tells you just once to do something. If you ought to know how to do it but just want him to sort of lead it past you at a halter walk, then you're out on your ass. He don't explain nothing twice."

"It all worked out in my head," Sam told them, "when Mr. Boudreau came up with the news about his daughter missing. I remembered that I'd been thinkin when I saw the Indians ride away, *they won't go far,* because I saw a couple of them stop to get the two that was wounded—"

"You saw that durin the fight?" Coffey interrupted.

"Yes sir. Right afterwards. I was watchin careful because I heard somewheres that Indians won't stop for one of theirs that gets wounded; they just let them stay behind."

That's right," said Coffey, "they just go unless they got a reason for needin more hands down the road." "Well, I didn't know. All I knew is that I was wishin we had an extra rifle intead of the axe, and then I got interested in seeing how they attack. I counted three kills—they're the ones still lyin out yonder—two of them dead right away and the other one that went a while later. And I saw two sure hits. I expected them to leave them there, but they didn't. They circled back and got them."

"You saw all that in the middle of a fight?"

"Yes sir."

"Mr. Hume," said the wagon leader, "your son's got a head tied on him stronger'n a good many soldiers I fit alongside. Most of the officers, too."

"Never mind that." Hume was ill at ease in the presence of praise, even though it was directed at his son. "Go on, Samuel."

"Well, Pa, once I saw them taking along their wounded, it seemed to me that they weren't going to go too far before they made camp for the night. And the best place that I seen since we been traveling from the fort is that little crick we passed about two miles back.

"Then, when Mr. Boudreau said they got his daughter, I figured that's why they gathered up the two that was shot. It came into my head that it might have something to do with his daughter . . ."

His report was broken into again, this time by the Frenchman. "Your son, he is right. Absolute! I wager the woundeds are needed for guards and for my Elva while the others go back to the post and let the news come to me, maybe through their women to my woman, that Elva can be ransomed. They do that. And by then they will be at the fort without blame. Son of a bitch!"

Sam waited a few seconds for other interruptions. Then he went on. "So while everybody was millin around after Mr. Boudreau told us about his daughter, I snuck out and went back to the crick to see if my guess was right. I'm sorry, Ma, that I didn't say nothin about it, but I figured I'd be back before long, and this way nobody would be telling me not to go buttin into other people's business."

His father, understanding that his son was really describing the distance that lay between them, said again, "Get on with your story."

"That's it, Pa. The girl is back there with them at the crick."

When it was clear that he was not going to add anything more to his account, Coffey slapped his gun and barked, "That's it! We talked enough! Right now we go back there and finish 'em up. It'd be loco to sit around waiting for them to move. They probably got a scout staked out in the hills over yonder, keepin count till we bed down for the night, so we got to make it look like we're doin what they expect. I'll go get the men in the other wagons ready and tell the women how to make it look like it's only the usual that's goin on. Mr. Hume and Henri, I'll want your help.

"As for you, boy, you done good. But that's enough for tonight. We need you and the other young 'uns to stay here with the women in case they outflank us someways."

After the three men left, Phoebe Hume said to her son, "I know you'd like to have gone with them, Samuel, but Captain Coffey is right. You've done us very proud."

"Pa didn't think so."

"That's just him. You know that by now. He's so pleased, he didn't know where to look."

It didn't seem that way to Sam, but he had learned on this trip that his father would always be a separate world, foreclosed to him.

Within a half hour after the men had ridden quietly away in the darkness, the few older boys remaining in camp squirmed off to their lookout positions. The women, wearing their men's clothing to mislead a watching spy, banked their campfires and pretended to make ready for bed although, of course, there was not the slightest possibility of sleep anywhere in the camp. They lay with their children in the wagons, alone in the nighttime sounds of the plains, lying wide-eyed, rigidly stretched out, waiting for their men to return.

Even when the first hoofbeats came from the distance a few hours later (although it seemed much longer to these wives and mothers), the immediate reaction was a scared certainty that it was a band of victorious Indians returning for them.

Their fears did not dissipate even when the first man, Captain Coffey, rode back into the camp. They searched his and the following faces for a sign of how the mission had gone, but the grim expression worn by all the men kept them silently concentrating on finding their own husbands and fathers in the posse.

Finally, as Coffey swung off his horse, he said, "We done it. We didn't lose nobody and we killed every one of them varmints. Boudreau over there," jerking his head at the Frenchman, who seemed reluctant to disturb the clasping arms of his daughter perched on his horse behind him, "he seen to it that they, every last one of them, was finised. When he ran out of gunpowder, he slit the throats of them that was left."

Later the men built a bonfire, and while all the small community gathered about it they began, at last, the story of their second battle. The third time that the part that Sam had played in the victory was mentioned, Elva ran over to where Sam sat with his mother and father, bent over, threw her arms around him, and kissed him. Sam Hume showed his first confusion of the day at this but, after all, he was only seventeen at the time.

Next morning the wagon train resumed its trek to the western coast. It wasn't until seven months later, when Boudreau and his daughter came to Jacksonville, that anyone heard about the fate of the rest of the trader's family.

The Indian who had been posted as a lookout after the first battle returned later to his campfire, where he found his dead brother warriors. He jumped back up on his horse and rode through the night to Fort Laramie, bringing the news of the carnage to his tribe. In revenge, those who had remained at the fort slaughtered Boudreau's wife and their other two children. The mutilated bodies were waiting for him in the living quarters at the rear of the trading post when he came back to it.

3

TO REACH MARGUEY'S HIGH, take the western road out of Jacksonville for perhaps a half a mile until you reach the fork bearing sharply off to the right. This will be Pair-O-Dice Road, named in honor of a drunken gambler who staggered this far before he shot himself.

Now follow the fork out to a stream where the road turns into a trail climbing and winding upward through a series of creekside clearings. The creek disappears underground halfway up to the High, but the trail continues on through fields of decomposed granite. Persist on the path, taking another sharp turn at the end of the granite croppings, and you eventually reach a hidden forest of pine and fir that might appear impenetrable but isn't so long as you continue always up toward the mountain's crown. Once there, you find yourself in the acre or so of velvety grassed mesa that's known as Marguey's High.

The first whites to find it were a man named John Marguey and his wife, Christina. She was ten years his senior but just as convinced as he that the handful of tents and shacks of a town about thirty miles away represented entirely too much civilization. They lived here for a year, glorying in the 360-degree view of the Rogue River Valley. As they wished, they saw the Siskiyou Mountains, a range of the Cascades, or the green glen through which they had ascended. From this vantage point, even the granite fields in the glen were simply brown elements on a cool green tapestry. They loved the High because they felt it was where they belonged. If an artist, painting this panorama, had placed them there for further balance on his canvas, a viewer might have agreed, "Yes, that's right. They fit."

The sun shines almost every day on Marguey's High. Even in the winter, the few snows that fall on the Rogue Valley began and drifted a thousand feet below the cabin of John and Christina, and they celebrated them with a delighted pointing out of each fresh pattern of beauty. When a rare storm blew in from the Oregon coast, severe enough to reach up to them, then their little home became a warm and cozy refuge away from a world that neither interested nor concerned them.

But in the winter of 1849, they froze to death. John had broken his leg in a fall from the great madrone tree that still stands at one end of the High and could not go out for the firewood they needed. Christina, too old to swing an axe for any length of time and not able to drag up enough of the windfall from the forest below, burned every stick of their handmade furniture for warmth on the afternoon before the night that the cold crept in and killed them.

An Indian found them a week later, not in each other's arms as the storybooks would have had it but lying peacefully side by side in the same rough bunk where they had taken so much delight in each other. He brought them down to the town, one at a time, and they continued their sleep on the hill that is now set aside as the Jacksonville cemetery.

After that, neither the Indians who used to go to Marguey's High in order to stir up the power in their loins before battle nor the white settlers who generally had enough problems to keep them busy on the valley floor ever came there again, thus leaving the place and its abandoned cabin solely to Sam Hume, Tony, Chung Lin, and myself.

Tony and I had found it one day while out on a trip to gather herbs—which was our excuse to our elders for ducking work on a nice summer day. We'd heard the stories about the spirits of John and Christina refusing to leave the place but, of course, that made it an even better bunkhouse for us away from the town. We assured each other as we patched it into weatherproof shape that it was going to be a perfect place to bring young women—if we ever found any amorous or stupid enough to agree to the long hike to the pine bough cots we had built into it. Naturally, Chung Lin never mentioned that he shared that ambition, but since we suspected that he probably had something along those lines tucked away in his head, we didn't feel too guilty about making him pitch in with the repairs.

In short, it was absolutely logical to head for the cabin in order to celebrate our rescue of Billy Tell. Chung Lin wasn't with us because Tony was still angry at our Chinese friend's latest misuse of his trust in some minor affair or another, so when I suggested to him that we bring Chung Lin along, he just stared at me with that frozen look that comes over him when he's snorting inside. That disappointed me because I thought our triumph was the right time for the two of them to make up. I should have known better. It always takes Tony an ungodly long time to work his way through an anger.

He was still nursing the grudge as we turned off the creek path and began threading our way through the granite fields. Sam was well out in front of us on the trail and, being Sam, he was aware that Tony hadn't simmered down as yet, but he said nothing beyond "watch it" whenever he thought he saw a rattlesnake slithering away ahead of us. Ordinarily, rattlers don't care overmuch about spending too much time in granitic soil, but when it gets warm enough they'll go anywhere in search of water. In August, it wasn't uncommon to find them nesting under the houses in town.

I felt badly that Tony's temper was keeping him from enjoying this marvelous day, so I tempted him into one of those conversations that I knew he'd like in spite of himself. "Tony," I said, "I wonder how much of our lives we waste in sleeping?"

He shrugged, but although that pinched look was still on his face, I could see that the idea interested him. Finally, he asked, "Would you say eight hours a night?"

"That would be normal, I guess"

Without breaking stride, he began the figuring that he enjoyed just about as much as anything else. And, while doing it, he eased out of the burn that was spoiling the day for all of us. "Let me see. Eight hours a day—that's fifty-six hours a week. Three hundred sixty-five days in a year . . ."

"Sometimes there's 366. Every seventh year, I think."

"Bugger off. It's every four. Now, dammit, Collis, let me think. Do it by weeks: fifty-two weeks a year times fifty-six hours would be 2,912. Right?"

"Of course it is," I said.

"Now a man lives to be seventy, doesn't he?"

"Most do. Sam won't. I understand that people racing up a hill like he's doing never get past thirty."

"I heard that, Collie," Sam called back. "Next time we come up, I'll carry you if that's what you want."

"That's what I want," I agreed. "How about doing it the rest of the way?"

"How about kissing my ass the rest of the way?" was Sam's last statement for the balance of the trip.

I had hooked Tony. He went on as if he hadn't heard us say a thing, "An average seventy-year-old man will have spent 8,645 days sleeping. That's almost twenty-four years. Of course, in your case, that amount should be doubled. By the time you're seventy, you'll have spent sixty-nine years sleeping"

"Great arithmetic," I said. "Your figures are dead wrong."

"You ass! Show me where."

"I couldn't be bothered," I answered. "Right now I'm figuring out how much time the average man spends sitting in the average outhouse."

As far as I've been able to conclude over the years, Tony is absolutely without a trace of the lyric in his spirit, but he once described to me his feelings about Marguey's High. Looking at the breathcatching view of mountains and forests on all sides, he said, "I think of the beautiful, orderly green fields of England and I know being here has been the luckiest trade of my life."

That's the kind of a day this was. Sunlight was flooding the small plain, but a gentle breeze kept the heat away and the occasional clouds floating through the sky could have inspired any man, even one as prosaic as Tony, to try to get it all down on a canvas or a piece of paper. It all had such a special kind of majesty that it became pointless to consider crowing over our rescue of the Indian boy. Instead, we spent the remaining daylight hours gathering enough firewood for a comfortable night's stay at the cabin and making our plans to go bow hunting the next morning. We started the fire just after the sun came down, and it didn't seem right to rehash the day's events until we finished cooking and eating the chicken we had brought with us and the potatoes we kept in the cabin's larder.

I said, as we sprawled in front of the cabin's fireplace, "It worked. Damned if it didn't work like a whistle."

Sam and Tony, basking in the warmth, were too lazy to respond for a while, but they knew exactly what I meant. Then Sam answered, "It sure did."

"Do you think the boy's tribe might take out after Jacksonville in order to get even?" I asked.

"Maybe. But if I was them, I'd be glad to stay away from here."

"You aren't them," Tony pointed out. "You aren't quite intelligent enough to be an Indian."

"I'm smart enough to stash away something up here in case we ever had a reason to celebrate." We watched as Sam got up and went over to the foot of one of the pine-bough bunks. Rummaging around in its base, he produced a jug of the whiskey that some local farmers produced. Holding it up, he said, "Just in case we ever got snakebit."

Tony, narrowing his eyes, identified it. "Tanglefoot. I believe it's supposed to be deadly."

"Is that a fact, now?" I asked. "Well maybe we ought to get rid of it. Or maybe first I ought to take a sip to make sure that it's poisonous before we throw it away," and I gulped down an enormous swig. I was going to follow with some lofty observations about the brew's year, bouquet, and lineage, but I couldn't because my throat and stomach were suddenly on fire. The swill was almost as lethal as Tony had described it. I passed it wordlessly over to Sam.

We were all still too young to know much about drink, but after we forced down a second swallow—each of us felt that we'd be damned if we appeared less manly than the other two—the tanglefoot got to us and emptying the jug began to emerge as not only a fine but also a logical goal.

Tony's reaction to the stuff was, well, uncharacteristic. He giggled, couldn't stop, finding irresistible humor in the sparks from some of the green limbs in the fire or the way I seemed to be bumping into things and even the sight of his own toes. But Sam grew more dour and uncommunicative with every drink. By the time the jug, which originally had contained almost a full quart, was finished, it was as if he were there by himself, sitting and staring into the fire, its shadows changing his face into something carved by an aborigine.

As for me, over the next week or so Tony saw to it that I was made fully aware of the way I had acted: "You carried on like an absolute idiot! No sooner was the bottle finished, than you were out the door and racing about the mesa. You asked the moon to sustain you in battle because you probably thought it the rightful Indian thing to do.

"Your lunacy fed on itself. Instead of the prancing about helping to quiet the alcohol in your system, you became even more frantic. When you finally halted, it wasn't exhaustion, it was because you ran squarely into the giant madrone. A normally squiffed sod might have slumped to the ground. But not you, Collis Gibbs. You stretched your arms as far as they would go around the tree's trunk and, while rubbing your cheek against its bark, you crooned some kind of a gibberish prayer to it.

"I couldn't understand much of what you said, but I had the impression that you were telling it that it was your God and if it would watch over you, you in turn, would wade through whatever fire that might ever occur in this forest in order to save it.

"When you noticed Sam and me watching from the doorway, you told the tree that, with its permission, the three of us would be indivisible for the rest of our lives. Then you amended your prayer to 'four' and added that no matter how cruelly I had treated Tommy, he was one of us and, being a heathen, especially needed watching over.

"Up until then, I had found everything to be quite comic, but I was rather touched by your plea and in that moment all my anger at our

Cantonese friend evaporated. I remembered thinking, *Of course, Tommy acted as I should have expected.*

"I've been too unfeeling. I'm sorry and I must make it up to him."

He stopped himself and for a short while stared steadily at me. I guess if a stranger saw the two of us at that moment he would have wondered what had happened that the sandy-haired boy was regarding me so frostily. But that's just the expression that comes over Tony when he's thinking. He really isn't even seeing the other person, and if there's disapproval on his face, it's because he's inwardly reviewing something that *he's* done that displeases *him*. Self-dislike is one of the few emotions that causes him to forget to keep his guard up.

With his background, Tony couldn't have failed to have had private convictions of his own superiority to a backwater place like Jacksonville, and yet I'd seen times when he'd been fazed by the smug belief that most Americans on the frontier had in themselves and their country. Now he was putting that together with the contempt dealt out all through the West to Tommy and his fellow Asiatics and understanding that they added up to the fact that he really hadn't been acting very well. Tony's basic decency is one of the reasons I've treasured him all these years. I don't think I have it, but, because he does, some of it (occasionally) rubs off on me.

"Just after your prayers to the tree became so garbled that it was impossible to understand a word of what you were saying," he continued, "you broke into tears, slid to the ground, and went to sleep. When you began to snore, Sam said, 'We might as well get the booger. If we leave him out here, he'll be using stiffness as an excuse not to go with us tomorrow.' So we gathered you up and carried you inside.

"I will confess, however, that our progress was just a bit hampered by the childish fit of giggles that had returned to plague me. They even affected Sam. He lost that dour look and began to grin and, before long, both of us were roaring with laughter. Actually, Collis, it really *was* rather funny. We swung you up onto your bunk as if we were sailors at sea dumping a body overboard.

"You showed absolutely no signs of distress with this treatment. As a matter of fact, you continued to snore until we left and headed for our own beds. But you stopped us by sitting bolt upright and, in totally sober, almost angry tones, said directly to Sam, 'You talk all the time about the way you and your mother remember the Sweetwater River country that you passed up in Wyoming, but you're dead wrong!' Then you leaned forward to add in a whisper, '*This* is Sweetwater land, my

boy, and don't you ever forget it.' With that, you fell backwards in a
state that anyone might describe as death if your nose hadn't been trum-
peting such abominable noises."

Tony's kindly attempt to paint me as a total ass didn't even come
close to stacking up alongside the foul feeling I had when I woke up the
next morning. There was a crust inside my mouth and a sourness in my
stomach that made me think right away about the farmer who had
distilled the mess we have drunk. I was consigning him, his family, and
even his casual acquaintances to hell when Sam brought me back to
total consciousness with a tremendous whack across the soles of my
feet.

I jumped up, really angry. "Of all the dumb damn things!"

"You'd a been sawin away there all day," he answered, but I could
see he realized he had hit me harder than he intended.

"Well, I don't think you're very damned funny," I said, limping out
the door in order to relieve my overloaded kidneys.

Intending to nurse my grievance long enough to let me duck out of
the scheduled morning's hunting trip, I stood in a peeing position for a
long while after I had actually finished, and I would have stayed out
there for at least another few minutes if I hadn't noticed someone walking
up the trail and entering onto the mesa. It was the first time since we
had adopted the place that anyone but us had come to the High, so I
yelled back to Sam and Tony, "We've got company! Somebody's on the
way up here."

"The son of a buck's still drunk," I heard Sam say.

I walked back to tell him to stop being so damned smart, but a voice
behind me—the stranger—called out, "You're swearing, too, is that it?" At
first I couldn't place it, but when Sam came to the door I realized that
it was his father.

"I said, 'son of a buck,' " said Sam, stepping outside with Tony
behind him. I remember thinking how curious it seemed to hear the
note of youngness in Sam's voice.

The older man, without shifting his glare from his son, said, "Sure.
Swearing and running off with these two loafers who wouldn't know a
day's work if it bit 'em in the ass."

"There's no call for that, Pa," Sam said.

In answer, Mr. Hume walked over and, with a sweeping, almost
bearlike roundhouse blow, knocked his son to the ground.

For a few moments Sam lay there where he fell. Then he raised
himself up on his arms and, staring at the patch of grass below him, said
to it, "Pa, that wasn't right."

"The hell it ain't!" And his father lunged forward to get his arm around Sam's neck.

At this, like a coiled wire let loose from a box, Sam jumped up, flinging his father off and then backing away. There was a plea in his eyes, but it wasn't cowardice. "No more, Pa. I'm tellin you, no more."

His father began to advance on a line that included Tony and me. We stepped back, not in fear, but to keep from becoming part of the ugliness.

There had never been any warmth between Sam and his father but, in spite of the gold madness that had characterized the older man's every waking moment since he had come to Jacksonville, Sam had never failed to show him respect. Right then it was a sad thing to see him trying so hard to let his father hold on to his stature in front of us.

Mr. Hume didn't feel any of this. Heading for his retreating son, he said, "You never been any damned good! Now that I'm close to the strike we come for and you could be helping, you're off mooning with these two nellies!"

Sam just shook his head, and we wondered why his father was so blind to what was in the gesture.

"You're no cursed son of mine!" he said, still moving heavily toward Sam.

"Oh shit, Pa," said Sam, quitting his retreat. Stepping forward, he hunched one shoulder down, shifted his weight, and his fist flicked out so quickly that it was almost like a snake striking. It connected flush on his father's jaw, and the man dropped in his tracks like a steer that had been poleaxed.

Sam stood over his father then, holding his hands to his sides but his fists were still clenched. He looked down, jaw muscles working convulsively, and the only emotion in his face was gravity. After the older man began to stir, he said in a flat, quiet voice, "You're right. I'm not your son and you're not my father. No more, you ain't. You was my father when I was growing up and when you did all the things you did to bring us out here safe. But no more. When you can be so rotten hungry for the gold, then you're nothin to Ma or me."

I glanced over at Tony and I wondered if my own face showed as much desire to be anywhere but here. He caught my eye and although neither of us moved from the positions we had stiffened into, each knew what the other was thinking: that we would have given anything we owned not to have been forced to watch this. But we stood there until Sam released us by saying, "Come on. I don't want to stay here no more, let's go down."

We wanted desperately to get away, but we hesitated because it would have been even more brutal to leave the old man stretched out alone in sunlight that had turned from friendly warmth into something hot and oppressive. Sam must have understood this because the frightening gravity left him and he added, "All right. You two go. I'll wait here and help him down."

"You don't have to," said his father, struggling to his feet. "Just get. Leave me be and don't be in my home when I get there."

Sam didn't say anything else. He walked over toward the trail leading back through the valley, not turning to see if we were following him, although, of course, we were. For at least a hundred yards, we kept our eyes fixed on the trail, and I don't think any of us would have broken the silence for the rest of the way if we hadn't heard Mr. Hume's voice calling frantically, "Sam! Sammy! Come here!"

We turned and ran back up the trail, Sam racing past us and again in the lead. When we reached the clearing there was no sign of his father, but we heard him shouting again, "It's here! Over here, it's the goddamn over here!"

And there, just down past the edge of the mesa's brow, was Mr. Hume feverishly gathering up an armful of loose rocks that had broken away from a stone outcropping. When he had as much as he could carry, he began scrambling up the side to where we stood. "Look," he yelled, "it's quartz! It's the real quartz, and here's the veins running all through it!"

In his excitement, he couldn't wait for us to react. "It's the quartz," he screamed again, his normal rumbling tones completely gone. "It's gold, goddammit. I found me a Glory Hole. Sammy, I found us the gold!"

4

NOW, ABOUT ME:

My father, John Gibbs, was a successful and quite popular physician in Philadelphia, and I've always heard that my mother was one of the city's beauties. These blessings, plus the joint wealth of their two families, would have guaranteed them a lifetime of pleasant envy from their friends except that a serious illness took possession of my mother after giving birth to me, and since neither my father's success nor charm was as medically effective as ability, she died.

Now what can an inept and newly widowed man do with an infant son? Well, if he's at all like Father, he develops an obscure medical complaint of his own. In his case, it was weakness of the lungs, and it was so successful a dodge for avoiding responsibility that no Philadelphia burgher attached blame to his decision to hire an English governess to act as the buffer between us.

My father was also an indecisive man, so it took the next seventeen years for him to convince himself of his lung problems to the point where he was certain that he had to get away from the Philadelphia air that, depending on the season, is either cold or damp and infernally humid. Finally comfortable with that diagnosis, he then prescribed a better climate for himself—some place that combined the balmy sun, the dry air, and the undemanding living style of a place like California. After searching and sifting through all the areas in this country that might resemble what he had heard about California, he decided to move to California. My father might not have been the smartest man in Philadelphia, but he was certainly among the most methodical.

I was another of his discoveries in the year of 1852. There was no urgent need to enroll me immediately at (of course) the University of Pennsylvania, and so, *by George, Dad and his son were striking out for the West!* This was the way he relayed the news to his cronies in the First City Troop, and every one of them responded with admiration for our virility and daring. Between the time of his decision and the time of our boarding the French brig *Cachelot*, I was taken everywhere to offer my

31

goodbyes to his friends, a group that I identified even then as the worst set of bores God had ever created.

The next decision was the route. We could have gone overland like so many of the others, but there were more attractive reasons to board a ship bound for San Francisco. Travel by ox cart would have been uncomfortable, undoubtedly dangerous, and the people who rode in wagon trains were certainly not the types with whom Father or his friends would care to spend all the months the trek required. To put it another way, the books, magazines, and papers of the time invariably described those who traveled by boat as Argonauts, while the people journeying by ox cart were most often identified as people traveling by ox cart.

Once it was made, the decision proved remarkably easy to execute. He sold his practice to a friend and put the proceeds, plus all the assets he and his wife had inherited from their parents, in the hands of another friend, a stockbroker in the city. This gentleman was as competent in his profession as father was in his own, so it took a bit less than three years for the brokers' letter to arrive informing us that every one of Father's dollars had been lost in an investment opportunity that had seemed to be gilt-edged because of the limited number of "insiders" who were being allowed a share.

Father never blamed the man for this catastrophe. He had been just as excited by the idea of constructing a tunnel under the English Channel. After he learned that the project had sunk without a trace, all Father said was, "Poor Jack, he must feel horribly about this," an example of noblesse oblige for which I could have cheerfully killed him.

This was the kind of judgment that caused Father to book passage on a French boat rather than any of the sturdier American ships that, by 1852, knew what they were doing when they headed out of the Port of Philadelphia for the 13,000-nautical-mile trip down the east coasts of the United States and South America, around Cape Horn, and back up to San Francisco. I believe he fancied that we'd be traveling in a preparatory way for the amiable kind of life waiting ahead of us—a vision that, like so many of his others, turned out to be slightly flawed.

Along with all the other well-fixed emigrants who chose to sail to California as Argonauts, he found that the voyage was a nightmare of boredom, bad food, overcrowding, and seasickness that lasted the full five months of the trip. Poor Father! During all that time I don't believe he had two days in a row where retching at the rail wasn't the final mealtime activity. I felt so much sympathy for him that I occasionally refrained from gulping down my food in front of him.

No, I wasn't seasick at all. While the rest of the Argonauts suffered from our tub's eternal pitching and rolling, my dispostion got sunnier. In fact, several of them told Father that they intended to strangle me whenever they got back enough strength to reach their hands around my throat. Fortunately, the general intent to shorten my journey was abandoned when the other passengers, with the exception of Father, gained their sea legs. Father was a Philadelphian to the bone, so he didn't easily accept change. He began the voyage by throwing up and he was still at the rail on the last day of the trip.

At the same rate that they got to feeling better, the passengers became more resentful of the atrocious meals they were being offered. The boat's advertisements had stressed French cuisine, and if that's what it was, then it's no wonder the French are such swine. They get it from their diet if the food aboard the *Cachelot* was anywhere near being a reliable yardstick. I heard one passenger tell his still-sick wife, "You aren't missing anything. The salt pork is rusty, the dried beef is rotten, and there's two bugs for every bean."

Another passager, keeping count of the weevils infesting the pilot bread and navy biscuit, tried a wry brag to make Father feel better: "What the hell, we're sailing aboard the only ship on the California run that offers fresh meat three times a day." That sent Father to the rail again, even though the last meal had been served two hours before.

There were repeated servings of *lobscouse*, a hash made of salt pork, onions, navy biscuits, water, and thickening. The desserts—plum duff, mince turnovers, and a pudding called Dandy Funk—all had the same pasty, greasy taste. The water that had been stored for months in the ship's hold developed a remarkably foul taste but, luckily, one of the passengers discovered that it could be swallowed and, quite often, kept down after it was mixed with molasses and vinegar.

I realized later that the conditions aboard the *Cachelot* were fairly representative of all the passenger ships making this voyage. In fact, it was probably better than most. I once met a man who made the trip aboard a ship where the passengers slept three abreast on platforms barely two feet apart, one stacked above the other. Seasickness combined with the difficulty of getting out of such a bunk resulted in a mutiny that stopped only after they reached the nearest port.

In spite of all this, I was having a lovely time. Can you imagine a more delightful situation for a teenage boy than having an entire boat to explore and exploit? The passengers were too sick to chase me out of the social quarters and the crew, resentful of the generally low opinion in which they were held, welcomed me as the one paying fare aboard who respected their skills. Quite a few of the sailors went out of their way to be extra nice to me but these, of course, I avoided.

I was even able to establish a relationship with the Captain, a surly bourgeois named Bequette. He had me booted out the first two times I ventured onto the bridge, but on the third occasion I was made conditionally welcome when he took the time to notice that I had a bottle of Father's best brandy with me. *"Qu'est-ce que cest?"* he asked the mate standing by.

"Un garçon," shrugged the mate.

"Je parle français un peu," I interjected.

"Allez!" thundered the Captain.

"Regardez," I countered, thrusting the bottle of brandy in his direction.

"Allez," said the Captain again, this time to the Second Officer, who left grinning.

The Captain carefully examined my bottle and then, baring his remaining teeth in a grimace meant to be friendly, asked, *"Quelle age avez vous?"*

"I'm seventeen, sir, and can we please speak in English? I'm afraid I've about run out."

He agreed by answering, "For only the age, you have the good cognac."

"It's from my father, sir. He admires the marvelous way you have been steering this ship."

I'm tempted to linger on this conversation because it was the first complete triumph I'd scored since we left Philadelphia, but it's enough to recall that the old pig spent a few more minutes showing me around the pilot house, allowing me to pull or turn knobs until I became bored, and for the rest of the voyage he demonstrated his expectations of another bottle by occasionally diverting some of the decent food that he and his fellow officers enjoyed to our tiny cabin. These meals were enormous improvements over the swill served to the passengers and the crew, so I ate both Father's share and mine with considerable pleasure.

Father didn't feel well enough to question either these treats or his depleting liquor stores until long after we had landed. And, as far as I know, he never noticed the absence of the pair of his cufflinks that I presented to M. Bequette after he took me ashore when we docked briefly at the Island of Saint Catherine, just off Brazil's coast. It was an enjoyable stopover during which he introduced me to several very interesting, well-painted, and (to my young eyes) elderly ladies. If I knew then what I think I know now, the stopover would have been even more pleasant.

When we finally reached San Francisco in August, it wasn't at all the way I had expected it to be. Instead of a sleepy harbor with perhaps a few whaling or merchant ships, it seemed to be swarming with ocean-going craft from every corner of the world. There were steamers, big sailing ships, schooners, brigs, and Lord knows what else. A dozen vessels were anchored in the roadstead and what seemed to be twice as many more milled about while waiting for a clear space at the docks. Streams of small boats shuttled between ships and shore crammed with passengers and goods. These last were dumped in helter-skelter heaps on the piers, and the human cargo, once landed, lost no time in hurrying off to reach, I guess, the gold fields before all the loose nuggets were gone.

Most striking of all was everyone's good nature. Even our passengers shed their scowls, and although they stopped short of rubbing their hands in anticipation, that was the general sense of their attitude. One of them, who had often greeted me aboard by offering to break my neck, said as a genial goodbye to Father, "Doctor, I wish you all the luck you're looking for. And if you keep that boy of yours with you, you'll find it, too. He's a natural-born sniffer after the main chance if I ever saw one!"

Taken aback, Father answered, "Yes, he's quite a lad," and shook the man's hand. A few moments later I saw him wondering whether the man had been an accomplice or a victim in one of my schemes, and since there was no point in discussing it, I diverted his attention by making a great show of our need to get into the line of passengers waiting to be ferried ashore.

San Francisco was apparently capable of supporting the activity promised by the boats in the harbor. Everywhere we looked, we saw busy wooden shacks, most of them just erected. Later, I learned that only a few of these were the first buildings to occupy their sites because of the city's tendency to catch on fire every few months.

On the way to our hotel we passed one section of the docks that had not survived a conflagration that had occured there several weeks earlier. Ruined supplies were everywhere. I saw gun barrels lying in the ashes, twisted and knotted like snakes; tons of nails had been welded together by the fierce heat and still stood in the shape of the kegs that once contained them. An iron safe had burst, and its contents, whatever they had been, were now charred beyond redemption. Spoons, knives, forks, and crockery lay fused into gray masses, and the stores of preserved meat recently shipped and unloaded here had exploded out through their packings in every direction.

Our hotel, unlike most of the lodging places we passed along the way, seemed to be a cut above a pigsty, but our room cost an unholy thirty dollars a night, and the meal served us that evening consisted of two slabs of anonymous meat fried just short of leather, for which four-teen dollars more was nicked out of Father's wallet. As we left the dinner table, I said, "Father, it seems to me that if we're going to stay in this city, we're either going to have to send for all our money or else head for the gold fields. I don't see how ordinary men can afford these prices."

This was forward of me. Back home we had rarely discussed money matters, but even this brief exposure to the cost of living in San Francisco was enough to shake my father's normal delicacy. Instead of freezing the subject out of our conversation, he looked worried. "I just don't know, Collis. I thought that opening a medical practice here wouldn't be too different from Philadelphia. But people like these . . ."

His voice trailed off into uncertainty. I wasn't sure whether he meant that the San Franciscans didn't need or that they wouldn't pay physicians. But I knew that either way we had to do something, so I persisted. "Well, what are we going to do if being a doctor here doesn't turn out?"

"We really have to try it, but if it isn't practical, I imagine we'll just book passage home."

If the expression on his face had been as positive as his words, I might not have ventured my next suggestion. "Did you ever think about becoming a gold miner?"

Then, for one of the few times in my life, I saw my father laugh heartily. "Collie, Collie," he said, almost sputtering his way through the words, "can you see me with a pick and a shovel and a mule?"

Even though the romantic idea had been at the back of my mind ever since we had left Philadelphia, the picture of my gentle and inef-fective father gotten up in a heavy flannel shirt, dungaree pants, rubber boots, and a sourdough hat—unshaven and searching through the wil-derness for a gold strike—was, after all, wildly funny. I began to roar along with him.

And then I stopped laughing and abruptly shelved the idea I had been nursing because it was as impractical as anything that had ever interested my father. If he ever decided to go gold hunting, where would that leave me? Either I would be left in the charge of a stranger in this jerry-built place, or else I, too, would be included in that comical tableau of the dusty prospector and his mule.

These alternatives weren't nearly as attractive as the vision I'd also entertained of living an untrammeled life as the only son of San Francisco's leading physician. For the first time I realized I had inherited more than I wanted from my father. By thoughtlessly calling attention to this place's expense, I was acting squarely within his style.

Fortunately, while I was whirling around in my mind searching for the best way to get the idea of our residency here back on the tracks, he said, "Well, perhaps we're making a premature judgment because it's late and we're tired. Maybe there's a whole San Francisco out there that's totally unlike the one we've seen so far. Let's explore it in the morning."

Hoping that my face showed awe at his good judgment instead of relief, I nodded my head vigorously in agreement as he went on. "One of our Quaker friends at home gave me a letter of introduction to a Dr. Ritchie who is the chief of a hospital here. He'll certainly be able to tell us what kind of a welcome a solid physician can expect in this city. As a matter of fact, before I turn in tonight, I'm going to try to get a message to him to expect us tomorrow."

And then, making me feel even better, he added, "Besides, if the merchants here want to be paid such ungodly prices for their goods, then it's only fair that they should also expect to be charged on the same scale for medical attention. It may be that we'll do quite well here, after all."

5

W E STILL WEREN'T SURE that we were at the right place even after we reached the hospital next morning. It wasn't big and it wasn't of brick or stone like a Philadelphia medical building, and, in fact, it wasn't much more than four or five wooden shacks connected by a series of corridors that must have been slapped together out of mill-end scraps. There was a faint reassurance in noticing the word, "Hospital" lettered on a shingle nailed over one of the doors, but it was discredited by the piles of trash and slops surrounding the small compound.

We paused before going in, and I felt better after I noticed my father drawing a deep breath. He was as worried as I. "It will be all right," he told me in pretty much the same tones he had used the night before Mother died.

The interior wasn't much of an improvement. We were in a small chamber that must have been the receiving room, although there was a total absence of any trace of human activity. There were no decorations, no indications of any type of medical facilities, and the only furniture was a desk made of a plank supported by two kegs on which documents were scattered at random, and a bench along the far wall. Seated on it was a young man who raised his eyes to a spot on the wall somewhere above us immediately after we entered. His remote expression said that, for all he cared, we could go back into the woodwork to rejoin whatever other residents there were in the area. This was the first time I ever laid eyes on Anthony Johnstone.

At that moment it wasn't a good bet he would ever become my lifelong friend. In fact, his apparently instinctive dislike came damned close to being the straw that could have scared me back to Philadelphia if my father, oblivious as always to hostility (because he never dreamed it could be directed at him), hadn't asked, "This *is* the hospital, isn't it?"

Tony let his stare down enough to bring us into focus and said, "Yes."

When it became obvious that he didn't intend to add anything else,

Father went on, "It's quite interesting but it really doesn't seem to be very active."

Tony almost thawed at this polite confession of puzzlement, but then his eyes swung to me and I saw him freeze up again. I wondered if it was the brown corduroy Norfolk jacket I was wearing.

Under usual circumstances I might have smiled or done somthing equally friendly to show a stranger that I was on his side when it came to being benign about my father, but right then I wasn't going to let this supercilious son of a bitch know he had me intimidated. "Are you one of the orderlies?" I asked him.

"I'm afraid not."

"Are there any around?" I persisted.

He surprised me by being civil instead of irritated. He stood up and said, "A nurse ought to be out quite soon. She's going to tell me about a friend who's just been admitted."

"A friend? What happened?"

For some reason, he was aware that I'd given up trying to bait him and was honestly interested in knowing what sort of a friend he'd have in a place like this and the kind of injury that could have brought him here.

"Well, actually not a friend. A boy that someone beat quite badly and left lying in the street. I had to bring him here, didn't I?"

The blush that accompanied the answer wasn't embarrassment—it simply underscored that he was really telling me that he, too, was wondering what he was doing here. And, also, I knew that this wasn't a request for my opinion. I had been exposed to enough Englishmen in Philadelphia to have become familiar with their perverse habit of putting the simpliest of declarative sentences as a question.

He was about my size—medium height—but much thinner and maybe a year or so older than I. His hair was just a few shades darker than blond, and his almost delicate face was set in so fair a complexion that I doubted he shaved with any regularity. Glancing quickly at him from a distance you might have thought him girlish, but you would have missed the toughness I read in his eyes during the moment we stood and faced each other.

"Of course you couldn't," said my father. "Do you mind if we join you on the bench? There doesn't seem to be any other place to sit."

"Please do."

He moved over to the end, but before we could seat ourselves, a very short and unquestionably very harried man came pushing pell mell through another of the doors in the room. He was heading for Tony, but when he saw Father he abruptly changed directions and thrust out his hand, saying, "Dr. Gibbs? I received your note! Sorry to keep you waiting but we've got no people—totally undermanned—and no time. This is the first chance to breathe I've had all morning!"

Father stepped back, almost stumbling over the bench behind him, and shook the outstretched hand that seemed to be about to claw his navel. He said to its owner, "Not at all. You must be Dr. Ritchie."

"I am." Over his shoulder, to Tony, he said, "Your friend will be fine." And then he asked, "Why are you smiling young man?"

Realizing this last had been shot my way, I answered, "Sorry, sir, I was thinking of . . ."

But before I could finish manufacturing a polite reason to hide the fact that this little man bouncing in place as Father towered over him was a marvelously funny sight, I found myself talking to the back of his neck. Neither caring nor waiting for my explanation, he threw his arms up around Father's shoulder saying, as he steered him out toward the hall, "We can talk better in my office, Doctor."

"Really, Dr. Ritchie," said Father looking for all the world like a liner being towed out to sea by a tug, "I haven't been here but a moment. And my son . . ."

"He'll wait," Ritchie reassured him. "I'm afraid we won't have that much time before the lad begins to miss you."

For the first time Tony looked amused instead of remote and when, after they disappeared into the hallway, I added, "That's probably also the way Father got married," he let out a howling loud laugh.

"Perfect!" he said, beginning our friendship.

"What's your name?" I asked the other boy.

"Tony Johnstone. Yours?"

"Collie Gibbs. How old are you?"

"Eighteen."

"That's a year older than me. Who's your friend in this hospital?"

"I'm afraid I don't know him at all. Seems to be Chinese, actually. Couldn't even give his name when I brought him here. I imagine he was done by some of the thugs that infest this place."

"I've seen them on the streets." I shook my head. "Awful. If that's all there is in San Francisco, I want to go back to Philadelphia."

"That makes a pair of us."

"You're not from Philadelphia."

"Of course not. London. You *are* a fool, aren't you?"

After considering this, I said, "You must like me."

"What a strange thing to say."

"No, it isn't. You called me a fool and you don't know whether I am or not. But if you honest-to-God thought I was, then you wouldn't say it."

He nodded his head in mock gravity. "Of course. But then again . . ."

"Now, if you had called my father a fool, that would have been different."

"That's not very pleasant of you."

"Don't be stuffy and English. You don't understand that I'm not saying my father is a fool. I only mean that if you *had* said that about him . . ."

"But I wouldn't have, would I?"

"It wouldn't have been very friendly if you had."

"I see. Of course."

We shook our heads soberly at each other until I added, "Of course. My father *is* a fool, you know."

At this, he let out another loud whooping laugh. "What a cruel thing to say!"

We were young enough to be overly delighted by the discovery of an ally, and after the pleasure of it took full hold, I asked him, "What on earth is someone like you doing in this horrible place?" But something in his eyes told me that the question had touched a nerve so I tried to erase the subject by sighing and adding, "But I guess we're in the same boat."

"I doubt it. Probably not. I'm stony broke. I don't think your situation is quite as sticky, is it?"

I reluctantly admitted, "I suppose not. All Father has to do is buy us passage back to Philadelphia whenever it gets too grim."

"There you are," he said, meaning that we weren't quite the allies we had thought we were a few minutes ago.

I didn't have an answer for this, and while I was trying to think of some tactful way to break the gloomy silence that had suddenly stunted our friendship, Dr. Ritchie and my father came back in.

Father looked quite serious, but the short man had lost none of his briskness. "Now, Dr. Gibbs," said Dr. Ritchie, continuing what seemed to be a monologue as they entered, "you think over my advice pretty careful. No question, you're going to find that I'm right. You can go see your Chinese boy now."

The last sentence was directed at Tony, who then turned to me, a stranger again, to say his goodbye before going down the hall.

I said, "Wait a minute. Let me go with you."

Before he could answer, my father, who obviously wanted to get away from the place as quickly as possible, put in, "Collis, the young man would probably prefer to make his visit in privacy. And we really ought to be getting back to the hotel."

He smiled in the way that he always did when he was troubled. I knew that he was bothered by something Ritchie had said and wanted to talk it over with me but, right then, it seemed a whole lot more important to me not to lose this new (and only) friend. "Father," I said, "please, we won't be long. Will we, Tony?"

All his English reserve wasn't enough to hide the relief in his voice as he answered, "Not really. Do you mind terribly, Doctor Gibbs?"

Bless my father. He minded all right, but when he saw how much it meant to me, he said, "Dr. Ritchie won't object to putting up with me for a little while longer, will you, Doctor?" There would have been even more grace in the gesture if he had noticed Ritchie bustling back out of the room while we were talking.

I didn't wait. "We'll be right back, Father," I said, taking Tony by the arm and heading down the hall with him, although he didn't seem all that enthused over getting to see the patient he'd been waiting for.

Halfway there, he stopped. "What's the matter?" I asked.

"I don't know this Oriental. If there are two of them, I doubt if I'll be able to pick the one I've brought in."

"No problem," I said, "either one of them will be glad to see you. I've always heard that there's nothing the Chinese like better than visitors."

That brought a weak grin. As we began walking again, he added, "And you also realize that we haven't the faintest idea where we are going. Of course that won't matter. Whatever ward we reach will be ecstatic at the sight of us."

Fortunately, there was only one room at the end of the hall. It had perhaps eight cots crammed into it, and there was no question about which one held our quarry. He was the only boy in the room, and blood was still staining through the fresh bandages about his head. As we walked toward the bed, Tony muttered, "I don't know his name and I don't know a blessed word of Chinese."

Noticing where we were heading, a man lying in the cot just before it, said to us, "You take that Chink the hell outta here with you. This place is supposed to be for white men."

Tony glanced at him as we passed and answered, "Really?"

When we reached the bed, we saw that there were bandages on the boy's chest as well as his head. Tony smiled at him and asked, "How do you feel?"

It didn't seem as if the boy recognized either Tony or his greeting. Then I waved my hand at him in a small friendly gesture, but after a long stare at us (probably to make sure that we weren't another threat), he closed his eyes and, for all I knew, went to sleep.

We stood there uncertainly until we realized that there wasn't much point in prolonging the visit. As we turned to leave, the neighboring man reminded us, "Take that goddamn Chink with you, goddammit."

Looking thoughtful, Tony walked over to him and let his hand drop heavily on the man's leg, that was bandaged around the splint. "If anything happens to that boy," he told him, "I'm going to break your other leg." With that, he left, me following (and swaggering a bit) as we walked back down the hall.

6

FATHER COULDN'T WAIT until we got back to our room to repeat Dr. Ritchie's unsettling advice. On the street outside the hospital he said that the little man's words boiled down only to the suggestion that we leave San Francisco on the next boat; that there was nothing for us here, and if there was, we'd neither want nor like it.

Ritchie had described San Francisco as ungodly expensive, ridden with crime and criminals, and as a place where doctors were needed most often to administer to toughs with ears torn off, noses chewed, or bodies riddled by shot. The physicians with the best-paying practices, he said, were the quacks claiming expertise in the control and cure of venereal diseases.

A precise man, Ritchie's summary was based on statistics, not impressions. He told Father that the city averaged two murders and one fire a day. The unruly young population drank at more than 500 bars, gambled at 1,000 dens, and nothing but life was cheap. Eggs cost six dollars a dozen, and real estate values were correspondingly astronomical. It was a place where the small group who could afford a civilized life was limited to those who already owned their gold mines.

If a man was truly committed to the West Coast, said Dr. Ritchie, then the only reasonable alternative was to travel north to the towns springing up around the new gold strikes. In Oregon, for example, even though gold was everywhere, the mild climate in such areas as the Rogue Valley produced a gentle effect upon its citizens, totally unlike the yield of the raw fogs of San Francisco.

He concluded by saying, "If I were younger and hadn't already committed to the practice of medicine, I might settle in a place just south of the Willamette, called Jacksonville, where I hear it's as balmy as the Mediterranean, the citizens are law abiding, and the gold mines in and around it are the base for a solid and honest growth. That's where a doctor can live and respect himself the way he should!"

As Father relayed these observations, I began to suspect that he had already made up his mind. I became sure of what the next leg of our

44

journey was going to be when he ended up by saying, "Of course, it might be fun to write home describing ourselves as Oregonians."

The best I was going to do was to swap votes. "It might be even more fun," I said, "If we could get Mr. Johnstone to go with us."

We had just left Tony a few minutes ago, but Father hadn't the slightest clue to the reference. "Mr. Who?" he asked.

"That nice young fellow back in there."

When the blank look stayed on Father's face, I realized his mind hadn't yet come back from Oregon. "The English boy we met inside the hospital. He's still in there."

Reality returned. "Oh, yes. Seemed to be a very genteel lad."

"He's in trouble, Father. He doesn't have a friend in this place." I went on to describe Tony's loneliness, his unselfish helping of the Chinese boy, and his evident despair at whatever the circumstances were that had brought him to San Francisco. As I talked, I could see the seed I was planting take root—that Tony was the companion who would keep me from claiming too much of my father's attention while he was busy becoming a colorful Oregonian.

"Jacksonville sounds marvelous!" I enthused. "Of course, we could always go back home, but think how much better the Oregon air will be for your lungs!" I was sure that Tony would never consider Philadelphia as an attractive enough reason to join our company.

Tony came out of the Quaker Hospital while Father was on his way to agreeing with this offer of a trade, so without waiting for a formal assent, I ran over and excitedly extended our invitation. I know this all sounds schoolboyish, but not only was I faced with the prospect of being damned lonely, this was also the first friend I'd ever had who wasn't related to someone just outside our family's circle.

He must have felt something of the same. After hearing me out, he turned to Father and said, "Do you really wish me to join you, Dr. Gibbs?"

"Of course," said Father and meaning it because by now he considered the invitation to be his own idea.

"Then," said Tony, "I'll go with you. But I must be allowed to repay my passage money to you as soon as I find work up there."

"Of course," Father repeated, beaming so widely at the thought that I was going to have such a splendid example of self-reliance to follow that, for a split second, I wondered if I hadn't been too impulsive.

And that is as much about our stay in San Francisco as need be told here.

Oh, yes. There is one more thing: We took Chung Lin with us.

I'm not really sure why bringing him along seemed to me like such a great inspiration at the time, although it was probably because I certainly had no intention of adopting Tony's willingness to work as a personal standard. At any rate, after I reminded Father of Tony's reason for visiting the hospital, there was a period of hemming and hawing that ended in Father convincing himself that a Chinese houseboy could be an ideal addition to the home of a mining camp physician. This new twist must have added to Tony's uncertainty about us, but he was too well bred to mention that only a mighty thin thread connected him to Chung Lin.

My delight with the idea of having my very own Chinaman must have shown on my face because after we went back in and found a nurse who could communicate with him, the boy glanced briefly at Tony, looked longer at my father, and then, with his eyes resting on me, nodded and smiled his agreement to the offer. Of course, I might not have been so pleased with my own shrewdness in manipulating this deal if I knew then what has since taken a lifetime to learn: Chung Lin's smiles and nods are always inwardly directed.

Not that it matters. The point is that after a few days of waiting for Chung Lin to mend, the four of us sailed by boat northward to Crescent City and, from there, bounced by mule train over the muddy trail leading inland to Jacksonville, where, as Father assured us, "you can become the men that the Lord intended you to be."

Ah, Father. You meant so well.

7

UNLIKE SAM HUME'S FATHER or mine, Tony Johnstone's father didn't inspire fear nor an amused tolerance—he was, simply, a remote figure so committed to the English certainty that the youngest son was an item to be genteely disposed of at the earliest possible date that there was rarely any communication between them. That's why Tony was here in America, although the reason he was alone and without funds in San Francisco certainly wasn't his father's fault. Tony told me the bones of the story, but left it to me to flesh out the rest of it.

While growing up, he and his two older brothers had been sent away to Dulwich School as soon as each of them reached the brink of asserting an individual identity. Tony remembers that, in his case, this was sometime just before he was ten years old. Eight years later it occurred to his father that someone ought to be looking for some potential Johnstone investments in America and, as the youngest son, Tony was not only the likeliest, he was also the only candidate for the job.

This exile didn't leave him with any measurable amount of bitterness. He had followed his brothers through Dulwich and Harrow and was about to trace their steps through Trinity, but he had never been a real part of the family circle. His father and his brothers were what they had been bred to be: stiff, demanding, and incapable of the smallest display of sensitivity. His mother had been and remained a shadowy figure. Obediently accepting a childhood training that dictated an acceptance of her husband's will, whatever fire she had left was extinguished by the time it filtered down through her two oldest sons, leaving little warmth for Tony.

Not that Tony cared. He didn't share his brothers' interest in sports or shopgirls, couldn't have cared less about a career in the military or the church, and although he liked to imagine that the reason for his casual attitude was that he was more drawn to art or literature, the truth was that he preferred his own company and felt uneasy on those rare occasions when another member of the family showed a brief interest in whatever he might be up to.

As a result, he wondered only briefly whether his mother was disappointed over the interruption in his education, but then realized that she couldn't be expected to question one of her husband's decisions, especially when it involved the matter of her youngest son's going on to Cambridge being weighed against the incredible profits that some of the English gentry were taking out of America.

The decision hadn't been made as yet whether the family investments should be in land, railroad stocks, or the gold mines that seemed to be jammed next to each other throughout the entire western coast of the New World, but the discussions always ended with the question of the proper time to decide which bonanza to back. Of course, Tony was never included in these conversations between his father and his brothers, but, even so, he was aware that no action would ever be taken based solely upon his unsupported reports. He was to move to America, soak in the investment climate for a few years, and then send home enough raw information to allow the family to identify the point at which the notorious Yankee passion for the lion's share of profits had passed its peak. In short, his job was to function as a thermometer.

"Anthony," he was informed by his oldest brother, David, "you're a methodical beast, so you would have been picked for the scalping even if you hadn't been the youngest." This was an unkind reference to the books centering on savage Indian warriors that were so popular in England.

Tony thought about it for a few days, and after projecting it into a certainty that he was destined to be besieved by arrows while under the hooves of wild buffalos, he told his next oldest brother, Charles, "Well, it's going to be a short life but a merry one."

"You *are* an ass, aren't you?" Charles answered, as if just discovering a very important fact.

It was settled that he would be sent to live in San Francisco with one of his father's cousins. This was a man named Hawley who had left England shortly after he had tried to strangle his true love, a music hall soprano who, according to reports, had been much in demand, especially by several of Hawley's friends. The cloud under which Hawley left evidently possessed a silver lining because Hawley was now heard to be putting together a sizable fortune in the new land. This happy result was cited by both David and Charles as proof that the Dumbest Englishman Alive, which was one of Hawley's titles, was superior to the smartest Yankee. "If Thomas Hawley can make a go of it," went the reasoning, "then we need worry only moderately about Anthony Jeremy Johnstone."

His mother pecked a goodbye kiss at his cheek, his father shook his hand, and his brothers were elsewhere when Tony sailed from London during the first week of 1852. He reached the first leg of his journey, New York, a few months later. His stay there was so brief that his only recollection of the city was that it was jammed with bearded men boat-loading provisions and mining gear who periodically suggested that he get the hell out of their way.

Next, he sailed south to Panama where his ship unloaded its passengers at the mouth of the Chagres River, a fever-ridden region of swamps. Maps showed that the distance from there over to the west coast to Panama City was only seventy-five miles, so this was the route picked most often by those who wanted to reach California in a hurry. This choice was also the cause of Tony's cursing his father for the first time. The route might have seemed a logical one to someone in London poring over an atlas, but it turned out to be an unmitigated hell in the New World.

The first two-thirds of the shortcut was accomplished by native boatmen paddling long dugout canoes called *bungos*. These navigators, Tony noted, fatigued easily, so they took frequent seistas prefaced by long pulls at gourds that had been slopping full of native rum when the trip began and were all empty when it ended. None of them understood English, but on past trips they picked up gibberish versions of "Oh Susanna" and "Yankee Doodle Dandy," so, the drunker they got, the louder they squawked these songs. Another North American custom picked up by the natives was their frequent stops for the purpose of raising the price of the fares.

In the meantime, his fellow passengers amused themselves by drinking brandy and trying out their new firearms on alligators, iguanas, and the other wildlife of the river banks. After half the brandy was gone and the first few fare increases took effect, the passengers began to discuss the idea of shooting boatmen instead of alligators, but, fortunately, some of the less addled among them made the point that there wasn't a white soul aboard capable of navigating a canoe through the water's hidden dangers. One of these, an unusually tolerant Indiana chiropractor, wrote in his diary: "I should like to see a community of genuine Yankees enjoy the monopoly of owning a few canoes to transport a crowd of eager adventurers willing to pay almost any price to get ahead; I opine there would be such a fleecing as the Isthmus has not yet witnessed."

Tony loathed every minute of the trip, but, even so, it was probably better than most according to the other diaries and reports of the period since they escaped the cholera and malaria that had extracted fearful tolls from most of the companies that had traveled this route before them. The last half of the trip, accomplished on muleback, took only five days, and when they reached the cluster of decaying shacks named Panama City, they were lucky enough to find a ship anchored in the harbor that was willing to sell them passage to California. Many earlier groups had spent months in this miserable place waiting for a boat with space enough to take them the rest of the way.

Even so, it was an ordeal. Tony told me, "I was able to do it only because I kept reminding myself that I was a representative of Great Britain, and so never, not for a moment, could I ever give these crude Americans the satisfaction of believing they could conduct themselves in a better fashion than an Englishman. As you see, my brother Charles was correct; I *was* an ass!"

His innocence lasted only until he reached San Francisco. After landing and as soon as he regained possession of the enormous steamer trunk that his mother had stuffed with the clothes, belongings, and pictures she imagined essential to well-being in America, he looked about the pier for a cab to take him to the home of his distant cousin. Seeing none, he left the trunk where it stood and walked over to the shore end of the pier, where he found a dray driver and an empty cart.

He had twenty-five dollars in his pocket, a sum his family felt was more than enough to defray his incidental traveling expenses. Another two thousand that his father had drawn in American currency from their bank was hidden away inside the trunk. After cautioning him not to mention its presence to anyone, including Hawley, the elder Johnstone had sealed it in an envelope and glued it underneath one of its shelves.

When the driver heard Tony's destination, he demanded fifteen dollars for the trip.

"That's too much," protested Tony.

"No it ain't," said the driver. "It's in Sydney Town." When this didn't produce an impressive effect, he added, "That's along Broadway and Pacific Streets, away to hell and gone over by Clark's Point."

"It is?"

"Yep. You got fifteen dollars?"

"I'm afraid I do."

"Then either give it to me or git the hell out of my way. My time is worth too much money to go boogering around Sydney Town."

Tony had no choice. This was the only unoccupied wagon in sight, and the gaping hole the fare left in his budget could be repaired as soon as he reached the bosom of Mr. Hawley's family.

Under the driver's glare, he wrestled his trunk up into the cart and climbed aboard just barely before the driver lashed his horse off into a wild, careening ride through streets that were nothing more than haphazard separations of wooden hovels, at least every third one a saloon. They didn't pass one human being that Tony felt he might ask for assistance and expect to receive a polite reply. Instead, he saw drunken men, screeching harridans and whores, countless Orientals, and a number of gaudily dressed sports who seemed to have come directly from the race track enclosures that, back in England, were reserved for bookmakers and touts.

Tony thought, *If this represents America, I'd be happier the next ten years in Panama City where, at least, grass grows in the streets*. He thought this because he was trying to keep from speculating over the identity of the clumps in the mud that their wagon spattered over the wooden sidewalks as it bounced along. The driver, Tony belatedly realized, was as drunk as any of the cursing pedestrians they befouled as they passed.

And then they stopped in the seeming worst of all of it. "There it is, younker," said the driver pointing, "435 Jackson Street."

Looking around, Tony saw a row of frame shanty houses, some with red lights in their windows and the rest with crudely lettered *Rooms to Let* signs pinned to the doors. "This can't be where Mr. Hawley lives," he said.

"That's Mr. Hawley's problem," the driver answered. "This is the address you give me, so git the hell out. My time's worth money, which I already lost on this trip."

Stunned by these surroundings, Tony could only say, "This is wrong."

"Keep me palavering and I'm a gonna hold on to that trunk of your'n for what I already lost on this job."

Worried by arriving at an obviously incorrect address, frightened, and tired, Tony finally lost his temper. "One more word, you blighter, and I'll smash your head in," he said.

The driver was barely sober enough to realize that Tony's words were not a threat but a pious prayer that he start something so he said nothing more aloud about the extent of his losses although his face showed that he was still cursing under his breath. As soon as Tony had the bulky steamer trunk out of the cart and touching ground, he crashed his whip at the horse, causing it to bolt forward and down the street, in the process churning up and depositing what Tony hoped was only a muddy splash on his trousers.

One forlorn recourse was left. Walking up to the steps of the house that bore the address given him by his father, he knocked on the door and was relieved to see that the woman who opened it was a stout type who seemed, at last, someone capable of civility. "Is this 435 Jackson Street?" he asked.

In reply, she walked past him, went down the steps, and stared hard at the numbers painted on the glass over the doorway where Tony stood. Then, she turned, came back up and faced him. "Be damned if it ain't," she said in tones of wonder.

His last hope was gone. Slowly, and with care, he said, "I am looking for Mr. Thomas Hawley."

"He ain't here."

"Is this his home?"

"It was as long as he was paying room rent."

"Until when was that?"

"Last week."

"And now?"

"This ain't his home."

He didn't know what else to say or ask but, during the pause, she softened because she read in his face that although he didn't realize it yet, he had just become a lost boy. "Come on in, young gentleman," she said, "and I'll give you a cup of tea. You're English, ain't you?"

He would have been even more upset if he had been aware of the sadness in his nod of assent.

"I thought so. I can always tell when they're talking English. You coming in or not?"

"It would be most kind of you," he answered, "but, you see, I have my trunk out here."

"The big steamer trunk?"

"Yes."

"Don't worry about it no more." And, with this, she put one arm around his shoulder.

Following her eyes, he looked to the curb. The steamer trunk, that enormous carryall, had simply vanished!

She said, "While you was talking to me, two men pulled up in a dray, jumped off, and grabbed it and left."

He shouted, "Why didn't you stop them?"

"How did I know it was yours till you told me?"

Even though he still hadn't thought through the full extent of his loss, there was a shadow of an adolescent treble in his voice. "So quickly. How could it have happened so quickly?"

"Now dearie, it wasn't all that quick. I was watching you from behind the curtain while you was taking your time looking at the numbers. Then you took even more time to knock on this door. And they just whizzed down the street, popped down off the cart—the two of 'em slung it up faster'n you can say Uncle Sam—and they was off before you got around to asking me if Tom-Tom lived here"

"Hawley. Mr Hawley."

"Never mind. He was a crazy man and you're better off."

Then the awful realization hit. "Dear Lord," he said, almost gasping out the words, "my every shilling was in that trunk!"

8

UNDERSTANDING FLOODED IN; the loss of the steamer trunk meant that he was left with only ten dollars to carry out his family's mission, there was no benevolent cousin to cushion and carry him through, and, worst of all, he was without money in a strange land whose residents were now more than rudely provincial—in a flash they had become frightening antagonists.

To add to his distress, Hawley's former landlady, Mrs. Costa, was losing her friendly air at the same speed with which she was finding out that he had only a few dollars left in his pocket. In her frame of reference, these were the only separations between Tony and the urchins and young ruffians infesting San Francisco's streets, alternately cadging and stealing from the city's population of opportunists and would-be gold miners.

Fortunately, he had not lost his wits along with his money. After the first shock wore off, desperation told him that he needed this woman's help and the only way to get and keep it long enough for him to figure out what he was going to do next lay in her obvious attraction to his English accent and gentility. So, he broadened both of these assets until they reached the point where she repeated the invitation that he come in for a cup of tea.

Within the first few minutes of their conversation, Mrs. Costa was revealed as a harpy who wouldn't have hesitated for a second if she felt she'd earn an extra quarter by turning her home into a brothel. Tony spent no more than a half an hour in that parlor, but for the rest of his life he was able to recall every detail of her bloated face, although this was probably due to the appallingly dramatic difference between the Thomas Hawley he had expected to meet and the "Tom-Tom" she described.

It was true that for a while, Hawley, as the prosperous owner of one of the city's busiest saloons, had made money hand over fist. Then he arrived at the answer to Omar Khayyam's question, *I often wonder what it is the vintners buy one half so precious as the goods they sell?*

In this case, the answer was that there was nothing, absolutely noth-

54

ing, that he came to want as much as the rotgut whiskey he had been selling, and not too long after this discovery, Tony's father's cousin was just one more common bum who had drunk and gambled away his money. The job Hawley found after hitting bottom was acting out Tom-Tom, The Authentic Wild Man in one of the cheap arcade exhibitions that the miners mistook for entertainment. This role required daubing his body with grease, covering it with feathers, and biting off the heads of live chickens.

When he could no longer be relied upon to rattle the bars of his cage on cue, he earned his whiskey through the only talent he had left—numbness. He would travel from bar to bar receiving whatever the drunks would pay for the privilege of hitting him as hard as they could. After he struggled back up to his feet, he'd shout "Tom! Tom!" and prove a lack of pain by baring his few remaining teeth in what was supposed to be a smile. By the end of an evening's work, he had almost always reached the degree of intoxication needed to release him from what he had become.

During this last period, he occupied the lean-to behind Mrs. Costa's home, paying for it, Tony supposed, through doing the few chores he could still negotiate and in speaking "English" for Mrs. Costa. She had already indicated, that this last item touched one of the few soft spots in her bulk by giving Tony the tinted hot water she called tea.

While he sipped at it, she told him that after noticing Hawley's disappearance a week or so ago, she had thought no more about him, accepting that all that had happened was that he finally absorbed one beating too many and had crawled into an alley somewhere and died. Now that she thought about it, she said, it was probably while he still owned the bar when Hawley had sent those letters to England that described his prosperity, but since that was some time back, maybe two years or more, she didn't think that Tony's father had much more sense than his cousin to be sending Tony so far on such a skimpy notion.

Ordinarily, Tony wouldn't have dreamed of allowing someone like this to judge his family, but he was learning fast that his survival depended on keeping quiet. So long as she confined her comments to the one estimate of her father's conduct with which he could privately agree, he didn't intend to say anything that interfered with her offering him Hawley's shack until he found a way to get back to England. But when she continued on into a discussion of the stupidity of turning his back on his trunk, he interrupted, asking, "How much rent will you charge me for the use of Mr. Hawley's room?"

"What difference does it make? You ain't got no money anyhow."

"I will have," he answered, projecting a confidence that he didn't feel in the least. "And then you will be paid in full."

"Lordy, son," she said, "I already been through this once. Whenever Tom-Tom was taken sober, which you can bet wasn't often, he was going to bring me back to London with him."

"Mrs. Costa, I shan't promise to take you anywhere. But you have my word that a fair rental will be yours as soon as I land a position."

"Do I, now?" she said in what seemed to her to be a fine approximation of his accent. "Well, your highness, I don't need your word any more'n I need to go to London. The rent is ten dollars a week and that's dirt cheap."

By now, Tony had found enough self-control to keep from pointing out that she had just delivered a fair description of her lodgings. "That is exactly all that I have left," he said instead. "Let me give you half that, and if I haven't secured a position within a few days, you can ask me to leave."

"Can I now?" she said, still mimicking him.

It took Tony a few seconds to continue in a civil tone, "Yes, Mrs. Costa, you won't have lost anything because I'll pay in advance and not stay a day beyond the money I have given you."

"For all your fancy talk, you're a pretty smart businessman, ain't you?"

Tony thought, *I'm going to have to do it. I'm going to hit her*, but aloud he said, "I'm glad you think so. It's your guarantee that I'll keep my word." Wanting to shut off the discussion she was so obviously relishing, he went on, "I won't worry about seeing the room now. I'd rather be out after work while it is still daylight." And he put his hand into his pocket for the dollars that would seal their deal.

Surprisingly, she sighed. "Never mind, Mr. Johnstone. You got just about enough money left to buy you one meal in San Francisco. Get back here by dark and I'll feed you some supper. You can pay when you find work." Then she shook her head in sad wonder at her own generosity.

Tony turned and left without saying anything further because he didn't want her to see the tears that started into his eyes. At that moment he thought they were caused by anger at the realization that he was so nakedly dependent on the goodwill of a creature like Mrs. Costa. He understood much later it was because of the unexpected display of humanity.

He felt himself trembling as he walked down the street, thinking, *This accursed country! These horrible barbarians!* Then, remembering his family and their smug belief that all their decisions were rightful because they had made them, he added, *God damn my father!*

He may have actually voiced this last statement because he saw a man turn and look at him.

I'll hit him if he says anything at all! was his next thought, but the man hurriedly continued on after seeing Tony's glare.

Opportunity to vent his fears and frustration came on the very next street. Turning the corner, he saw three young toughs viciously beating a Chinese boy whose blouse was already covered with the gore dripping from the cuts and bruises on his face. Scooping up a large stick lying nearby, Tony ran toward the assailants, yelling with all his might, "You bloody, bloody bastards! You filthy Yankees!"

The toughs fled before a threat as savage and mindless as this, and after Tony had chased after them for perhaps a half a block, he stopped and returned to help the Chinese boy get to his feet. This was Tony's introduction to Chung Lin.

9

SINCE CHUNG LIN PLAYS as big a part in what we did as anyone else, I suppose I should mention how and why he happened to land in San Francisco.

Understand now, I can't vouch for any of what follows except for what I've seen and been able to dig up—or to extract from his nephew, Chung Po Fong, who's been working all these years as his scribe. Incidentally, Chung Po Fong has always considered Chung Lin as the beginning and end of everything a man is supposed to be, so I guess a few of that heathen's virtues have escaped our notice.

Anyway.

The Custom House records for 1852 show that 20,026 Chinese came to San Francisco that year looking for the same thing as the rest of us. Most of these were immigrants from the three districts around Canton in the Kwangtung Province. In 1848 that area had been devastated by flood, famine, and political terror, so thousands moved away from their farms and into the city. It was in Canton that they heard the stories about the mountains in California being made not out of rock but of pure gold.

Some of them paid for their passage to America by selling whatever scraps of property they had been able to hold on to or by borrowing the money from relatives. The rest had no families left and were penniless to boot, and these, the majority by far, indentured themselves to an Immigrant Aid Society known as the *Hui Kuan*, which provided them with transportation, food, and shelter until they found jobs in the mining camps. Naturally, every dollar they earned during the first few years after they arrived here went back to the Society as repayment. Later, certain enterprising Chinese were able to pile up considerable personal fortunes by competing with the Society to provide this service, but, since Chung Lin was not among them, that's another story.

The miners who arrived in America under these conditions would never have left home in the first place if they'd only had to contend with the famines and floods of their native districts because these were normal

58

in the life cycle of each generation of farmers. But when the bloody civil wars broke out and were added to these cyclical catastrophes, their lives became too much for them to bear. As a result, almost three million left their country to make this long and dangerous journey. Many of the travelers found it tempting to settle in the first stopping place, which is why many of their children now populate the Hawaiian Islands.

The 300,000 who persisted and reached the American mainland were known as the Sojourners since they intended to stay just until they made enough money to return home to an easier life for themselves and whomever in their families was still alive. The term was a reminder among themselves that they were not here as pioneers, settlers, or adventurers, so there was no need to assimilate; they brought their culture with them and kept it intact during their stay.

Their wives never came with them. This was a condition generally demanded by the Society or the entrepreneurs advancing passage funds. The women left at home became the guarantees that their men would return, and as a result, the Chinese reputation among American railroad mine owners for industry and all but inexhaustible perseverance was generally based on the simple need to make good a compact with the family, the gods, and the people who had loaned them money.

Chung Lin was much younger than most of his fellow Sojourners when he arrived here in 1852, but he was just as determined to return home a rich man. As an orphan in Canton, his earliest lessons were what it was like always to be alone, poor, and hungry. Even the worst farmer manages an occasional good meal, but the city's alley and wharf scavengers like Chung get an early start in learning that sentiment, allegiance, or dreams won't fill your belly. It never occurred to him not to lie about his age to the *Hui Kuan* secretary who had the power to send him to a place where food, clothes, and money could be had for the earning. Chung Lin was a scrawny sixteen at the time, but he swore to the official by all the gods he knew that he was five years older and that every member of his nonexistent family back in his unknown ancestral village wanted to volunteer as a hostage against his return.

His trip to America was no better nor worse than that of any of his fellow Sojourners, meaning that the old tug on which they sailed was unbelievably filthy and so overcrowded that no rancher in his right mind would ship his animals that way if he wanted to get any price at all for them at the market. When he arrived in San Francisco, having no other place to go, he reported to the Yu Chuy Lung Company, which was an associated organization of the *Hui Kuan*. These people sent him to a shoe manufacturer where he became one of its 375 "Yellow Men" laboring force. Like the rest, his pay was a dollar for each ten-hour working day.

But, unlike the others, Chung wasn't willing to accept the life of a passive workhorse. He didn't have a family back in China that could be disgraced by his failure to live up to his passage agreement, and his years of survival as a Cantonese alley rat had honed his senses sharp enough to let him figure out that the daily dollar brought just enough shelter and food to allow him to exist until he reported back to work the next morning. So, he slipped away one night and became another faceless Oriental in the city. If anyone missed him, it was the accounts keeper at the Yu Chuy Lung Company who probably marked down the absence as one more Chinese death at the hands of a drunken Occidental.

He wasn't particularly distressed by being alone or penniless because that was the only state he'd known since he was seven years old. But survival might be another story in a city where he couldn't speak the language, so he set about finding someone to teach him a smattering of coolie English.

The friend that he found was a young girl who worked in one of the fifty brothels jammed into the three Chinatown alleys named Spofford's, Stout's and Sullivan's. Her name was Loi Yau, and she became Chung Lin's protector because he was the first person to regard her as a human being since she arrived in America. Sep Sam, a woman who owned a whore house in Sullivan's Alley, had bought her from her family for $503 along with the further agreement that the girl's passage money was still owing and had to be paid off under a contract for fifty-four months of prostitution.

There had been some other sales provisions. If she ran away and Sep Sam had to send men to catch her, the passage debt was increased by the cost of the search and chase. Every day of sickness was to be made up by two additional days of work. And, of course, the contract was assignable; if Sep Sam quit and went back to China, Loi Yau could be sold to another brothel keeper, but her debt wasn't lessened by any profits from the transaction.

The possibilities of living through the fifty-four months of the contract without a disabling venereal disease weren't good. Her probabilities of achieving a normal life in America or back in China were even worse. Her only prospect was abnormally quick old age, and who cares what happens to an old prostitute? It wasn't any wonder, then, that when Chung Lin happened to speak kindly to her in the street, she responded with the delight of a gutter puppy finding a bone.

Although she was only fifteen, he immediately became the younger brother whom she could love and give the few pennies she received as tips from her coolie patrons. For the first few days after their meeting, she squirreled away a portion of the food she received at Sep Sam's table and brought these scraps to Chung Lin in the sleeping shack where he was one of twelve who paid ten cents a night. After he found out he could make money working the piers as a porter, he deepened her feeling for him by the occasional gift of a rice cake.

Naturally, there was no way for their emotion to mature. Even if Chung Lin ever found enough money to buy her from Sep Sam, it wouldn't have occurred to him to do so. As for Loi Yau, there was no way she could agree to disgrace her family by running away from the contract they had made with the brothel keeper. However, a fortunate accident fixed each of them forever in the other's memory; they never saw each other again after the afternoon that Tony Johnstone saved Chung Lin from the three toughs who were going to beat him to death.

10

THERE WAS NO DOUBT that Chung Lin was impressed by the way my father set about outfitting our party. Father rarely questioned a shopkeeper's advice, bought the best of everything without haggling, and was totally oblivious to the looks that wondered why some of these purchases were being made for a Chinese boy. That doesn't mean that I saw any gratitude or even warmth in the owlish stare with which he watched Father. Rather, it was a passive acceptance of one of the facts now in his life and, if anything, I had a hunch that there was a trace of scorn in our Oriental at the sight of such an easy mark peeling off so many bank notes in store after store.

Chung was wary of Tony Johnstone but more comfortable with him than anyone else. He felt that this young Englishman instinctively knew the line, so whatever treatment he got from him might be harsh, but it would also be logical. Chung had been a loader on the Cantonese piers long enough to understand that the non-Chinese never concerned themselves with the people behind the services they demanded.

It was a different matter where I was concerned. He didn't like me even a little bit during those first few days. When it came to punishment, he figured that my father would have administered it with forgiveness in his eyes, that there would have been no emotion at all in Tony but, as for me, he was certain that I'd enjoy dealing it out. Worried by what he considered as my cynical manipulation of Father, he expected it to be only a short while before he'd be on its receiving end. Right then there was no question in his mind that my treachery was someday going to lead to his losing the unimaginably easy berth he'd fallen into.

But, as I understood later, this low opinion of me went up a bit right after we left San Francisco on the boat bound for Crescent City, where we were going to hire the mules and carts to take us to Jacksonville. I knew Chung had been doing his peculiar best to learn our language because every once in a while he'd repeat (but only to Father) a word or phrase he'd overheard us using.

It was the morning of our first day out, and I saw him standing alone at the rail. Walking over, I heard him quietly singsonging something to himself, but I had to stand there almost a minute before I realized he was at work again on his English. When he finally realized that there was someone behind him, he whirled around, and seeing it was me, his eyes went blank and he began to edge way. I stopped him by putting my hand on his shoulder, and then he just stood there waiting for me to indicate that he could go.

"Come on," I said, "I'm not going to hurt you." I said it with the friendliest smile I could muster, but he didn't give the slightest indication that he understood.

I tried again. "I want to be your friend."

No reaction, but I had an idea. "Say this: *I am an American.*"

His eyes remained blank, so I tried again, speaking very slowly and exaggerating my lip motions. "I am an American."

Now he was looking directly at me although he still didn't say anything, reading, I guess, that I didn't intend any immediate problem.

"I am an American!"

Very tentatively: "Melican?"

"*American.*"

"Melican."

"Ame *r* ican. *R-R-R*, damn you!"

"Arl."

"Are!"

"Are-uh-el."

"That's closer. Are."

"Ahr."

"Right. Great!" I almost crowed with triumph. "Say it again. Ame *r* ican."

"Amerilucan."

"American! I-am-an-American."

It was almost too great a hurdle. His tongue just couldn't twist away from the L it wanted to put into the word, but he was damned if he was going to give up. He thought long and hard before trying it again, and then, speaking so slowly that it was a sentence instead of a word, he said distinctly, "Ah Mer Ee Can." My elation must have told him he had succeeded although of course he didn't know what it was that he had just correctly pronounced.

"That's just marvelous," I said, as happy as if I had been the one who had turned the trick. Then the two of us went on with words and terms for another hour or so, he pronouncing them and me using gestures to explain their meanings.

We tried it again next day. He seemed to have lost his suspicion of me, but now I saw something oddly different in his manner. Of course, there was no way I could have known that he had spent the night first repeating with pleasure all the words I had taught him, but then, while drifting off to sleep, the accomplishments had become alien things and the dreams that followed were riddled with the fears kept down while he was trying to stay alive in San Francisco. They surfaced in his sleep because aboard this ship there was nothing to fight and he was a sixteen-year-old boy who was getting time to realize that he was badly frightened by this new country and these strange people.

I had brought a periodical with me. Opening it, I pointed to the picture of a young lady in one of the advertisements. I said, "This is a *girl*."

"Gurl-ah."

"Girl."

"Gel."

"*Girl*."

"Guh-rul."

"Right. Fine." And then I saw tears in his eyes. "What's the matter, Chung Lin?"

He didn't answer but turned away and looked out at the sea because he was ashamed.

I didn't know what to do with this. I'd begun by regarding him as something into which I could pump information and maybe as the object of a game I could win and brag about to my father and Tony. Now it wasn't sport anymore; it was a boy crying because the picture of a contented, safe girl had reminded him that he had no safety, no family at home, no way to relate to his present situation, and the only doubt about his future was whether he'd be strong enough to stand up against those who were going to beat and exploit him. Suddenly, learning English was a long and hopeless path, because even if he successfully negotiated it, what was at its end that would ease his loneliness?

The picture had triggered the memory of little painted Loi Yau who had known that when he offered a rice cake he was also offering human exchange. No one since then had understood his rice cakes until I had come forward, and that's why he cried.

Of course, I didn't understand any of this then, but I sensed the fear and loneliness, so I put out my arms and held him until he stopped sobbing.

Chung Lin and I never referred to that time again, even after we became men. But I came to know in my bones how much my reassurance had meant to him and how much strength I'd found in comforting someone who was even more afraid than me.

11

"**T**HIS IS THE LIFE, eh boys!**"** Father observed with delight for perhaps the fifteenth time while we were bouncing over a pair of parallel ruts that was the trail between Crescent City and Jacksonville. After the fifth or sixth time, I noticed even Tony began to clench his jaw.

There was no diluting my father's delight in our new adventure. Whenever the rains teemed down, which was every few hours, he'd pull the atrocious sombrero that he had come to love a bit farther down over his head, wrap his poncho more tightly, and as soon as his chattering teeth permitted, he'd whistle to show his oneness with nature.

Nor did I agree with his idea that it was both manly and colorful to relieve ourselves by squatting under a tree. Agree? Hell, it was sheer terror! My bowels became a constipated solid block because I couldn't rid myself of the idea that the forest was full of snakes waiting in line to snap at my bare fundament.

I've never been so tired of anyone in my life as I got to be during that trip of My Father the Frontiersman.

Tony, of course, was too polite to offer any comment beyond occasionally shooting a quizzical look in my direction. But Chung Lin was another story. I was afraid that our putative houseboy was going to be as irrevocably ruined as a dog that's been abused in puppyhood. When the storms pelted us, he'd hunker farther down into the clothes we'd bought him and which seemed to be getting bigger on him by the minute, and he'd stare straight ahead, never saying a word either in Chinese or in the bits of English I'd drummed into him. I didn't doubt for a minute that he was praying to his heathen gods for delivery from this happy lunatic.

Father's romantic fog didn't lift even after we reached the tents and makeshift shacks of Jacksonville. He felt we had reached Camelot, so I should have known how useless it was to argue when we saw the double shanty he was about to pick out as our new home. The wretched place had neither windows nor floor, and the fireplace in it couldn't seem to make up its mind which way it intended to lean.

The man who offered it to us was quite proud of what he obviously considered a baronial holding. "Ye'r lucky, Doctor, that yer driver knowed me. Soon as I'd be letting it out that I'm ready to sell this place, it'd be grabbed right up. For two hundred dollars, yer buying as snug a home as there is in the hull valley!"

That miserable son of a bitch, he didn't even own the hovel! We found out later that its original builder had moved on to presumably richer diggings up at the Applegate River, and if he'd ever returned, we'd have been driven out at gunpoint, and there wasn't a man in the town who would have done anything but laugh at us for being such greenhorns.

When our seller saw he had his pigeon squarely within his sights, he finished Father off with, "All's you gotta do, Doc, is build some scaffold over t'other end and yer boys and you'll have some mighty snug bedsteads."

How he ever fitted Chung Lin into the role of the doctor's son is one of those leaps that I suppose only real estate vendors can make, but Father couldn't have cared less. No sooner had the man left with our money tucked away in his back pocket than my parent, with a light in his eyes that said he was ready to accept congratulations for his resourcefulness, said, "There you are boys—once your beds are built on the other end, we're going to have some mighty snug bedsteads!"

We didn't answer. We couldn't. Instead, Tony and I walked outside for our first real look at this raw little settlement that had been born less than a year before on a day in either December or January when the two itinerants, Cluggage and Poole, stumbled over the watercourse they named Rich Gulch and which was the scene of Oregon's first gold strike. After the news of their find reached California, almost overnight a thousand miners were jostling each other out of the way in order to stake their claims as close as possible to where Cluggage and Poole found their paydirt.

Naturally, when a swarm like this descends on a place, one of its earliest needs is a local source of supplies. Fifty miles away in Yreka, California, two packers, Appler and Kenny, heard about it and, after loading their mules with whiskey, tobacco, rough clothing, and food supplies, headed north to set up store in a tent. Not too long later, I believe in March, someone named Fowler built a log cabin, and that was Jacksonville's first real house.

A mining camp multiplies before your eyes in the first aftermath of a big gold strike. Within weeks, even days, other stores opened, more cabins were built, and a respectable (I use the word loosely) number of women had arrived. And, while the place was mushrooming into shape, even though none of its citizens were sure whether it was located in Oregon or California, it took a few minutes off to honor Andy Jackson by naming itself after him, although if he had seen the "city" he might have doubted that this was the high point of his presidency.

Some of Jacksonville's new citizens soon found out that putting up buildings was often easier pay than finding a place to pick gold nuggets up off the ground, so they turned to whipsawing logs and opened a mill from which they sold dressed lumber for $250 a thousand board feet. That brought clapboard houses with sawed doors and frame windows into being, and by June 1852, when the Humes and a few other families arrived, the place had begun to look like a community that could recognize a respectable household even though there were already seven saloons in the town and four more under construction.

The population was up to about 1,500 and more appearing daily when our little group reached there a few months later. The Chinese miners hadn't yet appeared in force, but Chung Lin didn't draw much notice because everyone was too busy mining, talking about mining, or getting ready to sell things to miners. Our first day there might have consisted of just settling in if Father could have resisted making another of his lighthearted observations. He said that he didn't have to touch anyone's forehead to tell that the town had a fever, all he had to do was wave his hand in the air.

I was still nursing my exasperation at the hovel he had picked as our new home, so I answered, "Father, waving your hands around isn't going to turn this pigsty into a decent place to live. And it isn't going to be all that much help in starting up your practice, either."

It was too mean a thing to say. Tony looked at me as if he were having second thoughts about being stuck in this raw place with a spoiled brat. Chung Lin didn't understand the words, but he got their sense because his face assumed that blankness that came over it every time he heard me pull my father up short. Realizing I had taken petulance too far, I added, "What I mean is that . . ."

"I know you didn't mean that quite the way it sounded, Collis," said Father, "but sometimes I can't help wishing you'd spend as much time studying your own speech as you do Chung Lin's." The gentle smile with which he said this turned the blurting out of my stupid statement into the reaction of an eager boy with an unfortunate way of expressing good intentions. Occasionally, Father's proper Philadelphia background was not the total handicap I may have made it out to be.

"I'm sorry," I said. "I was trying to understand how we are going to fix up all those beds the man told us about. I didn't say it as well as I might have and I'm truly sorry."

"No, it was a proper concern. I should have been the one to consider that problem." Then, in a graceful change of pace, he added, "I imagine the first thing one does in a situation like this is to get some tools and lumber. Do you know how to use a hammer, Anthony?"

My friend confessed, "Well, not really. But I've seen it done, and it's not very complicated, is it? I'd like to have a go."

"So would I," I chimed in with what I hoped was enough enthusiasm to balance out my childish behavior.

"So, gentlemen," said Father, "it's ho for the bedsteads!"

Then we all looked at each other. Where on earth would we go in this strange place to find hammer and nails? And from whom would we buy lumber and how much did we require? Since none of us had the answers, the only thing left to do was to go into the town with the hope of finding someone who wouldn't skin us too badly while filling our needs.

Fortunately, the solution arrived while we were still stowing our gear into the cabin's various corners, crevices, and holes. It appeared in the person of a young giant who almost blotted out the light as he came through the doorway of our new home. "Afternoon, sir," he said, addressing Father.

"A good afternoon to you," my father replied. After it became apparent that our visitor was stuck for whatever was supposed to be said after greetings were exchanged, he added, "Are you by any chance a resident of this place?"

"Live over to yonder," he said, pointing to a cabin on the hill just above us.

"Good! You're a neighbor. I'm Dr. John Gibbs and this is my son, Collis and his friend, Anthony Johnstone."

I filled the next long pause by saying, "And this is another friend, Chung Lin, who's helping us." I put out my hand and after a slight hesitation, he shook it.

"I'm Samuel Hume," he said, "and I live over . . ." he was about to wave toward his house again, but then, scowling, he acknowledged, "I already said that."

"No harm in repeating it—we're strangers here and we need all the introductions we can get." Father shook his head gravely and then smiled.

An answering grin of totally unexpected sweetness broke over Hume's

face. "Everybody's a stranger here," he said. "My folks and me just
came a couple of months ago." He looked about the cabin and, for some
reason, we all felt better when he added, "Won't take you no time to
get set."

Then Tony, ever the practical one, asked, "Perhaps you might help
us cozy in?"

The phrasing might have been unfamiliar, but Sam had no question
as to Tony's meaning. "I'm here to help," he said. "Ma sent me over
when she seen you unloading your wagon."

"That was quite thoughtful," said Father, "but I think we could
handle it all very well ourselves if we knew where to go to buy lumber
and a few tools."

"What for?"

Tony answered, "We've got to build sleeping cots for ourselves."

"Him, too?" He nodded his head in the direction of Chung Lin.

"That isn't a problem, is it?"

By now I had a glimmering of the fairly short fuse on Tony's temper
so I was about to step in to turn the conversation into another direction
when Hume answered, "Not too many like him around here just yet,
but there's some of the miners already studying about what'll happen
when they come swarmin up from California."

"Does it make a difference?"

He grinned again. "Not to me. Nor my folks. Fact, we never saw
our first Chinaman until on the way here we passed one on the trail and
we stopped to ask him which way it was to Jacksonville. He didn't even
look at us, he just hunched up his shoulders once or twice and said,
'Grackson no no,' and kept on walkin. Ma told Pa that was the queerest
Dutchman ever. Seein your friend reminded me of how funny we thought
it was that he talked that way."

The flush left Tony's face, but he didn't return the boy's smile. Being
Tony, he wanted to tack down exactly where Sam stood. "Then you and
your family won't mind our friend living here with us?"

His shrug indicated he'd lost interest in the conversation. "I guess
it'd be up to him if he don't mind livin with somebody that talks like
you." Turning to my father and me, he asked, "What kind of tools did
you have in mind?"

As I explained the "bedstead" idea of the cabin's former tenant, I
saw he was wondering how far he should mix into our affairs. When I
had finished, he thought for a moment longer and then, hesitantly,
observed, "Sawed lumber and nails cost lots of money here and, if you

don't mind, sir," he said to Father, "we might be able to lash some poles together into pretty fair double bunks."

Father was anxious to accept this courteously disguised offer of direction although I knew he had no idea what Sam was talking about. "That sounds like a fine idea, Samuel. By all means let's go ahead and lash some poles."

Our new neighbor nodded and began walking off, calling over his shoulder, "First let's go get the boogers." We stood in place for an uncertain moment, but when he showed no sign of returning to shepherd us, we turned and trooped after him as he headed for the thickest part of a nearby stand of pine trees. After reaching it, he looked about him and told us, "There's lots of good poles layin around in here. Let's tote some of them out." Picking up one log that measured about four inches around, he slung it over his shoulder and carried it to the clearing. We followed suit and when we had accumulated a dozen or so that he considered usable, he bucked off their limbs and set us to peeling the bark off the trunks that remained.

When he saw the question in my eyes at what seemed to be a long and tedious job, he said, "It's better to find out now if they got beetles or bugs than later when your blankets are all over them."

Then he turned to Chung Lin, initiating the easy communication between them that lasted from then on. "Tommy," he said—and I don't know how he settled on that name but it was the one that stuck—"we need these to fill up the mattress ticks." And not waiting to see whether his words were understood, he bent down and scooped up a big handful of pine boughs from the forest floor. These he held shoulder high, while resting his face in their soft needles to show that they were to be used to cushion our bodies.

Tommy (I'm more comfortable with that name now that there's been a proper identification) stared back for a lot less time than it generally took when we tried to tell him to do something and then, without further instruction, began bringing armfuls of the fragrant stuff over to our cabin door.

"Now, Doctor, sir," he continued, turning toward Father, "about all else we'll need is some sailcloth you could buy in town at Appler & Kenny's to make mattress ticks for the pine needles, and they've got some hides in there that we can cut into strips so's we can lash—tie—the poles together."

That night we all slept snug in beds that cost just a few dollars and a few hours' work.

12

TONY LOST NO TIME in getting to be a pain in the ass. The first thing he wanted to do next morning after our pine-bough bunks had given us the sweetest sleep you could ever imagine was to go out and look for a job.

I tried arguing with him, but after a while I realized that all my pointing out of the fun we could be having poking around this new town was just increasing his certainty that Anthony Johnstone's most important order of business was to pay my father the money he owed him for his clothes and the trip to Jacksonville. He finally cut me off by saying, "You don't understand. I feel poor!"

"What?"

"Yes, poor, you sod and don't look quite so appalled. If your father hadn't put out his hand, I'd still be floundering about in San Francisco. It isn't a nice thought."

Someone like Tony should have regarded Father's gesture as normal civilized behavior—but the feeling of being helpless back there in the city had been a totally new kind of thing for him. I saw then that he couldn't live with the idea of gratitude being the basis for his friendship with us.

So I dropped my arguments against him becoming a member of the laboring class. "What are you going to do," I asked, "go to work down in one of the mines?"

He had the grace to grin. "Not quite. I don't see myself just yet as a mole for hire."

"Would you like to be the mayor of Jacksonville? I understand you get to keep at least half of what you steal."

He thought that one over and then said, "It doesn't sound too ambitious, does it? To whom do you think I might apply for the post?"

"To me, of course."

"How stupid of me. Of course."

Within two more days a man named Stoltz, who was working the banks of a creek not too far from our cabin, taught him how to be a coyote miner. The training took less than a morning, but Tony was so grateful and in such a sweat to be self-sufficient that I kept the guess to myself that this was probably Stoltz's way of keeping the neighbors away from his own claim.

Next to pulling rocks out of a crevice by hand, coyoting is the most primitive kind of mining. You dig a hole some five to six feet wide and if you're in the right kind of soil, you'll find a strata of brown clay. This might be embedded with small cobblestones among which, with luck, there are some things in it that look like pumpkin seeds but are actually coarse gold flakes worth anywhere from a quarter to several dollars. Whenever the gods really want to raise your temperature, every so often you'll find a big yellow eye looking back up at you from the clay.

But, without the leaven of luck, coyoting is just plain drudgery. After several weeks, Tony had thirty-eight dollars, a wrenched back, and wasn't quite so deaf when my father said, "Anthony, I wish you could forget about the few dollars I've loaned you."

"I really wish that I could," Tony admitted, "but it *is* there, isn't it?"

"Then, for goodness sakes, at least wait until a more civilized job comes along."

"In Jacksonville?"

"Yes, here." He thought for a moment and his face brightened. "Do you remember that man Sacks that Collis brought around? The one who supposedly had so much knowledge about the medical use of herbs?"

Tony remembered old Sacks because, as he told me, I had bored him numb with my claims for the drifter's medical expertise. I'd met the man early one morning in front of a saloon in town while he was still sober, and I'd been excited by his descriptions of first learning about herbs while living as a trapper among the Indians and then by thumbing through some dog-eared manuals on the subject he found in his later stays in various mining camps. It was the kind of a mixture of moonshine and a few grains of sense that has never failed to snare my interest.

He was barely comprehensible a few days later when I brought him around to meet Father, because by that time it was noon so he already had enough tanglefoot in him to stun a mule. His one clear statement was delivered after my father put a simple question to him about the specific value of some herb or another. Old Sacks answered with an air of perfect logic, "You're a son of a bitch," and staggered from the room. He couldn't have said anything more calculated to cause Father to wonder whether a man so sure of himself might not be on to something valid.

Actually, I didn't think that much more than a tenth of what the old man had preached had any truth to it, but there was enough left to allow me to convince myself that Father's practice suffered from a severe herbal deficiency, so I set about fanning the tiny flicker of doubt aroused in him by Sacks into a sturdier flame. Over the next few days I found several ways to mention to my father that perhaps the reason dispensing herbs had never been discussed in his training was because none of his teachers had ever heard about them; and if he jumped on the opportunity to learn about them here, some day he could carry this knowledge back to the Philadelphia medical community, who'd then stand in line to clap him on the back in congratulations.

It worked better than I had hoped. Not only did Father adopt my final suggestion that I become his herb collector, he also hired Tony to help me. It happened during one of the times he was changing the bandage supporting Tony's sprained back.

"You know, Anthony," he said after he had finished, "Collis might have been right about the herbs. Not all of them, of course, but there seems to be enough in the few species I've examined to warrant their occasional use."

"That must be gratifying."

"You mean I should be pleased that my son hasn't been just working another of his sells?"

"Oh, no," my friend answered thinking *oh yes*, "Collie has a good instinct for these things."

"I'm impressed that you feel this way," said Father. "Why don't you join him?"

"In herbal collecting?"

"At the same wages I'm paying Collis. And I'll credit half of it against our bill."

"But I don't know a blessed thing about herbs or medicine."

"Neither does my son, but I'm sure he's going to learn in quick order."

Tony said, reluctantly, "Doctor Gibbs, I'll confess that I'd like never to see a pick and shovel again. But I can't help but believe that you are finding an easy way for me to settle my debt."

"Not at all," said my father earnestly. "I'm convinced that I've stumbled over a golden opportunity to add to my professional knowledge."

Tony began to shake his head again, but this brought a sharp enough twinge to his back to finally dislodge his pride. After a brief tussle with his conscience, he gave in. "Well, if you're certain . . ."

For the next few weeks Tony and I ranged the fields and hills around Jacksonville, cramming just about everything that looked interesting into our bags and having one of the best times we'd ever known. Most of our collectings turned out to be worthless junk, but this didn't bother Father because it turned out that he enjoyed using the books he'd brought with us to try and identify the flowers, weeds, and herbs that we dumped onto his office floor each night. He began teaching himself the names of the various species, and he'd lovingly catalogue each and every item, keeping even some of the marginal stuff in the hope that he'd learn a use for it.

After a while, the tiny medical office that he had rented on California Street got so crowded with strange smelling piles that it threatened to burst and spill out onto the sidewalk, so Tony and I had to become more selective, and this finally forced us to face the fact that neither of us knew what he was doing. We were bringing back everything that appeared remotely medicinal, but we didn't have the foggiest idea about their uses or effects. I figured it wouldn't be long before Tony went back to being uncomfortable over taking his weekly salary.

To head off this feeling that we were getting about as much results as a couple of monkeys trying to make love to a soccer ball, we spent extra time trying to find a miner or housewife who might be a bit more lucid about herbs than old Sacks. No luck. Although some people claimed they knew a thing or two about the subject, there was never a speck of reliability or even logic in what turned out to be their fragments of folklore. Even so, we tested almost every remedy and formula they described up until the point that Tommy drove us and our foul-smelling concoctions out of his kitchen.

"We're wasting time, Collis," Tony told me one morning. "We can keep gathering every strange plant we stumble over, but unless we know what it can do, your father is going to earn a name for poisoning his patients."

"That's been our problem. If we knew some Indians, we could learn everything there is about herbs by getting them to betray the innermost secrets of their sacred culture."

"That sounds splendid. You *do* speak beautifully."

"I know," I said and modestly explained, "it's from a book I read back in Philadelphia. It's called, *The Betrayal of Our Red Skinned Brethren.*"

"Fascinating." He stared solemnly at me for a moment and added, "More than anything else in this world, I'd love to betray some Indians. Where do you think we might find one to practice upon?"

"I've thought of that, too," I answered. "Let's go hunt up Sam Hume. If there's anyone in Jacksonville who'd know an Indian ripe to be betrayed, it's Sam."

The grin finally crept onto his lips. "Absolutely. Just the right scoundrel to keep us in the evil ways of the white man!"

We hadn't been seeing much of Sam because after he'd gotten tired of helping his father mine the dry holes he kept coming up with, he'd gone to work as a carpenter for Henri Boudreau. At first I thought it was strange that Mr. Hume didn't put up a bigger squawk at this, but then I realized Sam's wages must have been a big help to the family's table money.

It was just after Henri came to town in late August that he opened the Bella Union, a saloon that right from the start did just about twice as much business as its competitors since it never closed, not even in the early morning hours. Sam was building a bowling alley addition next door to the bar because, according to what Henri had heard, this was the latest thing in just about every mining camp in the West that had advanced past being more than a collection of tents.

Our large friend was sitting on the ground, his back against a tree, eating a sandwich when we arrived. If a stranger had watched us walk up to him, he might have thought we were enemies because, as usual, he stared at us without offering a word of greeting.

I spoke first. "How much is Boudreau paying you to hold up that tree?"

The stare was diluted by a flicker of disgust. "Don't be talking that way to somebody who works for their livin.'"

"He's right," Tony told me. "You are showing disrespect to one of nature's noblemen."

Sam grunted through a mouthful of his sandwich. "What are you two weasels up to, anyway? I wouldn't guess that you drifted over here to help out."

"Weasels!" I said indignantly. "Do you mean to tell me that somebody lying around on the grass has the guts to call us hardworking herb experts, weasels?"

Sam didn't bother with a reply. He finished his sandwich off in one last gulp and then stretched out prone, one elbow crooked over his eyes to shield them from the sun. Then, after lazily drawing in a deep breath, he announced to the sky, "Don't worry, God, there's no way they'll keep on fightin you. Soon as you show Tony, here, the paths of righteousness, he's goin to turn his back on Collie Gibbs and help me get a man's job done."

"He can't," I explained, also to whatever spirit was listening. "He owes us a fortune and it's only my goodwill that keeps Father from having him locked up for owing money that he's not dreaming of paying back."

"The sod is right," Tony told Sam. "A thirteen-dollar balance to Dr. Gibbs is all that keeps me in bondage and away from joining you in your honest toil."

"When does that get paid off?"

"If the good weather holds—and I'm certain your Lord will want to do me this courtesy—just a few more weeks."

Then he became serious because a new idea had occurred to him. Or, maybe he'd been thinking about it for a while and this was the time to announce it to me. "Collis, I really believe I'd like to learn something of carpentry. Do you think your father would mind?"

His wanting to join Sam caught me off guard. I thought for a moment, but the best I could do was, "Well, sure, Tony, he'd understand. But he really does sort of count on you for the herbs. He's using more of them than ever these days."

"Really?" By that he meant we both knew that my father wouldn't have run out of herbs for the next three years if we stopped collecting.

I wanted to, but I honestly couldn't fault Tony. The reason for our afternoons in the fields was becoming fairly thin, and once it wore through, there was no way he'd accept staying on as a paid companion. I gave in by saying as bitterly and reproachfully as I could, "One of these days there'll be an epidemic and the whole damned town will die for lack of enough herbs. Just you wait and see."

Sam asked, "Did I start something?"

"Not really," Tony answered. "Collis is just being . . ." He never finished the sentence because that's when Mrs. Jabez Witham came striding up to us, disapproval of our indolent sprawling showing in every corner of her dark face.

"Samuel," she said, ignoring Tony and me, "I hope you realize how anxious Mr. Witham and Mr. Boudreau are to get this building finished!"

Witham was our town banker and the source of the funds for the building of the saloon and bowling alley. The fact that his wife towered over him by a good foot and a half caused quite a bit of idle sexual speculation in the town.

"I sure do, ma'am," Sam answered. "But I'm just takin a short spell for lunch."

Pursing her lips even further at the sight of so many idle hands, she noted, "Well, it does seem somehow that talking to these boys all the time isn't part of eating lunch." She was holding her thin body rigidly erect, but she couldn't have been sending out more sparks than if she had been spinning like a windmill.

"Don't take on so," Sam said, getting slowly to his feet. "I'm just about to start workin again, so there's no call to be frettin about your husband's grubstake."

It wasn't like him to talk like this. Ordinarily, he showed a grave courtesy toward his elders that was the combination of his mother's training and his father's iron hand, so I thought that maybe being spoken to this way in front of his friends had set his teeth on edge. Then I thought again and realized, *damned right this isn't like him!* Something way out of usual was going on.

I sensed the drift right after she left a few minutes later, but it took another week of badgering Sam before I got to the point where I could put the whole picture together.

Well, maybe it wasn't just my pressing that brought him to confide in me. After all, it was his very first go-round for sex, and even a stoneface like Sam Hume had to be bursting with the need to tell someone. Tony might have been prissy about it, but he'd cover with a superior smile because Mrs. Witham was so much older; Chung Lin would have wondered why Sam thought it was so important; and that left me, although he knew that I'd probably (and I did) slaver over the details.

Of course, Sam didn't tell me everything. In a disjointed sort of way he just told me the bits and pieces, but I was able to get it all into order by supplying the rest of the items I knew had to be there, too. From the start, I've always known what comes next in the kind of thing that happened between our friend and the banker's wife.

In a place like Jacksonville, anyone who doesn't know everyone else is set on being a hermit, so Mrs. Witham had seen Sam around but didn't really notice him until he had taken on the job of building the addition to the Bella Union Saloon.

He'd been working there for almost two weeks when along came one of those ungodly hot days we sometimes get in the late fall where the sun sends the thermometer up high enough that anyone working out of doors is going to be wearing as few clothes as he can get away with before being declared a public nuisance. Sam, stripped to the waist, was digging postholes for the building's corner supports when Mrs. Witham arrived.

He remembered: "The sweat was just pouring off me, so I figured I ought to try and keep as much distance as I could between us. I mean, she's the wife of the richest man in town and I must have smelled like a bear with porcupine for supper. But when I moved over to another corner, doggone if she didn't follow me. She kept talkin about how important it was for me to get this job done right because it meant so much to Mr. Boudreau, and all the time she kept starin off over my shoulder. A couple of times I turned around to look but there wasn't a thing there.

"At first I thought to myself that this is a lady that's really interested in her husband's business because there wasn't any question in my mind that she was thinkin a touch more about Mr. Witham's money than old Henri's bar. In fact, she was doggone tense about it, but since she's got a name for bein a high-strung woman I thought she was just being the way everybody always says she is. Nervous.

"She kept after it like a cat worryin a mouse until I started to wish she'd go away and let me get my postholes dug, but, no, she wasn't about to do that. If anything, she was gettin worse.

"Finally, I figured the hell with it and paid her no more attention than a 'yes ma'am' or a 'no ma'am,' and the next thing I knew, when I was raising one of the corner poles to set it in place, there she was tryin to lift up the other end to help me. I swear, I was purely shocked because it certainly wasn't right for her to do that, especially since I didn't want the damned other end up anyway, and if anybody had happened by, it would have been just awful lookin.

"So I said, 'Mrs. Witham, it's nice of you to want to help out to get this job done quicker, but I'm getting along pretty fine and, to tell the truth, you wobblin around with that other end ain't assistin me all that much.'

"At this she got steamin mad. She let the other end of the pole down so hard I could feel my end buck up and jam a big splinter in my thumb.

"You know, Collie, I try to be polite most of the time, but this just about tore it. I yelled, 'Goddammit!' and dropped my end, too, and yanked out the splinter, and then I'm a son of a buck if she didn't come hoppin over to me and sayin, 'Oh, I'm so sorry, Samuel! Here, let me . . .' And she took my hand, putting my thumb in her mouth to suck away at the blood that was comin from where I had pulled out the splinter. And, at the same time, she had her hand slidin up and down my wet back.

"At first I didn't know whether to shit or go blind, I was that surprised. And then I jerked my thumb out of her mouth—I think I even scraped it more on her teeth—and then I backed away. I mean, I know I always been dumb where women are concerned, but there ain't no way anybody is ever goin to stay that dumb when a lady like Mrs. Witham is actin so much like a bitch in heat that she's doin everything but drag her ass along the ground!"

That was about all of the story he wanted to tell me, but over the next few days I was able to extract most of the rest. Wherever there was a gap, my enthusiastic imagination closed it by coming up with whatever he tried to leave out. I don't think I've missed too many of the details because his reactions were a pretty good check on just how close I was to the bull's-eye.

After Sam had pulled away, Mrs. Witham's next move was to tell him to come along with her.

He said, "I can't do that, Mrs. Witham."

"Why not?"

He tried to think of a way out, but the best he could do was that someone was bound to see them no matter which way they went. Her answer was not to pay any attention to his words. She said, quite severely, "I don't know what on earth you're up to! I'm worried about you, Samuel!"

He said her breath was coming short and heavy while she was saying this, and there was nothing in what she was telling him that had anything to do with what was on her face. "You're going to get yourself into a pile of trouble, Samuel, if you don't learn how to behave!"

By now he had the sense to listen only to what was in her voice, so he just nodded.

Pointing to the side but not taking her eyes off him for an instant, she went on, "I'll tell you what, you meet me at that clump of trees yonder, and I'm going to go there now, not spank to the front of them but over to the middle, and after a while you'd better be marching there, too. I'm going to be a friend to you, Samuel, even if it's not what most people would do to take this much trouble, but I will. I'm going to try and tell you how you mustn't ever misread people when they mean only good and to be helpful. You hear, Samuel? I'm just hoping that I can talk some sense into you." She paused, no longer looking at him but again at somewhere over his shoulder. "Now you come on, but not right away because anybody would jump to thinking the wrong things if you was to be tailing right after me." And without waiting for a reply, she turned and walked, stiff and straight, toward the trees.

He stared at her retreating back and shook his head, saying softly to himself, "Be goddamned." Almost mechanically, he walked over to the pole they had been wrestling over, picked it up, and set it down in the hole he had dug.

Steadying the swaying pole with one hand, he reached down for his shovel and, at the same time, kicked dirt in the hole for the log's support. Then he said again, this time explosively, *"Be goddamned!"* and dropping both pole and shovel, he wheeled about and walked as fast as he could without running to where she had disappeared among the trees.

He couldn't find her at first, believing that the gleam of white he saw in his first look around was a shaft of sunlight. But, of course, it was she, already naked, and as he ran toward her, his last thought before he was there and she was pulling him to the ground was that even then her eyes were focused at some point beyond him, but by that time he didn't give the slightest damn as to what it might be.

Her need was so great that when he exploded almost before penetration, she kept pawing at him, and the soft crooning sounds that welled up from her throat didn't quit until his vitality returned and then their lovemaking became the deep thrusting drives that she rocked him into maintaining. This time they shared the climax.

He rolled over, the breath coming from him in gasps as if he had run a mile, but she lay quietly on her back, the severe expression not leaving her face until suddenly she arched, and it seemed to him that her features blurred into a dreamy ease that flitted away so quickly that he had to doubt it had ever been there. Then she lay back down again.

Turning at last, she saw what was in his eyes as he looked at her body, so she twisted away but not before he could wonder at seeing swelling curves instead of the thin angularity that anyone might expect after meeting her as a fully dressed matron of the town.

My Lord, she's something! he thought, awestruck by the first nude woman he'd ever seen other than those on the creased tintypes that were passed around in the saloons.

"You stop that!" she said, brushing off the arm he had reached out in a caress and, scrambling to her feet, backside toward him, she dressed, and before he could think of anything to say that might make her lie down again beside him for even a few minutes more, she was hurrying away out of the woods.

She stopped just before where the trees gave way to the clearing and called, "Samuel!" although she didn't turn around.

He answered, "Yes ma'am?" and immediately cursed himself for sounding so much like a gawky kid after his splendid accomplishment.

"I've a good mind to talk to your ma and pa," she said sternly and passed from his sight.

13

THE ENGLISH have a history of disinheriting every child but the oldest son, so Tony was suprised that he was left anything at all when his father died. It wasn't much; the entire legacy fit into the packet his brother sent him containing the old gentleman's lesser cufflinks, some miniatures, the pen he had whittled as a boy, an unexceptional collection of military figurines, and a sheaf of yellowing notes and letters tucked away in the pigeonholes in the escritoire he kept in his bedroom. But the fact that his father said in his will that he wanted him to have the desk's contents was a gesture Tony found quite touching.

The death occurred quite a while after Tony had come to America and become our friend, so I mention it here only because among the contents of the packet was a letter Tony had written home during our early Jacksonville days. He was grudging (". . . too personal, too vulnerable and, also, I sound like a stilted ass") about allowing me to use it here but relented when I pointed out that, as well as anything else, it describes exactly what we saw and felt during that time.

Here's the letter:

3 January 1853

Dear Father,

Please forgive the weeks that have gone by since my last letter home, but so much has happened of concern only to me and so little that could be of interest to all of you back in England that I have been at a loss as to what I might write. But, since you suggested regular reports, here is one more. If I become too tedious, please let me know and I'll avoid the less interesting subjects in future letters.

I am still living with Dr. Gibbs and his son. I have finally repaid the monies he advanced me, and although I appreciated your offer to retire this debt, I thought it better to accomplish this through my own efforts, which, surprising as it may seem to all of you, have been productive enough to cover the loan as well as my daily costs.

Of course I agree with the point made in you last letter that I acted in

83

panic after discovering the loss of the funds you placed in my care. I should have gone to the nearest San Francisco banking house and certainly its manager would have written immediately to your New York agents, and then I should not have had to accept a stranger's generosity.

But, I must also add that even if I had not been so badly rattled by the theft, the time required to establish communication between the bankers and yourself might still have left me with the need to accept any offer, no matter if it were far less than the decent one made by Dr. Gibbs.

However, there seems to be at least one advantage in this misfortune; someone earning his way through this country may very well end as having been placed in the best position to gather and pass on the information that I have been charged with furnishing. You see and hear so very much more on the streets than from a seat in the office of someone anxious to persuade you of whatever situation offers him the most benefit.

This possibility, of course, does not excuse my carelessness, but, if you permit me to follow this path, I will do everything I can to make certain that you receive value from your decision that I make this trip. As you suggested, I shall not attempt to weigh any of the information I glean but will include it all in these letters home.

So, here follows the first omnibus from one who toils for his wages!

I am not certain that the growth of Jacksonville as a gold-producing centre will retain its present hearty rate. Although new mines continue to be discovered, I wonder at the speed with which old claims are abandoned.

The richness of the soil here in the Rogue Valley attracts an increasing number of farming families. Their major crop is the wheat that is ground into flour and sold at a prodigious price to the miners. Therefore, the farmers become as prosperous as most of the miners. But if the veins of gold that caused this place to become what it is are ever exhausted, the miners will leave. Then what will happen to the granges of southern Oregon? The more farsighted people here suppose that land values will tumble quite sharply if the farmers are ever forced to consider the difficulty of transporting their unsold crops through the mountains that surround them.

I mention these gloomy prospects only because of your last letter in which you spoke of the high regard at home for the Oregon country.

On the other hand, if Jacksonville continues to find new gold mines, or if more efficient methods of operating old mines are employed, it is difficult to believe that there is another area in these territories that offers a better return on investment capital.

Since I am still unqualified in these matters, whenever possible I try to become aware of the opinions of the city's more successful men of property. I was in the company of one such man a few days ago. He is the town banker and his name is *Jabez Witham*. The occasion was the Witham family Christ-mas party. The Withams occupy the only home in the area that possesses more than three rooms.

I was included in the invitation extended to Dr. Gibbs and Collis. The few others I knew among the visitors were our houseboy, Chung Lin (he wasn't a guest, of course—the American fondness for democracy we hear so much about doesn't extend quite that far—he was lent by the doctor for the kitchen) and Mr. and Mrs. Hume and their son, Samuel.

The party, attended by residents from every part of the Valley, was con-sidered by all as an enormous social success. The Witham home, well lit by tallow candles (here, they are known as "dips"), was the scene for much dancing, which began at seven in the evening and lasted until the following morning when the farmers returned home to milk their cows, a necessity even on Christmas Day.

The music was provided by a rustic down from one of the nearby hills who sawed at an ancient fiddle (violin) to produce airs with such names as "The Arkansas Traveler," "Pop Goes the Weasel," and several others that I seem to remember having heard before, although I could not identify them in these surroundings.

A lesser group chose not to dance to the calls of a freckle-faced boy who, as the evening wore on, became hoarse in the attempt to make himself heard over the endless shuffling and prancing. They sat before a spacious and blazing fireplace, matching colorful stories of pioneer experiences and hairbreadth escapes from "Injuns" and "varmints."

Some others remained at the dining table for the entire evening, even though they could eat no more food, in order to hear the observations of the various territorial politicians who attended because of the esteem in which they held Mr. Witham.

I relate all this so that you may place in its proper context what I shall tell you later in this letter.

Our host, as is the custom of the wealthier men in the area, purchases his whiskey by the barrel. Several of his kegs were opened in honour of the occasion, but, having heard many lurid descriptions of the various methods by which this stuff is manufactured, I chose not to sample their contents. However, no other gentleman present, with the sole exception of Mr. Witham, showed the slightest inclination to share my doubts.

My opportunity to chat with our host occurred as the entire group united to sing the carols of Christmas. I was feeling quite honestly touched by the sincerity of these people when I heard his voice in my ear. "What's the matter, young man, don't you know the words?"

"I do, sir," I assured him.

"Well, then, don't you like to sing?" His attitude was that of one who earnestly cared that I enjoy myself in his home.

"I do, sir," I assured him, "but, after all . . ."

"After all what?" he interrupted, knowing full well that I meant I didn't feel sufficiently at ease with this group to join them in so communal an activity.

And then I thought that perhaps the question was his form of reassurance. After all, I had been in residence here as long as many and, probably, longer than most. What is more, I realized that I am attracted to these people. They accept me, not (I can see you smirking at this, Charles) for who I am but rather for what I am.

Do you find this attitude a distressing one? I hope not. I would be so pleased if you would not regard it as marking one in the course of losing hold of his standards because that is certainly not the case. I wish I had the skills to express these sentiments more clearly (I admit that even I find them a bit surprising), but I am afraid this will all have to wait until it can be sorted out when I return home.

At any rate, let me continue by describing Mr. Witham at length since I am aware of the interest you have in information that involves a potential associate.

The gentleman (?) is quite short, slight, probably just entering his middle years but has already lost every strand of hair that ever graced his head. He is so bald that it is rather difficult to believe that he was ever anything else. His wife, Helen, is much taller than he, but no one in the first meeting with them would doubt that he dominates her, so bullying is his manner.

Now add a pair of steel-rimmed spectacles always at the point of sliding off his pinched nose, a fussiness that keeps the dust away from his person on the driest of days even though the rest of us walk about as if we had just passed through a bin of flour. And, finally, a voice (I'm certain he's cultivated it to compensate for his lack of height) so deep that it might be rumbling down from the mountains.

This is not persiflage, Father. This is Jazeb Witham, and I am certain that his present appearance is not much different from what it was when he departed his native Boston bound for San Francisco. He is locally considered a Pacific Coast pioneer, an honour that is given additional weight by virtue of his reputedly having spent several years as a California miner.

The claim of having been a miner rests on his unsupported word, although it has been generally regarded as a truth in Jacksonville. For myself, I find it easier to accept the estimate of the cynical few who maintain that he laid down his shovel soon after having picked it up in order to become the proprietor of a service that transported packets between San Francisco and Yreka, a community several hundred miles to the north. I would also believe that he

*was an employer of those who rode horses rather than one who himself rode
horses.*

*He arrived and established a small bank in Jacksonville shortly after the
discovery of its gold was first noised about. Due to the substantial flow of
nuggets and bags of precious dust that began, and continues, to flow across
his counters, he is considered as the area's ultimate word in the matter of
mining. I have heard veteran prospectors repeat and accept his evaluation of
the possible worth of a claim, although I do not believe that he has ever spent
an entire morning in any local digging. It may be that this authority is due
an much to his voice and certainty of manner as it is to his money.*

*This much I knew before my visit to his home. I was made aware of ever
so much more after he suggested that we repair to the small sitting room off
the large parlour in which the carolers were congregated.*

*He began our conversation by pointing to a paperweight that signified his
affiliation with Wells Fargo, a large and well-respected western financial
institution. He explained that this connection was managed in tandem with
the operation of his bank and that it had made a substantial contribution to
both his wealth and the world of further opportunities.*

*You are doubtless wondering by now why a man like Mr. Witham would
discuss such personal matters with a young visitor in his home? So did I until
I recalled the propensity of most Americans to discuss their financial affairs
with anyone; net worth is a commonly accepted index to real worth in these
communities of newcomers.*

*Incidentally, that observation does not mean that I have become a phi-
losopher at nineteen. The custom of bragging about money is so widespread
here that its genesis would be obvious to anyone not caught up in the practice.
Actually, in the following few minutes, Mr. Witham also introduced me to
the cost of the Christmas party, the value of his home, and the success of his
latest financial coup that caused an investment of $2,000 to grow into a sum
that would have satisfied most men as a lifetime's earnings.*

"But you aren't," I said to him.

"Aren't what?" he asked.

"Satisfied with what you have made so far."

*"Tarnation, no!" he answered so loudly that those still at his table turned
from their glasses and speechmaking to stare into the room where we sat.
Curiously, this encouraged him to raise his tones to a pitch that carried even
further as he added, "I'm only satisfied in finding the best gold mines in
southern Oregon and then in setting the best men here to do the digging!" He
smiled in the direction of the table of listening guests, and not a man there
disappointed him. Every one of them smiled back in approval.*

Father, it is quite possible that, as I have described him, Mr. Witham may appear as a crude provincial and nothing more. As you will see, this would be but a partial portrait.

As I have learned, his banking methods are unorthodox but efficient. His institution keeps no account books save for personal records, receives no formal deposits, and issues no cheques. Anyone offering him funds for safekeeping is given a small bag on which he is expected to write his name or mark. The bag is then closed and securely tied, whereupon Mr. Witham takes it into his stone vault, and there it remains until the "depositor" requests its return. The profit to the bank for this service is gained by the charge of a fee in keeping with the amount entrusted. Because no records are kept, there are no book-keeping expenses involved. Everything Mr. Witham receives for this service is his. And, since these funds are never commingled, no possibility exists of their being swallowed up by the demands of apprehensive depositors even if they should all descend upon the bank within a single day.

It is safe to assume that Mr. Witham is well aware of the size of each savings bag, and those clients whose funds show healthy growth can expect that someday Mr. Witham will invite them to enter into a partnership with him to exploit whatever potentially profitable situation has lately drawn his attention. In this manner Mr. Witham has created ties to almost every other prosperous man in the area. After our conversation (or, I should say, after being addressed by him for a good hour) I surmised that the majority of the guests at the Christmas party were partners with our host in one enterprise or another.

Do you remember how unerringly our dog Bobbins would sniff out rabbit warrens in the field? Mr. Witham seems to have the same ability to sniff out money, and this is how I account for his having spent so much time that night with one whom he knows as neither family friend nor customer. I am certain that he has sensed that I represent investment capital.

So, expect my later letters to contain more of Mr. Witham. This one has gone on too long, but I suspect that you will find that it has not been unproductive because, inevitably, my Yule host will suggest a situation that I ought to transmit to you.

My love to Mother and affection to David and Charles,

Anthony

P.S. Another example of Mr. Witham's grasp of the area has just occurred to me. Through some mysterious means, Chung Lin, the houseboy brought to the party by Dr. Gibbs, recently came into the possession of a nugget of gold. He asked Collis to accompany him to the bank to have it exchanged for currency. Mr. Witham, after weighing it, asked, "Where did this come from?"

Collis, having been prompted by Chung, answered "Walker Creek."

"Where on Walker Creek?" was the next question—and one whose answer Chung had (perhaps conveniently) neglected to brief his interpreter, so Collis could only answer, "Up in the hills."

Mr. Witham scowled. "That sure is strange. It's all granite out there and no gold has ever been found on it." But, even so, he pushed seven dollars in silver over his counter, which was a very fair price for Chung, who, as Mr. Witham guessed, had never in his life dipped his hands into the waters of Walker Creek.

14

THINGS CHANGE. Just when you expect tomorrow to continue on with today, something happens, like Father feeling that he had to fire Tommy. The reason for Father's change of heart first surfaced on one of those raw February mornings when any miner not suffering from terminal ambition stayed in town because the creeks were icy enough to numb the beefiest man after ten minutes of tending his sluice boxes and whatever else that hadn't been swept away by flood waters.

Although Tony had gone back to coyote mining instead of taking up carpentering (when he thought more about it, Sam's thing with Mrs. Witham was too sticky to fit into his English set of rules), he was neither ambitious nor stupid enough to be out working on a day like this. He and I were in our cabin, stretched out by the fireplace he'd repaired under my careful supervision, when Sam knocked at the door.

His way of saying hello after we let him in was, "How come you're not out gatherin herbs?"

Concerned, I asked, "Are you crazy?"

"Not a mite." He walked over to the fire and stood, warming his back. "I just wanted to shut off your smart talk about why I'm not out helpin my pa or Boudreau."

"You're not misleading Collis," Tony put in, "he knows you've already been digging away for hours and you've just stopped by to warn us that it appears much warmer outside than it really is."

Ignoring him, Sam asked me, "Where's the doctor?"

"Out doctoring. Mrs. McLaughlin is dropping another bairn, and Father thought it would be very professional of him if he were there to catch it."

"He sure admires his business." He thought for a moment and then added, "They won't pay him, neither."

I shrugged. "So he'll just charge your father twice as much to make up for it."

"Huh! Right now, Pa's over to Appler and Kinney's gettin rid of everything we made last week to buy everything we'll be needin next week."

Tony asked, "He really does have the fever, doesn't he?"

Whenever we got on to a subject that made Sam uncomfortable, he'd change the subject. "Where's Tommy?"

"Out back, building a shack," I told him.

"Doin what?"

"Building a cabin. A shack. A place for himself. You don't understand English any better than he does."

"What on earth for?"

"You *do* ask questions," Tony said. "I believe he wants more privacy."

"He must want it real bad. Can't get nothin done in weather like this."

"Then," I suggested, "you tell him. We've tried every way we know how to convince him to at least wait until it gets warm enough for us to want to help him."

"You must of been ridin him."

"Not at all." Tony was too comfortable for a proper show of indignation at this charge. "Tommy simply has this thing in his mind that he wants a hearth of his own. For the past week he's been slapping together broken boards and poles like a demented beaver."

"If he's been at it that long, how come he's not done? A week to build a shack is pretty long."

Out in the back we found Tommy working away in the cold rain. All we could see through the three or four layers of clothes he had on was his beet-red face and two white and frozen hands as he pawed over the stockpile of shattered boards and baling wire he'd salvaged from the discarded scraps that littered every street in Jacksonville. Sam walked over and, sighting down the one wall that Tommy had managed to keep standing, said, quite seriously, "Not too bad, Tommy. You'll get it done this way, but it'll take forever."

The Chinese boy paid him as much attention as he had when we walked up, which was none at all. Grunting and exhaling in a hiss that steamed into the air, he began struggling to work a board into the ground that, I guessed, was supposed to support the second side.

Sam said nothing more. He stood watching until Tommy stepped back to look at the board teetering in every gust of wind, even without additional weight. But when an especially violent blast came along that would have toppled it to the ground if Sam hadn't caught it and set it up again, he said, "Look, you stubborn little weasel, if you want to spend the rest of the month putting together a mess of splinters, that's all right. But why don't you just once listen to somebody?"

At that point, Chung Lin proved how well he'd mastered his new language. He walked over to the swaying board, kicked it hard enough to make it bounce after it fell over flat, and said, "Dirl-uh-ty son of bitch!" It was the first time we had ever heard him swear, but we didn't laugh because it would have been too cruel. He would have thought we were poking fun at his efforts.

"Let us help, Tommy," Tony said. "It will go more easily."

"Sure, Tommy," I chimed in, "the faster we get you a house, the quicker we can all go back inside." I looked around and found one of the least damaged posts. "Want me to put this back up?"

By waiting for Sam to make the decision on this sorry piece of lumber, Tommy showed that he was finally willing to accept help and direction. "I find no better wood," he explained.

Sam nodded. "Shouldn't wonder, the way folks use it up around here. Everybody's buyin planks as fast as they can be whipsawed."

I asked, "Can he ever get anything built out of this junk?"

"Nope."

"I didn't think so." I considered the matter for a moment. "You don't expect us to go into the woods in this kind of weather to cut poles, do you?"

"Nope. We'll do what the good Lord would suggest after he thought about a case like this. We'll swipe them."

"Sam," I said, "that would be dishonest!"

"Sure would."

"Not only would it be wrong," Tony pointed out, "but everyone watches their lumber pile too carefully."

"Not on a day like this. Anybody with sense stays inside. So let's get goin. First stop ought to be the pile behind where they're building the hotel. We could get the whole job done out of what they'll never miss."

"I refuse to steal," I said, "especially in the face of the danger that we'll freeze our butts off just carrying boards back and forth."

"You're near close to right, Collie," Sam agreed. "I don't know what got into me. It'd be downright crooked to try this in the daylight. We'll have to do it later on."

All went well that night. Sam changed his plan so that instead of requisitioning our supplies from the pile behind the hotel, we distributed our trade to just about every new building in progress. A few boards here, a fistful of nails there, and next day no one questioned the fat store of materials that had grown in our backyard. Even Father didn't mention it, but perhaps some wisdom in his bones directed his attention elsewhere.

In four more days the cabin was completed, but, of course, our heathen friend showed neither surprise nor delight. The only time he altered his passive acceptance of our labor was on the first morning when Sam explained to him that the reason his walls kept falling down was that he had never built a framework onto which they could be nailed. After that, he saw the logic to the construction, and more than once he came up with ideas for shortcuts and improvements that Sam said we ought to use, so we did.

We worked at the job like all get-out, and, to be honest, it was fun every step of the way. When it was done, we felt we had accomplished something pretty fine and that each of us had a part of it.

We couldn't have been more wrong. Tommy took possession as soon as the last nail was hammered into place. He moved in his few belongings, barred the door with an old rusty lock he had scrounged somewhere, and never after invited us inside. From then on the place was his sole and sacred castle.

His only visitors were some of the Chinese beginning to stream into the area as workers for the mines. But, even though we often heard sociable singsong chatterings coming from inside and, on one memorable occasion, voices lifted in a drunken reedy melody, Chung's place remained off limits to us three Occidentals.

In all fairness to Tommy, however, I've got to admit that this new desire for privacy got in our way only where his shack was concerned. He worked harder than ever at keeping our place clean and our meals prepared. He was almost insistent about taking on any of the chores we didn't particularly fancy, and after they were done, he'd cheerfully go along with us on whatever excursion seemed like a good idea on a given day.

In our earlier days, he'd prepare a meal out of anything that was lying around or that someone brought home, but now he shopped at every farmhouse, store, or stall in the area with supplies for sale. He made a point of picking out the best vegetables and meat and got them at the lowest price the seller would stand for. It wasn't long before our table was envied by just about every one of our neighbors lucky enough to be invited in to share a meal.

Even Jabez Witham, pushing back his chair after a hearty supper in our home, asked, "Doc, do you always eat this good?"

Father admitted that although we weren't always certain of the origin of some of the dishes Tommy put before us, they almost always tasted first rate.

"Most folks around here are proud to settle for some meat and a mess of boiled greens."

"Chung Lin does the shopping as well as the cooking," my father told him.

"Cost you a pretty penny?"

"Not at all. I think we spend less on the table now than we did when each of us took turns buying what we needed. And then quite a bit went to waste because so much of it didn't fit everyone's taste."

Witham didn't seem to find this example of Father's acumen very convincing. "You mean the Chinese boy does all your shopping?"

"I give him the money in the morning and there's a good meal on the table that night."

The banker's barely concealed sniff at this claim told Tony and me that it would be a cold day in hell before he allowed a Chinaman so much leeway. We thought the reaction was funny at first, but, later that night, after we discussed it, it became a different story. *How dare that pompous little bastard insult our friend at our table!* was the way it went.

We felt like idiots two mornings later after Tommy's cabin caught fire. The banker's estimate of our friend's potential for thievery turned out to be right on the mark. We were walking home from some chore or another when, suddenly, Tony yelled, "Smoke! Over there behind the house—Tommy's place is burning!"

Tommy was away on one of his tours of the neighboring farms, so if Tony hadn't seen the smoke, and if we hadn't been lucky enough to catch it before it broke into a blaze, the whole place could have burnt down, probably taking our cabin with it.

We ran out back and broke through the door, which was still kept locked even though he ought to have understood by now that we were willing to respect his territory. What we saw was a crude workbench he'd built at one end of the shack on which a tiny heap of charcoal was still glowing under a pot of something that looked like lead. An ember had fallen from the pile and was smoldering away in the center of the tattered piece of rush carpet he'd picked out of someone's trash pile.

After we ground out the live coal and pulled the smoking rug into the yard, I began to wonder what was he doing with a workbench. "And that old drill affair," I said aloud. "Where did he get it and what was he using it for?"

"Drill?" Tony asked.

"The old drill. I've seen things like them back home in our dentist's office. Want to go back in and look at it?"

"Why on earth is it upsetting you so? Certainly I'll stare at it with you if dentists' things make you happy."

"I'll bet Tommy is up to something shady that he doesn't want anyone to know about. It's probably why he keeps the place locked."

"The sod," said Tony, still not understanding that I was being deadly serious. "And he's left us out." Then he took a good look at me. "I've never suspected you of this much purity, Collis, my lad."

"It isn't a joke, Tony. He's up to something that could get him hurt, maybe hanged around here. You know how these people feel about the Chinese. What would he be needing a drill for, a workbench . . ."

"And a pot of lead," he said, now as puzzled as I was.

"Sure," I said. "He couldn't drive a nail in straight when we were building, and now he's got himself a mechanical set-up." We looked at each other, both of us mystified and then beginning to worry in earnest.

We had our answer a day later, when Jabez Witham bounced a gold coin more than once on the marble surface of the counter in his bank right after his money instinct told him there was something queer about the quarter eagle that was among the gold coins being offered him by some farmer for change into a double eagle.

I'd better explain about our currency, which was mostly in gold. An eagle was ten dollars, a double eagle was twenty dollars, and an Indian head was a dollar. These were all that Congress originally authorized, but then the federal politicians went on to pass so many other confusing laws concerning weights and minting that, to make it simple, a whole new batch of smaller coins of all sizes and shapes were born and handed around without anyone regarding them as anything but a convenience.

For example, the first half eagle, worth five dollars, originally had to contain 135 grains of gold. This was reduced to 129 grains by another law in 1834. And since Congress also kept on changing its mind about other denominations, it wasn't long before only the experts could tell if any particular coin was short-weighted.

Naturally, old Witham was just such an expert. After he'd finished ringing the coin that worried him, he gave the same treatment to the rest of the pile. Next, he took all the coins from his safe that weren't tied away in bags and bounced them, too. About a tenth of these sounded as far off as the first one he had tested, so he took a strong reading glass, turned his lamp up to its brightest, and began minutely examining one of the double eagles that had sounded suspicious.

That night we had Witham in for supper again. He'd invited himself to the house with the excuse of wanting Father's opinion of a deal involving the kind of mercury used in mining, and he kept the subject going long enough to be asked if he'd like to join our evening meal. This wasn't something that got by Tony or myself, because both of us knew that although my father might be aware that some of the drug companies back East used the material in making their patent medicines, as far as he was concerned, the conversation could have been in Greek when it came to how much they paid for it in bulk, their sources of supply, and the daily market prices.

So we kept fairly quiet at the table, adding no more to the talk than asking to be passed a dish. We were sure that there was no such thing in Witham's book as purely social talk and that whatever it was that really brought the old fox here would be aired sooner or later.

It came right after Tommy cleared the table. Witham, lifting halfway out of his chair as he searched through his vest pocket for a toothpick, said, "Well, we can talk all we want about the easiest ways of separating gold from dirt, but today I seen the slickest way yet of getting it without straining your back."

For the first time since the opening five minutes of the man's visit, the glassy look left Father's eyes. "Something new, Jabez?" he asked.

"New to me, anyway." He vented that cackling laugh of his that had nothing to do with humor. "Slickest windy I ever seen."

He didn't require much pressing to tell us the rest of it, and before he had gone any distance at all, Tony and I recognized the real reason behind his visit. As I said, there was no such item in Banker Witham's lexicon as a casual visit.

He told us that he'd been coming across quite a few gold coins that had been doctored in a mighty interesting way; somebody had bored a thin, deep hole sideways into each one of them and then filled up the cavity with lead. Whoever did it must be a pretty smart craftsman, he opined, because he'd even taken the trouble to dust the top of the lead core with a few grains of real gold, and this had hid the bore enough to keep anybody from noticing the trick for some time because an awful lot of those coins in his bank had been milked, and that meant nobody had ever tumbled until he, Witham, had gotten his suspicions roused just that very day.

"Funniest thing about it," he continued, although the cackling had stopped and it was clear from his suddenly grim expression that he didn't find anything at all funny in the matter, "it's the John Chinamans who're getting stuck with a lot of the bad money. Almost every storekeeper I asked remembered, after I pressed him, about getting some of it from them, and those coolies sure don't see enough wages to want to go doctoring the pay they got left from what they make. And I don't know even one mine owner that would take the trouble to steal the bit of dust that could be bored out of a teeny hole in an Eagle. There's too much of it still laying in the ground.

"I estimate that crook has stolen at least darn near a thousand dollars, and if nobody stops him before the news gets around, there'll be nobody in Jacksonville trading with anything but barter." He kept his eyes on Father as he said this, but I'm sure he didn't miss the red creeping into Tony's face and whatever was happening to mine. Jabez Witham wouldn't overlook the trembling of a leaf where cash was concerned.

Tony's and my eyes met, and Witham caught that, too. Standing up, he said, "Well, I'd better be getting along. Tomorrow's another day, and the job's waiting for me to work out whoever that scoundrel is that's doing this to the town. Doctor, I'm obliged. Mighty fine meal. That Chinese boy of yours is a real treasure."

We waited until Father had gone to bed before we dared talk about the warning we had just received.

"It's Tommy," I said. "The drill." The lump in my stomach felt like it weighed a ton.

"Of course."

"We'll have to get him out of town. They'll shoot him, for sure. How in hell did Witham figure it out?"

"It wouldn't take that much thought for a man like Witham, would it?"

I was too close to panic. My mind just wouldn't work. "How so?" I asked. "I don't follow you."

"After he realized that someone had been buggering away at the cash, there isn't much more to it than asking the people who make change or deposit at his bank where they've gotten their gold coins, and he heard a bit of Chinese in every answer, didn't he?"

"That doesn't have to mean just Tommy! They're all over the place."

"Be reasonable, Collis. Witham is certainly aware that Chung buys our food from every merchant and farmer because that is precisely what your father told him. Everyone about here knows that the coolies rarely leave their Chinatown except to shop and visit his shack. Add them together and there's no other total but Chung. He's impressed the coolies into passing bad coins for him."

The truth was there, but I just couldn't swallow it. I was almost pleading when I answered, "All right, Tony, but so what? So he pinched some dust here and there for himself, but you can't blame—"

Tony broke in, anger and disgust in his voice. "Collis, it is utter nonsense to go on! You are about to offer all sorts of reasons to excuse him—'the poor boy is *so* alone,' 'he just didn't realize,' and all that rot— but, before you do, let me ask just one question."

I tried to head him away from what I was afraid he was going to say next. "Ah, come off it. You're acting as if Tommy—"

"*Tommy*, my foot! He's a bloody damned native, and you're a fool for thinking of him in any other way!"

That hurt me, really hurt, but all I could think of in protest was, "I don't like your saying that, Tony."

There was a pause and then, with less anger, he asked, "Will you say again whether you dislike it after you've answered a question?"

"What question?"

"Where does your father keep his money?"

"You know very well—in the chest under his bunk."

"So does Chung."

"My God!" I said.

"Exactly. What do you think are the odds of there being one untampered coin left in that chest?"

Involuntarily, I shook my head, trying to rid it of the image of my father accused of being involved in the counterfeiting. "My God," I repeated, "they hung a man over in Sailor's Diggings for trying to pass queer money."

"Yes."

"But no one would believe that Father . . ."

"No one but drunken miners. And there's enough of them around at any given time isn't there?"

"We've got to tell him!"

"Of course. And as quickly as possible."

The realization made me almost sick to my stomach, but I still couldn't help adding, "Maybe there's a way of letting him know without getting Tommy—"

"Collis," he interrupted, the harshness coming back into his voice, "he's a damned native and Dr. Gibbs is your father!"

15

. . . the slings and arrows of outrageous fortune.

IT HAS TAKEN ME a long time and a raft of mistakes to understand that phrase. It took many bad judgments and too much resentment and dismissal of other human beings because I couldn't see that I was condemning them for having been minced and ground and outraged by whatever fortune that ruled them. I had to lose much that I loved and be hurt by strangers who didn't know or care what they had done before I was hammered and bent and finally burnished enough to where I could grasp the godliness in that line of Shakespeare's.

We are all what we are because of fortune's outrageous slings. No sane man gets up in the morning set on doing evil. To judge him by what he does that day is to be a presumptuous damned fool, because what he does that day is the product of all his days back to his birth and probably even beyond that. Of course, every man has to be held accountable for his evil, or our world disappears, but I've learned that it is enough if he is punished. I've learned not to judge him.

You bang your forehead by bumping into a door. You kick the door because of your hurt. Punishment enough. Don't judge it for being a door or for leaving itself ajar.

Chung Lin was just such a door when we were young together. It has taken the books I've read, every sling I've suffered, and the few words or reactions he forgot to guard to let me understand why he became a counterfeiter and we became damned fools for judging him as having betrayed our trust.

We saw his actions only from the white Jacksonville viewpoint. We didn't know, nor would Tommy have ever thought it worthwhile to tell us, about the kicks and curses and mindless threats that came his way just about anytime he wasn't with us. Naturally, he had to consider what it was going to be like if we ever abandoned him as impulsively as we'd taken him in.

Most Chinese are proud. They set a great store on self-respect, and it isn't easy for them to accept a beating when the only claim to have the right to deal it out comes from having the "proper" shape to your eyes or the color to your skin. He certainly had enough sense to know that doctoring American gold coins was wrong, but that wasn't very important after it was measured against the lesson drummed into his bones in the Cantonese alleys that money was the one friend he could depend on not to toss him overboard.

When Father fired him, he said, "Chung Lin, you are a thief."

What answer could Tommy make? The older man's tones told him that the decision was based purely on identification, so there was no possibility of appealing it. After all, he *was* a thief.

"Pack your things and get out." Now the tones were impersonal. Chung Lin was being discarded as an unsatisfactory article. Of course, Father didn't realize that this might also turn out to be passing a death sentence on a boy in a strange, hostile land.

But Chung Lin knew it. He also knew that a plea would be useless. He didn't even say goodbye to us. Tony wouldn't have wanted to hear it, and it would have been too much to expect anything of me. He couldn't see me standing up alongside of him to face my father, the banker, and the town, and he was right. I found it easier to look the other way as he tied his few miserable belongings into a bundle and left—small, friendless, and scared.

So how could I fault him later after Witham began using him in his plans for trading with the Chinese of Jacksonville?

16

TOMMY MUST HAVE BEEN STANDING at her back stoop for at least ten minutes before she saw him. Out of fear, he hadn't done much more than tap softly every so often at the door, but if she hadn't needed more water for the stew she was preparing for her husband's noon meal and come out meaning to go to the pump, he might have gone away without her ever having known that he'd been there.

Or, maybe he couldn't have left. His fellow Chinese wanted all the work they could get, so there wasn't much chance that they'd offer him any help. Especially when he probably wasn't from their district back in Canton or even someone who'd been herded together with them at Gum San Dai Fow—the Big City in the Land of the Golden Hills, which was the Sojourners' name for San Francisco.

No, he wasn't about to leave Jabez Witham's back door. There was no other place to go. The stares in his direction at dinner the night before he was fired told him that the banker was the architect of his ruin. But, thinking about it while my father was cutting him off, he remembered that there'd also been a hint of appraisal in the man's glances, which was certainly a flimsy base for the scheme he then hastily concocted, but, as I said, it was the only one he had.

"What on earth are you doing out here, boy?" she said, almost as startled as he was.

"Fo Missy Wit-tam," he answered, thrusting toward her the seven eggs he had in his hands.

She drew back. "I'm not buying anything from one of you! Certainly not eggs, anyway."

"Buy no."

"Go away! If you don't go away this minute, my husband is coming home right now and he'll give you what-for, do you hear me?"

"Buy no," he insisted, continuing to stand there, and after a while she saw that he meant them as a gift.

"And I don't want them neither." Then, when something about him seemed familiar, she walked a step closer to peer at him. "You're the Chinese boy who works for Dr. Gibbs. Sure you are. You washed dishes for us last Christmas."

"Kliss-mas," he agreed.

"Come on inside," she said. "No. Wait a minute." She walked out to the pump, drew her bucket of water, turned back, and, as she went inside the house, added fretfully, "Come on," and motioned him to follow her.

He stood silently in the kitchen as she hustled about preparing Witham's dinner, and although she didn't look at him again, she was conscious that his eyes never left her. She was glad when she heard her husband at the front door. "Wipe your feet!" she called, and after he was seated at the dining room table took his meal out to him, saying, "Dr. Gibbs just sent us some eggs. I don't know what on earth for, unless you acted foolish last night at his house and he wants us to know he didn't mind."

She often started their conversations by accusing him of misconducting some affair or another that she wanted to know more about. Because he was familiar with the tactic, he took his time spearing and chewing a lump of meat from the stew before he answered, "I caught his boy stealing. Told him about it last night."

"Collis? That's the dumbest thing I ever heard! The boy's shiftless, but there's no earthly reason he'd steal. The doctor gives him anything he wants."

Another maneuver. Tell him he's dead wrong about something and he'll go on all about it while he's defending whatever it was he'd said or did. She clasped her arm more tightly about herself as she stood in the doorway waiting for his answer.

It wasn't often that the little banker had such a clear-cut victory in the offing. He methodically shoveled more of the stew into his mouth until he judged that her impatience was just about to peak. Then he put down his fork and, for the first time, looked up at her. "Weren't Collis. I never said it was. His Chinese boy, that's who it was. I'd tell you how I caught him if you'd quit jumping at me."

"Hah! China boy, my foot! That's how smart you are. He's in the kitchen right now with the eggs the doctor sent over. Fired him, my foot!"

Witham got up from the table and brushed by his wife as he walked into the kitchen where Chung Lin, never having presumed to seat himself, stood by the door. As the banker advanced toward him, he held out the eggs still cupped in his two hands. His sensed that a placating smile would be way out of order, but, even so, he was so nervous that he damn near couldn't keep from baring his teeth.

His instincts were correct. Witham was able to weigh all the shadings in any gesture, no matter how slight. He would have survived on the Cantonese piers. After studying Chung's grave face for a minute, he understood that the boy knew he was the one who had gotten him fired, so the sober stare meant that the gift was a way of saying, *only you would have seen through what I was doing, so maybe you can use someone like me.*

"Anyone can give merchandise away," said Jabez Witham. "Question is, how good might you be at selling it?"

Sam had just finished work for the day and was walking toward home when Tommy came by, carrying the shovel Witham had given him to peddle.

"What've you got there?" he asked.

"Shov-err."

"Thanks, Tommy. I wouldn't never have recognized one if you hadn't told me. I was askin what kind of work you figured on doin with it."

The answering shrug was too elaborate. It told Sam that the meeting wasn't accidental—the diminutive Chinese boy had been waiting to brace him with some deal he had in mind, so he said, "If you want, you can walk along with me while you figure out some reason for that thing that I'd believe." He slung his tool kit back over his shoulder and started off, shortening his step so Tommy could keep up with him.

Tommy shrugged again, but this time honesty was in it. "You buy shov-err?" he asked.

"One thing I don't need is a shovel. Where'd you get it?"

"Mebbe you father buy?" Tommy insisted.

"He's up to his ass in shovels. Where did you get it?"

And that's where Chung Lin came clean, because Sam was his only potential customer and he saw that the story he'd concocted about a drunken miner shying it at him wasn't going to work even a little bit. If Sam didn't already know about his being fired for thievery, he'd hear about it shortly from one of us, and since he knew Sam was absurdly honest, he would conclude that he'd also stolen the shovel.

So he told Sam about offering to go to work for Mr. Witham after being fired because he had no other place to turn; and how the banker had agreed to put him on once he proved he could sell for him and that this probably meant that he was going to be used as a pipeline to collar all the coolie retail trade in town; and being a storekeeper was a career

of grandness unimaginably beyond anything he'd ever dreamed for himself. Of course, he said all this in pidgin English, but Sam understood
every bit of it.

When he'd finished, he took heart from the grin on Sam's face. His
friend wasn't going to judge him as Father, Tony, and I had—he was
willing to help. He knew this was so when Sam asked, "How much did
the old buzzard tell you to get for this busted-up spade?"

"Fo dollas."

"Figures. It was worth maybe a dollar when it was new." He looked
at Chung Lin. "But it's the price of the job, isn't it?"

Since Sam didn't have the four dollars, he briefly considered offering
it to his father, but that was only for a moment. Even if Mr. Hume had
the money and actually needed another shovel, he certainly wouldn't
buy it from anyone his son brought home. *It's getting so Pa grudges sayin
good mornin to me.*

The next recourse was Boudreau. The Frenchman would buy a jack-
ass with three working legs if it seemed like it could help him sell an
extra glass of whiskey. *I'll tell him that it belonged to Cluggage or Poole,*
Sam thought, *and that after I wax it up, it'll make a whoppin fine decoration
over the bar.*

So, with Chung Lin trotting along behind, he headed for his employer's cabin. Luckily, he was in, sitting at the table and staring moodily
over at the fire while waiting for Elva to give him his supper. He didn't
bother to do much more than briefly look over at the pair after Elva let
them in, and Sam wasn't halfway through the explanation of why they
needed this particular shovel before Boudreau cut him off by saying,
"Yes, buy it. Come to the bar tonight and I'll give the *Chinois* his money."
He was deep into one of the blackest of his depressions, and it was clear
that he wanted to be left alone by everyone, including his daughter. He
didn't raise his head from the plate set before him as she slipped outside.

"Is he always that way at home?" Sam asked after she joined them.

"Mostly. Sometimes he's even worse." Then, to get away from the
subject, she said, "I never knowed you to be the most awful liar I ever
met."

"Who, me? Oh, the shovel."

"Yep. The one belonging to the first miners. Or maybe it was owned
by some Russian duke—the way you sounded, you wasn't that sure."

"It was Tommy who told me about it."

"Another fib. Samuel Hume, you don't quit that, you're going to
end up in a terrible place as soon as you die. Putting it on poor little
Tommy! I'd be ashamed."

He grinned. "Tommy," he said, putting his arm around the boy's shoulders, "tell her who it was that made up this monstrous story that I believed only because you said it with real tears in your eyes."

He didn't understand all the words, but the meaning was there to make him unaccustomedly happy. They were poking fun, and he was included. He was going to sell his shovel and become a merchant prince, and these were his friends.

17

PEOPLE IN THE ROGUE VALLEY get damn near lunatic with relief when spring comes.

In most places there isn't any question about winter being long and bitterly hard, but here it's a woman who nags at you right at the moment you're about to make love to her. On any one of those marvelous days we get toward the end of the year, winter can remind you that she's out there by sending in a thick pea soup fog that can last, sometimes, until the middle of January.

Then, after that, when the mercury really sinks, it might be a beautiful sight when the fog mist crystallizes and then sparkles on the trees in the morning sun, but you're shocked by the rawness you feel when you go outside because you were led to expect pleasant company and, instead, there's someone cold and nasty waiting for you. On other days the temperature can be warm enough to help you forget your coat and then drop down to below freezing at night.

After January's cold, the rains arrive, cutting great gullies through the granitic earth in every trail in the valley, and getting home from anywhere, maybe just down the road, is never more than an even bet. You get so damned tired of mud, but the rains are reassurance that spring is coming, and if there's been a fair snow pack laid in the mountains around the valley, we know it's going to be downright spectacular living here right up and into the dead of summer. Winter is a nagging pain in the ass, but when she shows signs of slackening her grip, everyone quits praying and starts pumping.

And all this is by way of saying that Tony was at the point where he was getting ready to pump. It had been too cold for coyote mining, not that he could have returned full-time to it anyway because of his back. There was no excuse left to be fiddling with herbs because he'd paid Father the last of the money he owed, and no self-respecting man made his living doing chores, so the need to learn a trade left him with the option he finally took of joining Sam at carpentering, no matter what he thought about him and Mrs. Witham.

They were still working on the bowling alley that Henri Boudreau wanted next door to his Bella Union saloon. The job was slow going because Henri came up with another idea just about every time it was ready for the finish work. Not that it bothered them—the work was steady, they were learning new things every day, and there wasn't any reason to feel guilty about costs because he was certainly taking in enough at his bar to keep the two of them on the payroll all year round if he wanted to. That bar of Henri's was more like an ocean than anything else. A big wave of whiskey would pour over it toward his customers and an undertow of money came rolling back.

At first, I agreed with the rest of Jacksonville that although Henri was a hard worker, his grumpy lack of appreciation for success was just greed. Later, when it became clear that he honestly wasn't getting the slightest bit of pleasure out of what he'd accomplished here, I realized that driving himself like a mule was the only way he had of trying to lose the demons that the killing of his wife and other children back in Fort Laramie had left inside him.

Elva saw it, too. One day while she was walking with me over to the building site, she remarked, "Pa don't like me bein around his saloon."

"I don't know that I blame him," I answered. "If I had a daughter, I wouldn't let her get anywhere near a place as rough as the Bella Union."

"No, I wish that was it, but it ain't. He don't care to be seein me all that much around our cabin, neither. It's gettin so that as soon as I make supper, he's just as pleased if I get over to my bunk right after." She thought for a moment and added, "It's like he doesn't even want to know I'm there. Most of the time now, I just pull the blankets over my head and go to sleep, and he's always gone by the time I get up, no matter how early it is."

Then she fell silent, and for all I counted, she could have been walking by herself because she wasn't the slightest bit aware of my silent study of her sweet, solemn face. She was sixteen then but already tall enough to just peer over the top of my head. She probably wasn't ever going to match Sam's height, but I had to admit to myself that in a year or so she'd be up there in his neighborhood.

When I described her before as a redhead, I should have explained that it was also a little like saying that flowers have a nice smell. Her hair was an orange gold and her skin was pure buttermilk cream, and in her happy innocence she never understood that her body was as great and generous as one of those goddess statues they keep digging up on some Greek island or another.

Speaking of pagan deities, it also ought to be noted that she carried herself with Juno's grace, and if all this sounds as if I'm idealizing a freckle-faced country girl, I would defy anyone tagging along with us not to have felt the same heavy, hopeless lump that was inside of me as I looked at her and knew that, in spite of what Tony thought, her love for Sam Hume was always going to be as much a part of her as her beauty.

"There they are," she said, but I kept looking at her rather than in the direction of her wave, which was to one side of the lumber piled at the building site.

"Over yonder," she repeated impatiently because I hadn't answered, "but—who's that?"

I recognized Helen Witham talking to Sam as Tony stood by. As we walked over to them, I heard her say, ". . . and, Samuel, whether you like it or not, every board you lay has to be kiln dried."

"We know it," said Tony. "Mr. Boudreau has told us several times that we aren't to use green lumber."

Ignoring Tony and certainly not acknowledging our presence, she continued with her eyes still on Sam, "That's it. If it shrinks, the balls won't run true."

"Mrs. Witham," said Sam, "you think there's a man in the whole Rogue Valley that gives a damn about a wobbly bowling ball?" Then, by way of greeting us, he said to Elva, "Mrs. Witham, here, is sort of worried about the job we might be doin for your pa and her husband."

I jumped in at that point because I was afraid that the tone in his voice was going to tell Elva some things she shouldn't know. "Mrs. Witham, they're pretty careful about their work. I'll bet you're going to end up with the best bowling alley north of Sacramento."

I might as well have saved my breath. Smiling at Sam in a way that I guessed was supposed to be maternal, she finished with, "You know you promised, Samuel, that there'd only be boards dried out real good."

Ordinarily, Elva wouldn't have butted into a situation like this, but she sensed Sam wasn't being treated right. I saw that she was puzzled by whatever it was that was happening, but she certainly wasn't going to let it take place without her standing alongside him. "Ma'am," she pitched in with that sunny smile that should have melted anyone this side of an oil painting, "Sam *always* keeps his promises!"

For the first time, Mrs. Witham shifted her attention away from Sam. Pursing her lips at Elva in a way that meant that young people (especially young halfbreeds) ought not to interrupt serious conversations, she said, "Missy, this is my husband's business I'm talking about, and Mr. Witham knows how many pennies there are in a dollar even if your father doesn't!"

Having delivered herself of that dollop of venom, she sniffed and walked away, leaving Elva staring after her, the understanding slowly creeping into her eyes that the woman had just filed some kind of claim on Sam Hume's attention and wasn't going to take too kindly to anyone that mixed in. At least, that's the way it seemed to me. I had a fierce conviction that I ought to stretch out my arms and hold her, but that feeling was immediately replaced by the desire to shoot Sam when he laughed and said, "Boy, she just don't stay away!"

Tony showed that he felt pretty much as I did by looking at Sam with that dead expression that came over him when he was about to remove himself from a situation he didn't particularly fancy. Then, bending over, he scooped up an armful of boards and headed toward the half-finished floor.

"Hold on," Sam said. "Leave some for somebody else." He turned back to Elva and me. "We got to get back to work. You see how close they're stayin on us."

"Sure, Sam," she answered, trying to smile in a way that made me want to hug her more than ever. "Collie and me didn't have business to be botherin you, nohow."

"Well, I don't want your pa or Mr. Witham gettin mad at me."

"I don't blame you," I said, trying to save a situation that was growing lame. It hadn't occurred yet to Sam that the girl had any idea of what had been left unsaid, but, being Elva, she wouldn't be able to hide her hurt for much more than the next minute or so.

He showed he didn't need my approving words by picking up at least twice as many boards as Tony in one armful (I thought: *showing off!*) and calling over his shoulder as he left for the building, "Why don't you'n Elva go over to Tommy's store? He's got in a whole batch of new things. Chopsticks and them little bottles she likes."

She watched until he had caught abreast of Tony and then turned to me. "Oh, let's! I love his store. It's so scary."

"What's scary about it?" I asked as we started the walk up the hill to Oregon Street, where the Chinese had their shacks.

"Oh, you know."

"Oh, *that* scary. Sure, everybody knows that."

"You think you're so smart."

"I certainly am."

"You would be if you didn't go tellin everybody about it."

"I don't like you, Elva," I said.

"Yes you do."

"No I don't. I only let you hang around because your father's got a whiskey store."

"Big, bad drinker." The sun was back in her smile. "Is Tony still mad at Tommy?"

"Not since I talked him out of it."

"I'm bound to admit that's one thing you're good at."

"Thanks."

She was immediately concerned. "Oh, Collie, I didn't mean that the way it come out. I meant it nice—nobody can change people's minds like you, even when they're dead set."

I thought back to the night I had gotten drunk up on Marguey's High, wondering if it really had been my words that brought Tony around to seeing that anyone in Tommy's place, given the opportunity, would have used it in pretty much the same way. *No*, I thought, *Tony would have come around by himself. He likes Tommy too much to hold a grudge.* Of course, I didn't dilute the credit she was offering me by mentioning this aloud. Instead, and making sure my modesty was transparent, I allowed, "Well, to be honest, Sam helped me a little in showing him the light."

Mentioning Sam was a mistake because it set her to thinking about him again. "Well," she said after a pause, "I don't care what all."

"What does that mean?" I asked, knowing damned right well that she was turning over in her mind the connection between Sam and Helen Witham.

"Nothin."

"Sure it does." I was skunk enough to want to drive home the point of my friend's all-round unworthiness.

"No it doesn't. It really doesn't," she insisted, smiling brightly.

The tears in her eyes were just about to level me. "Come on, Elva. Don't do that."

"You mind your own business, Collie Gibbs!" she yelled and then ran away.

I stood there for a moment, feeling terrible. She was really crying when I caught up with her. "Oh Collie," she said, "she's such an old lady!"

The best I could do was, "It doesn't mean anything. Honest, Elva."

"That's what you say," she said, sobbing harder than ever.

"It's just the way human nature is," I said, miserably aware that I was probably telling the truth.

"Would you do it?"

"Not in a million years."

"Pooh. She's a very pretty old lady." She thought for a moment and then shuddered, "Ugh!"

That was the end of her tears, and it was like the sun coming out after a quick summer storm. We started walking again in the direction of Tommy's store, but within a few steps it occurred to me that my good friend Sam didn't deserve this quick an absolution, so I thoughtfully mentioned, "After all, it's not that Sam wanted to marry her or anything."

Again, being Elva, she let out a whoop of laughter. She had the heartiest laugh of any girl I've ever known. After a while, I joined in—tentatively, of course, but enough to prove that I wasn't being its butt.

"Oh Collie!" She was bending over now, holding her stomach. "I swear you ought to have seen your face when you said that!" We both knew exactly what she meant, so she didn't have to forgive me aloud for trying to use the situation.

I've never done more than kiss Elva Boudreau on the cheek, but there wasn't a day in any of those years that we weren't close enough to make explanations or even conversation unnecessary. Generally, whatever I thought or felt was an open book to her. On the other hand, I can't claim the same prescience where she was concerned, because no one ever had the slightest difficulty deciphering whatever she was thinking or feeling. If there was a totally honest human being, it was that girl.

So I let the matter drop and the laughing trail off, and when it was over, she said to me, "The hell with old Sam Hume. It's too nice a day to go inside that dark store of Tommy's."

I had no trouble following this conversational leap. "All right, what will we do?"

"Let's go to Marguey's High."

"Sam's father would think that's the worst idea you've had all morning. Company is exactly what he doesn't want ever since he staked out his claim up there. Richard Mulligan told me the old man ran him off with a shotgun last week when he accidentally came through it while he was out hunting."

"Accident my foot," she answered. "That Richard Mulligan was probably sniffin around for someplace nearby to file for hisself. And then he'd have the reason to go there nights and next thing Mr. Hume would have to be figurin where all his quartz was gettin to."

She rightly took my answering silence as indecision. "Come on," she coaxed, "let's head for it, anyway. We don't have to go all the way up. Unless maybe you got chores or some important things to do."

"I don't."

"And neither do I. Pa is over to Phoenix for more lumber. He said he'd eat his supper there." A cloud flitted over her face again. "I wish Pa wasn't so dead set on workin all day and night like a steam engine. He's not like he used to be."

"He'll come around. Wait and see."

"Seems like it'll take forever." She was quiet until we had turned onto Pair-O-Dice Road, and then she asked, "It ain't ever easy for anybody, is it, Collie?"

"Maybe me. But that's all."

"You sure?"

I looked at her, wishing again as I had so many times before that she were my girl. "I'm sure. About the only thing that bothers me is when it'll be that my father tells me he's got enough herbs and it's time to go to work."

"Then what?"

"Maybe carpentering with Sam and Tony."

"Better hurry. Sam said as soon as they finished the bowling alley they might be takin up as hunters. There's heaps of money to be made sellin meat to the miners."

"When did he tell you that?" Now damned if I wasn't jealous about Tony, too! They were supposed to be my friends, and neither had even mentioned the plan to me.

"Oh," she said, "it was just mostly like an idea that might someday be worth thinkin over."

Seeing that my feathers were ruffled, she added, "But I'll bet they never do it. The way Sam said it, he wouldn't ever be really serious until there just was nothin else for them to work at."

I was still angry. "Then why doesn't he go back in with his father? Everyone knows that the claim he got away from us is the richest around."

"Collie, you know he wouldn't do that. Sam wouldn't even still be at home if it wasn't for the way his ma carried on."

"No I don't! You know more about Sam than I do."

"Now don't get huffy."

"I'm not the one that's flustered. Look how red you're getting."

"I'm goin home," she announced. "I don't like it when you turn nasty." With this, she wheeled about and started back.

"Wait a minute, Elva," I called. "I'm sorry. I didn't mean anything."

She kept on, giving no sign of hearing me, so I was left standing there, disgusted with myself for being so pettish and mostly for letting my jealousy show.

I waited to see if she'd return to laugh at me for being dumb, but she disappeared around a curve, and when there were no sounds left but the screeching of a buzzard circling over the meadow, I started following her on the path back to Jacksonville.

And then I heard her speaking to someone. As I came nearer I heard her say, "You hadn't ought to be tagging after me, Kientpoos." That's when I began running, and as I came up to them, I saw it was the Indian boy we had saved from her father and the lynch mob that day—the boy the town knew as Billy Tell.

He didn't seem surprised or upset at my doubling back on them. Nothing showed on his face until I was within a few steps, and then he said to Elva, "Not good."

"You're damned right," I told him. "Skulking around this close to town is going to get you hanged for sure next time."

When he kept staring at her and not saying anything more, I added, "And you keep away from Winema, too," which is what she had once told us was her mother's name for her.

"Not me," he said. "You. Not good for you." He and Elva looked at each other for a long minute, and then he repeated, "Bad for you." With that, he turned away and disappeared through the manzanita bushes.

After the sounds of his departure were lost, I fairly yelled at her, "I just wish there was somebody in this whole valley you're not smiling at and playing up to!"

But she didn't get mad in return. It was as if I hadn't said anything at all. With the most worry I'd ever seen on her sunny face, she said, "Collie, he was tellin me that his tribe is about ready to fight."

18

TOWARD THE MIDDLE OF THE YEAR 1853, seven white men were murdered by a minor chief named Taylor and his gang of Indians, and right after that people began trying to draw a line between Indian loafers and those who were spies for the war party that wanted to wipe Jacksonville off Oregon's face. This kind of thing snowballs, so it wasn't too long before all of us were watching every red man, woman, and child out of the corners of our eyes.

It's hard to say which side deserved the most blame for the bad feelings, but there's no question but that it all began a few years back when most of the Willamette Valley settlers threw their hoes into the bushes and headed southward for the California gold mines. They had to come through the Rogue Valley for the trip, but whenever they stopped near the ferry points to fashion the boats and rafts they needed, our Indians went after them for everything they had.

This interruption of their God-given right to move in on their neighbors was something they found intolerable. Even the would-be miners who hadn't been molested began firing off complaints to Washington as soon as they reached California, so, in 1850, the army sent General Lane out to meet with Chief John of the Rogue River Indians.

John was a sensible as well as a seasoned warrior. He didn't require much more than a short look at the soldiers and guns that had come along with General Lane before agreeing to a peace settlement—a decision that never reached much popularity with his braves, who were doing too damned well robbing the palefaces passing through. And so, after the general went back to Washington, the chivvying went on.

Not that the miners were without fault. I've unearthed one of the army reports from this area, which said, in part:

> . . . the discovery of gold attracted many of the most unprincipled and ungovernable white men from all countries. With few exceptions, but for these wretches, it is believed the Indians of Oregon would have been the most peaceable, friendly, and easiest managed, with proper care, of any uncivilized tribes within the bounds of the United States.

114

The hostility between the two sides became really aggravated when gold was found close at hand in Oregon. The "wretches" mentioned in the army report began to pour into our area, and, without a doubt, they treated the Indians a hundred times worse than the farmers and settlers who had been trekking down from the Willamette Valley. After the Pitt or Modoc Indians retaliated by ambushing some lonely prospector, there were few miners who wouldn't join a party to go and blaze away at the next bunch of redskins coming down the trail.

The evils and the infringements were just about equal. Once the undeniable fact was passed that this originally had been Indian country, it was hard to excuse the other side from their wanton destructions and continual stealing of settler property. But, as autumn was turning into winter in 1853, the killing of Thomas Wills in Jacksonville raised the whole thing into something way beyond harassment and nuisance.

Wills, a popular merchant, had decided to take a walk after supper just to the edge of town. When he didn't return within the hour, his wife and some of their neighbors went looking for him. They found him dead, his head bashed in and his body bearing some other mutilations that were known to be the handmarks of those Indians who were particularly savage. For the next few days, every buck in town was suspect and treated accordingly, but when that didn't give enough satisfaction, the miners fanned out to the hills, heading for whatever Indian encampment was the closest.

They weren't trying to find the murderers—they were bent on an indiscriminate vengeance that wasn't slaked until they stumbled over a group of six redskin women and children hunkered down near Jackson Creek, their men probably out hunting for food. The miners slaughtered every one of the six, and the report they sent in to General Lane's deputy was that they had fought and beaten a large party of hostiles. That's when the skirmishes stopped and open warfare began.

The warriors were better armed than the townspeople at the outset due to an old habit of the miners of trading their guns and ammunition to the Indians in exchange for skins, shells, meat, or just about anything that could be later swapped for whiskey. This probably accounted for the first beating that a Major Phil Kearney and his soldiers took when they attacked one of the strong Indian positions located out near Table Rock Mountain. The major came back from that engagement cussing the citizens of Jacksonville every step of the way, and, after that, gunswapping was quit by even the dumbest drunk we had.

It still wasn't formal war, but Jacksonville began seeing itself as a besieged camp. At the time, there wasn't a building in it that couldn't be easily approached under cover from nearly every direction, and, as I said, because of the miners' eagerness to trade for tanglefoot, there weren't that many guns left in the place. If the hostiles had risked an attack in force, they could have easily taken and destroyed our little town.

Everyone was scared just witless. The biggest braggarts among us walked carefully during the day, guards were posted on picket duty every night, and even with all this vigilance a man was shot dead within rifle range of California Street. Some of the married miners took to bringing their wives and children out with them to their claims each day, probably under the theory that misery likes company, because there certainly wasn't any sensible reason for it. The only weapon most of them had was a hand axe.

It might not have reached this point if it hadn't been for the past excesses of the miners. Most of them were young, full of beans, and no matter what background had originally produced them, none seemed to find any trouble in sinking to the level of the lowest end of their group, which was, unfortunately, trash. I've seen the same thing happen in military units because there's a kind of anonymity involved that whispers to a man that he can do anything he really wants to because no one sees *him*, they only see the uniform.

Then as well as now, this holds especially true where sex commerce is involved. Very few of the miners showed regard for the amenities when it came to forcibly or otherwise availing themselves of Indian women. If the squaws wanted to sell, that was fine; and it was even better when they allowed themselves to be seduced because then the miners not only had the fun of doing it, there was also the bonus of shooting an irate Indian husband or father who fussed too long about the matter. And, if there wasn't a gun handy, there were always a few friends around to help him beat up the brave who was registering the complaint.

Most of the folks who stayed back East never understood that a terribly sharp edge was put on the Indian's hatred of us because so many settlers, miners, and ranchers thought that seducing, buying, or raping squaws wasn't anything to stew about. It wasn't just money and territory that caused the wars. Too many of us treated them like animals without rights.

I may have gotten a bit ahead of my story, but without mentioning the bitterness, it might be hard to grasp the things that happened after

Tony joined Sam as a carpenter for Boudreau and Witham and had taken to tracking game up in the hills on Sundays or any of the other days that it rained too hard. At first, Tony used Father's clumsy old Sharps on the trips, but when he found out how much he liked hunting, it wasn't too hard for him to convince himself to put most of his new wages toward a first-class muzzle-loading percussion rifle of his own.

Our local gunsmith, a German named John Miller, introduced it to him by saying (I'll spare you my version of his accent), "This is lovely engineered. A thing of beauty. But it is a weapon and nothing else. These people here make a big mistake about guns. They think guns are their friends. A gun is not a friend. It is a rattlesnake that will bite you as soon as you get careless. But if you respect this weapon, it will bite other things for you very nicely."

Unlike most of Miller's other customers, this advice struck Tony as a serious matter. After taking a week or so to study the rifle, he came to know every bolt, pin, and assembly in it. Then he turned into an expert marksman by systematically blazing away by the hour at the targets he and Sam posted in a granite field just beyond the town. From that point on, they wasted very little powder. The squirrels and porcupines—their meat isn't too far away from pork—and even the occasional pheasant they got were rarely so riddled with shot that they couldn't be eaten.

Between the two, Tony was the better shot, but he never touched Sam when it came to tracking. As a matter of fact, if Sam hadn't been able to teach himself to recognize almost every sign a man leaves in the forest, Tony would have never doubted that it was they who found Billy Tell each time they came across him in the hills instead of it being the other way around.

This happened three or four times, and most of the time the meeting wasn't any more than a "Howdy Billy" from Sam and a few nods or a short salute in return. But it was enough. Sam told Tony he guessed that the Indian boy had been tracking them because he figured there was some kind of a friendship between them.

"I shouldn't wonder," Tony answered. "After all, we did keep the blighter from being hung, didn't we?"

"Maybe not. There's somethin else goin on in his eyes. Maybe about the war pow-wows."

"I wouldn't know. He never looks my way."

Sam grinned. "I wouldn't neither if every time I come up, you just stand there stiff as a board."

"Am I supposed to kiss him? You can grunt along with him in Chinook, which is something that, odd as it might seem, I neither can nor want to do. So I simply stand by appearing as grave as possible, hoping he won't think I'm not being civil."

"No," said Sam, "you got to kiss him. Maybe pat his ass a little. Me'n Kientpoos do it all the time to each other when you're not around."

"Billy Tell" seemed to fit him better than his real Indian name, *Kientpoos*, so that's what we most often called him, and he didn't seem to mind. As for *Chinook Talk*, it was a bastard combination of English, some French, and a dash of Spanish. The Indians of the Washington Territory, Oregon, and northern California had learned it from the Hudson Bay Company traders, and it was what they used for fur bartering. The boys in our own area took to learning and speaking in it because certain words took on some very dirty meanings if they were properly mispronounced.

Now, to backtrack: One day, just before they were ready to finish the Bella Union bowling alley carpentering job, Jabez Witham and Boudreau's bartender, Richard Mulligan, showed up. "That's it, boys," the banker told them while Mulligan stood by ready to head off anything more than sore-headed words. "We have to let you go. Your work isn't turning out anywhere near the way that Mr. Boudreau and I thought it would."

Tony was mystified, but Sam got the drift right away. "Mr. Witham, it's all just the way you said you wanted it." Nothing showed on his face, but Tony recognized the anger in his lowered tones.

The banker shook his head. "Fraid not. You aren't finishing it the way real carpenters would. If we let you go on, we'd just have to pull out all the work you're doing now, and that's going to cost us double."

Sam thought this over and then, with about as much expression in his voice as if they had been discussing buying another keg of nails, answered, "Mr. Witham, you're welshin on our deal. You promised a bonus if we got done by the end of this week."

"Samuel, that meant if it was properly completed."

"Is there any way we'd of satisfied you?"

"Certainly." The little banker was being as brisk and businesslike as if he were standing behind his counter. "All you had to do is what's needed, and this isn't it." Turning to Mulligan, he said, "Let's not be wasting any more time, Richard. Please get your tools down out of the wagon."

"Yes sir, Mr. Witham," said Mulligan and limped over to where he had hitched the banker's rig. Richard walked with a limp because he had once fallen while oiling a windmill back in Wyoming; but the way it came out when he explained it to valley newcomers was that there had been this terrible gory Indian battle that ended with him winning hands down and smiling while they cut an arrowhead out from deep in his calf. He had the scar to back it up, but after the newcomers were here for a while, they were apt to agree with the general opinion that Richard Mulligan was more full of shit than a Christmas goose.

"Now, let's see; I owe you boys four days at nine dollars. That's thirty-six dollars apiece." Witham frowned to show how deeply he was thinking out the equities of the situation. "Tell you what. Since it looks like there's been a misunderstanding, I'm going to give you each an extra dollar. How's that?" He announced it with the air of a man whose only aim was to be fair with the world.

"Thirty-six dollars will do it," said Sam. "And we'll take it now instead of waiting to the end of the week."

"Not possible," Witham answered, looking over to Tony for the help he needed in explaining the sacred laws of business. "My bookkeeping just isn't geared that way. I'm set up to pay all my bills on Fridays, which is the way you've always been paid, right on the button."

"Pay it now," said Sam, in a voice so low that only Tony heard him, although the banker clearly got the message because he dug right into his pocket.

"I don't like this way of doing business. I'm afraid I won't be hiring you again, Samuel."

Sam waited until the money had been counted out and handed over. Then he said, as he stuffed the bills away, "That sure is a shame, Mr. Witham, because I thought we was doin a good job. Just look how straight the balls would roll even before we got the sanding all finished." With that, he picked the banker up in the air, swung him back, swung him forward, released, and the man went sliding and sprawling almost half the length of the bowling alley.

After watching Witham's lurching and spluttering path down the lane, Sam turned to Tony and noted, "We should a done a mite more sanding."

"You learn something new from every job, I suppose," answered Tony as they picked up the tool kits they hadn't been given time to unpack that morning.

Richard Mulligan, returning from the cart, passed them as they left the building site. He winked, holding up his hands, palms outward, in a mute display that he knew he was only a bartender. Unimpressed, they didn't return the salute and kept walking.

When they reached the outskirts of the town, Tony asked, "Now what?"

Sam shrugged. "First, let's cache the tools." And, as they looked around for a hollow log to shelter the kits until they got back, he added, "Guess we're about to get into the meat business for real."

For the past few weeks they had talked, not more than half in earnest, about hunting as a full-time job, but Tony's naturally conservative nature had to have its say once the opportunity was actually in front of them. "Do you think there's enough money in it for the two of us?"

"There's sure enough miners around too lazy to hunt their own food."

"And Collis?"

Sam grinned, the sting of the banker's unfair treatment all but washed away in the dawning knowledge that now they were free to do what they liked the most. "Collie's a weasel," he said. "He'll spend all his time explainin what we're doin wrong."

"But he'll be so hurt if we don't ask him along."

"Then let's do it. He won't last more'n the first few days, anyhow."

"It would be a bloody shame if he doesn't. If the three of us were to go about it properly, we just might end with a very good business. Whatever else was happening here wouldn't concern us at all, would it?"

Sam stopped and eyed Tony for a moment. "Anthony, you're tryin to tell me that there ain't goin to be anybody hirin us for wages anymore for fear of gettin on the wrong side of old Witham."

Tony nodded. "Perhaps. But there really would be enough work for all of us if we were serious about it."

"Hell, let's get Billy Tell, too, while we're at it."

"No one in Jacksonville would trade with an Indian. Not these days."

"Don't have to. All we need be frettin about is usin him to track the herds. He knows how to run deer better'n anybody else."

"I doubt he'd be willing. His tribe might not like the form."

"They don't have to know anymore'n we have to let the people here know we're all in cahoots. He tracks, we kill; he skins, we sell."

"And Collis?"

"I wish you'd stop sayin, 'and Collis.' Sure, Collis—he'll be in charge of doin the sellin."

"We have a company!" Now that the doubts were gone, Tony was delighted with the possibility of turning a hobby into a career. As a bonus, there was an immediate mental picture of his stunned family reacting to his new role of frontier meat packer.

This turned out to be the last bit of fun he had out of the idea that there'd be the Company. When the project was broached to Billy Tell, he didn't dignify the proposal with even a Chinook grunt. He stared steadily at Sam and then over to Tony for a bit, and then he went gliding back through the thickest part of the forest, which was the last they saw of him for a week.

Looking at the path he had taken, Tony said, "I get the feeling he doesn't fancy us as business associates."

Sam agreed. "The next worse thing we could've asked was how's his sister comin along."

They didn't fare much better with me. I was in my father's office when the two of them came trooping in, and when they saw I had my eyes closed, they banged the door and clumped around loud enough to wake the dead, let alone a man who just might have nodded off in the middle of serious thinking. "This is a professional office," I pointed out to them. "I hate to think what would have happened if a patient had been in this chair."

"It's scary," Sam admitted. "I wish I was ashamed of myself."

"Collis," Tony said, "rub your eyes and wake up. We have a plan that just might rescue you from this stink in here. That is, at least for as long as your lungs can take in fresh air without shriveling."

"You've already forgotten. That stink is life-giving herbs."

"He hasn't," said Sam. "He's trying to get you out of it before it gets into your bones."

"Sure," I told them, "you two worry about me all the time."

Looking at me carefully, Tony said, "As a matter of fact, we do. We've just decided to hunt and sell the meat to the townspeople as a trade. We want you to join us."

I yawned as elaborately as I could. "I couldn't stand the bloodshed. If it wouldn't be one of you accidentally shooting me, it would be the other shooting me on purpose."

"Because of what?" Tony wanted to know.

"Just because. You English are so damned envious of your betters that almost any reason would be enough to aim at me."

Tony considered this. "It might be giving up the best part, but suppose we promise that we won't. Then would you be our partner?"

"Not a chance! I knew last week that you two were thinking about starting up as hunters or something. Elva told me. And she also said that if you really want to feed the miners, you ought to be opening a restaurant next to her father's saloon, because as far as she was concerned, the only thing either of you should be trusted with is a popgun."

"She really said all that?" asked Tony, realizing that maybe I was put out by Elva being in on it before they got around to discussing it with me.

"Sure she did," said Sam. "Not the popgun part, because Collie'd anytime rather lie than stop at the truth. But she didn't miss tellin him the other. As soon as I said the littlest thing to her, I should a known she'd be in a sweat to blab. Collie wouldn't a gone along anyway, but that dumb kid—she's always buttin in where it don't concern her."

Those days he was always quick to jump on her. "She didn't mean anything wrong," I told him, starting to get angry in addition to being hurt by the way they had kept me out of this marvelous idea until now.

He didn't want to be the least bit forgiving. "Anything that goes through her mind comes right out her mouth!"

"Well," Tony observed, "being honest isn't actually the world's worst trait, is it?"

"I'd just as leave she was less honest and had more sense."

I was about to blurt out something really nasty at this, but Tony caught my eye just in time, and what he said without saying it aloud was, *Let it be.* And he was right, because anything more I did to tell him how wrong he was would only cause him to come down even heavier.

So, I changed what I was going to say into, "You oughtn't be so hard on her, Sam." And, in spite of my own feelings where Elva was concerned, I found myself wishing I could get him to realize how much more worthwhile she was than all the others he'd been laying with ever since getting it off with Mrs. Witham. That thin biddy must have triggered something inside of him because every free minute he had in town these days went to figuring out how to get the nearest girl onto her back.

It was worrisome. The appetite he was developing was bound to land him into a raft of trouble. If old Witham didn't find out about Sam and his wife, then some other farmer would when it came his daughter or wife's turn, which was the kind of situation that every self-respecting man here settled with a gun. It had to end up with either Sam or a farmer getting a bullet, and that was bad medicine no matter which way it came out.

Damn Helen Witham and the way that starved bitch had smelled out the sex in Sam! Her skinny fingers must have fairly itched until she got it tapped and going. Double damn her for backing off after she got scared because that landed him squarely on the prowl. It flashed through my brain that maybe he'd do it to Elva, but it went right away because no decent man would be that mindless, no matter how much of the old scratch he had in him.

As far as we knew, so far he'd kept away from the whores, but the way he was going, it was only a matter of time. As for the Indian girls—well, Tony told me the rest of what happened that day.

19

THE REST OF THAT DAY—this is what happened, just as Tony described it to me:

After the two of them left Father's office, they got their guns and headed for Walker Creek, not saying much to each other until they were halfway there. Tony guessed that Sam knew he'd acted badly by lighting into me about Elva but was keeping glum because he didn't know how to go about setting things straight. The hunch was confirmed when Sam finally said, "For a fact, that Collie sure does think a lot of Elva."

"I know," Tony answered, letting it go at that. As much as he liked Sam, he thought it was time he learned that saving face wasn't always necessary.

They continued a few more paces in silence until Sam, kicking a fallen branch harder than was needed to clear it out of their path, said, "Damn!"

When Tony just kept walking, he went on, "If I told her once, I told her a dozen times to leave me be. But she keeps at me, and that ain't what I got in mind. She'd be better for Collie, anyway. He's always moonin like a calf after her. I mean, I don't ever want to hurt her feelings, so I wouldn't tell her that, but, gee, if she only had some sense about the way things are."

Tony relented, just as he always did whenever his friend's vulnerability surfaced. "It isn't your doing, Sam. Really. Collis is old enough to understand what he's about, and, as for Elva, she'll certainly be the first to tell you that her attachments are her own concern. But, for heaven's sake, don't lead her on."

"I'm not. I honest to God wouldn't, Tony."

"Then that's it. These matters always work themselves out just so long as you don't keep poking away at them."

"You sure?"

"Not a bit. But it did sound splendid, didn't it?"

They grinned at each other, and neither offered anything more until they reached one of the bank bends in the creek and Sam said, "Shit! There's some Indians. Even if they ain't trouble, they probably already snared or spooked away whatever game was around."

Tony didn't see anyone. "Where?"

"Over to yonder," Sam said, pointing to a place upstream. "Two of 'em."

Tony stared steadily at the spot until two forms took shape apart from the foliage behind them. "It isn't a problem—just women," he said. "Don't take on so."

"The hell it's not. It's old Mary and her girl."

"And?"

"The girl's bad luck. Her tribe drove her away for whorin with the miners. Mary went with her, nastier'n a polecat. Before they left, the buck that was her husband put out one of her eyes. It's what they do when they catch 'em droppin their drawers for strangers."

"You know her?"

"Yeah. Looks like Mary's still cluckin like an old hen over Me-Huh-No-Lush."

"Is that her name?"

"It's the one she got at the campfire. Means 'she is blind.' Come on, let's go over." As they walked to where the women stood, he added, "The miners call her somethin else, but she's never cottoned that. It's real dirty. I called her Little Mary the times we crossed each other."

When they reached the women, Tony thought, *She must have been beautiful before they punished her.*

Sam greeted them in Chinook and followed by asking if they'd seen any deer-herd tracks in the area. Old Mary just shook her head, and since there wasn't anything else to talk about, they stood until the girl announced, "You, Sam."

He nodded amiably, "Right you be, Little Mary. I'm Sam Hume."

She turned to rattle in Modoc to her mother, who appeared upset by what she was saying. The girl persisted until she won something that looked to Tony like resigned agreement, and then, turning back to Sam, she asked, "A dollar?"

"Yeah, I got a dollar," he answered. And, with his eyes still on the girl, said to Tony, "She's got the old lady to let her whore with us because they're flat busted."

"Sam," said Tony, "please don't."

"Why not? It'll do them and us both good."

"Let's just give them the money."

"No. Neither of them are gonna mind, and I always admired that Little Mary, one eye or none." Misreading Tony's distaste, he added, "Hey, wasn't you just tellin me that people ought to be let alone to do what they want? Why not this squaw?"

Tony shrugged. "All right, go ahead if that's what you want. But I won't. I'd really rather not."

"You sure?"

"I wouldn't have said it if I weren't, would I?"

He nodded. "That's right. You do what you want and I'll do what suits me." And not looking again at either Tony or the mother, he went over to the girl, put his arm around her shoulder, and, after a moment, they walked off.

When they had disappeared around the next upstream bend, Tony turned back to Old Mary, but the woman gave no sign of caring that he was still there. A minute passed and then she stood and walked off through the bushes at a right angle to the path taken by Sam and her daughter.

Tony was alone, the taste of bile in his mouth. The fun of tracking or hunting was gone for the day, and there didn't seem to be anything left to do but go on home by himself. *So damned ugly!* he thought, and then there was the gnawing idea that maybe *he* had behaved childishly— that if he were really mature and independent, he'd either have gone with Sam or, barring that, simply shut up and waited. *She was so beautiful. How could she have done that? A dollar!* Then, the picture of Sam and the girl and what they were doing began creeping into his mind.

In an attempt to dispel it, he shook his head sharply, which is when he saw, staring at him from perhaps twenty yards away, an antlered buck carrying enough meat on him to feed a dozen miners. Instinctively, he lifted his rifle, sighted, and dropped the animal with the first shot.

The elation of the good kill committed him. If he left now, Sam might miss the carcass when he came back this way, and that would waste a first-class opportunity to begin the business they had planned. What's more, even the darkest thoughts about Sam's ungraceful conduct weren't enough to make him abandon this fine a trophy. *At the very least, it's a six-pointer*, he thought.

He drew his knife as he walked over and knelt by the buck, which was much larger than it appeared from shooting distance. The job of dressing out the carcass was going to be a long one, and he'd better get started if he was going to crow to Sam, *Look at it! Killed, skinned, and cleaned—and I didn't have the slightest need for your lecherous help*.

The job became so absorbing that it took too long for him to hear the crashing sounds in the underbrush behind him. When the noise got loud enough to make him turn, an enormous bear was already out of the clearing and moving rapidly on all fours toward him. Ordinarily, bears avoid human contact, but this one must have been ungodly hungry and unable to resist the smell of hot animal blood brought to him by the afternoon winds.

In the moment of leaping to his feet, Tony realized he had neglected to reload his rifle, but peril set his mind to working like fury. Remembering that Sam hadn't taken his cap-and-ball Navy pistol with him, he raced toward it, but this action caused the bear to change course to follow him with what seemed incredible speed.

He got the pistol, snatched it up, and began firing it. He was sure that he got all five rounds into the monster, but they had no more effect than if they'd been a swarm of flies. He turned to run, but the bear, now towering erect, was on him. As he was pulled into a crushing embrace, he threw his left arm up to protect his face, smelling the fetid breath, and then the huge jaws crushed his arm as if it were a matchstick.

After that, he remained conscious long enough for a blurred sight of Sam jumping onto the bear and plunging his knife in and out of its back. He felt himself released, dropping to the ground, and the last thing he saw before he fainted was Sam leaping forward through the outstretched paws and driving the knife full into its heart.

Later, Tony learned that Sam saved him from a fatal loss of blood by tying his belt into a tourniquet next to his shoulder and, after slinging him across his back, carrying him back to Jacksonville, where Father finished the job of keeping him alive. But there was nothing that anyone would ever be able to do about the arm Tony had lost.

20

AFTER FATHER cut the remaining shreds of muscle from his shoulder, something more than a physical change took place in Tony Johnstone. The impersonal courtesy, the easy smile that overlaid his toughness, and the occasional flashes of wild humor were all still there, but now they didn't seem to have anything to do with what was going on inside of him. Our friendship—and this included Tommy as well as Sam and myself—was undisturbed, but now he was never the one to suggest a lark, he simply went along. The one difference we could put our fingers on was that he took to watching over Sam as if he were a rash younger brother.

One day I called him on it. "Tony, I can't help wishing you'd worry about me the way you do Sam. He's twice as big as any of us and yet you're always stewing about him getting into trouble."

"I seem to have been cursed with the job of keeping all of you from blotting your copybooks."

"Especially Sam," I insisted.

"Not true. He blooms on his own. And, despite your doubtful face, so do I. Our hunting business prospers and, more important than the lovely wages, I'm going about what my family wanted when they sent me to this nasty place: accumulating knowledge."

"Like how to skin a squirrel? That kind of knowledge must be in big demand over there."

"There isn't a better way of discovering the farm and mining potential here than to deal with the people who are doing it, is there?"

"Oh, sure. Your father and brothers especially have to understand why Sam Hume has to be kept from getting a shotgun blast in his back from some farmer who just found out why his daughter is getting so fat. No question about it, that's *really* important knowledge."

"Collie," he said, shutting down our conversation, "you're a survivor. You ask everyone's help and advice and then you sort it all out, using just whatever suits the thing you've had in mind all along. Tommy does anything he thinks he needs to do, and it often turns out precisely right for him—if for no one else. But Sam simply hasn't a clue to any of it. That rather opens him up, doesn't it?"

And that's the way it stayed from then on. Most times it was Sam and Tony settling on one side of an argument and me with no company on the other, because Tommy was now working full bore both in his shop and at a whole raft of mysterious other things that we knew nothing about except that the bankroll for them just had to be furnished by somebody else. We didn't question that this meant that Jabez Witham had come in as his partner because there wasn't another local citizen who could (or would) have financed the trip Tommy took back to China to recruit coolie labor for the mines. This left me pretty much all alone during that awful winter of '53 and '54.

About that winter. Oregon always has been known as a place of extremes—and one of the prime reasons for the reputation is its weather. The rain can fall like Niobe's tears for two weeks straight, and then every morning for the next month you'll wake up to the kind of day that kept Adam and Eve so blissful before the subject of clothes came up. We had a taste of this climatic foolishness in the beginning of December when the skies and soft breezes of what seemed like an endless Indian summer disappeared so abruptly that we were sure God had been called away to tend to other matters.

The snow started in the late afternoon of a day that began just as lyrically as almost every other since June. The one reported comment on the clouds gathering on the horizon was, "Well, maybe we'll get a mite of rain after all," which was followed by the answer that, by then, had become a ritual: "We sure can use it, them hills are as dry as a bone." The man who delivered the judgment was, at the time, picking the corn still on the stalks in his vegetable garden.

After the snow stopped falling four days later, even the most optimistic among us understood that it was going to be a long while before the packers and their mules would be able to struggle through the passes with our supply of staples. And then, every so often for the next six weeks, the snow fell again.

Luckily, Sam and Tony discovered that the cold had produced a top crust on the snow that the sharp hooves of deer would pierce but was strong enough to hold a man. They'd crunch over to where one stood sunk up to its belly in a drift, and while the poor dumb animal was staring up at them, somebody would swing his axe—and then there'd be fresh meat for a while.

I didn't see how they could bring themselves to kill these helpless, sad-eyed beasts, but, of course, in spite of my qualms, I ate as heartily as anyone until the steady diet of venison without salt or bread or bacon or beans began to make the idea of starvation not quite as desperate as it had appeared during the first few weeks after the snowfall. About the only people the lack of salt didn't bother were the Chinese. They turned the meat they trapped into something edible because they still had stores of the rancid butter no one else in Jacksonville wanted. One of them had figured how to render the brine out of it.

It was a nasty time, and during the days of Christmas, no matter how often someone tried to raise a spark of Yuletide feelings, it never caught. We were too hungry and cold and miserable to do much more than dream about and regret leaving the places we had come from. Father quit rhapsodizing over the hardiness of "we pioneers," and Tony, looking rheumy and pinched and British beyond belief, summarized the situation as "fairly grim" in a way that, for once, didn't sound like snobbish understatement. Never before or since has Philadelphia seemed such a marvelous place.

On one of our worst days, a trace of relief finally appeared in the person of a whipcord old packer who brought his mule train up from Yreka, fifty miles to the south. He'd beaten the Siskiyou Pass by plodding on ahead of his train while the mules inched though the path he made as he shuffled the snow away. But even that blessing wasn't unmixed. Dan Kenny heard through the mysterious grapevine known only to retailers that the old man was on his way and went to meet him two miles out. He bought the 250 pounds of salt packed in the train for eight dollars a pound, and by the time the load came to Jacksonville, Appler & Kenny had the price jacked up to just under the point where they might have gotten lynched.

This was the one bright spot in that dreary winter. Those who had hung on to their gold dust had salt for their meat, which made it tolerable. The rest, especially the farmers, did without, but eventually this was solved when most of them got a bit of the precious stuff by scrounging up one item or another for swapping with those miners who could afford to buy it.

The Indians didn't mind not having salt because they were satisfied sprinkling gall as a seasoning over whatever grub they could get their hands on. However, this amounted to damned little since the snow was too thick for them to scratch up any of the vegetables they had planted, and no white man was about to give them any of the meat or provisions he'd put away, no matter if they had anything left to barter, which they didn't. And since they had even less experience than us in traveling through snow drifts, their sustenance was the slim pickings of whatever they found right near their camps.

These hard times for the Rogue River Indians were aggravated after some of the harder cases in the town, not being able to farm or mine, figured that they ought to be using their time to even up whatever scores were left over from the hostilities. Parties of these "exterminators"—which is what they called themselves—went looking for redskin camps, and whenever they found one that wasn't too full of able-bodied warriors, they'd do what they'd come for. This meant killing mostly women, children, and the ancients who weren't able to go out foraging for food among the drifts.

A party of these hoodlums, led by gimpy Richard Mulligan, came back one morning shepherding a captured bag of women and their papooses. Mulligan was proud as punch over his trophies. "They're hostages," he bragged to the people who crowded around them on California Street. "We'll send word to Chief John that we're not gonna let go of any of his squaws or their whelps until he comes in and guarangoddamtees that him and all of his devils is gonna clear out of these parts."

There were very few citizens who didn't regard bringing in the captives as a stroke of genius. No matter how tough the Rogue River Indians had proven themselves to be in combat, no one thought they'd be savage enough not to trade their families for the small favor of knuckling under. So Mulligan's gang picked the oldest of the male captives as a messenger, fixed his attention with a dozen kicks to make sure he'd memorized their ultimatum, and let him go.

The treatment must have been effective because he returned the very next day with the Chief's answer that he was willing to come in and talk it over, and he appeared not long after that, alone except for a very young brave whose job it was to interpret in Chinook. Only the three of us recognized the interpreter as Billy Tell, even though most of the men in the crown had been the very ones who'd been thirsting so to hang him last summer.

Looking every inch the fierce old warrior we'd heard about, the first thing John wanted to know was what kind of care was being taken of his tribe's women and children. Twice he made Billy repeat the question and Mulligan's answers that they were just fine and dandy. All through this, Billy gave no sign that he felt he was anything but a message center. He didn't show the slightest bit of interest in what was going on, even when he looked over to where Tony, Sam, and I stood. Most of the time he kept his eyes up over everyone's heads and at the hills, which gave the effect that he, personally, didn't believe a damn word of what he was supposed to translate.

Billy's attitude worried Mulligan even more than the Chief's few gutteral sounding comments because being considered bright by the town's citizens was a new place for him, and he didn't want to lose it by having the hostage scheme fall through. So he stepped up his protestations that the captives were being fed and housed just about as well as anybody in town, which wasn't saying much even though it was fairly close to the truth. He became so vehement about it that it was clear to even the dumbest among us how much Richard Mulligan wanted his name entered into western lore as the "Saviour of Jacksonville." When he got to where he was sweating in spite of the cold, Billy finally brought his gaze down.

Seeing this, Richard, punched even harder. Billy listened until he'd finished and, turning to the Chief, took so long to translate that we were sure he hadn't omitted a syllable of the claim. While we all studied his face, the old man digested this news in silence for a few minutes and then delivered himself of a few grunts, which Billy interpreted back to us as, "Chief John has heard you out. Now he will make talk with his warriors." With that, the two of them got back up on their cayuses.

Before they rode off, Billy, for the first time, looked straight at the three of us. He still didn't show a flicker of recognition, but we agreed later that, inside, he was grinning from ear to ear.

They returned for three of four more powwows after that, and it went the same way each time. By then, most of the women in the town were urging their menfolk to return the Indian women and children in exchange for a compromise so everybody could live in peace. And they might have gotten their way, but Richard Mulligan stopped it by insisting that it would be even better for Jacksonville's (and his) reputation if the warriors were driven clear out of the area. "Otherwise there's nothing to prevent 'em from goin after us again next spring," he told his admirers, and his argument swung the rest of the men in town around to agreeing that no matter what the women wanted, the best thing Jacksonville could do was to use the situation to earn the name of being a place that redskins better not be fooling around with.

"The damned fools," I told Tony and Sam as we walked away from the latest meeting, "don't they know it's a shell game? You'd think that at least the merchants would be bright enough to see that the tribe doesn't care how long they keep on talking so long as their women and kids are warm and eating regularly. They want to palaver about a treaty until the winter's over."

Sam shrugged. "So?"

"It's just not right. It bothers me."

Tony shook his head at my idealism. "Collis, me boy, I see no skin scraped off your nose. If our Indian friends want to play Jacksonville for fools . . ."

"They're not my friends," I said, "they're yours."

"Fine. If Jacksonville wants to support the squaws and papooses of my friends through a bad winter, I couldn't be more in favor of it."

"Don't argue so much," Sam told me. "If the people here weren't so sure that an Indian smarter'n 'em doesn't walk, Chief John wouldn't be able to pull the windy like he's doin. It's purely their own fault."

Actually, I agreed that what the Indians were doing to Jacksonville was funny, but the two of them were getting on my nerves by the way they sided together against me in every argument. So I stood my ground. "Wait until one of you has to take his turn in the barrel, then tell me how much you bleed for poor Lo." *Lo* was the name some of our newspapers pinned to all redskins. It came from *Lo, the noble Indian,* which was a phrase an idiotic eastern writer had adopted for the stories he churned out.

"We shall keep it in mind," Tony assured me. "And, in the meantime, you keep polishing your ties to dear old Jacksonville. Come scalping time, we promise to put in the good word for you with our red friends."

Then I stopped arguing because a perfectly beautiful dodge had just come to me. It was so great that I could hardly keep a straight face. "Very well," I said sadly, "I just hope that someday the two of you will see that reds are reds and whites are whites," and, not waiting for an answer, I turned and walked away.

Tony called after me as I headed toward California Street, "Come off it, Collis, you're acting like a child."

Normally, this would have been good enough to get me to return and defend myself, but the scheme was already whirling into shape in my mind. I simply drew up my shoulders as if I'd given vent to an enormous sigh and kept on going.

The key to my plan was Richard Mulligan, who was sure to be at the Bella Union, which is where I was headed. If either of my friends called anything after me, I didn't hear it because I was too busy refining my idea, and by the time I reached the saloon, I knew exactly how it was going to work. The project must have had the gods' approval because

Mulligan was just coming out the door as I reached the place. "Henri fire you already, Richard?" I asked casually.

"Shit, no. Frenchy couldn't get a Siwash to work as cheap as me."

"You work cheap because you steal a lot."

This was the kind of talk he understood, so his ugly monkey face split into a smile as he answered, "Shee-it, the next dollar I steal will be the first."

"Ah, Richard, you're the cunning one. Does anyone ever get ahead of you?"

"Not so you can notice. Before I got me this wound . . ." And then, remembering that I'd been here long enough to know the truth about his gimp, he changed his brag to, ". . . this accident, I'd give anybody cards and spades. Still can."

"No question about it," I agreed. Since Mulligan was one of the no-goods whose idea of sport rarely went beyond tying a kerosene-soaked rag to the tail of a stray dog and then setting it on fire, I didn't have to worry about over-elaborating my trap. "Richard, what if I were to tell you I know of an idea that would keep us in money all year long without ever having to do a red cent's worth of work in return?"

"I'd say you're full of shit." Richard Mulligan's small talk had a certain amount of monotony to it.

"The hell with you, then. I'll find someone else to go in with me."

Greed struggled briefly with his distrust of anyone who could speak two consecutive sentences without referring to a bodily function. Greed won. "Come on, Collie. I done you plenty of favors."

"Like what?"

"Plenty of things." He thought for a moment and the monkey face brightened. "Like the time I come woke you up when your father was asking where you was."

"Well," I said, considering it judiciously, "that was certainly being helpful." Then I frowned. "But you really oughtn't to be telling a man he's full of shit when he offers you partners in a first-class claim."

"You mean it's a mine?" he asked, his enthusiasm dampening. "I thought you said there wasn't no work involved."

"I didn't say it was a mine. All I said was, it's a claim. A lucky strike."

"What in hell are you talkin about, Collie Gibbs?"

"Fighting Indians."

"Oh shit."

"I'm serious, Richard. I know that you just about broke the back of the Indian war when you brought in those hostages."

"I sure did." He frowned. "Be nice if some others cottoned to it, too."

"You can't blame them. Most are still scared to death that Chief John is going to run out of patience and sic his braves back on us with everything they've got."

"They ain't about to do that."

"How do you know?"

"I know Injuns, that's how. Cut 'em off from their squaws, and you're cuttin 'em off from poon tang. They don't like that even a little bit. They'll do anything to get their females back."

"Exactly!"

"Exactly, what? Collie. You're talkin in goddamn circles!"

"No, I'm not. Listen carefully, Richard. If we formed a militia to put down whatever fight was left in the Rogues, there wouldn't be much for them to do, would there?"

"Goddammit, I already told you there was no fight left in them Injuns."

"Exactly."

"Exactly, what?" he repeated, but this time interest had replaced frustration in his voice. My fish was hooked.

"That's my plan. If we form a militia to save the town from the redskins, the government is bound to support us. Right?"

"Sure they are. That's what they been doin in Yreka since before I left there."

"Every member of the militia gets paid by the federal government, right?"

"Right! And they get uniforms, too. Hell, they even got thereselves some bugles in Yreka."

"Now do you see it?" I asked.

"I think so. We're gonna form a militia."

"Right. And . . . ?"

"And we're gonna make it official! We're gonna get the War Department to make it official!" Now that the drift was clear, he was so excited that it was all he could do to stand still.

"You're smart, Richard. Nobody has to put their finger in your mouth for you to get the idea. But let's make sure. The most important thing is who does our militia have to fight in exchange for getting uniforms and money?" His broad, snaggle-toothed smile was enough to tell me that he didn't require further priming, so I went on. "It's just talking that we'll be doing instead of fighting because there aren't any Indians around who really want to fight, are there?"

He burst into laughter. "Goddamn me for a son of a bitch! It's slick as frog hair! We'll draw rations 'n quarters! It's . . ." And then he stopped laughing, and the look he gave me was suspicion mixed with a plea. "But you're gonna want to be captain, ain't you?"

"Oh no," I answered, plainly shocked and hurt. "How on earth could I handle a job like that? I've never been a soldier, and I wouldn't know how to even begin ordering around a military unit." I shook my head, amazed that he could have been so blind. "So far as I can see, there's only one man in Jacksonville for a job like this, and that's Richard Mulligan. We need you. It's why I'm here."

Swelling up before my eyes, he answered, "You got a head on you, Collie."

I shrugged. "I don't call having common knowledge being so re-markable."

For a moment I was afraid that was too broad, even for Mulligan, but he insisted, "No, you've got a good head. If I told your father once, I told him it a hundred times."

"The best I might be able to do," I answered modestly, "is maybe help you with the recruiting."

"Sure. A job like that, I'm gonna need all the help I can get."

"Richard, that's marvelous! I knew I could count on you for a square deal. You'll be the captain and I'll be your adjutant."

"How high is that?" True to the military heritage he had just dis-covered within himself, Richard Mulligan wasn't about to brevet anyone not properly qualified.

"Just a lieutenant."

He thought for a moment. "Over to Yreka they only had one captain and one lieutenant."

I was going to argue a bit further, but I saw he'd already figured out that he couldn't expect me to bribe him for the job with either cash or whiskey but that there were certainly others in the town who would. So I asked, "sergeant?"

My appointment was confirmed with a no-nonsense nod. "Sergeant. If you do good as sergeant, I'll do what I can to get you a raise."

The cadre had been formed, and now it was time to implement the next step in my plan. "Will you tell Alben Hensley, or is that part of my job?" I asked.

"That drunk? What for?"

Alben Hensley, who took whiskey aboard like a thirsty sponge, was the editor of our newspaper, the *Jacksonville Sentinel*. He hadn't been here long enough for there to be much known about him except that he wrote editorials that riled half the town and would dog a merchant up and down California Street for a paid advertisement for rotting meat. The *Sentinel* missed publication just about two weeks out of every five, but since it was the only paper we had, my answer to Mulligan was, "We need him to let everybody know that the Indians are just as dangerous as ever, no matter what they promise to swap for their families. If he gives us the right story, every man in town will be ashamed of himself if he doesn't join up."

Richard saw my point. "All right—but you talk to him. He mought be holdin it against me because I throwed his ass out of the saloon day before yesterday for startin an argument before he bought anything."

"Yes sir, Captain," I answered. "I was right about you. You really are one shrewd son of a bitch!"

"Go ahead. You go on about your business, and I'll start in formin the troop." And with no more farewell than that, he wheeled about and headed back into Boudreau's saloon, a picture of the career military man off on important War Department affairs.

I watched until he had passed through the swinging doors and then set out for the *Sentinel* office that had been established in a small shack down where the street tailed off into bushes, brush, and trees.

Its editor was in, randomly squirting oil at the innards of the rusty, flatbed press he had brought with him to Jacksonville. "Morning, Mr. Hensley," I said in what I hoped were the tones that alerted a journalist that he was about to get an exciting piece of news.

He'd heard the song before. He squinted at me and, turning back to his machine, asked it, "What do you want?"

"I'm Collis Gibbs . . ."

"I know. You're the doctor's son. You getting married or something to that half-breed girl?"

"How would you like to mind your own goddamned business?"

"That is my business. News. You want me to announce a wedding or something?" He cocked his head back to me, warned, I guess, that my reply might mean he was just before getting into a fight with the son of a prominent citizen. It wasn't too far from the case. At that moment, fetching him a clout across his big nose seemed a lot more attractive than getting his help with my scheme.

Then I realized it was probably just a professional attitude. I obviously wasn't an advertiser, and since it was a small town, everyone in it must have seen me mooning after Elva at one time or another, so he had concluded that I was there to offer the only piece of news in my possession. I've met quite a few reporters and editors since then, and most are just as rude once they make up their minds that you aren't going to give them anything they can use.

The thought drained away my desire to hit him. "Let's start over again. I'm here to tell you that a militia is being formed in Jacksonville to fight Indians."

"Who's running it?"

He bent over to pick a proof page from the floor, and while he was smoothing it out so that its back could be used for notes, I said, "Richard Mulligan."

"That benighted bastard." He crumpled the page and threw it back on the floor.

"Listen, Hensley. This thing is serious. I don't know what you've got against Captain Mulligan, but he's one of the few men in this place who's been through an Indian war. We all need him. If he doesn't get a troop together, our town could be wiped out before any army detachment heard about it and got to us."

"Who'd boost the little ape up high enough for anybody to see him?" he said, stooping down again for his note paper, an action that allowed me to realize it wasn't going to be too hard to sell my story after all. The editor of the *Sentinel* needed a circulation-builder as badly as I wanted him to have it.

He took my story, peppering me with questions for details I obligingly manufactured while ignoring his disgusted snorts of disbelief. When I'd finished, he offered me a job as a reporter, which was a bonus I hadn't even considered getting. "I'll pay you five cents an inch for anything we print," he said. "And if you're as shrewd as all this moonshine tells me you are, in no time at all the two of us can make this the fattest weekly north of San Francisco. You can take my word that you'll be sharing in it every step of the way."

This last statement made me happy. Not only was I going to be paid for prying into other people's business—a job that, so far, I'd been cheerfully doing for nothing, but, even more pleasing, I loved seeing a situation develop where I was the fish being offered a bait full of hooks. I thought, *Everybody is out to diddle everybody*, which is an understanding that has helped me all my life.

However, I didn't want him to land me too easily. "Five cents an inch isn't much," I answered. When he shrugged at this, I went on. "But I feel it's my duty to do anything that will help our city. If there's one thing we need to fulfill our destiny, it's a first-class newspaper. When do I start?"

"Oh, Lord," he said, mostly to himself. "Now, if you want."

"Fine. May I have a pencil and a notebook?" I needed these to prove to Elva and, of course, to Father, Sam, and Tony, that I could be as productive as anyone else—I'd just been waiting for the right job.

"Get your own supplies," said my new employer. "And while I'm setting the tripe you've just delivered, you go see Edward Hume. I've wanted to talk with him ever since I heard he's sitting on nuggets bigger and yellower than a Chinaman's head. Ask him how he plans to keep the rest of the thieves in town from stripping his claim once the spring thaw starts."

21

WHEN I HEARD HIM bustling about the cabin, I opened one eye just wide enough to confirm my suspicion that it was still dark outside. These days, Father left for his office before dawn in order to patch up the night's casualities among the miners. The town was going to heave one long concerted sigh of relief whenever the weather improved enough to let the sourdoughs get back to their diggings.

He caught me. "You're awake, aren't you?"

"Barely. I'm at death's door."

"You may, just may, have a slight cold. I do wish you'd get up and dress."

"Are you saying that you'd prefer that I die with my boots on? Really, Father."

He regarded me with that expression of pained impatience that he and my friends had taken to ever since I'd gone to work for the *Sentinel*. "Collis," he said, "I find it hard to deny the feeling that you may be just a bit overcome by your new employment. You were up until an ungodly late hour."

"We journalists have deadlines to meet."

"Unfortunately, I've just read your night's output. It seemed to consist of a letter to Captain Alden at Fort Jones requesting a charter for that preposterous militia you've organized with Mr. Mulligan." He stopped his stirring about and sighed just long enough to make sure I'd seen the picture of a concerned parent that, every so often, he enjoyed painting. "I worry about you. I do, you know."

I wrestled myself more snugly under the covers. "It isn't very nice to be reading a reporter's correspondence behind his back. Beside, I don't think it's lawful."

"Why did you leave it on the table? I assumed you wanted my opinion."

"Absolutely," I said, although of course I knew he didn't care one way or another. "I thought you'd like to see how community-minded I'm getting to be."

"Collis," he answered, shaking his head, "you'll either end as a territorial politician or in being hung, and I'm not at all certain which will be the worse fate." He sighed. "I suppose that the responsibility is at least partly mine. I should never have had children."

I thought his good humor might have reopened a door, but when I asked, "Father, don't you think it's time you forgave Chung Lin?" the smile left his lips.

"I do forgive the boy. But if you are suggesting that we take him back, of course the answer must still be, absolutely not. He abused our trust in the most shameful way." When he saw that I was about to remind him again of Tommy's loneliness and fears, he added, "I'd rather you didn't press this. If you want to continue your friendship with the lad, I won't object even though I find it difficult to approve. But I really wouldn't want him in our home again."

"He's working for Jabez Witham, you know. And he's the one he actually stole from."

"I'm afraid that says more about Mr. Witham than it does about Chung Lin. Please don't go on with this, Collis."

He was being as stiff-necked as he could, but I'd grown up a bit since coming to Jacksonville. "You're absolutely right," I told him. "I'll kill the damn Chink next time I see him."

He smiled, mostly in relief because I had skipped the opportunity to put up an argument. "You don't have to carry it quite that far," he said. "The boy wasn't quite that bad."

"Yes, he was," I insisted. "He wronged my father, so he's got it coming to him."

His answer was another and more elaborate sigh meant to indicate how sad he was to learn that his son wasn't quite right in the head, but the small smile remained on his face as he went back to putting his things together to take to his office.

Incidentally, his "things" were the drugs he needed to replenish the supply chest in his office. This was a daily chore because, in those days, doctors leaned heavily on items like calomel, which was the most popular cathartic around. Prescribing a laxative was generally the first recourse of just about every frontier physician when faced with something other than broken bone. He also used a solution of tartar emetic to produce vomiting and perspiration, which was an added specific in some cases. Another standby was "Spanish fly," a drug derived from a small beetle that he administered to produce a blister or act as a counterirritant in some of his more delicate situations.

Naturally, Father also practiced surgery. All the frontier doctors did.

They had to. Much of it was amputating the toes and fingers of frostbite victims, and that winter alone, Father lopped off twenty-three toes and nine fingers from among his various patients where mortification had set in. Bloodletting, up to twelve ounces at a time, wasn't uncommon, and if someone was too weak to undergo it, Father applied live blood-sucking leeches to his patient's skin.

It wasn't an easy time or place to be ailing. Appendicitis was diagnosed as "knotted bowels," and the treatment was, well, I'd rather not recall all the details. As a matter of fact, this is just about as much as I want to say about Father's practice, except to point out that the country doctors did as well as they knew how, and most of them came to be recognized as symbols of hope and service. he was the only man the pioneers and their families could turn to when things were at their bleakest.

So much for Father. He left and I went back to sleep and didn't wake up again until somewhere around noon, which wasn't particularly good timing because this was the day of Chung Lin's going-away party, and I had a bottle of tanglefoot to buy. Champagne would have been better, but since there wasn't any around, nothing less explosive than our redeye would do to celebrate Tommy's having sold old Witham on both the idea of going into the labor-recruiting business and then paying his fare to China to get the business started.

The party was scheduled for that afternoon at Sam Hume's house because Elva wouldn't have been allowed to hold it at hers, and Tony and I had a hunch that my father wouldn't have been particularly warmed by the idea of playing host. That left only Mrs. Hume, whose heart was always big enough to accommodate just one more. The one small problem was that she was a diehard teetotaler, so the solution, which of course I didn't mention to my friends, was quietly introducing tanglefoot into the gentle punch that was Mrs. Hume's idea of a fit drink for a celebration.

I bought the bottle at Lohmeyer's saloon rather than the Bella Union because I didn't want Boudreau pairing two and two together if Elva should come home and mention how much fun the party had been; especially if she happened to slur a word here or there.

"There's the weasel, now," Sam said as I came through the door.

"Collie, what on earth's been takin you so long?" asked Elva. "Tommy and Tony'll be comin along any minute now and what kind of a surprise would it be if we wasn't all here to holler?"

"Give me time to catch my breath before you start in nagging," I told her as I struggled to get my coat off and hang it on one of the pegs behind the cabin's front door in a way that the bottle would be in the handiest pocket. "There were three rattlesnakes in the path not a hundred feet from here, and I had to kill every one of them before I could get through."

"In the winter?"

"Sure. They knew about the party since last summer and they'd been hanging around hoping to be invited."

"Pooh," she said, sailing back into the center of the room where Mrs. Hume had moved the table. I couldn't read the message decorating the big cake on it, but I saw something that looked like a ship iced on its nearest side, so I guessed it was a goodbye sentiment for Tommy. It was just the kind of thing Mrs. Hume would do, even if she hadn't liked Tommy so much. It was enough for her that he was Sam's friend.

My opportunity to slip the pint of whiskey into the punch came right after we heard Tony's knock on the front door. He'd been entrusted with the job of steering Tommy here in a way that wouldn't let on that he was getting a going-away shivaree. Elva, almost beside herself with the fun and excitement, motioned to us to be quiet while Tony rapped two times more. Then she jumped forward and flung open the door, yelling, "Surprise, Surprise!" full into Tommy's face.

Tommy didn't get it at first. He stepped back, looking scared to death, but when Elva threw her arms around his neck and kissed him, and he saw Tony smiling at him, and Mrs. Hume and her son joining in the yelling with Elva, and me pouring my own surprise into the punch, a big grin came over his face. He knew right away what it was all about. His English had gotten to where he was just barely intelligible to someone beside us, but there was never a minute when he didn't know exactly what was going on around him.

"Suh-plize!" he yelled back. "Me. Suh-plize!" suddenly looking inches taller, and that's when Mrs. Hume kissed him, too.

We all crowded about him then with our presents of warm clothes that we figured he'd need on the trip. In addition, Tony had the sense to get together a gift of hardtack wrapped so that it could be hidden away underneath his jacket. Tony rightfully figured that the food would come in handy long before Tommy was back on Chinese soil.

"All right," Mrs. Hume called, as caught up in the fun as anyone else, "let the poor boy breathe. You'll smother him." Then she busied herself cutting the cake and pouring the punch and making sure we all had one of the cloth napkins she saved for her best dinners, if her husband ever stayed down off Marguey's High long enough for her to have one. When Elva served Tommy his cup, he looked over at me in a way that showed that even as excited as he'd been when the door opened on his party, he hadn't missed my contribution to the festivities. As I said, there wasn't much that got by our little friend.

Mrs. Hume also wasn't too apt to overlook things that weren't quite right. After we'd all had two or three glasses of the punch, she must have seen that our faces were getting a bit flushed and our voices pitched a mite high, but rather than remark on it, she excused herself from the party by declaring that she had to go into town to fetch something or other for her husband's supper. When Sam was about to suggest that he do the errand for her, she shut him right off with, "No Samuel, I won't be but a minute and it's plain manners for you to stay with your guests." Guests. Just as if we weren't all over there just about every day.

After she left, Elva really got into the spirit. She kept talking, jumping up and down to make her point, and became more excited than ever when we laughed. "You don't listen!" she wailed at one point. "None of you ever do 'cept Tommy." She leaned down and kissed his cheek, and he blushed while we all clapped. "He's the only one of you who's ever goin to amount to somethin, you wait and see. You all think you're so big and slick, and only Tommy's got sense enough to . . ." and she paused because she'd lost track of what she was about to claim for our guest of honor.

"Hear, hear!" Tony called while she searched for some virtue whose lack would make us all ashamed of ourselves.

This was enough to shunt her just-begun solemnity over into anger. "You stop that, you Mr. Johnstone. You think you're so fancy and the way you 'n Sam take advantage of all them farmers, and if'n it was me I couldn't sleep at nights."

It wasn't the first time she'd gone after them for the high prices they put on the meat they sold to settler families. Tony had the grace to look guilty, but Sam put in, "Pipe down, Elva. They wouldn't be gettin any provisions at all if it wasn't for us. It's only good business to be chargin a fair price when things are scarce and—"

"Hush up, Sam Hume!" she yelled, her face getting red as a beet. "You go ruttin around, thinkin you're so damn big and all you got inside is a little boy trying to be big and important, and you're so mean, and I just don't like you at all!" With this, she broke into tears, leaving the rest of us bewildered by the sharp turn our party had taken.

"Aw, Elva," Sam began, and then he stopped because her cheeks were turning from red to chalk white right in front of our eyes.

"Lordy," she said looking startled, "I feel awful sick," and she ran outside. We could hear her retching through the open cabin door.

"I'll take care of her," I said, feeling like a skunk as I went out.

The party ended not long after that. We washed the dishes and put away what was left of the cake, and then Tony and Sam walked Elva home. My excuse for not going with them was that it wouldn't be fair to let our guest of honor wander off by himself, and, beside, I didn't see any pleasure in being around if any of them got to wondering why I dumped what was left of the punch into the bushes on the far side of the house.

On our way back to the Chinese camp, I said to Tommy, "It was a real nice party, wasn't it?"

"Yes," he answered, not taking his eyes off the path.

"We're going to miss you, Tommy. Take care of yourself."

"Yes," he said again and then stopped. He reached up, patted my shoulder, and added, "Me back home soon."

I was pretty sure he meant Jacksonville.

22

I 'VE ALWAYS ENJOYED the unfolding of the human comedy, but, for the remaining six weeks of that winter, I watched what was going on in Jacksonville with the real happiness of a man finally being paid for doing the very things that, up until then, his family and friends had been suggesting that he quit doing and go to work.

I watched Chief John's warriors as their families were released from their imprisonment on the top floor of the Masonic building, and I noted that none of the braves snickered and how well their wives hid their thankfulness for being allowed to get back to their manual labors around the family campfire. I described it as "typical Indian stoicism" in my account of Captain Mulligan's moment of triumph, and if any of my readers had the sense to see that he had forced the Indians to promise exactly nothing and all that Jacksonville had to give in return was a winter's worth of warmth and food to their families, it wasn't mentioned around town.

I observed and reported Richard's savoring his accomplishment of the "peace" and only hinted that he might have enjoyed it even more if there had been a photograph taken at the formal signing of him flanked on one side by painted warriors and on the other by his uniformed militia. Actually, the photographer's absence didn't really dilute the moment since the Indians hadn't bothered to wear anything to the occasion but their usual greasy rags, and the U.S. government, typically, hadn't yet got around to sending uniforms or pay or even a measly bugle.

Not wanting to dampen our peerless captain's enthusiasm, I didn't point out that the War Department bureaucrats hadn't done much beyond nod their heads that there was probably a need to form a troop and write a letter saying that as soon as their channels became unclogged, the unit, if it were ever authorized, would be certainly placed on official duty. This was enough to lead Richard to expect the golden federal stream to spurt any day now, although some of his men were beginning to wonder whether it might start at least a few days before the time of the Second Coming.

But, most fascinating of all, I saw a mining town shake itself to life after a hard winter. The old troubles with the Indians (who were now too busy with getting their own lives back on the tracks to start anything fresh) were pushed from everyone's mind because with the coming of spring, all that counted was getting gold out of the earth.

There's a reek that comes from gold mining camp that smells almost like sweat because it's produced by a frenzy whipped up out of hope and greed. The miasma hangs over the entire place, affecting even those who aren't burrowing into hillsides or sifting creek waters, because the luck of the miners feeds or kills the town that springs up to serve them. It doesn't matter whether the name of the place is Jacksonville, Sailor's Diggings, Yreka, or Nome; they all smell the same while the miners are out digging in the fields around them. Newly arrived veterans from other places can walk down any of their streets and tell by the smell whether its prosperity is in front or behind, but the residents can't make this kind of judgment because not one of them ever expects that their gold will run out.

And why should they? More of it is produced every time they learn another way in which the ground can be forced to disgorge the stuff that caused their ailment in the first place.

In Oregon, in the beginning, almost all of the gold was panned from its waters by the placer method, but that was too slow because there are just so many times a day that miners can scoop their pans into the creek before they drop over from exhaustion or a locked back. So they taught themselves the rocker and sluice-box systems, and these brought the prospectors out of the streams and onto solid ground, where they found their first really big strikes.

That's when the smell of instant wealth became really strong, and it loaded the air even more heavily when the prospectors turned to hardrock mining after discovering there were rich veins in the quartz running underneath the earth's surface. When chipping away at these by hand wasn't fast enough for them, they took to dynamiting the quartz and then carting the broken-up rock to their jerry-built stamp mills where it was smashed into bits and run through enough water or chemicals to leave the gold sitting by itself in a pile that could be scooped up and stashed away in leather grouch bags.

As soon as the businessmen heard about all this, they came hurrying in with their hydraulic equipment. They bought off and shoved aside those miners grubbing by themselves and those who might have paired up with a few other souls and set their engineers to directing blasts of water through enormous hoses against the hillsides, washing the gravel down to sluices that never stopped working. They installed their dredges in the river beds and these, like gargantuan hogs, began sucking up great gulps of ore-loaded materials, digesting them on the spot and regurgitating the waste material out into disorderly piles along the river banks. Of course, this caused considerable fouling of the sweet stream waters, but no one cared. They got the gold, didn't they?

It's been estimated that somewhere around $30 million was taken from Jacksonville's hills and streams while the gold was everywhere and begging to be taken. In the early days, with the fever burning at its brightest, some prospectors, using only knives and spoons, were scooping $500 to $700 a day out of the crevices along the creeks, and this was nice, bright, coarse gold already formed like drops of molten lead.

But miners are a restless breed. If a claim quit paying at least $100 a day per man, they thought about moving on to the next strike. It never occurred to them to get together in their own big company because most of them were too restless and all of them too miserable-natured to pool their resources into anything that smacked of a long-term obligation. Only those with the deepest infections stayed on. People like Sam Hume's father never leave a gold field so long as there's still a few yards of unclaimed ground around. They won't ever believe that the vein will peter out although it always does.

So the miners move on and, generally, the others follow, and often, but not always, the camp disappears. In some, the few farming and trading families left in it find that their stakes have been pounded deep enough to hold and that this cluster of cabins and tents has turned into an honest-to-God town.

That's what happened to Jacksonville. Its location along the road leading from northern points like the Willamette Valley and heading down to California settlements of Yreka and Sacramento to the south made it a handy place to stop and buy supplies. Then, too, we had the trail in from the coast, along which came most of the goods that fed southwestern Oregon. So, the town held its own, even apart from the gold. Within a year or so after we arrived, 1,800 people were calling it home and it had become the county seat.

Of course, all this didn't happen just that winter and spring, but I had the best seat in the place to watch the start of it, and no matter how many times Alben Hensley asked me to bring in stories saying what farmer's wife was expecting what relative from back East, I only wrote about the things that I found colorful. Some unrecognized sense was telling me exactly which story was worth watching.

This caused friction between us, but since my pay schedule was about as erratic as a dog trying to pass a peach stone, I wasn't too upset by my editor's unhappiness. It reached a head a month after I became his reportorial staff, when he asked, "What ever happened to that piece I wanted on Edward Hume?"

I could have lied and said that both the nugget and the size of Hume's strike had been exaggerated, but it seemed like just the right opening for establishing my independence. "I'm sorry, Alben," I told him, "but the Humes are friends of mine and I'll be damned if I'm going to start a stampede their way."

"A reproter has no friends. Besides, everybody already knows about it."

"Then why print it?"

"Because we are a journal of record," he answered, and for some reason I believed that he believed it, so I gave him the answer that I thought might close off the subject: "Well, so far it's just mining camp talk, not anything official. But if people see it printed up in a newspaper, they're going to think it's gospel."

"Doesn't matter, it's news. And thank you for the comparison."

"Since when is it also news when some merchant stays home with a carbuncle? But we'd print that in our journal of record, too, if he wanted it known bad enough to pay for an ad in the same issue."

After considering this attack on his journalistic integrity, Hensley asked, "You know of any merchants with carbuncles?"

"I'm glad you see it my way. Now, do you want me to get shot?"

He didn't have to think over that one. "It would make me a first-rate feature. Certainly."

"Then put me on a straight salary instead of space rates and I'll go right up to Marguey's High to interview Mr. Hume about his claim. Afterward, we can both pick the buckshot out of my ass on company time."

"Collis, are you trying to tell me you feel there's no story in old man Hume?"

"That's about the size of it, Alben."

He thought it over, and I knew that from then on I could do what I wanted when he said, "Then perhaps we ought to redirect your efforts. What would your qualms be about doing a piece on how far that loafer bastard Mulligan has gotten with his militia organization?"

"None at all," I assured him. "It's the kind of story any reporter is dying to get his teeth into."

He said, "It's gratifying to see the printer's ink begin to course through the veins of so young a man."

My friends were doing some watching, too, but most of it was of me. They talked about it one night at their campfire after the day's hunting was over. The way Tony remembered it was that he brought up the subject by telling Sam that he had bumped into me the previous day "zipping up and down California Street with his notepad and pencil at the ready."

"That weasel sure has changed."

"I suppose for the better, but I do miss his nonsense. Since he's begun scribbling, the only signal he sends that he knows his father and I are about is an occasional grunt in our direction after dinner. I rather believe he feels he's at work for the London Times."

"How come you say 'dinner' instead of 'supper?' "

"Because it happens to be the proper term for the evening meal."

"Is that a fact?"

"That's a fact, my boy."

"I'll try to remember it."

"You will," Tony told him, knowing he would, "but, unfortunately, I may be the only one here to understand what you've said."

"Who cares, long as I know it's right." He threw a branch in the fire. "I'm glad to see Collie workin, I truly am."

"Now it's my turn."

"For what?"

"To ask about your grammar. You never fail to omit the last letter of a participle ending, and I wonder why."

"What in hell is that?"

"You say 'workin' instead of 'working,' 'goin' in place of 'going.' That's slovenly. Your mother was a schoolteacher, wasn't she?"

"Sure. She keeps at me the same way you do. The thing about Collie, though, is the way he's choked up about bein—kiss my ass—being one of the town's workers. It make him different some ways. Hell, all ways. Anymore, it don't seem like there's one thing the three of us agree on."

Tony said, "He fancies he's become one of them. But, knowing Collis, this too shall pass."

"If he don't do some damage before he gets over it. He talks like they do about Indians bein only a bunch of bad animals."

"I've heard you do the same."

"Mostly in joke. And I don't work for the *Sentinel*, neither. These days I wouldn't put it past him to write one of his stories about how the braves swindled the town with their windy about ransoming womenfolk and kids. The first thing those simple seeds in the militia will do about it some Saturday night is go after them and start the whole damn thing all over again, just when they're being quiet."

"He wouldn't do that!" Tony was shocked at the thought that Sam might feel I was capable of descending so low. "Collis has too much feeling for others. He'd never want to see someone else hurt. Don't you know he's been upset because of what we've charged some of the farmers for our provisions? He actually made me feel ashamed of myself. And he certainly refused to write that story about your father's claim!"

Sam was more surprised by Tony's vehemence than I'd have been had I been there. Once Tony decides to give you his loyalty, it takes your doing something really awful before you lose it. Of course, he thinks a long time before he offers friendship to anyone.

"Well," Sam conceded, "I guess so. So far, he's turned right side up after he gets done with being crazy." He thought for a moment, staring moodily at the fire, then added, "I wish my Pa would. Maybe Collie would've done Ma'n me a favor if he had put it in his paper about the claim. It's all Pa thinks about. He don't act much like a human bein any more. He won't come off that hill except maybe to eat or sleep at home once in a while, he's that afraid somebody's gonna walk off with a peck of his dirt. Ma'n me talk about how much better it might be if we had stopped and homesteaded back in the Sweetwater country like she wanted."

Recognizing the pain, Tony thought for a moment and then said, "Well, you've told me how hard things have always been for him, so I don't doubt he sees this as the first spot of luck that has ever come his way. And perhaps he hasn't changed quite as much as you think. When a man shows hunger for property—and I don't believe it matters whether it's gold or land—it always may have been there. If you and I were to be honest with each other, we might admit to showing the same sort of thing when we took advantage of the settlers who bought our goods." Tony didn't have to say that it had been Sam's insistence that pegged their prices as high as the traffic would bear. Sam got the point although he didn't do much more than poke again at the fire. "Is your Pa that way?" he asked.

"It isn't quite the same. My father has always had whatever he's wanted. I've just begun to understand that he wants more only because it's expected of him."

"I can't see no difference."

"There is, though."

"What did they say about your arm?"

"I haven't written about it." Now it was Tony's turn to look back to the fire. Sam's way of dealing with his loss might have been too blunt, but it was also a knowing try to keep Tony from feeling sorry for himself. Left alone, Tony would have buried the hurt, never mentioning nor even recognizing that it was festering inside of him.

"Well, you ought to. What the hell's the use of bringin home a surprise like that? Besides, you're a better hunter with one arm than most that's got two. That's somethin to be proud about."

"It's something, not somethin, you weasel. There is a *g* at the end of that word, isn't there?"

23

THE FOLLOWING MORNING when they were back in Jacksonville, Tony didn't argue when Sam said, "I feel too doggone restless to be out peddlin," so they sold their whole bag of venison and quail to Hardy, the butcher, instead of following their usual route around the larger mining claims where it would have fetched better prices. Sam's next suggestion was, "Let's go roust up Collie and see if there's some trouble we can get into."

"I doubt that he'll be up and about this early."

"Then we'll yank him out of bed. Come on, let's go."

They hadn't moved more than ten feet from Hardy's butcher shop on the corner of California and Oregon Streets when a wagon pulled up alongside of them. "Hey, lady!" Sam yelled, "your horse is sloshin mud all over us!"

His words were to the woman holding the reins, but he had his eyes fixed on the girl sitting in the seat beside her and he grinned when she called, "Then why don't you watch where you're going, farm boy?"

The older woman said, "Mind your mouth, Celina." Addressing them, she said, "I'm sorry. Please excuse us." Then she asked, "Do you know of a hotel with rooms to rent? We've just come to town."

Sam was busy gawking at the girl, so Tony answered, "Madam, you might try the United States Hotel. It's just at the other end of this street." As he pointed the direction, he noticed that the girl, instead of showing discomfort at Sam's stare, was looking back just as steadily. After a while, she informed him, "None of it's for you."

In telling me about this meeting, Tony said, "Her face was unusual. Especially for this area. This girl is something quite apart from our ladies— a slender body, pale green eyes, a nicely chiseled mouth, and a smooth, almost ivory skin. I thought I could be quite comfortable in her company in England, but when she spoke to Sam, her tones were as rude as her words. After that I didn't doubt that she would be at home in Jacksonville."

Her words didn't leave Sam with the same feeling. He was probably too used to the way girls talked here, or maybe he was too stunned by his first sight of Celina Sewell. "Did you get a good look at her, Tony?" he asked, still watching the cart as it turned and headed back down the street to the hotel. "Did you ever see such an angel?"

"That's a rather quick judgment isn't it?" Sam was so bemused that Tony didn't have the heart to tell him what he told me.

"Oh no. She's different. She's very different." As they resumed walking toward our cabin, Tony felt he could see the thoughts whirling around in his friend's head—an opinion that was confirmed when Sam stopped and said, "Tony, you go on. I'm goin back to do somethin about that girl."

"Sam, I'm afraid that would be foolish."

"No, it won't. The way she looked at me, I know there's a thing between us we can work out."

Tony began, "I think you may be wrong . . ." But Sam had already left to follow in the wake of the wagon.

Damn him! Tony thought as he kept on toward our place.

Father met him at the door. "You've just missed Collis," he said. "He's gone off for a walk with Charity Witham." There was pleasure in my father's voice. He'd recently developed the idea that I was getting sweet on the banker's daughter.

"You don't know which way they went, do you Dr. Gibbs?"

"I'm afraid not." His manner was as gentle as ever, but in it Tony sensed the wish that he'd let Charity and his son alone for a while. It wasn't so much Father's regard for Charity as it was that he kept hoping that something would distract me from my feelings for Elva Boudreau.

Tony thanked him and left but, despite Father's hopes, when he bumped into me right after getting back to the center of the town, it wasn't Charity I was with, it was Richard Mulligan.

"Goddammit," I said, raising my voice as I saw Tony coming up, "that's one hell of a way for a militia leader to be acting!"

Mulligan wasn't about to bluster back because he knew I had him dead to rights. "Now Collie," he said, trying to soothe me, "don't be takin on like this. It sure didn't mean nothin."

"The hell it didn't!" I shouted. "God damn you and your stiff pecker, you're going to ruin our whole plan. If any of the army soldiers hear about it and get to talking, it's not just you that's in trouble—it's all of us!"

"Stop yellin so, Collie." I had him near pleading. "Everybody in this place is gonna hear you."

"That's better than seeing me bargain with a redskin, isn't it? At least I'm not swapping a government rifle for ten minute's rent of a squaw. What an awful excuse for a captain you've turned out to be!"

"Ah, shit, Collie," he said, turning to Tony who was standing by. "Tony, tell him . . ."

"Tell him what?" Tony asked. He'd never found the fun in baiting Mulligan that I did, but right then he was willing to go along with anything I had in mind since he didn't have anything else to do.

"That he's a damned stupid skunk!" I put so much heat into it that I saw Tony wondering if some of it was genuine. "It's bad enough when the drunks and loafers in this place do it, but the commanding officer of the Jacksonville militia himself!"

Tony caught it and promptly looked horrified. As if this accusation just couldn't be true, he asked, "You don't mean to say . . ."

"Absolutely," I assured him. "I caught him on this very spot offering to trade for no more than two bits worth of a squaw's most priceless possession the very rifle given by our government to defend our city. At least, [here I pretended to have been suddenly struck by a small doubt] that's what it seemed like to me."

Richard fairly leaped toward this small patch of hope. "I did not! I wasn't gonna do even a mite of it. What I was doin was findin out where her tribe is ratholed. I was only shammin that I'd give her the gun."

I stared at him long and earnestly and then said, quite slowly, "I want to believe you, Richard. I don't want to have to turn you in. I honestly don't."

"Give Richard the benefit of the doubt, Collis," Tony urged me.

It was all the help Mulligan required. "I know it peared wrong but, honest, ever since me'n you started the troop, I been takin it dead earnest. Me'n the boys are meetin just about every day over to Lohmeyer's on our strategy. Last thing I'd ever do is somethin that'd sell the boys out. Honest to God. I swear by my mother."

I couldn't resist one more turn of the screw. "And that's another thing. You've got the troop so they don't come into the Bella Union any more. Do you think that's fair?"

"It sure is! That simple Boudreau is tellin everybody outside the troop that they're damn fools to be expectin more Indian troubles, that the bucks have just about quit. And the next goddamn time he buys a drink for the troop is gonna be the first time, not like old Lohmeyer." There was righteousness in his voice as he added, "This ain't no dodge, Collie. No more it ain't. They's varmints ready to go on the warpath out there, and all that's standing between them'n the town is us militia and the couple of guns Captain Alden just turned loose of. You got to tell everybody that!"

I waited long enough for him to see that the gravity of his words had gotten through to me. Then I said, in much softer tones, "Richard, damn it, I may have been wrong. This Indian menace is turning out to be just as real as we thought in the beginning."

"You're goddamn right I'm right, Collis Gibbs," he answered, matching my sincerity, "but I don't blame you for not understandin why I was funnin that squaw. You meant well." He was shrewd enough to recognize he was home free and that he didn't have to say anything more. But he couldn't resist patting my shoulder in a firm, manly fashion before swaggering (a hard trick when you've got a gimp) away.

After he'd gone, Tony asked, "Now what?"

"Next comes Indian troubles. The braves go on the warpath and we of the militia begin to earn the wages that a fine and benevolent government will be sending us."

"Really? You'll be able to arrange that, also?"

"Really. I can."

"How?"

"Well, actually, what I have in mind is for Billy Tell to manage something that looks like a threat."

"He won't oblige you. I doubt that Indians want to fill their lives with so much fun."

"The hell they don't. What do you think all that palavering over ransoms was all about?"

"But that's over, isn't it? All he can gain from your scheme is a spot of trouble before his friends are ready for it. Of course, you might daub yourself with warpaint and personally mount the attack."

"Not a bad idea, but I'll think of something better."

"You will, Collis. I have great faith in you. For a moment, there, I thought you were going to salute your Captain Mulligan."

"It crossed my mind. Where's Sam?"

"Sniffing after a girl. It's what he does when he isn't at work."

"What girl?"

"Someone new." He went on to describe Celina, finishing with, ". . . and when she told him that he had absolutely no prospects where she was concerned, it was all that was needed to convince him that he'd have her skirts over her head as quick as Bob's-your-uncle."

"Is that English talk?"

"No, you fool, it's Dutch. I've translated it for your benefit. And

I'm surprised to find you here talking nonsense instead of wooing Charity Witham as your father so devoutly believes."

"Oh, you've seen Father."

"I'm afraid so. He seemed hopeful that I wouldn't waste any of the valuable time you might be spending with our local heiress."

"I know. He's awfully set on it. So is she. I got rid of her as soon as we saw Mulligan and that squaw. I told her that important military business had just come up."

"She's a desirable young lady."

Tony was being deliberately pompous, so I said, "I've already diddled her, you know."

"Have you, honestly? What awful taste!"

"For diddling Charity or talking about it?"

"Both. I'd really rather not discuss it."

"I know. You're such a fine young man, Johnstone. I wouldn't dream of giving you the details."

"When did it happen?"

"Day before yesterday. But I don't want to shock you with my bad taste. Let's talk about something different. When do you think spring will be here in full bloom?"

"You ass," he said. "If you leave anything out, I'll kill you."

24

CELINA AND HER MOTHER had disappeared inside by the time Sam reached the U.S. Hotel. The rain was back soaking the street and, since the afternoon was getting on, he figured they wouldn't be out again until next day. He didn't know where they had come from, but wherever it was, it had to have been a long ride.

Another man might have quieted the randiness the girl had fired up in him by going off scouting for someone else, but that was never the way Sam Hume's mind worked. Instead, he thought, *Maybe tomorrow— Jacksonville ain't all that big*, and then considered doing some work in the little shack behind Hardy's market they used in part payment for supplying the butcher with fresh meat. He walked back down the muddy street thinking, *For a change, Tony'll be satisfied.*

When he walked into the shack, he was hit by the reminders of past kills: the fetid odor of meat scraps decaying on the floor, smears of dried blood that were relics of their first butchering attempts, and the chunks of discarded organs that hadn't yet been thrown out to the stray dogs that roamed the streets and alleys. *Phew! If I do one damn thing worthwhile, it'd be to clean this place up.*

He opened the barn doors of the shack as wide as they would go, although on a day like this the most he could hope for short of scrubbing the whole place down was to move the smell as far as the doorway before it was driven back by the rain. Looking around him, he said aloud, "Ah, what the hell," resolving to get the scouring done that the filthy place needed. He took off his jacket and shirt and hung them on the stub end of a limb that had been bucked off one of the logs used as door frames.

Sam's way of tackling a job was to immerse himself so thoroughly in it that everything else was blotted out, so she must have been standing there for quite a while before he realized he wasn't alone. Even then it took a few seconds for him to shift his mind from the table he was scraping to the realization that the girl watching him from the open doorway was really the one who had so bemused him a few hours ago, and now there was a half smile on her face instead of the cocky indifference she'd shown while seated in the cart beside her mother.

"It really stinks in here," she said.

He straightened up, conscious of the sweat on his body, and for a moment wondered if she meant him. Then he didn't give a damn because the sight of her drove out everything else. His voice sounded thick in his own ears when he answered, "Yeah. But I got to do this. Need another wire brush and get the place cleaned up and . . ."

"What the hell are you talking about?" she asked.

"Tony. Tony n'me. We work here."

"Doing what? Executing criminals?"

"We're hunters. This is where we cut up the meat." He thought, *What am I goin on like this, for?* and then, *What is she doin here?* He began another, more coherent, explanation and then broke it off, grinning, "I'd ask you to come in but I'm afraid you'll get the place all wet and sloppy."

"I wouldn't want to do that," she said walking in and to the other side of the table from him. Taking her time glancing over his body, she added, "The mess you look, you're lucky somebody ain't out hunting after you."

Something clicked in his mind. Without realizing how instinctively he knew what to do and say, he walked around the table and stood so close that her eye level was just about to his chest. "Come on."

She stared up at him for a long while. "Not here." The ugly shack and its odors and the smell of this big young man in front of her must have combined to produce something she had to struggle against. She closed her eyes and repeated, "Not here."

"No," he said, "sure not." He lifted her and put her down across the long, newly scoured surface, leaving her legs dangling over the table's edge as he hiked up her dress. She opened her eyes again to watch him as he stripped off the rest of his clothes, and he didn't stop for a first kiss as he entered her.

Their coupling was wild and rocking, and not until he was straightening up from his crouch over her did he realize that the shack's doors were still wide ajar. Walking over and slamming them shut, he said, "My Lord!" which was as much about what had just happened to him as the sight they must have presented if anyone had passed by. Turning back, he saw her body trembling violently each time a wave foamed again, but neither that nor her awkward position mattered because he was lost, really lost in wonder. It wasn't just her lovely face or breasts or the grace of her belly and thighs—it was the way all of them joined into rare physical beauty, and, even then, he had the sense to recognize and be awed by it.

He stood, staring at her, until she opened her eyes and brought him back down from where he was by saying, "We ain't finished, yet."

The town girls he'd had before this taught him many things, but none of them had prepared him for this swift a descent, which was something she seemed to understand because there was little-girl mischief in her voice as she added, "We'll go to the hotel. I'll get rid of my mother."

It wasn't until he had brushed her off, dressed himself—her helping—and they were walking on the street, that they spoke again. "Be damned," she said. "What's your name, farmer boy?"

"Didn't I introduce myself?" And they both stopped and roared with laughter. "Sam Hume," he told her.

"Big Sam Hume. I'm Celina Sewell."

"No, you're not. You're Sam Hume's girl."

"Am I now? We'll see, big Sam Hume."

When they reached the hotel, he waited as she went up the stairs. He didn't care who else was in the lobby or what they thought about his standing there because all that was in his mind was the beauty of her on the table back at the shack. Her mother came down a few minutes later, ignoring him as she walked out the door.

She hadn't told him the room number, but there were only four doors in the hallway so he knocked at each one. No one answered until the third. "What took you so long?" she demanded with mock gravity.

"I had to finish up sandin the table."

"You ain't funny. You're just funny looking."

"Am I now?" He walked in and looked around. "I been studying, Celina. Did you come down to the shack specially seekin for me?"

"I did."

"What for?"

"For this," she answered, leaning up and kissing him for their first time. "Anybody as big as you ain't all that hard to find."

"You asked about me in the butcher shop."

"Sure, I did," she admitted. She carefully closed the door, slid the bolt in place, and then tried it in a pantomime that recalled the open barn doors of the shack. When she had finished, she leaned her back against the door, arms folded across her chest, and said sternly, "If they didn't see us the first time, they'll have to pay the second."

Thinking that she looked at the moment no more than twelve, he kept his face as straight as hers. "What do we charge? How about if we . . ."

"Shut up and come on," and she kissed him again. He felt her tugging at his shirt and, after it was free, at his pants.

Picking his head up from hers but not untangling her tight embrace about his neck, he said, "I'm supposed to be doing this." When she didn't quit, he added, "I got to undress you, Celina."

"You're too slow." She backed away, unbuttoning the top of her dress. It slid to the floor before he could get to her, leaving her stark naked and confirming the memory that, finally, had become hazy down in the lobby.

This time it wasn't a violent blotting out of time and place. She wouldn't let it be. She slowed him by arching away whenever the violence in him became too insistent and guided him into understanding that what they were doing was for the both of them. There was no need for a single spoken word. He understood her sighs and the deep welling noises in her throat and did whatever she wanted. He had been born with a deep sexual drive, but this was the first time it had ever been returned redoubled.

For Sam Hume, this was a new world filled with rosy shadows that became real only when an intermittent flash of clarity brought him back to the girl twisting and turning underneath him. Its end was a thick, almost suffocating curtain made of something that seemed like velvet.

Afterward, a long time passed before they spoke. Then, Celina, lazily taking the lead, told him that they were here because her mother needed relief from San Francisco's fogs, that if this place helped her mother's health, she would probably look for a job to keep her occupied and, yawning, asked, "You have a girl?"

Elva was in his mind for no more than a split second before he answered, "Nope."

25

WINTERS SELDOM HOLD OUT once the new year turns in the Rogue Valley, but this one didn't quit kicking back with rain squalls and winds until almost April. It was just the kind of weather Sam could latch onto as an excuse to spend most of the week butchering and delivering in town.

I called him on it one morning while we were sitting on a bench under the shed roof in front of the Jacksonville bakery. "Not that it's any of my business, but isn't Tony ever bothered by being out in the woods doing most of the hunting?"

"Beats me how you can be so absolutely right all the time."

"He's getting fed up?"

"No. About it being none of your business."

"And it's also none of my business about that new girl you're supposed to be sparking?"

"That's about the size of it." He yawned and got up from the bench. Stretching like a tomcat who'd been out prowling all night, he asked, "Goddammit, Collie, ain't she the prettiest thing ever?"

"How do I know? You don't bring her around and, so far, I haven't seen her on the street. I'm starting to believe that there's not any new girl at all."

The truth was that while I'd been running around interviewing every third ragged-ass farmer, miner, and merchant in the valley, I'd heard more than once that Sam had picked himself a real whizbang. She'd even wangled a job right off in Jabez Witham's bank, which probably surprised him as much if not more than anyone else. The way I heard it in the Bella Union, she had just waltzed in, blinked those green eyes once or twice, and that little bantam cock tumbled face forward into the dusk.

But the decision to hire her, like all his other deals, didn't take long to produce a profit. Not only did he find about twenty reasons a day to squeeze past her in that narrow space behind his counter, she was also attracting considerable new business. Miners from as far away as Willow Springs rode in through the rain in order to push their pokes across at

162

her, which turned out to be all to the good for some of these sourdoughs since it was the first time they could remember their money being in the bank instead of in some saloonkeeper's pocket.

From what everyone (naturally, this was just the men talking) said, she had a way about her that was as enticing as a summer dip in the pond, but, except for Sam, no one heard of anyone getting nearer than arm's length to her. The speculation was that scarcely a night went by that she didn't disappear somewhere with our friend. He might turn up sleepy-eyed, but she was always at work next morning, bright eyed and unruffled as if she'd just come from the mint.

And all this left Elva—well, about half the girl we'd known. She couldn't miss hearing about what was going on, so these days there wasn't much sunniness in her and she had no heart at all left for the easy conversations we used to have. After a few times, I quit trying to bring the smile back to her face. That's why I took after Sam that morning. I couldn't argue that it was his business what he was doing with Sewell and even how he was getting along with Tony, but this was an entirely different matter.

"Sam," I said, "I don't doubt that this new friend of yours is the world's best, but how about Elva? You know how decent she is and how she feels about you. It isn't fair not to tell her straight out that you're gone on another girl."

He surprised me by not bridling. "What can I do, Collie, shoot a gun at her? I've done everything just short of it."

"I'd bet that you haven't. You can't talk to any girl without joshing and flexing and acting up."

"No, I don't," he said (but there wasn't much ease in his voice), "do I?"

He waited for me to answer, but when I didn't, he started to shut off any more talk by saying, "Well, I'm not about to change my whole self just to suit her. Besides," and he thought for a moment, "I really do like old Elva. Maybe one of these days . . ."

"Maybe one of these days nothing! Why don't you let go of her? For Christ's sake, isn't that Sewell poon tang enough for you?"

"Collie, I'd just as soon stay friends, so don't you be talking that way again." He stared levelly at me and turned and walked away, leaving me sitting there feeling just terrible.

I stewed for a while, thinking about going out to see if I could get Tony to help, and then I realized that even if he were the type who mixed into another's affairs, which he wasn't, Tony wouldn't cut any more ice with Sam than I had. Worse, he'd probably tell me something I already knew: There's precious little anyone can say in these things that carries even as much weight as the pillow underneath the girl being diddled.

So I thought some more and finally figured that what was left to me beyond doing nothing was to go meet this Celina and take a stab at convincing her that there were other trophies in town beside Sam Hume. The kind of barroom talk I'd heard suggested that her emotions might not reach down as deep as the ocean. I got up from the bench and headed down the street toward Witham's bank.

She was behind the counter when I walked in, and the only customer there was just concluding his business. As I took my place behind him, he was saying, "Miss Sewell, I guess I must be one of your big depositors. This is the fourth bag I've put in this week."

"I know it, Mr. Bernhardt," she told him with a smile that said that if he'd just be patient a while longer, the sun was going to come out and the birds would start singing—not now, of course, but surely one of these days real soon. "Mr. Witham was saying just the other day that you're one of our most important customers."

"Well," the hardware dealer noted as he puffed up, "I wouldn't fret too long over whether I'd allow you to help tell me what to do with some of the profits."

"My Lord, Mr. Bernhardt. What a generous thing to say!"

He thought he heard the birds already faintly chirping. "Say when and we'll be having more fun than you can shake a stick at."

"I'm sure I'd love shaking a big stick," she answered, her face remaining perfectly demure. It was obvious that the double meaning didn't get past the old goat, but, before he could split apart at the seams, she added, "I swear your wife must be one of the luckiest women in the valley," which was another two-layered observation that told him she knew he was married but couldn't help being impressed by him, anyway.

I didn't see his face but his lowered tones told me he was certain he was just about there. "Girl, you name the time."

"Let me think about it." Her smile said that he'd made an interesting point but, nevertheless, he'd finished his business for the day. "Now I've got to get to this gentlemen."

He turned and when he saw it was me, he said, "Oh, hello, Collie." Halfway through the greeting I heard his voice turn from oily warmth into the tone that merchants use with a local reporter who also sells advertising space. As he brushed by me on his way out the door, I saw that the bees humming inside his head were raising such hell that it was doubtful whether he'd remember if it had been me or Chief John standing in line behind him.

"Morning, sir," she said, and now all the invitation in her smile was for me. "And what can we do for you?" Mr. Bernhardt had never happened.

"Good morning, Miss Sewell. Lovely morning, isn't it?" Tony had been right about her looks, but he hadn't said nearly enough to prepare me for transluscent skin, the mane of raven hair sweeping back from a high forehead, the tilted button nose and, from what I could see of her body, the reason why it wasn't too hard to imagine her turning every night into Christmas morning for Sam Hume.

"If it don't rain," she said, watching me take inventory. "I'll bet you're just chock full of business."

"Two items."

The smile stayed but a question came into her eyes. "What's the first thing? Then," and the smile turned generous, "we'll see if we get to the second." I believe that girl was incapable of meeting an old drunk on a muddy street and telling him to get out of her way without making it sound like an invitation to the dance.

"Well, I need change for this," I said, sliding a quarter-eagle across the counter.

"We just might be able to handle that," she observed, "if you don't go telling everybody where you got it."

"I wouldn't do that. I'm not going to be the one who starts a run on your bank."

She nodded in a way that said she appreciated my joke but let's get on with it. "And that takes us to your second problem."

"I'm Collis Gibbs. Sam Hume's friend."

"You don't have to convince me. I already seen you on the street, Sam told me about you, and that's what the man called you just now. So how is that supposed to get us into trouble?"

"No trouble. I've just heard so much about you that I wanted to meet you personally."

"And now you did." She shoved my change farther over the counter to me in a way that said our affairs were now complete.

It seemed to me that even if she didn't find me as attractive as creaking old Bernhardt, she at least owed being friendlier because of my closeness to her beau. "Thanks, I guess," I told her.

"You look like somebody grabbed away your all-day sucker."

"I've given you a bad impression. I was too excited by finally getting to see you."

"What does that mean?" she said, narrowing her eyes to study whether I was poking fun.

"Doesn't mean anything. I just heard so much about you that I wanted to meet the famous lady."

"Heard from who? Sam?"

"From everybody."

"Like who?" she insisted. "What was it you been hearing?"

"That you're gosh-awful pretty and bright."

"I know all that. What else did Sam say?"

"I told you, it wasn't just him. Half a dozen men told me they'd pass their chance at salvation if you'd go out with them."

This kind of joshing was familiar ground. The intensity left her voice as she answered, "Well, now, does that include you, Mr. Collis Important Business Gibbs?"

"I wish it did," I said, sadly. "But it wouldn't do either of us much good. Ever since that bull gored me, all I've been able to do is shake hands with pretty ladies. Most of the times they just laugh at me when my voice gets too high, that damn bull."

"I'll bet. I'd just bet that you don't have to be watched every minute. I been hearin things, too. From the way it was told, not even a female snake is safe if anybody's around to hold her still for you."

I smirked as expected but, inside of me, there was a mile-long grin. My hunch had been absolutely square on the button! And it wouldn't be too long before Sam also recognized the chippy strutting around down there, not so far beneath that angelic face and figure.

Another piece of truth was unveiled in the next moment; I realized how much I actually cared for Elva Boudreau because my first feeling after getting a clear sight at Celina Sewell was relief that the unhappiness was going to be lifted. Sooner or later Elva was going to have Sam back. The nobility of this understanding was then diluted by something that may have been more typical: *When Sam finishes with this girl, there's no reason why I shouldn't get some of it too!* So I said, "Whatever you heard about me is dead wrong. Maybe one of these days I'll earn the chance to prove it to you."

"Maybe," she said, looking more seraphic than ever. "And maybe also I ought to tell your friend how long it takes you to get fresh behind his back."

"I'll tell him myself."

"Sure you will. I can just . . ."

I lost whatever it was that came next in the catechism that was second nature to her because that was when Edward Hume came out of Jabez Witham's office. I doubt I would have heard a gun go off in the amazement of seeing Sam's father and the little banker in a conversation that seemed to be giving each of them such enormous satisfaction.

"Edward," I heard Witham sum up, "I'll get the order down to the city on the next stage. We'll have the machinery back right about the time the trail is dry enough to cart it up there." Then, when he saw me, he closed up shop and gave me a smile that was expansive enough to remind me that, as a prospective son-in-law, I was another deal of his he thought was about ready to start bubbling. "Howdy, son," he said.

For his part, Mr. Hume evidently had been pleased enough by the banker's remarks for him to recognize me with something more than his usual grunt. "Been keepin busy, Collis?" he asked, which was no more like him than if he had stepped forward to straighten my tie.

I could only nod. This was the first sentence he'd directed to me in all the time I knew him, and here he was acting like he cared what I'd been up to. He was actually calling me by name.

Witham, probably because he wanted me to feel like we were already family, next did something that wasn't like him, either. Instead of keeping his cards close to his vest, which was how he generally did business, he said, "Collie, you can offer us your congratulations. Mr. Hume and I have just agreed to jointly develop the Sweetwater mine."

Edward Hume showing sentiment enough to name the claim on Marguey's High after a place that meant so much to his wife? Edward Hume and Jabez Witham partners?

"Don't forget your change," said Celina from behind me, but I couldn't take my eyes away from the bobcat and the grizzly bear who had just gone in business together.

26

THE HALF-YEAR IT TOOK Tommy to reach China, get his coolies together, and return home to Jacksonville by September of 1854 was actually a good record for the trip. He could have spent at least three months at sea each way, let alone all the weeks required to complete the job ashore, but he was able to cut that schedule by a third after convincing Jabez Witham to lay out the extra dollars required to book his work force on one of the fastest ships carrying Chinese labor to America.

The decision made good business sense. In those days, the American and British shipowners who dominated the yellow cargo field had given their sailing masters strict orders to wring every possible dollar out of each square foot of space. On one of that era's runs, 500 coolies were loaded aboard and only 400 were alive when the ship reached San Francisco. Remember, those were human beings who died from lack of food or medical attention or who just plain suffocated in the stinking hold. They weren't animals; these were men with dreams and fears and families.

That's why lessening the coolies' ordeal below decks finally appeared prudent to Witham. As Tommy pointed out, the longer the trip, the higher the mortality rate. There were no fare refunds for dead passengers, and Chinese diggers were bringing a premium in our labor market ever since the big gold strike a few months before at Sterling Creek just outside of Jacksonville.

There was another bonus for our friend in this agreement to buy passage aboard a responsible ship. As the businessman aboard in charge of the project, he wasn't herded in with the Chinese down below. His sleeping quarters were with the ship's crew, so by the time he returned to Jacksonville, his hold on the English language and its obscenities was at least a wagon-load better than when he left. As his nephew Chung Po Fong observed, "My uncle was never a man to waste the slightest opportunity. His dealings with Mr. Witham showed him the great advantages available to men of trade who spoke this new tongue, so he used every waking moment while at sea to practice on those around him."

The trip was a commercial success. He recruited four dozen young men, all champing at the bit to bring honor and prosperity to their families and, in addition, purchased four sturdy farm girls for the whorehouse he intended to open in Jacksonville. Of course, he hadn't cleared this last civic improvement with Witham, but he was sure the banker wouldn't object so long as he didn't officially know about it. After all, their services would certainly help bank the normal restlessness of these robust miners-to-be.

The four girls were carefully chosen from among the hundreds offered him. Each was in her early teens and impressed with the importance of fulfilling the contracts he made with their fathers or uncles. Because American law frowned on importing unattached Asiatic females, he disguised these joy-girls in rough coolie clothing, personally smeared their faces with dirt, and mixed them in with his labor force as they were being loaded below decks. Since their costs were carefully hidden in his recruitment expenses, he didn't stew too long over taking the two risks involved in this masquerade; if the females weren't detected by the authorities and confiscated, once they were happily identified they might be out of working order by the time the voyage was over.

He was lucky. No one noticed the females being loaded aboard. The almost continuous attention they received below decks from the coolies didn't permanently impair any of them, and the only problem that arose after they set sail was because one of the girls forgot the solemn compact her father had signed for her services. She proved weak enough to encourage the interest of a fellow cargo-mate named Ah Ling to the point where, at debarkation, he sought out Tommy to suggest that the rest of his wages be held back until they amounted to enough to buy Precious Jade (the name she adopted to fit her for her new career) as his wife.

Of course, he was refused. Even if Tommy could be tempted by a marriage broker's profits, such a move automatically cost him a fourth of his female work force. He couldn't take that kind of loss because, looking ahead, he'd figured a ratio of one girl to fifty laborers, and while in Canton he had arranged with a resident recruiter to ship him 150 more coolies next spring. Worst of all, agreement to the brazen request set the kind of precedent that damaged his plans for his own future, so, as soon as the group reached Shasta City, he sold Ah Ling's contract to a local farmer.

All of his cargo reached Jacksonville alive and reasonably well, and although he didn't show us the slightest sign of pleasure over what he'd accomplished, inside of him he was rubbing his hands in happiness. At that point, neither he nor anyone else caught the miscalculation that was going to end up forfeiting the lives of many men.

Much much later he admitted to me, "I was too young. I was a toad swollen with pride. I knew that most of the Chinese already in Jacksonville were from Hong Kong while those I brought with me were Cantonese. I should not have closed my eyes to what was known to the most ignorant peasant: In China, each side hated the other."

Naturally, Witham didn't introduce Celina Sewell to Tommy when he came to the bank to deliver his report on the trip's success, but she was in the room with them long enough for him to get a good look at her. I would never have known that he was immediately certain of who and what she was if, while welcoming him back, I hadn't mentioned that Sam was giving us all a bad time over this gal who had gone to work for old man Witham. He wanted to know more about how that came to be, so I described as much as I knew about it at the time.

My recollection of his comments is probably polished a bit better than the actual words he used. There were still the problems (which he never lost) with r and l, and his vocabulary hadn't yet grown to where it matched his intelligence, but there was no longer the slightest difficulty in understanding exactly what he meant.

"I see her," he admitted when I'd finished.

"What did you think?"

The first thing I'd noticed after going into his shack was that, somehow, he looked different, and I realized what it was while I waited a few seconds or so for his estimate of Celina Sewell. There'd always been a small hint of apprehension in his eyes, but it wasn't there anymore. Now his face was, well, not passive but maybe placid. It was as if he wasn't worrying any longer over the things that the rest of us took for granted. So I was more annoyed than surprised when he shrugged slightly and answered, "She is not my rice so I how can I say?"

Growing up was one thing, but turning his back on Sam was another. "That's one way of putting it, Tommy," I said, "but a better one might be to show that maybe it matters a little bit to you."

"Shall I say that Sam should be only with Elva?"

"Something like that wouldn't be too far off."

"Then I say it."

"What you mean is that it isn't your concern, is that right?"

"Would Sam listen if I speak?"

"Dammit, Tommy!" I said, "you haven't seen Sam yet so you don't know what a mess that chippy is making out of him. Now all he does is hang around town waiting for her to finish work. He hasn't been out hunting in weeks, and when he does go out, Tony says he just puts in the time until he can get back to her. Their meat business is going to hell."

"I hear of the thing that came to Tony."

"Well, he's still ungodly touchy, so don't say anything beyond being polite. He's convinced it makes him half a man. If it wasn't for Sam keeping him busy out in the field by himself most of the time, I think he'd shoot himself."

"Then there can be right in what Sam does?"

"If he was doing it just because it helped Tony, then it'd be great. But it's not and it's turning out to be just about the last straw for his mother. He doesn't come home, and his old man won't come down off Marguey's High except to talk Witham into buying another pump or something, and that leaves Mrs. Hume keeping everthing going all by herself with only Tony and me going over to give her a hand every once in a while."

He thought that over and then said, "No blame. Sam only does like young men does. You are hard with him."

"You ought to see how hard it's hitting Elva. Maybe then you wouldn't have so much infernal patience."

That blew away the goddamned Olympian attitude he'd been sporting and brought him right back to being one of us. If Chung Lin had a soft spot anywhere in his body, it was for Elva Boudreau. He literally worshipped that girl. I've seen him do things for her he wouldn't have done for his own sister if he had one. Maybe more—I'm still not sure how long he'd have hesitated in those days if he got the right offer for any relative. "I think I know this Sewell," he finally agreed.

"And?"

"She is a joy-girl in her face and her heart. Sam has bad trouble. Many sad stories are told to Chinese children of the warrior who trades family and honor for the favors of a joy-girl."

"That's the way I feel about her, Tommy. She's a whore, that's all."

He nodded. "One with good business in her head. Were Mr. Witham to tell her to work with me, I would think her good to look after the four girls that somebody cheats me and puts among the strong men I bring here from Canton."

It was the first time I knew he was going to open a whorehouse, and it made me feel good because it was proof the success of his trip hadn't changed our Chung Lin all that much. "You're saying Celina could be a madam?"

"I not know that word."

"Your English suddenly broke down, is that right? It means the lady who manages the place."

"Madam," he said, testing it on his tongue. "Not a good word. But if it is correct, then I now know it."

"It's correct. And quit stalling."

"Stalling?"

"God damn you, you ugly heathen. What are you trying to tell me?"

He was only eighteen then, but when he answered, he looked more like eighty. "I am saying that I am scared with this Sewell. I am saying that not you, not me, not Anthony can help our Elva. And, most, I say that we can do no help for Sam. His mind is between the legs of a joy-girl. Try to send it another place and Sam is no more friend for you."

27

TONY WAS AS GLAD as the rest of us to see Chung Lin back in Jacksonville, but the news he'd received from England just the week before kept him from greeting our traveler with little beyond an absentminded smile. It was a very short letter to have dealt so much hurt:

My Dear Anthony,

It is my sad duty to inform you of the deaths of Father and David.

It happened just two weeks ago, and although we are not certain of the exact cause, we believe that it was occasioned by a dinner at Father's club where Colchester oysters that seem to have been tainted were served. Eight other members were stricken the same evening, three of that number suffering the same fate as Father and our brother. One of them, Nigel Hardy, was, I believe, in the form preceding yours at school.

As you can well imagine, Mother is quite desolated by this loss, and while I am doing my best to comfort her, the demands involved in assuming management of the estate are such that they rob me of much of the time that I would like to spend with her.

Our father was a truly remarkable man. His love and respect for his country and family shall always remain a model for us all. This untimely loss leaves a space that will be difficult to fill.

But we cannot mourn the past at the expense of the future. Since the funeral services have already taken place, there is little reason for your early return, and, because I consider it my duty to complete Father's plan to initiate a sensible investment program in America, the need of the information you are developing is more urgent than ever. I would like you to complete as good a file as possible before booking passage back to us.

Again, Anthony, this is a sad loss for us all. I know that you share in my prayers that our mother's remaining years be as untroubled as Father would have wished.

Sincerely yours,
Charles

Ordinarily, Tony wouldn't have shared as private a thing like this with anyone, but the lack of feeling in it for him as a human being must have leveled his normal defenses. My own reaction when he showed it to me was anger. "That's awful! What right does he have to take over directing your life just like that? Why don't you tell him to go to hell?"

What I didn't ask was why the letter came from his brother instead of his mother, but he must have read it in my face because he answered, "Collis, that's the way it is." Then, drawing in a deep breath as if he was trying to get over a punch in the stomach, he added, "But *she* could have written it, couldn't she?" He was asking for reassurance and then for the first and last time in my life I saw Tony break down, crying as he never could when the bear tore off his arm.

You don't put your arms around someone like Tony, so all I could do was stand helplessly by until he had control of himself again. I knew he was going to be all right when, instead of trying to raise his usual cool smile, he looked gravely at me and said, "Sorry. Why on earth do I miss them so right now? Why do I feel that I want to be there instead of here?"

"It's very simple," I told him. "You're a snob."

"There is that," he agreed, the naked pain beginning to fade from his face. Eyeing me, he shook his head again, saying, "If only Charles were half so kind as you."

"No one is—so don't hold it against him."

He thought for a moment, "It's all done and over, so I'll just have to accept it, won't I?"

"About me being so marvelous?"

"No, you ass. About my being so sentimental. They aren't unfeeling. Unchanging, is more like it, and she'll write as soon as she's able—and I expect too much."

My silly response had worked, and it flashed through my mind that I may have seen him get a bit older right before my eyes. Now serious, I said, "I think perhaps you always have. They are the way they are, and when your mother writes—and she will, you know, you're asking a lot to believe she could put pen to paper this soon—you'll see how she really feels."

"Poor Mums." And there was a long, quiet sigh.

"I once read in some book about Africa that once a man stands in a river, neither he nor the river are ever again the same."

"You're being cryptic. And that's a bit much for me at the moment."

"I'm sorry. I don't mean to be. Did you ever know that Sam had an older brother named Ned who died on the way out here?"

"No." He studied me, trying to read what all this had to do with him.

"Mrs. Hume told it all to me some time ago. I don't guess she'd have ever said anything about it, maybe for the same reason Sam's never mentioned it—the hole it tore out of their lives must have been too big. I'm sure the only reason it spilled out of her while I was there was because she's so lonely and scared over the way what's left of her family is carrying on. I mean, Sam hardly ever home and the old man so loony over that damned gold mine.

"Poor lady. In the middle of telling it to me she was sobbing so hard that I tried to stop her, the memory was hurting her so; but she insisted on going on, and after she was finished, she made me promise never to say anything more about it. It was too private. I wasn't ever going to mention it to you, but I know she'd understand once I explained what I've just realized—your brother Charles, in his own way, is acting pretty much the same as Sam's father."

"I don't think I want to hear this," he said.

I knew he meant he felt he just couldn't handle another ache, but telling him about it was the right thing to do at that moment, even though repeating the story broke my word to Mrs. Hume.

Edward, Jr., the brother nicknamed Ned, was two years older than Sam when the family set out for Oregon, and, as Phoebe Hume described him to me, there wasn't any question but that he'd been the apple of the old man's eye. Because it was such a wearying and boring trip, Ned, like many of the other young men, had taken to stunting about—things like climbing along the wagon's sides and onto the back ledge step to call out to whomever was next in line. That's what he was doing while their wagon train was approaching the North Platte River, and he fell off after they hit one particularly bad rut, smashing his leg against a jagged rock in the trail.

Luckily, it was late afternoon and close to the time to make camp because otherwise there may have been sentiment in some of the other wagons to keep on going until nightfall. Arguing whether to stop and rest for a while, especially on the Sabbath, caused more splits along the Oregon Trail than anything else, so a boy had to consider himself fortunate to have his accident when there wouldn't be too much dissent against halting while he could be tended to. Of course, what happened to Ned couldn't be considered as lucky in any other sense because there were no physicians in the train. Three doctors of divinity, but no doctors of medicine.

After one of the cattle drivers who had worked as an orderly in an army hospital set his broken leg, the general interest in the incident died down except, of course, for his mother and father. Mr. Hume was angry enough to have cuffed the boy for the results of his high spirits if his wife, in one of her rare shows of defiance, hadn't stopped him.

Next day, Ned was arranged as comfortably as possible in the back of the wagon, and an hour after the journey was resumed, Mrs. Hume climbed into the back to check on her son. She stayed there until the halt that night because the boy was burning up with fever. When her husband only nodded and went about cooling the horses after she told him about Ned's condition, she understood that he didn't know how else to cover his frustration. There was no question in her mind about how deeply he loved Ned.

The fever stayed on for the next two days. On the following day, a Sunday that was one of the few Sabbaths that the train stopped for along the trail—not for religious purposes but to rest the livestock—the cattle driver came over to look at Ned's leg. Afterward, he called Mr. Hume out. "It looks to me like the gangrene," he said.

Mr. Hume asked in a soft voice, "Are you sure?"

"I seen too much of it in the war to say somethin like this without being danged sure."

"What do we do?" he asked, even though he knew the answer.

"The leg has got to come off. Otherwise your boy is goin to be just as dead as if he broke his neck when he fell off."

As it turned out, the cattle driver was afraid to perform the operation. He had an idea of how it was done, but, sober, he couldn't bring himself to actually do the cutting, and Mr. Hume wouldn't let him drink the whiskey he needed to get drunk enough to try it.

After failing to find anyone else in the train with the knowledge or even a glimmer of familiarity with the technique of an amputation, Mr. Hume went off by himself to pray for a minute and then he told his wife that there was no other choice but that he would do it. In answer, she looked at him long and steadily before saying, "May the Lord be with you, Edward," and went back aboard their wagon to sit alongside of Sam who was watching, owl-eyed, at everything that was taking place but having the sense to keep quiet. From then on she never stopped asking for divine help nor ever shifting her stare away from the horizon out beyond the knot of people gathered around her husband.

Mr. Hume, casting around at the other people, asked if anyone had a very sharp butcher's knife, and three or four women scurried off to bring him blades and whetstones.

They made Ned ready by tying him to a plank and then laying him down as easily as they could on a blanket that covered a pallet made of leaves and twigs. His leg was set up on a small box so it extended over the plank, not touching anything else.

While Mr. Hume took a long time to pick out one of the knives brought him, and even longer to hone it, the cattle driver dosed the boy with laudanum, but, as far as anyone could see, the drug was producing little effect. Ned simply lay there, his eyes closed tightly and once said, "Father, please make it fast." Only the closest to him heard the words, but no one watching missed what was in Mr. Hume's eyes that was his silent answer to his son.

Then he began the operation, cutting about three inches above the fracture. He cut all around the leg to the bare bone, and the smell and the look of the matter that appeared in addition to the naked bone convinced those who could stand watching that the diagnosis of gangrene had been correct. After it all drained, one of the women loosely fixed a tourniquet above where the stump would end.

Throughout this, Ned scarcely moved a muscle. He bore his suffering in a way that gave his father strength to go on. Sometimes there'd come a spasm of pain over his deathly pale face, but as if to compensate for it, he'd whisper a few words of encouragement.

It was only when the lady who was holding a phial of spirits of camphor to his nose let it slip away in her fascination with what Mr. Hume was doing that Ned showed the real extent of his suffering. His lips became bloodless and he fluttered his hands trying to get at the phial, saying, "Oh! No. No! Let me have it!"

Finally, the leg bone was hacked off, and the cattle driver, forgetting his nerves, secured the arteries and brought the flap of flesh down to cover the raw meat that had been a knee.

Ned lay back then, his eyes closed. The operation had taken an hour, and every second of it had been blinding pain. Now he was depleted of all feeling. His father, seeing this, put down the knife he was clenching so tightly that his knuckles were white and brushed his hand briefly and gently over his son's forehead, after which he went to the far side of their camp where Phoebe Hume saw him vomit and then kneel to the ground, his hands clasped, his face lifted toward the sky.

She went over to join him, neither of them saying anything to the other, but it was clear to the people watching them that they were holding and speaking to each other through God. Even after they heard the sudden murmur of the crowd, they gave no sign beyond intensifying their prayers, although they knew the sound meant that their oldest son was dead.

When I had finished, Tony nodded his head in a way that told me he understood why I had violated Sam's and Mrs. Hume's privacy by repeating this story. He said, "Death can force a new life on those it hasn't touched just yet, can't it?"

"Yes," I agreed, "somehow people have to go about filling the hole it leaves, and sometimes they don't do it very well."

28

SINCE THERE WASN'T ANYTHING in Tommy's background that could convince him a love affair was much more than another childhood ailment that had to get worse before it got better, he put Sam's conduct off to one side of his mind while he set about preparing for the meeting he had that morning with his partner, Jabez Witham. There were several situations that required immediate resolutions to keep them from growing into serious problems.

First of all, he knew the banker was bound to hear of the whorehouse operation in the fairly large frame home he'd rented at the far edge of Oregon Street, and, in light of his well-publicized contributions toward building the new Methodist Church, he might feel obligated to choke it off before its stream of profits had time to wash away his scruples.

Next, even though the house's new tenants had been named Precious Jade, Golden Precious, Precious Moon, and Far Off Star and dressed in every piece of finery he could scrape up, there was a good chance their customers were going to recognize them for just what they were—farm girls to be used only after a man's loneliness and sexual needs became unbearable. He just plain didn't know how to minimize their large hands and feet nor soften the coarse and stupid attitudes that were more typical of Hong Kong boat girls than the ornaments he'd hoped to bring to Jacksonville. That meant that somewhere he had to find an old lady who could be relied on to keep both the house and the girls in order, and the nearest place for such a turtle woman was San Francisco—which brought him back to Mr. Witham.

Would the banker understand that this extra, unforeseen expense amounted to just small change alongside the partners' half of the two dollars every customer was going to pay as passage for his trip upstairs with one of the girls? If Witham would listen long enough, he might agree that this was sure to result in sizable piles of cash since, as Tommy saw it, working hours would involve a seven-day week, stretching from two in the afternoon to whenever in the morning, with time off only for dinner and a midnight snack.

179

Tommy needn't have been so concerned.

Right after he sat down in the bank's back room to outline the situation, Witham just blinked and said, "Of course, my boy! All the money we might make in this enterprise is nowheres near as important as our Christian duty. We've just got to provide companionship for these lads who left their families and loved ones to find an honest day's work. And certainly these females deserve and need mothering. You'll find as you go through life that people work so much better when they're happy at home—and that's just what you're trying to give these (here, he paused to clear his throat) girls—a happy home!"

Naturally, Tommy was pleased by how quickly the little man could calculate their profits.

That left only one more problem to discuss, but, in light of Mr. Witham's genial greed, he no longer saw it as a major hurdle. Tommy intended to allow his joy-girls to sew, knit, or sip tea in the downstairs reception room when business was slack, and, in exchange for this privilege, he wanted them to make their personal purchases only at the store he had opened with his partner's money. At all other times, they had to remain on the premises because, in addition to the profit, there was no point in reminding the rest of the town of their presence.

But how could such a rule be enforced in this land where a loud claim for freedom had already been made. Precious Jade had shown traces of rebelliousness. True, there wasn't much chance that any of the girls would ask for the protection of Caucasian law, but what if one of their miner-customers turned into a suitor? And then wouldn't the other Sojourners be tempted to slip through this first breach of a solemnly entered-into contract? The memory of his own success in ignoring just such an agreement after he reached America was too fresh in his mind to allow anyone else to try it.

Unfortunately, just as he was about to suggest to his partner that he might use his influence to stimulate the sheriff, Mr. Westheimer, into acting as official restraint for their working force, male as well as female, Celina Sewell walked into the room where they were discussing these business decisions. "Mr. Witham," she said, "we got a problem."

"What is it, Celina?"

"Another one of them merchants just hinted that it was gettin unhandy to be dealin with us. All of them say they need their small change early to open their stores, and the ones like the saloons want to put their money away right after their evening trade's been done. They think it's just mortal temptation to be keepin their receipts around all morning while the town is filled up with drunks that went broke durin the night."

"Girl," said the banker, "I'm already at it from ten until midnight, and I'll be hard put to add another three hours before that."

She frowned to show her concern. "Well, then, we got some real trouble, because if we don't do it, it won't be long before somebody else opens a bank that will."

There was no way for someone as alert as Tommy to miss the intimacy filling the pause that occurred while they studied each other's faces for an answer. She had spoken in a proprietary manner, and he'd responded with the air of a man who wasn't the least threatened by her almost conjugal interest. He also noted that, as far as they were concerned, he'd ceased to exist while they talked. This didn't make him angry, just sad. He was sorry to see fresh evidence of his associate's provincialism because he found so many other qualitites of shrewdness to admire in the man.

In our conversations down through the years, Chung Lin never hinted resentment at the grossness of this kind of conduct, but his nephew once told me that our friend, while in the bosom of his family, often speculated why the Americans of that time foreclosed themselves from the talents of certain newcomers while going all out to welcome others with more familiar faces or forms. He admitted that the Chinese of the era originally came here for no other reason except to get their wages and return home, but if they had been treated, not necessarily with warmth, but maybe with elementary courtesy, he wondered whether they might not have contributed something to arts and sciences.

Celina broke the silence. "If you don't come in early, then I ought to."

"Now, Seelie, I wouldn't want to load that on you. You work hard enough as it is."

"There's no help for it. If you feel bad enough to cry about it, I'll leave an hour earlier."

Much relieved by this offer, the banker said, "Maybe I ought to be the one that comes in early."

"I don't think that's very sensible. People don't need you to make change or put away a deposit. But when they come in to talk business, it's you they're after."

"You're right, girl," he said. "I'll get you a key to the front door." Then, after a moment's hesitation, he added, "Or, better still, you come by the house in the mornings on your way to work and I'll have the key waiting for you."

"That's the best idea," she agreed. "I just as soon not have the responsibility."

The note of courtship in their voices told Tommy that they hadn't gone to bed together just yet, so he guessed that this early-morning arrangement was going to last only so long as it took Mr. Witham to feel easy about someone else holding the key to his place of business.

"We'll start tomorrow, Seelie." He nodded briskly to indicate that the matter had been settled and now their business was done, but he didn't take his eyes off her until she had left the room.

Tommy's presence was reacknowledged when the banker turned back to him with a smile of pride in this display of loyalty from such a superior source. "Well, my boy, what else do we have to talk about?"

"No more," Tommy answered, "but sell our coolies to the mines. But this is what you fix."

The banker looked thoughtful. "Maybe we've got a better way of going about it. What would you say to you using them in a mine that you owned with me behind you?"

"If it not idea of Mr. Witham—not good."

The banker had no prejudice where profits where concerned, so he missed Tommy's meaning. "Why not? There's nobody to beat you people for being industrious. If you had enough work gangs going, I'll bet we'll still be taking gold out of these hills long after all the American miners move on to something easier."

Out of respect for his own safety, Tommy rarely debated someone else's decisions, but he wanted to be sure his partner had considered the big problem that an all-Chinese mine operation in a white world was going to spawn. "Make white miners mad," he pointed out while shrugging in a way that said that no matter how splendid this idea might be, it would never get the chance to see daylight.

"Most of the time you'd be right," said the banker, and Tommy breathed an inward sigh of relief because these first words indicated that the obstacle had been considered and dismissed as not necessarily fatal. "But who in tarnation is going to object to a bunch of crazy Chinese grubbing away for the few pennies left in the tailings of a mine that's been worked over and abandoned? Nobody but me and you are going to know how much those pennies can amount to. White miners are too thundering lazy to get out all the good that's in a mine. There's too many other places for easier digging around here."

Tommy had begun mulling over exactly this kind of a project right after he'd recruited his troop of coolies back in China, but no matter which way he turned it around in his head, he always came back to the certainty that even if he were ever permitted open operation of a mining claim, the slightest rumor of productivity was going to be enough to get him forced away from it at gunpoint. The idea was feasible only if the mines were held in a white man's name. "How could a Chinese own?" he asked.

"Well," said the Witham, "I've heard talk of making it against the law, but there's nothing yet on the books against it. I'd put the properties in my name, but it'd hurt the bank. It's not so bad my being in partners with a miner, but owning it all by myself wouldn't look right. My customers might say I was going in competition with them. So let's try it. Worst could happen is that if you got closed down we could still sell your crew to the other mine owners. Besides, next to nothing is what I'll give for a worked-out claim—so we'll buy you one or two. That's how much I trust you, son."

Tommy kept quiet, waiting for the banker to develop the idea that he, himself, had considered with such longing.

He wasn't disappointed. "And we won't worry about any legal problems later on, neither! Anybody wants to contest your title, it's my hunch that the judge won't be too shy about deciding in our favor."

The banker might be counted on to protect their mine with the sheriff's guns, but what good would weapons do in a court of law? "No judge," Tommy answered, shaking his head to indicate that he thought it too much to expect.

"Don't be too sure. Suppose when we get around to electing one, it turns out to be Gibbs?"

This was a bombshell. "Mister Doctor Gibbs? Father of Collis?"

"Why not? Fine upstanding citizen. One of the best we have. Next election I'm going to get his name put up, and if I don't miss my guess, it'll be unanimous—meaning nobody'll vote against him."

Tommy thought fast and hard. He didn't want to remind the banker about the reason my father fired him, but if it wasn't put on the table right now, later on he might find that his returns from the project amounted to exactly nothing. "Mister Doctor Gibbs is mad with Tommy. He would not vote with me, you think?"

The banker smiled, looked up at the ceiling, and then back to Tommy. "No offense, son, but you don't count that much. I do. All the doctor has to know is that it's really my property at stake. Him and me have something mighty good brewing between us."

When Tommy's worried look didn't go away, he added, "I'd expected you'd know about it, you being such good friends with Collie. But in case you're not playing possum, don't be too surprised if Collie and my daughter Charity aren't thinking about making arrangements for a date at the church we've been building."

It wasn't often that Witham felt he had to amplify his words to Chung

Lin. Ordinarily, their conversation was limited to business matters where they had an almost perfect communion, but this was different. "Boy, our kids are fixing to get married!"

Tommy's answer was an explosive hiss of congratulations. For the first time since the meeting began, his face reflected something beyond anxiety. Smiling broadly, he said, "Mister Witham, Mister Witham, you think of everything!"

That cleaned up their agenda for the day, so Tommy left, privately wondering how and when he was going to withdraw his share of their profits from this bank without antagonizing its owner. Any man who would give the keys to his vault to a Celina Sewell or would expect a Collis Gibbs to marry his daughter was not the man with whom he wanted to deposit his savings.

29

I'VE GOT A COPY of the license right in front of me. It's dated September 20, 1854, and made out to Henri Boudreau giving him the right to operate a "bouling alley" in conjunction with his saloon. I suppose this moldy old paper is as good as anything else to establish the benchmark when Jacksonville became a real town, keeping records of marriages, births, deaths, and—wonder of wonders—elections that were something more than a way of settling the arguments of a pack of drunken miners. Local citizens, John Ingleman and Elizabeth Winkle, were officially married that year, and the McCullys registered their baby, the first to be born here, into the book at the shed we set aside as the Town Hall.

The people who wanted this place to be their home were taking over from the miners without a battle. Jacksonville had turned out to be a "shallow camp," meaning that most of its gold lay near the surface. The first wave of prospectors scraped it up and then spread farther out along the creeks while the more farsighted among them went to work in the hills. New miners coming in traveled directly out to join them. What was left in the town was business, and because merchants beget merchants, we became the supply center for northern California and southern Oregon in addition to all the Rogue Valley camps around it.

All this brought more settlers to the outlying districts, and it wasn't long before Jacksonville was the county seat and the government scheduled us a Circuit Court judge named Matthew P. Deady to preside here on a regular basis. This was a heartening mark of confidence in our future, but it opened the doors to a whole new set of civic troubles. Even then, Oregonians weren't overjoyed by the idea of outsiders running our affairs, so a general agitation for statehood began to brew. The orneriest among us wanted to go so far as to secede and establish a new country called "Jefferson." Sometimes I hear rumbles that this kind of sentiment still persists, but, unfortunately, I'm not around to help keep it bubbling the way I did in the old days.

Yes, I was still at it. After we finally received official permission to organize a militia, I put in about two weeks snuffing out opposition to Richard Mulligan's appointment as captain. It worked, and we were in business, putting us right up there with other settlements that had grown past being a clump of tents and shanties. Of course, no one with good sense slept better at night because of the presence of our own military unit, because just about every one of these ragtag outfits followed the same pattern. They'd pick out some abandoned log cabin that was close enough in to where they could keep their eyes on their land claims, name it "Fort Something or Other," and hold roll calls in one of the saloons in town. Whenever the need to actually fight Indians came up, it was generally followed by a quick vote to contact the nearest army encampment for a detachment of honest-to-God soldiers.

So we had new settlers, merchants, as good a militia as anyone else, and, very shortly, the one sure sign that a mining camp had become a town—a bakery. Along the frontier, the one thing that everyone had in common was a sweet tooth, and Phoebe Hume and Elva, in all their innocence, were the ones who started the great Petticoat War by going into the business of satisfying this craving.

Mrs. Hume was one of the best bakers around. There were very few neighbors who didn't find some reason to look in for a visit whenever the aroma of one of her pies or cakes was in the air, and once it even caused a group of itinerant miners to knock on the door to try to buy whatever was inspiring the heavenly smell coming out of her kitchen. So, it was a very short step for her to think about opening her own shop.

"What's wrong with the idea?" she asked me. "I don't mind cooking for friends, but there's no sense in making up a batch of pies just to feed the town. No dollars, neither."

I waited until I finished the mouthful of Pear Surprise and then smiled to prove I'd caught the little joke. The minor delight she called a Fruit Surprise was another reason we'd look forward to any birthday or holiday. She'd take a few shallow tin platters about ten inches wide and sixteen or eighteen inches long, pour into each a quarter of an inch or so of crushed fruit, most often pears or peaches or berries, always with skins and seeds carefully removed, and then set the pans out in the sun to dry. After that, they'd be dusted with sugar, rolled up, and cut into pieces about an inch long.

The stuff was bliss to be chewed long and lovingly, but the idea popping into my head just then made me gulp the rest of it down. "It'd be wonderful, Mrs. Hume, and it'd make slews of money! The only thing," and I frowned to show how seriously I was considering what came next, "is that it'd be so popular that it's bound to turn into an awful lot of work."

She turned from the pan she was scrubbing long enough to dart one of her shrewd looks at me. "I already thought of it, Collis. I'm going to ask Elva in to come in with me. She's been around this kitchen enough times. Maybe she doesn't need the money as much as me, seeing as how her father is doing, but it's something to keep her busy."

She meant that being a partner in the bakery might take Elva's mind off the way her son had been acting since Celina Sewell came here. "Marvelous idea!" I enthused. "And I can help. I'll put something in the *Sentinel* every week about it."

Eyeing me and nodding in sober agreement, she answered, "Certainly you will. There won't be one baby born or miner bruised up that didn't happen in the bake shop. I knew I could count on you, Collis."

"I'm serious, Mrs. Hume. There's lots of ways I can pitch in."

"There sure are." The brief smile that followed said she loved me even though both she and I knew how long were the odds that I'd be somewhere else whenever grease had to be scraped from an oven or there was a barrel of flour to be moved.

That put me on the defensive. "I'll go right out and find you the best spot in Jacksonville! I know every place in town that'd be good for a store. We'll find a big, empty lot, maybe right next to one of the bars— maybe I'll even convince Mr. Boudreau to let us have the one behind the Bella Union, and we could build a first-class bakery in no time! All we'd need is an oven and I think I know . . ."

"Whoa," she said.

"I'm only trying to help. What's wrong with that?"

"Not a thing. You're bright as a dollar, and there won't be any Pear Surprise left if you keep gobbling away at it, and maybe if you were to drink another cup of milk, you could finish the pan." For the first time she interrupted her quick movements in cleaning up the kitchen to face me squarely. "To tell the truth, boy, we've already worked out most of it. Elva's found a place and . . ."

"I thought you said you were just thinking of talking to her about it."

"Never said that. I only said that I was about to ask her to come in with me. And that's what I'm going to do. But we've chatted about it real serious off and on, and last Thursday when she was out after flowers she found a place near Sterling Creek that's just right."

"Mightn't a place that far out be a problem?"

"Sure it might be. But there's too much good to it, too. It's a cabin that somebody moved on and left, and it's even got a big old cast-iron stove in it that must have been too heavy to carry alone. And, Collis, there's the prettiest stream running not a hundred feet away from it, and it's right spang near all the miners, so they won't have to be traipsing all the way into town whenever they get their mouth set on a piece of pie."

I didn't have the heart to point out the problems that Indians or drunken miners might visit on two females in the kind of unprotected spot she was describing. Besides, so much hope and fun were shining in her face, that for the first time I saw the pretty girl who had captured dour, crabby, Edward Hume.

Well, not more than three weeks later they had the bakery going. Mrs. Hume and Elva had Sam, Tony, me, and, more often than you'd believe, Tommy, all working away like beavers at fixing and cleaning and lugging supplies. For a while even Sam and Elva lost the strained feeling that had come between them. Once I heard her teasing about Celina although, of course, she didn't mention her by name.

"Sam," she said, "you got enough strength left to trundle this old sack of apples over by the stove?"

I could tell he caught her drift right away because his face became more solemn than ever as he bent by the big bag, scooped his hands under it, straightened his back, and puffed out his cheeks without picking it up an inch and then collapsed on it to show that she'd been right; the load was just too heavy for a weakling like him to move.

She walked over and said with mock severity, "I declare, that female is going to be the death of you yet!" which was a cheeky statement for someone like Elva, who was supposed to be wondering what was going on when the birds and bees were buzzing around each other.

The old Sam glinted through again after it occurred to him, too, that the bake shop was located in an awfully isolated place. One day he showed up with a pepperbox revolver he'd bought for them. "Just in case you need to be signalin somebody," he told them. "But don't try aimin it and thinkin you're going to come anywhere near a mark."

The gun was one of the first of their new implements to be put to use. They had been open not much more than a week when, during one of the infrequent slack periods (the miners had taken to their wares like an army of ants trailing to a drop of spilled honey), Elva looked out the door and said, "Aunt Phoebe, come here. Don't it look like somethin's there over yonder behind that clump of trees?"

"More customers?" She walked over to where Elva stood and peered out the door.

"Customers don't hide. Somebody's hidin."

Now Mrs. Hume saw the Indians, three or four of them, as she recalled, moving slowly in their direction. "Quick, girl," she shouted, "get back!" She slammed the door shut and jammed the limb that stood in the corner into the supports Sam had put up on both sides of the doorway.

They stood behind the barricade, frightened and immobiled until the first arrow smacked into the side of the cabin. Then they realized it had been aimed at the cut made for a window and it was only a matter of time before the missile was going to be followed by attackers.

That galvanized Elva. Gathering strength she didn't know she had, she picked up the table in the middle of the room, intending to block up the window hole, but another arrow sailed through at that moment, not hitting her squarely, but grazing close enough to rake a long, bloody line in her arm. She grabbed at the wound, and in the moment that she wasn't aware of anything but the blood welling out, Mrs. Hume snatched up the pepperbox, positioned herself in front of the window, and began blazing away at the hostiles.

Evidently the Indians weren't prepared for anything more than scaring two women into submission, because the gunshots caused them to hesitate, and while they were deciding on their next move, some miners who had been ambling over there to buy pies, picked up steam after hearing all the noise. The sounds they made scrambling through the brush convinced the redskins to head for easier prey.

It was a close enough call to eliminate the need for a formal decision by Elva and Mrs. Hume to quit the idea of running a bake shop out where they could have all the retail trade to themselves. And, although neither woman ever mentioned it to the other, both of them had the same thought: They had almost paid a nasty price for Sam and his father being so busy elsewhere.

Then came the Petticoat War I mentioned earlier. Something close to panic occurred among the women in the town after they heard about the narrow escape. Those who weren't married to members of our militia got on those who were, and among all of them the demand became damned near overwhelming that their men march out to start and win an Indian uprising. They even held a meeting about it in the Methodist Church, Mrs. Hume being appointed recording secretary, and the repository of the most hysteria, Clara Barstow, was elected chairlady. After swapping several wagonloads of pent-up indignation, the women, under Mrs. Barstow's direction, unanimously passed the resolution that if the Jacksonville militia didn't get up on its hind legs and fight, they would send a letter to Washington insisting that it be cut off the federal payroll.

This turned out to be a notably futile gesture. As should have been expected, the militiamen didn't spend too much time in whipping themselves into a warlike pitch. After hearing that there were actually some warriors in the neighborhood who were seriously considering shooting arrows in their direction, all the discussions became confined to the quickest way of getting in a troop of professional soldiers. Finally, to keep these powwows from becoming an end in themselves, I brought the matter to a head during one of the regular musters that were being held every afternoon at the Bella Union.

"Mulligan," I said to our leader, "it's my opinion that we've got to settle on something right now to get ourselves out of this barrel. You probably know this better than anyone else, but it's my duty to mention that there's only two choices: fight or disband. If we just put in a call for help, somebody in the government is bound to start asking embarrassing questions. We might even have to pay back the money they've given us."

"Collie, goddammit," our doughty captain exploded, "stop tryin to force somethin down our throats!" No one in the bar missed his relief in finding a focus for his frustration, and there wasn't a man among them who wouldn't have marched with him toward the conclusion that somehow this dilemma was mostly my fault. My brothers in arms had been drinking for three days now while mulling over this problem.

"Well, now, Captain," I retreated, "I didn't mean to say we had to do something this very minute. All I meant to suggest is that you and your senior officers might find it sensible to make *your* decision pretty soon."

By now, Elva and Mrs. Hume had moved their bakery to a place well inside the town's limits, and since there wasn't much more than the normal wear and tear to be expected from passing rogue redskins, I added a pat on the head. "Best thing to do might be to leave tactics as important as this to our leaders. Richard, maybe you and your staff can take a little while by yourselves tonight to figure out what we ought to do. And I, for one, say right here and now that no matter what order you come up with, I'll follow it to the letter, no matter how much risk might be involved. I'd follow you anywhere, Richard!"

The general murmur of assent that immediately followed left no question in my mind that there wasn't a man in the place who expected any decision from Mulligan except the one that didn't involve fighting.

Next morning, passersby noticed a pair of Clara Barstow's bloomers fastened to the flagpole that stood in front of our City Hall. Once the news of the unique pennant got spread around, it was rightly seen as a symbol of the willingness of gallant men to forfeit their paychecks rather than leave their womenfolk untended.

Later, Tom Barstow swore that if he ever found out who had dishonored his wife this way, he'd make certain the culprit was punished. And if he personally wasn't big enough to accomplish the job all himself, then he'd hire as many men as it took to do it. The declaration would have had even more impact if Tom had been able to keep from winking in my direction when he said it.

30

THERE'S ONE PART of the story I've been trying to piece
together that might never have found a place here if I hadn't
sent Tony Johnstone a note asking what had been going through
his mind during that time when Sam had been so obsessed with Celina
Sewell. The answer must have been written awfully late in the evening
because over the years I've grown to know that the best time to get
through his defenses is while he's having his two or three drinks before
turning in.

But, no matter how late the hour, if we had been sitting face to face,
I'm sure he wouldn't have told so much of it to me.

This is the letter he wrote many years later:

Dear Collis,

*Contrary to the opinion of most of the people who knew us in Jacksonville,
I did not feel the slightest bit ill-used by Sam's remaining in town while I
did our work in the fields. As a matter of fact, I preferred being alone during
that period, so it really didn't matter to me whether he wasted his time on
street corners or in wagging his tail after the Sewell chit.*

*I was hurt, inside and out. True, my shoulder had healed at the point
where the arm had been separated, but that didn't mean I felt restored to
manhood. In a way, I suppose, the willingness to hunt the forests without
other company was an attempt to convince myself that I was still whole.*

*So, occasionally losing my way in the woods became neither frightening
nor even unpleasant because those were the times when I could again be me
without experiencing the need to appear so for the benefit of Sam or you or
little Tommy. In fact, being lost became actually attractive because it so easily
happened that there was no need to accuse myself of hiding away. You knew
so little of the fields, Collis, that I doubt you were ever aware of how primitive
a western forest can be. Choked with underbrush, dead branches, and fallen
trees, its paths most often are simply gullies cut by the rainwaters washing
down from the mountains. There is rarely room or time to note pathmarks*

192

when just the simple act of getting through on foot is making enormous demands on mind and muscle. If you are lucky enough to find the slightest deer track or overgrown trap line, you must fix your eyes on it.

One morning I strayed just a few yards off such a trail and became so absorbed in the search for other signs, that it took me several hours to locate and return to the path I had been following. And then I saw I was no longer the only one on it. There was, just ahead of me, an Indian girl. My first inclination was to step back into the brush until she had gone from sight and then retrace my path to the camp I had established. She obviously shared the reaction. Upon hearing my sounds, she immediately sped on ahead.

For some reason, this spurred me to change my mind and race after her. Perhaps I was still too much in the grip of the need to hunt and prevail.

Her speed was such that she would have gotten away if she hadn't tripped in one of the slashes that the rains gouge across granitic soil. Before she could scramble back to her feet, I was there, and when she stood I remembered her as Me-Huh-No-Lush, the girl who had been blinded in one eye by the husband she'd cuckolded.

She also apparently recognized that she had seen me before because submission replaced fright in her face. Making no effort to brush away the twigs and dirt still clinging to the torn cotton dress she wore, she said what I suppose were the most important English words she knew, "A dollar?"

Need I describe my reaction? I wanted only to get as far away from her as possible. I was conscious of no bitterness within me, there was only the desire not to be further subjected to the reminder that her whoring had caused me to lose my arm.

But she wouldn't have it so. I had gone no more than a few paces when she caught up with me, and her look was so imploring that I stopped to answer, "I'm sorry, no dollar," and turned away again.

She wasn't to be shaken. I felt her arm on my shoulder, and, finally, my loathing of what I had become welled up and no matter how irrational it was to vent it on this poor ignorant girl, I fairly screamed, "You filthy slut! Get away! Let me be!"

I shouldn't have expected her to understand my anger. "Me Little Mary," she said.

"I know," I answered, finding control, "but I have no dollar and, God knows, no desire for you."

She said nothing in reply, simply waiting dumbly in front of me like a pony that had been beaten into obedience too often.

"Don't you understand, you poor clod, I want you to go away. I don't want to be anywhere near you."

At last, comprehension crept into her eyes. She shook her head sadly and said, "Poor clod Little Mary."

"Then go wherever it was you were heading." With this, I walked off.

But her words had been too woebegone. I stopped. She wasn't just another animal in the field, so, after staring ahead for a moment, I turned back to regard her.

She hadn't moved nor was she looking at me. She was simply there, more forlorn than any human ought to be. The total resignation in her stance told me that if I went on she would die of her hurts and starvation exactly where I had left her. "Oh, damn you," I said. "Where is your mother?"

"Not see since Sam."

I supposed this meant that the crone had abandoned her and gone back to the tribe. Or perhaps death had taken the old one and ever since the girl had been wandering through these woods living only on nuts and berries. I resented having this thrust on me, but I could not help asking, "Have you eaten?"

She shook her head.

"How long? How long hungry?"

At this, the girl sat down in the trail and stared dully at the ground. "Much hunger. Much long."

What was I to do? Leave her there to die? "Poor damned dumb thing," I said, "come on. Let's get back to my camp and I'll feed you." She understood when I turned this time, and there was no hesitation as she followed behind me.

I found my trail and we walked perhaps a mile or so back to where I had established a temporary base, and although this is a considerable distance in rugged terrain, I was conscious of her and my thoughts of her for every step of the way.

There were three fat pheasants I'd bagged and hung on the limb of a tree near my billet, and these she spotted almost as soon as we arrived at the site. She looked at them and then at me, and when I nodded, she went over and took them to the still-smoldering ashes of last night's campfire. While she busied herself with cleaning the game, I went out for more limbs and twigs, which I then used to bring the fire back and to construct the rough spit on which they were to be cooked.

The wretched thing was ravenous. The birds were barely done before she was tearing away at one of them. I asked at one point, "How long has it been since you've eaten, Mary?" but her attention wasn't to be diverted. She kept chewing away as if I hadn't said a word.

When I had finished my bird (long after she had cleaned hers down to its bones), I became aware that she was looking my way again, and, of course, there was no need for her to put the plea into words. "Go ahead," I said, pointing at the remaining pheasant in a way that signaled it was hers.

She shook her head in a negative gesture, but when I repeated, "Go ahead, I shan't want any more," she tore into the last one as if it had been her first.

I sat back and watched as she ate, wondering how soon she would go away. To be truthful, the prospect of her company was no longer unpleasant after I realized that it was the first time in many weeks I'd been with someone who was so much worse off that there was no need to feel the presence of a judgment. Who wanted Little Mary, the pariah with one eye? Absolutely no one. She was destined to be lonely and driven, never to be received back by her own people and to find companionship only when some beast of a miner was drunk enough to want an old Indian whore. She was still young at the moment, but she must have known that age would find her more quickly than any of the others of her tribe.

For the first time since my experience with the bear, I recognized that I had been wallowing in self-pity for too ungodly long a time.

It was well past noon before she had finished, and the hot sun above reminded me that in the coming night the traces of poultry grease on my hand and face would be considered most appealing by insect swarms no matter how well I might cover myself. I motioned my intent to return shortly and left her scraping a hole in which to bury the remains of our meal before they attracted more bothersome forest predators than the evening's gnats and fleas.

When I reached the stream that coursed perhaps a hundred yards from my camp, its waters seemed so inviting that instead of contenting myself with scrubbing away from a perch on its banks, I took off all my clothing and jumped in. It was much cooler than I had expected it to be on this fine a day. In fact, it took several minutes before I'd done with gasping at its stinging cold and found pleasure in the rush of the crystal-clear water flowing around and over my body. It was a moment of strange content because it seemed to me that much of my hurt was washing away.

Reality returned when I became aware that she was watching me from the banks above. Once again I was conscious of my stumped shoulder and, of course, my nakedness. I waded over to a nearby clump of reeds, hoping she would understand that I wanted to be left alone.

Instead, she stripped off the rags she wore and jumped in, swimming to where I crouched in the shallows. Then she smiled, not in invitation nor as a placating gesture but in a reflection of the well-being I had been feeling. Almost instinctively, I smiled in return.

For the next half hour the two of us paddled about, as solemnly pleased as two setters in a wading pool.

When I'd had enough, she followed me out of the stream and we stood on its banks regarding each other. Ordinarily, nudity brings forth the prudishness in my nature. In school, I had actively disliked the intimacy of the gymnasium dressing rooms, but now there was no such shrinking away. For the first time she appeared, not as a deformed thing (even her blindness did not jar) but as a magnificent female—young, nubile, and thoroughly desirable.

I put my arm out as she glided to me, and I clasped her as we sank to the ground.

But it was no good. No good at all. I could not respond physically to her beauty, and, after a while, I lay back, my one arm shielding my eyes from the sun and finding myself with the hope she would be gone when I took it away.

She would not leave. I could feel her sitting quietly beside me, and once, when our flanks touched, it was as if I had been touched by despair.

Finally, I felt her hand in my palm. Gently drawing my arm away, she leaned over and looked full into my eyes, and then she did something I had believed was only rarely performed by members of her race. She leaned over and brushed my forehead with her lips, and the gesture said more than any of the words we could not speak to each other; of her awareness that I, too, needed to be made whole.

Reaching up, I drew her to me, and my answering kiss was neither love nor desire but gratitude, and it was enough because she understood me.

I made no further attempt to take her. We lay together as two children until the late afternoon came up, chilling our naked bodies. We rose, dressed, and walked back to the camp, where I built another fire although neither of us was hungry enough to prepare a meal.

We sat by the fire until evening turned to night, and then we rolled ourselves in my single blanket and went to sleep, holding each other.

She was gone when I awoke in the morning.

Thank you, Collis.

Anthony

31

WHEN I MENTIONED that Mrs. Hume and Elva were the innocent causes of the Great Petticoat War, I meant that after the matter of Mrs. Barstow's bloomers flying from the flagpole had been talked to death by the town, a handful of wives still tsk-tsked about it whenever they met in the bakery shop. Nightmares centering on the way the Jacksonville militia had met their first test kept plaguing these good ladies.

Elva told me that Mabel Burke summed it up by saying, "It warn't so much the few redskins that were nosing around that old rickety cabin of your'n, Mrs. Hume—because they're gone and good riddance to them. But suppose it really had been a big passel up to some awful evil? The army might never have come here in time because they couldn't do aught else but figure that our militia would take care of the problem. After all, that's why the government's forking out all that good money to them shiftless rascals!"

At first, I thought it was funny, but then I began to realize that Mrs. Burke's words contained some real bad seeds. Suppose Jacksonville really were attacked by Indians and all we had between us and them were the ragtag J'ville militia boys? It had all been a marvelous lark, but it was time to bring it to an end.

But how? There wasn't any way on God's earth short of using an axe that anyone was going to be able to separate Richard Mulligan and his crew from their paychecks. They had to be put into some fix where they'd have no choice but to disband or be fired by Captain Alden, our nearest real military official.

The bright and shining answer didn't come to me until the next roll call at the Bella Union while Mulligan was addressing his troops in a long whine that ended with, "Goddamn them [meaning the solid citizens who'd been questioning whether our militia were worth anywhere near the cash they'd never stopped drawing], ain't one hellbent Siwash that's showed his ugly face here since last winter, no matter what anybody says, is there?"

There was a general grunting assent that meant only willfully stupid people would close their eyes to the fact that the place had been kept safe by the militia staying on guard in town instead of spreading out on a wild goose chase through the hills. All along we militiamen had privately entertained the same contempt for the town that its citizens were now developing for us. We were the ones who had it first because we were the ones who'd been signing the payroll.

I saw this and the rest of my plan in the same flash, so, after quietly drifting out of the saloon, I went to search for Billy Tell.

He wasn't too hard to find. Ever since the peace treaty was signed, he'd been hanging around the town, weeding vegetable patches, sweeping out saloons, and doing all the other chores for a few cents that a white man wouldn't do for a dollar. Anyone with half an eye should have seen he was smart enough to be above this kind of scully work, but no one mentioned it because it never occurred to anyone to discuss an Indian as a human being. Billy Tell was quite secure in his role as the spy in town for Chief John.

"Billy," I said, after I ran him to earth in Flora's Stables, "I've got a job for you."

He went on with his work, but I knew I wasn't being ignored. Over the winter, Billy and I had come to understand that neither of us meant any harm to the other and that we might very well have been friends if things had been different. So I told him about my plan, and although his only comment was a grave nod, it read as if he'd said, *Jesus, is there anyone that dumb? Well, maybe there is. After all, your friends took care of our families all winter in exchange for a scrap of paper we're going to ignore whenever we get around to it.*

Of course, I'm not sure this was exactly what was going through his mind, because Indians rarely smile, but I'm willing to bet it was pretty close. All he really did was to bob his head up and down just once to signify agreement. And then, in spite of his commitment to Indian stoicism, he showed his true feelings by slowly shaking his head from side to side, and this time I was mortally sure it meant he was thinking, *I'm a son of a bitch if this don't beat all!*

It was as good as if he had smiled and clapped me on the back. In return, I saluted him with my own Indian sign I'd just made up, consisting of placing a finger to my lips in a way that said, *You bastard, if my secrets aren't safe with you, then yours aren't with me*, and I left for my next move, which was acquiring a bottle of tanglefoot.

It's doubtful that there's anyone still drinking today who remembers just how potent that stuff could be. Its chief product was oblivion, and if you drank it steadily, that state became permanent. Every bartender made his own, so the recipes varied somewhat from place to place, but the elements were generally the same. Each batch was about three-quarters of a barrel of straight alcohol to which was ladled as many dippers of water as the saloonkeeper thought he could get away with. After that, a chew of tobacco was added for color, some caramelized sugar for body, and a handful of pepper thrown in to get the drinker's immediate attention. In some establishments, the practice of dropping in a rattlesnake head wasn't unknown, but this was mostly reserved for one keg that was kept for show and tapped only when a drunk greenhorn wanted to prove how utterly fierce he was.

After these ingredients were stirred together, the result was put aside to age, a process that always lasted just as long as it took the first customer to show up and grab for one of the tin cups that began and completed most bar furnishings.

I needed at least a quart of this swill if my plan was to work. I couldn't go back to the Bella Union to buy it because the boys were still there, and if anything went wrong, somebody, especially Boudreau, was bound to remember that a bulk purchase wasn't my usual style. At any other bar in town the best I could expect was a battery of crude josh about what girl I had in mind to use it on, and that kind of an exchange might easily come back some day to haunt me.

This left me with just one source: the little combination store and restaurant with the name "Chung Lin" scrawled on a board in front of it.

"Tommy," I said when I got there, "I need a bottle of tanglefoot."

He could have asked me why it was so necessary or why I didn't get it from any of the saloons in town, but, of course, he didn't. Not Tommy. He wouldn't have commented if President Franklin Pierce had shown up at his door to buy a pair of lady's bloomers. "No whiskey here," he answered. "Only the rice wine of my people."

"Do me a favor and look. You might be surprised to find you've missed a bottle here or there."

"You bring me trouble?" he asked. "You know what comes if town saloon mans find I sell same like him."

"Stop the horseshit, Tommy. If I didn't need a quart no one should ever know about, I wouldn't be here."

He sighed ever so slightly and went into the cubbyhole that doubled as a kitchen and storeroom and in a few seconds was back with a bottle that seemed to me to be still warm from the day's distilling. I asked, "How much water in it?"

He shrugged, which I took to mean there was either a lot or very little.

"Come on, Tommy. I need the strongest jolt I can get. I've got some very important business to do."

He shrugged again and, taking the bottle from me, once again vanished into the back room. When he returned, the contents of the new bottle he offered me were so pale as to be almost colorless. "Take," he said, "but no pay and no words to anybody where it was home."

"You are a credit to our town," I said, and left, knowing that the trace of a smile on his lips meant that whatever the reason I had for the tanglefoot, he was sure it would bear some fruit we'd later savor together.

The last and most crucial part of my plan turned out to be the most difficult to implement. No matter where I looked, I couldn't find Alben Hensley. I searched all the saloons and, as a last ditch, tried our newspaper office. He wasn't there of course, but I was encouraged after I felt the lamp and found it still warm enough to tell me he hadn't left too long ago, so I went back up into town, figuring he'd be either in one of the stores trying to sell advertising or in any of the whorehouses for exactly the same reason. When it came to scrounging for cash enough to quench his thirst, my publisher would have sold billboard space to a chief trying to recruit a war party.

No luck. No Alben Hensley anywhere, and it was getting dark. I was just about to pack it in for the night, hoping to set the plan going in the morning, when I realized that this required traveling out to where Billy Tell was waiting. If I didn't let him know about the postponement, I ran the risk of losing his services altogether. Because I didn't feel a damn bit like tramping out this late to Sterling Creek all by myself, I headed for the hotel in the hope of finding someone who had seen old Hensley.

Luck came back to me. He was in the lobby, talking to the manager, unattractive Mrs. Keely, who was one of the more challenging strongholds for the bachelors of our town because of her pretty receipts. I wasn't certain whether the conversation was based on business or romance, so I waited until she left him in response to a complaint floating down from one of the rooms.

"What's the matter, my boy?" asked my employer after he'd spotted me. "You look as if the world were teetering on your shoulders."

"Alben," I answered, "I think we're in for some bad trouble. Real bad."

He looked around and, after concluding that whatever it was I hadn't brought it with me, took my arm and began walking me toward the door fast enough to make it clear he didn't want my gloomy face hobbling his progress with Mrs. Keely. After we were on the street, he asked, "Now what's the problem? Who's after me?"

"For a change, Alben, it's not you. It's us. All of us. I don't think there's much time left before this town is going to come under an all-out Indian attack. Not just a couple of drunken redskins—I mean a real war party."

"Are you still singing that tune?" He turned to go back into the hotel.

"I'm serious, damn you," I said, letting my voice shake ever so slightly with fear and anger. "This afternoon, one of Captain Alden's soldiers was in Lohmeyer's and he said they're getting orders to move away from the valley because General Lane is so convinced that Mulligan has everything under control here, he's going to send Alden's command to some other place where the people can't handle their own fighting."

It was exactly the right lie. If there was anything constant in Alben Hensley's life, it was his unswerving belief in the stupidity of the army. "My Lord," he said, stopping in his tracks, "is there anything on God's earth dumber than a professional military man? Anyone who'd put a drop of faith into Mulligan or his loafers should be condemned to stay in a soldier suit for the rest of his life!" He thought for a moment. "Which, of course, is the heart's desire of General Lame Brain Lane."

"Being bitter is no answer, Alben. We've got to use the paper to keep Captain Alden's detachment, no matter what you think of them. We've got to do something fast."

"Like what?" he asked in a way that showed he could be convinced to forget his disbelief of an Indian uprising.

"I've got an idea," I admitted, "but I don't think this is the place to talk about it."

"You mean if anyone overheard us, it might start a panic?"

"Exactly."

"Oh Lord," he said, "Collis is at it again."

"This is no windy," I insisted. "There's no way you can ignore those redskins that tried after Mrs. Hume and Elva Boudreau. And no one knows better than you how our militia handled that one. Put them together and what do you get? You get trouble if the soldiers leave, that's what you get. I'm not fooling, Alben. This is serious!"

He thought for a moment, probably matching what I'd said up against the dollars-and-cents charms of Mrs. Keely, weighing the possibility that she might not come downstairs again that night, and finally deciding in my favor. "All right, lad. Let's go down to the printing plant. But I'm not going to give you more than a few minutes. This is thirsty work for this late in the evening."

"You're in luck," I said, producing Tommy's redeye from where it was nesting under my jacket. "A friend of mine just gave me this present."

He shook his head sadly as he took the bottle to examine it. "You know the rules, son. A newspaperman never accepts any gift that might influence honest reporting." He held the bottle up to examine it in the light coming through the hotel window. "And since this appears to be straight mule, someone wanted a powerful amount of slanting."

"It's only fair to share it with you," I said.

His thirst interfered with the caution with which he normally regarded me. "You're an honest man, Collis. Put this back under your jacket and let's get to the plant."

I couldn't resist. "You keep calling it a plant. It's only a shack."

"I refer to you as a newspaperman, too, so perhaps I should watch my analogies. They crucified the last optimist."

It was my turn to pause and think. "Maybe the plant isn't the best place for us to go. Someone might come in to place an advertisement if they saw a light in the place."

"God forbid," he answered, meaning that he'd be damned if he'd share the bottle with anyone else.

"I'll tell you what," I said, suddenly struck by the idea. "It's not a bad night. Let's go a little out of town, maybe just over toward one of the creeks. We can discuss this thing while we walk."

He was so busy concentrating on the lump under my jacket that there was no longer any possbility of the alarm bells going off in his head. "Certainly," he said, taking me by the arm, "let's go right now." At that point he would have agreed to the two of us shinnying up the flagpole for our talk.

It was easy enough to steer our path toward Sterling Creek because, every so often after we passed out of the town, we'd stop for a libation. Naturally, I was tonguing mine, but, even so, the few drops of Tommy's pride that slipped down my throat told me this was the kind of firewater that set men free. Spilled on a bar, it was capable of eating its way down through the wood.

Hensley didn't feel the need for restraint that I did. Every drink he took produced another dip in the clarity of his conversation. Since my plan required his being at least halfway sensible, I ended by holding the bottle away from him during most of the trip. Even so, he was fairly lit by the time we reached the tree I had selected as the night's arena but, fortunately, still sober enough to be horrified when I managed a stumble over one of its roots and spilled out a good part of the rest of the whiskey.

"Oh, my God!" he said. This wasn't blasphemy, it was the pious expression of a man appalled by one of life's tragedies. "What a bloody awful thing to happen!"

"It's all right, Alben," I reassured him, holding the bottle aloft, "there's still some left."

"Give it here," he answered, thrusting out his arm. "You're not the type who was meant to be trusted with this stuff." When I hesitated, he said even more urgently, "I've never trusted you with *any* stuff!"

I confirmed his belief that he'd put his demand logically by passing over the bottle, which was still about a quarter full. Carefully cradling it, he slid down to a sitting position, his back against the tree, and drained most of the rest.

That was just about as much fuel as he needed for the trip I was about to send him on, so I cleared my throat as loudly as I could to give Billy Tell the signal we had prearranged.

"What the hell are you doing that for?" Hensley asked irritably. "If your throat's blocked up, take a drink of this," and he made a move as to hand it over to me but quit as soon as he noticed that there was just about one swig left. "Never mind. If you've got a frog in your throat, go get some water out of the creek. Any doctor'll tell you water's the best thing for an ailment like yours."

Where the hell was Billy Tell?

I began worrying over how long it would be before the redeye's cumulative effect would stun my employer out of any ability to weigh civic problems. "Alben, the idea I had for our safety is going to require . . ."

It was then that my Indian honored our agreement by proving he'd temporarily forsaken his natural treachery. An arrow came singing out of the darkness and thwacked into the tree, quivering not more than four or five inches above where the back of Hensley's head rested against its trunk. The execution was so perfect that my first thought was, *Is he too drunk to notice?*

He was not.

With a yell that started from his bowels, he leaped up and ran to his left, reversed himself and ran to his right, then back to me, where he grabbed the lapels of my fleece jacket and howled, "Collis, Collis! They've got us! They're here and they've got us here and we're all alone!"

Prying away his hands, I said, "Easy now, Alben. Maybe they don't know we're here," a statement his hysteria prevented him from recognizing as probably the worst piece of reporting ever offered to an editor.

"Do something, boy! Which way should we run?" Now his voice was a harsh whisper.

I stepped forward and, cupping my hands about my mouth, I shouted into the darkness, "God damn you all, we're Americans! If you harm us, our people will be back with an army of sticks that shoot fire!"

"Oh Lord, *please* don't antagonize them!" The prayer laid on top of the panic in Hensley's voice told me how well the plan was going. The strangled snort I heard in the bushes was equally heartening because it proved there was a limit to even an Indian's lack of a sense of humor. These interesting reactions were followed by another arrow whipping uncomfortably close to my head on its way to bang into the tree alongside the first one.

"They're all around us, Alben," I said in low tones. "We'd better make a run for it."

And run we did. Scrambling, tripping, and falling through the brush, bumping up against trees and being scraped by their low hanging limbs, our escape was nowhere near the elegant finale I'd expected, although I should acknowledge that Billy Tell's rendition of a series of war whoops would have sent a racehorse into the blind staggers.

32

AFTER WE REACHED town, panting and disheveled, it was no longer necessary to convince Alben Hensley that we needed all the professional military protection we could get. In the saloons that night, his descriptions of our ordeal mushroomed to where there'd been a whole army of bloodthirsty redskins circling us, and if it hadn't been for their attention being diverted by a pack of wolves that'd heard the noise of the fighting, we would have never gotten away with our scalps. Hensley's account contained so many gripping editorial sidelights and flourishes, that there wasn't a man in any of the saloons he visited (I had gone to bed feeling the tale was safely his from then on) who thought of pointing out that no one had ever seen a wolf, let alone a pack of wolves, prowling through our area. Even better, the curlicues added to the story as it raced through Jacksonville next morning went miles further than anything I expected.

In fact, it almost worked too well.

To a man, the militia up and quit, which is what I'd originally had in mind. What I hadn't counted on was the women. When the *Sentinel* came out two days later with its front page screaming for every kind of military protection known to mankind, our matrons, sweet young things, and whores all got together in a temporary alliance to pressure their husbands, beaus, and customers into service. Not only did most of the militia reenlist, their ranks were swelled by about two dozen more recruits.

I was so proud of the way my plan had worked, I actually found myself torn between letting it roll on and the understanding that hit me every so often that there really were hostile Indians out there. They'd gone after Mrs. Hume and Elva, and if they ever did attack in force, all this new civic bravery would evaporate faster than a puddle in the sunshine. The loafers would quit again, claiming they'd never intended making Jacksonville their permanent home anyway, and the farmers would, as they always have, consider it government business and send out to General Lane for help, providing he wasn't headquartered somewhere else when and if a full-scale war blew our way.

Fortunately, I couldn't resist bragging about my success to Tony. He'd just come back dog tired from a hunting trip and was still asleep the morning I braced him. After five minutes of banging away at the breakfast dishes, I had him awake enough to complain, "Must you create such a damned stir this early in the morning?"

I walked over to the cot. "The limey hasn't died! He speaks. Thank you, dear Lord, the limey isn't dead."

"Even if I were, your bloody clatter would have roused me." He stretched luxuriously, looking at peace with himself, which was a nice thing to see for a change. "You weren't here when I came home last night and you're already up this morning. Is this a new Collis Gibbs?"

"It is. I'm surprised you recognized me."

"Your father must be a happy man."

"Father is in town. As a matter of fact, everyone but us is in town." I sat down on the edge of his cot. "And it all has to do with me being such a totally new man."

"Very well, Collis, tell us about it. We're awake and ready to listen to whatever it is that's set you banging away at pottery and lurching up against every bloody stick of furniture in the place."

"The Rogue Indians have gone on the warpath. They're just before attacking Jacksonville in force."

"Really?" he said, his head sinking back down on the pillow. "Please, by all means call me before they pass through the gates, won't you?"

"You aren't taking this threat seriously enough."

"Oh, I certainly am. Once out in force, those chaps are frightfully irritable . . ." And he closed his eyes to tell me he was preparing to drift off to sleep again.

"I'm the one who warned them," I said. "The new Collis knows his duties to the town, he does."

"New Collis, hmm," he murmured and then sat bolt upright. My answer reminded him that I'd had some sort of plan in mind for the militia before he'd gone on this last hunting trip. The grin I couldn't keep off my face caused him to remember most of what it had been. "Collis, you sod, don't tell me you've actually gone and done it!"

"I have, Tony, I have! I've got the town worried to death. They're seeing Indians behind every bush, and not only that, I've scared the militia shitless. Most of them quit for a while, but there's no way they'll stay on and the people know it and are hating them for wanting to duck out, and there isn't a woman in the place who hasn't called her husband a coward. I've been brilliant, Tony, absolutely brilliant!"

He let the words sink in and then slowly shook his head. "I've looked forward so to see you grow into manhood, but that won't happen now, will it?"

"No one knows but you and I."

"Sam?"

"Nope. Oh, there's Billy Tell, but he helped so there's not much chance of him mentioning it around."

Now the grin was on his face, too. "I'm not at all certain I should be privy to the evil facts, but, because of friendship, I suppose I must. You might burst if you continue to be the only one who admires you."

"Tony," I said solemnly, "it was just marvelous," and I proceeded with a step-by-step description, acting out Hensley's panic, the consternation caused by his story in the barroom; mumbling the excuses being offered by the militia; and I had him howling with laughter before I'd gone through half of it and wiping his eyes when I was done.

He was holding nothing back, so unreservedly enjoying every bit of the account that I couldn't help adding after it was over, "Tony, it's so great that you're able to feel good again."

It wasn't the right thing to say. For a moment the cloud I recognized as pain was in his eyes, but, thankfully, it left almost as quickly as it had come. Of course, I didn't realize then that it had gone away because of the Indian girl. Nor would I have had reason to know that he was wondering if it had really happened, whether the hours he'd spent with her had been only an enchantment but that, no matter what, he was grateful to be whole again.

The smile was creeping back. "I'm enjoying the prospect of your being hung right after someone pieces together your involvement at every point in this charade."

"Not a chance. They're all too dumb."

"How can you be so certain?"

"Because not a one of them has sense enough to think past his own hide."

"I wonder," he said, "if it ever occurs to you that these are real people, not paper cutouts. There's no question you've run a lovely sell, but just suppose they aren't quite as dull-witted as it's fun to believe. You've really caused them quite a disruption, haven't you?"

The question didn't come close to denting my smug pleasure in myself. "Anthony, you are an old woman. You think there's a thunderstorm coming every time somebody farts out in the bushes."

He studied me for a moment. "Jacksonville really has done wonders for you, Collis. There's such elegance to your speech these days. I'm certain your Philadelphia friends would be beside themselves in admiration of your manly vulgarity."

"See? You keep proving you're an old woman. Come on, Tony. Get up and get dressed and we'll go down to the Bella Union and watch the fun. I'm pretty sure Mulligan and his crew are there right about now trying to figure out the letter they want to send General Lane."

"What letter? You've lost me."

"About disbanding the troop. They'd give anything if I'd write it for them, but they know I wouldn't desert my uniform in face of danger for anything in the world."

"I thought the town had shamed them into seeing it through?"

"That lasted almost a day. Will you please get up! We're going to miss everything."

"Collis, can't you understand that all this just isn't the county fair?" In spite of his wanting to play Dutch uncle for me, the smile was back lurking around the corners of his mouth as he got out of bed and began dressing.

"Collie, my pal," was the way Richard Mulligan greeted me at the Bella Union. "I'm glad you come down, boy. I been wonderin where you were."

"You need me for anything special, Captain, sir?"

Maybe I'd put a shade too much staunchness in my voice because I saw him stiffen a bit before he answered, "Well, for a fact, me'n the boys has just about got set on the idea that mebbe you'd better be the one that writ to General Lane. Anybody else puts one wrong word in it and he's liable to be down here on us like a load of chicken shit."

"It's been worrying me, too, Richard," I said, judicially, "so I've been turning it over in my mind and I may have figured something out that will answer just about all our problems."

Mulligan's next question was as close to piety and prayer as he'd ever get. "Boy, you figured out a way to save our ass?"

"Maybe," I replied, paused to make certain I had everyone's attention, and then went on. "Now, it's not really anything you'd be ringing a bell over because it's just common sense. I can't see why we actually have to say we want to quit. Besides, there's no way to write any letter that won't leave him hopping mad over the pay we've drawn. The way I look at it . . ." and here I paused again and looked around me, letting my glance flicker briefly over Tony who, I noted, had put on his dead face for the occasion, but it didn't matter because I knew he couldn't help but be impressed by the way everyone in the bar was craning to hear my words, ". . . it just seems to me that we don't have to do a heck of a lot more than get word to him that we've got a lot of men down sick with some disease, something like smallpox or something else serious—I don't know right now what it is, but it'll come to me—and it's left us outnumbered by the Siwashes to the point where the town ain't safe."

Out of the corner of my eye, I saw Tony stiffen at *ain't*. Mulligan stiffened, too, but it was in disappointment. "What in hell good is that gonna do? He's already been contacted and he don't show no taste to come here, no matter what."

"We're a unit under his command, aren't we?"

"Well, sure."

"He's a professional military man isn't he?"

"Goddammit, Collie!"

"So he knows he's in trouble if our unit gets wiped out. He'd have to explain to whoever is over him that he let a town go under because he was too busy elsewhere to send replacements to one of his companies that needed it because sickness had it at half strength."

No one saw the big hole in this idea, but I didn't expect them to. They were all too scared not to grab at any double-jointed idea that saved them from fighting redskins as well as being charged with drawing money from the government under false pretenses. These worries weighed the same to the Jacksonville militia.

"Collie," said Mulligan, "would you do the letter saying how sick we are?"

"No."

"Why in hell not!"

I waited until the last second before frustration turned into something worse. "Because," I answered, "it's not the military way to do it. That's what the morning report is for. If Lane didn't read it right, it'd be his neck. All we have to do is send him a report showing the number of men fit for duty is way down, and, since everybody knows about the Indians turning ugly around here, if we don't get replacements right away, then nobody here can be faulted for not wanting to make a stand when we can't do anything but get wiped out."

"The kid's right!" someone yelled. "How in hell can anybody goddamn blame us when the Siwashes got us ten to one?"

The rest of them just about exploded into agreement, and, that settled, the obvious next order of business was a drink all around because certainly no government could be dumb enough to get on us for being sick. It actually might have turned into a celebration if just then the normal street noises outside hadn't swelled up into something that sounded like the entire population of Jacksonville exploding. It didn't take a moment before everyone in the saloon, Tony and me included, was shoving and spilling our way out through the swinging doors in order to see what was going on, which was most of our women marching down the street in a slightly military formation.

They were heading out of town, all of them with the same grim look on their faces, paying absolutely no attention to the crowd cheering and laughing, and some of them booing, too, from the sidewalk. The only indication that the females recognized there was anyone else on the street was the sign carried by two of them that read, IF OUR MEN WON'T FIGHT—WE WILL!

Just about everybody's wife or mother was among them and armed with muskets, pepperboxes, hatchets, pitchforks, or old fowling pieces that probably had been unearthed from barn loft junk piles. I think it was Mrs. Burke who was actually flourishing a rusty saber. I saw Phoebe Hume in the thick of the group, and there was Elva, marching alongside, awkwardly cradling an enormous navy pistol over her shoulder, the smile that always seemed part of her freckled face replaced by what probably seemed to her to be a ferocious scowl but wasn't. When I sang out as she went past us, "Hey, wait a minute, Elva! We'll go with you," she couldn't help glancing over and then whooping back, "Just don't you worry, Collie Gibbs. We ain't too yellow to fight, even if you'n your friends are!"

Of course, Celina Sewell wasn't in the ranks. She was standing in front of the bank with Jabez Witham to whom she said something right after Elva had yelled her defiance to me. Then she turned back to watch with more contempt showing in her face than there was in the whole crowd.

By then the group had reached the end of the street and was marching out of town, heading for those hills where everyone figured the Indians had made camp until it was time to strike.

Tony said, almost to himself, "Strange, half the men here seem to have the grace to show shame, and the rest think it's the funniest thing they've ever seen."

Since there was no expression in his face, I asked, "And what do you think?"

He looked at me and said, "No matter how much pleasure you take in this, Collis, those are gallant and decent ladies who prize their homes so much they are willing to fight for them. But the men—now, where are you off to?"

"Be right back," I called over my shoulder. "Got to see Alben Hensley for a minute."

Which I did.

When I returned, Tony asked, "What on earth was that all about?"

"I told Alben I wanted to go along with the women as a war correspondent."

"Oh, my Lord."

"What's wrong with that? He was willing to let me go, but he put up a fight when I told him it was hazardous duty so I ought get at least twice the nickel an inch he's been paying me."

"Collis," Tony said, "can't you see that the fun is over?"

"No, it's not. There's no one out there who's going to hurt them."

"That just isn't the point! There's no jest in frightening a band of women to where they feel it's necessary to place their very lives in peril. And after they find that it was all for nothing, do you think that any of them will ever forgive their men for allowing them to do this? Collis, it's all too sad and ugly, and we've got to do something before it goes any further!"

He'd ended by almost pleading with me, but even that might not have pulled me down from my lunatic excitement if, just about then, I hadn't also heard another nearby voice saying the same kind of things but with so much anger in it that I had to look twice before the identity of the speaker sank in. It was my father, actually haranguing the men remaining on the sidewalk outside the bar, and, while he spoke, even some of the men who had gone back inside came out to join the knot around him.

He was appealing to them not to let the town die. I don't recall his exact words, but they centered on the shame that from now on would be connected with this place no matter if the day ended without injury to any of the women who'd just proven their belief in it. This was Father talking, telling them that even their sons wouldn't evade disgrace by moving away because whenever anyone thereafter mentioned the name of Jacksonville, the laughter that was sure to follow would always make them remember their fathers with disgust.

I'd never been so proud of him.

There was no need for a head count when he'd finished. Everyone listening to him just nodded in agreement that they had to go, and even the remainder of the militia coming out of the bar didn't bother with anything but heading after the womenfolk.

Tony said to me, "Your father is an extraordinarily fine man."

"The best," I agreed, and we started off for the hills, too.

33

THE MILITIA BROUHAHA started out as a lark and ended by leaving the taste of bile in my mouth. I'd been so wildly exhilarated by the way everything worked, that it wasn't until the women and the parties searching for them had all straggled back to town that I realized I'd absolutely sailed past the line decency should have drawn between sport and the ridicule of honest people. My belated view of how I'd acted stayed sour even without the embarrassing recollection of Tony's earnest effort to point it out to me.

The bitterness grew even after Father and I returned to our cabin. In asking Tony's whereabouts, he said, "I thought he was in the group that came down from the hills with us."

"No, I'm sure he wasn't, but it doesn't prove anything. There were people strung all over the place." I couldn't bring myself to tell him I suspected Tony had been so disgusted with me that he'd gone off to stay at one of his small hunting camps in the forest. To shift the subject, I added, "Father, I was awfully proud of you today. You gave the people here a real sense of belonging to Jacksonville."

I thought this description of his role that afternoon would please him, but, instead, he seemed troubled as he answered, "I'm not at all certain of that. They had to be brought near to a tragedy before they accepted their obligations as citizens." He thought for a moment and then, even more subdued, went on, "I don't think those men represented the better element, do you?"

"Some were. Sure."

"But they all had to be pushed into defending their homes."

"Maybe they can't be blamed for that. Maybe, deep down everyone feels this place can disappear just like all those ghost towns down in California that stopped being anything but a bunch of broken-down shacks after the gold ran out."

"The farming families? The merchants?"

"The farmers might stay on, but merchants go where there's money to be made. I don't believe I'd count on the businessmen unless this

really becomes the permanent big stopping point on the trail from the
North they all keep bragging about. Why are you so upset about it? Our
home is Philadelphia. You wouldn't want to spend the rest of your life
here, would you?"

"I'm not certain."

It struck me as odd that the question seemed to increase his uneasiness. His background couldn't possibly mesh with a place as rough as
this—but he was actually hesitating over the decision of whether he ever
wanted to go anywhere else again. Then he asked, "How do you feel
about it?"

"Well, I've enjoyed the things we've seen and done, but . . ." I
shrugged the rest of the answer.

"I couldn't blame you for not wanting to remain here, Collis. There
would be no reason for a young man of your breeding [*that* sent a stab
through me!], imagination, and, yes, ability to accept a small village as
his be-all and end-all. It wouldn't be fair to suggest it to you, and, as a
matter of fact, I'd be against it. But, as for me . . ." there was a short
and awkward laugh, "today's events all but ended my doubts that I
might comfortably remain here. It just may be that Jacksonville can
become a major trading post and the people who make it so will grow
into sound and solid citizens. It might even be that, in spite of their
initial attitude, they proved it this afternoon."

I couldn't find it in my heart to point out that it might be fine for
someone else to wait around until solidity struck these diggers and apple-
knockers, but he was as out of place among them as a thoroughbred
pulling a milk cart. He must have sensed this because something came
into his voice that urged me not to think less of him. "They listened to
me, Collis! Those rough men standing in front of the saloon looked up
to me, and when I said whatever it was that made them agree to go after
our women, not a one of them saw me in any way but as someone who
had a right to speak. It was a very strange sensation, Collis. Those people
not only respected me, they liked me enough to listen to what I had to
say."

"You were respected and liked in Philadelphia."

"Certainly I know that. But it wasn't at all the same. At home there
was the family and our friends who'd been leading the city for ever so
long. None of that was here, today. Don't you see, those people liked
me!"

I felt uncomfortable at seeing him without his normal reserve, so I
tried to bring the conversation to an end by agreeing, "Well, there's no

question but that the kind of work you're doing here sure beats your practice at home. You've helped a lot of people."

"I have, haven't I?" He studied me for a moment and then said, "Jabez Witham has asked me if he might put my name in nomination for town judge at the next election. This was even before this afternoon. A few days ago, in fact."

"Father," I said, "that's marvelous!" instinctively thinking that it certainly wasn't anything of the kind. If Jacksonville ever elected unworldly Dr. John Gibbs as its guiding hand, there were more reasons than ever to wonder about its future. It was something I'd mull over later, but, in the meantime, I rushed on, "I can't wait to brag about it to Elva and the boys!"

"Elva," he said.

"Elva is going to be prouder of you than anyone."

"You really care for her quite a bit, don't you?"

"Well, sure. I like her very much. To tell the truth, maybe if it weren't for her being so sweet on Sam Hume, I'd like her even more."

"Sam will never marry her, you know."

Something had happened to our conversation. "Father, what's this all about?"

"You know I rarely concern myself with gossip?"

"Of course." I didn't know what was coming next, but for some reason I knew it was going to be unpleasant.

"I've heard a particular story enough times that it's no longer possible to dismiss it as only rumor. Please forgive me, but I suppose this is as right an occasion as any to repeat it, no matter how much it may embarrass you."

"Go on, Father."

"They say that you are head over heels in love with that girl, but that she is, well, only another of young Hume's blanket mates."

This awful accusation whipped the day's sourness into something that left me trembling. "What a horrible thing to say!"

He went on, underestimating the shock his words had produced, which was a rare lapse for someone ordinarily as sensitive as my father. "She's a half-breed, Collis, and none of them has ever demonstrated the slightest trace of moral character."

"I don't want to hear this! Not at all! She's a fine, fine girl, one of the best human beings I've ever met." For a moment, I was damned near ready to cry.

"Your heart is running away with you," he said, becoming in that moment a stranger instead of the father I'd known all my life. "You are certainly intelligent enough not to close your eyes to the problems that mixing bloodlines produce in these children. Men much more experienced than you or I have said—and you must listen to them, Collis—that sooner or later they'll act in a way that proves they've inherited the worst of each strain. No one knows better than you that I have no bias against any man. I accept Indians for what they are. Some are even capable of conducting themselves almost as white men. But certainly no one should ignore the mischief that occurs when they breed with Caucasians!"

He paused, expecting a defense I couldn't make because I was aghast at these words from a man I'd always believed to be of the finest instincts no matter how ineffective I thought him in other matters. Where was the Philadelphia gentleman who had made me so proud that afternoon? Did he want the approval of these people so badly that he'd taken on their bigotry?

When I remained silent, he delivered what he evidently considered the most telling indictment. "I have it on very good authority that she was the chief instigator of this afternoon's shameful episode. It was she who roused our women into that grossly unfeminine display. It was your Miss Boudreau—and mark this, son—who was willing to lead a raid against her own people in order to achieve a place among us!"

This afternoon he'd praised the women to the townsmen for their spunk. Now, calling it a gross display made it clear that any reason would do to debase Elva. "Father," I said very quietly, "let's not talk any more about this right now."

"Why delay a mature discussion? We owe each other that much."

What could I say? This man, my father, whom I'd always loved no matter how I'd occasionally behaved toward him, was telling me things I considered pure venom. Fury would have swamped any answer I'd have made beyond what I actually said, which was, "Please. Some other time. My head is just pounding with everything that happened today."

Even so, he'd have kept at it if I hadn't added, "I think I'll go out for a while. Maybe the night air will help," and I walked over and picked my jacket off its peg. With my back still toward him, I said, "Don't worry about waiting up for me, I'll be in as soon as I feel better," and went out the door.

Once outside, I wasn't sure where I wanted to go, but since I didn't want to be alone with the thought, *He threw out Chung Lin, too,* I headed for the saloons, which were the only places in town still lit up. I passed by Lohmeyer's because that's where most of the militia hung out and I certainly didn't feel like discussing the day's events with any of them. The Bella Union was just as full, but, by then, I didn't care. I went in and worked my way through the crowd up to the counter and signaled to Henri Boudreau at the other end that I wanted a drink.

The place was so full of smoke that he was almost over to where I stood before I realized the bartender wasn't Boudreau but Richard Mulligan. Henri must have needed him to work that night because just about every man in town was at one saloon or another hashing over the day's events. When he faced me, looking unusually sullen, I guessed that someone must have explained to him how I'd played him for a fool, but I couldn't have cared less. "Didn't expect to see you here, Richard. Thought you'd be over at Lohmeyer's with the rest of the boys."

He didn't answer while he poured a drink from the bottle that served most of the customers in the place. But after he pushed the glass toward me, he said, "You son of a bitch."

"What's that?"

"You heard me, you son of a bitch. Get your drink and get the hell out. I'll quit before I pour two shots for a louse."

It was too much coming after that scene at home. I leaned over the bar, grabbed his filthy shirt in one hand and said, "You talk to me one more time that way, you gimpy little bastard, and I'll knock your head off."

There wasn't a speck of fear in his face as he pulled back, just hate. "Don't ever be walkin alone by yourself, Gibbs," he said, "cause sure as shit you'll be gettin a dose of lead if I'm anywheres around."

Threats from this mangy excuse for a man were more than I was going to stand right then. Pushing the other drinkers out of the way, I raced toward the open end of the bar, my only thought to get behind it and put my hands around Mulligan's throat.

He had the same idea. Running to meet me and yelling, "The skunk got me into this!" he was like a man gone mad. This caused my own head to clear, which was lucky. In that second I saw he'd snatched up one of the pistols Boudreau kept loaded and lying on the back shelf.

Henri saw it, too. His attention had been caught by the sudden drop in the crowd's noise, and when he understood that his bartender had a gun and was going after someone—I'm not certain that he ever knew it was me—he left his place at the other end of the bar and dove forward, stopping Mulligan by crashing into him, and both men fell out of sight underneath the counter.

We heard one screamed curse and then an explosion that deafened in that crowded room. This was followed by a silence that was louder than the sound of the gun going off.

Then we saw Mulligan slowly rise and reappear. He kept staring down at the floor and, finally, around at us and said, "Oh, Jesus Christ, he's dead." And with that he threw the pistol away and ran out through the saloon's swinging doors.

34

CERTAINLY, Elva couldn't have run the saloon, and since Jabez Witham's sheaf of signed notes proved he was owed more than the Bella Union could be sold for, no one blamed him for taking over the place a week or so after Henri Boudreau was killed. Also, the banker made a point of letting everyone know that out of the goodness of his heart he'd settled quite a large sum on the girl.

She told Tony what it was, and he told me. One hundred and fifty dollars, the grasping son of a bitch.

No matter. Phoebe Hume had just about adopted her as the daughter she'd never had, and the two of them were in their bakery from early to late six days a week turning out the breads, pies, and cakes the town liked so much. They were earning good wages because they sold most of what they baked, and anything left over went to Tommy's restaurant, where it was either remanufactured into something his coolie customers could appreciate or put in front of whichever drunken Occidentals showed up with the idea that a Chinese dinner was a prime way to end the night. Only God knew what was in the rest of the slop he served them.

It would have been nice if everything was as honestly bright as that sounds, but it wasn't. Not for any of us.

Mrs. Hume tried her best to keep Elva too busy to think, but whenever the girl had a few minutes away from the oven, she'd sink deep into a sad silence. On top of the pain about her father, Sam, after a week of playing Big Brother, had gone back to Celina.

I didn't have the heart to try and reach her or even to be in her company. Not that she ever reproached me—I just couldn't ignore the guilt over Henri's death that wouldn't quit clutching at my insides. I tried putting in long hours at the *Sentinel*, even learning to set type whenever there wasn't a scrap of news left to report, but work had just about as much success helping me forget as it did with Elva, which was damned little.

As for Tony, there was a flatness that had come over him, too, that had him down to where he was just about ready to leave. He was still boarding at our cabin, but he was there as seldom as I was during that period. Even hunting wasn't the fun it had been. As he told Sam one day, "There's really not much point to killing animals whose meat rots before it can be sold, is there?"

They'd been walking together through the town on one of the rare mornings when Sam wasn't still asleep after being with Celina the night before. The sharp way Tony spoke shook Sam out of the tree for a moment. "What's the matter," he asked, "you sored up about somethin?"

"I don't think I'd use just that phrase. 'Fed up' might be a shade more precise."

"Over me? Hell, Tony, if it bothers you that I been doin the town work, let's switch off for a while."

"Would that include taking your place on top of Miss Sewell?"

"Come on, boy. Whoa up, there."

"Well put. That's one of the graces I've learned to admire in you Americans; your phrasings are absolute models of brevity. An Englishman might have gone on for ten minutes before suggesting that I tend to my own affairs."

The bewilderment instead of anger in Sam's eyes perversely increased Tony's frustration with the emptiness he felt in his own life. "Sam," he said, "I've had enough. I've rather decided to leave."

"Where to? Back home?"

"I'm not certain. Perhaps not England. But I've had it in this place." When he saw that Sam took this as if he were turning his back on him, he added, "It isn't you or Collis or anyone else. It's just that, for me, there's so little here any longer."

"What's the difference between today and last week? You weren't all that upset then. Is it your arm?"

"No. Or maybe it is. Oh, I don't know what the bloody hell it is. I feel so damned burnt out inside."

"You'll get over it."

"I don't think so. Not while I'm here, at any rate. Everything I'm about seems utterly pointless. If at least I were able to hold on to the pretense of accumulating investment information—but that won't wash much longer, will it?"

"Well, hell, Tony," he said, putting his arm around the other's shoulder, "you got to do what you think is right. I'll miss you like thunder, but there isn't a lick of sense in tellin you to keep on at somethin you don't believe in."

"Thanks, Sam," he answered, grateful for the willingness to understand and accept his malaise. "I suppose I'm acting the tiresome old maid that Collis always says that I am."

"Collie's only funnin. You know that. You don't take him serious, do you?"

"Of course not. As a matter of fact, I'd rather he felt well enough to point it out again for me."

"He's got his dauber down, that's for sure."

"And this just may be the winter of our discontent."

"That's crazy. It's already April."

"I know that, you bloody big fool. It was a quote."

"Your friend Shakespeare?"

"Probably. At any rate it's always trotted out to cover times like these when there doesn't seem to be anything else to say. Boring, actually."

The conversation had turned into an older and easier path, making Tony feel better because it no longer seemed to him that he was so isolated. One of the things that has always marked friendship with Sam Hume is that you never feel alone.

There was also that streak of awareness in him. Recognizing that Tony's feelings might not be so mired in the deep brown cods that they couldn't be raised again, he kept on with the better things that made up their days. "That Elva," he said, "her'n Ma don't have no discontent time. They sure hit it off. Ma says that up until that gal came, she'd only guessed how nice it could have been with a daughter."

"Are the other women still so spiteful to her?"

"Ma don't let 'em get even started. She tells anybody unsheathin their claws that if they weren't so mad at their men about the Petticoat Army, they wouldn't need to be takin it out on Elva."

Tony smiled for the first time that day. "She was quite the spitfire. That lovely military face she thought she'd assembled."

Sam laughed. "She sure as hell can be cute and spunky as a basket of pups." This must have set him to defensive comparisons because he added, "Tony, as good as Elva is, and she's champion good, I wish there was some way you'd get to know Celina better. She ain't, isn't the way you think at all."

"Which is . . .?"

"Well, you know. You all see her flirtin and makin up to people and then they gasbag about it to make themselves important. But that's just her way. Underneath she's one of the most shy people you'd ever meet. Tony, sometimes that girl hurts real bad over how some of the men talk to her. She'll never tell me who because she knows damn right well I'd be lookin them up, but sometimes I think I ought to just purely take her away from all these damn fools."

This was the last yank needed to pull Tony out of himself. "You aren't thinking of marrying her, are you?"

"Not fixin to marry nobody. I got a real long way to go before that happens. But one thing's for sure; if I was about to even get close to thinkin about marriage, I could do a hell of a lot worse than Celina Sewell. You can't even begin to believe how much love and sweetness and fun that girl's got in her."

He certainly was correct about Tony not having the capacity to accept Celina as the vision in crinoline he saw. Tony thought for a moment before saying, "You're probably right. Perhaps none of us are quite fair where she's concerned because we really don't know her, do we?"

"It'd be so great if you got to be friends with her."

"I'd like that," answered Tony, feeling that the only thing he'd like less was a toothache.

"Would you really?"

"Of course."

"Then I'll tell you what. No sense in thinkin about work today, so how about eatin supper with us? Me'n her are going to Tommy's, and it'd be just the three of us if you'd come, too."

"I'd love to, Sam, but really . . ."

"Oh the hell with goin up to the hills. You're the one that's said we got more meat than Witham's got money. Besides, look at the thunderheads all over the sky. By tomorrow it'll be rainin like piss pourin out of a boot and you'd be beatin back out of the woods like a drowned cat!"

I know all this because Tony told me some of it, Sam mentioned what he remembered, and the important part was observed by Tommy in his restaurant.

Dinner at Chung Lin's wasn't exactly the treat Sam had promised. For one thing, the coolies at the *fan tan* table in the back room were noisier than usual, or at least that's the way it seemed to Tony. He asked Tommy about it, but, instead of padding out to calm them down, he shrugged and said quietly, "They argue over more than the game, but not fight— just words." Tony rightfully accepted this as a reference to the growing rivalry in the area between the Hong Kongs and the Cantonese, although he couldn't help wondering how much wishful thinking was involved in Tommy's verdict.

His doubts also extended to the couple sitting across the table from him. Sam, oblivious to the sounds of the quarreling gamblers, was positively cooing with the pleasure of having Celina sit by his side. He'd occasionally offer her a tidbit from his plate and then sit back and watch her eat it as if something precious was taking place. Her running comments on the place, its food, snips of town gossip, or even the demand that he quit crowding so closely to her, all affected him as if he'd just heard some of the smartest observations anyone had ever perpetrated. Even the occasional apparently artless mentions of Jabez Witham's fumbles at her didn't put a ruffle in Sam's mooning.

Naturally, this made Tony acutely uncomfortable, but Celina was smart enough to try and treat Sam's behavior as a joke that they all shared. "Now you cut it out, Sammy!" she said after one of his clumsy attempts to rest his hand on her thigh. "Tony here is gonna be bound to think there's somethin serious goin on between us." She was looking at him while she said it, so Tony guessed this was supposed to indicate that these displays embarrassed her as much as it did him.

Out of civility, Tony gave her back one of those tight grimaces that said to anyone who knew him that he wished he were somewhere else, but she read it as signaling she'd completed another conquest. From then on, she didn't trouble to mask an amused tolerance that lasted until dinner was over and they were sipping the tea Tommy served them along with a bland smile that showed how honored he felt to have his establishment graced by such radiant young love.

Nor did she bother to speak more quietly as Tommy walked away. "I don't ever trust a Chinee. They're so darn sneaky."

Tony felt a gentle tug in his heart at this first gap in her shrewdness, so when Sam began explaining again their ties, he cut in with what he thought was a rather nice way of letting her dash herself on the rocks. "You may be right, Celina," he said, "about most of the Orientals here because, as I understand it, none of them possess the slightest loyalty to America. Except Chung Lin. And he worries quite a bit about this state of affairs." Tony estimated this was just enough to keep Sam quiet while letting the door stay ajar for her.

"I don't care what you say, all of them are the same. And that one most of all," she said, nodding her head toward the doorway through which Tommy had disappeared. "Whether you know it or not, he's in partners with Mr. Witham in lots of things, and no matter how often I try to get Mr. Witham to watch out, that dirty Chinee keeps bamboozlin him six ways to Sunday."

She continued, not at all understanding the silence that followed this description of Tommy. "I told Mr. Witham dozens of times that he's not gettin close to an honest whackin-up from the mines they own." She stared at each of them as if she were considering whether to trust them with the next momentous secret and then went on. "That goes for this very place, too! Of course, Mr. Witham is the main owner, he's got tons of money sunk into it, but that Chinee is the one gettin all the cream. The only reason I let you take me here was that I was hopin to catch that sneak at whatever he's up to, and them yellow monkeys gabblin out back sure prove that it's nothin good!"

Tony let out a low whistle to show how impressed he was with her brightness and loyalty, but Sam, after looking over at him in puzzlement, said, "Seelie, you got a pile of wrong ideas. Tommy—"

"I have not!" Flaring up because her knowledge of Jabez Witham's affairs was being questioned, she continued, "And I'll tell you somethin else, Sammy Hume, if I was you, I wouldn't bet that your pa is always gonna be the high muckety muck in his own mine, neither!"

The mention of his father caused Sam to withdraw into himself. "I couldn't give less of a damn," he said.

"You better had ought to. If you or your ma figure that Sweetwater mine to be yours someday, you'd be smart to be doin somethin about it."

"Seelie, let's get back to Tommy."

"Sure. Talk about your Chinee friend or anything else you want. But don't forget that man's got a hate for you [resurrecting the day Sam had thrown the banker down the bowling alley lane] and you'd be the last person in the world that he'd worry over if some kind of bottom was to drop out. I'm tellin tales out of school, Sam Hume, but you know why."

There wasn't fond doting or anything else readable on Sam's face now. He leaned back and said, "You're tellin me somethin besides old Witham doesn't like me?"

"Gee, are you ever dumb," she answered.

For the life of him, Tony couldn't understand why she was heading far beyond a flirt's normal encouragement of rivalry between her suitors. Now she was out to fan the strongest anger in Sam toward the banker that she could. Where was the gain?

"He's takin advantage of your family, Sammy." Her nod was an emphatic affirmation of her own judgment. "When that man gets through pickin your pa's bones, there ain't goin to be a thing left. Right now he's got so many notes signed by your pa—they even been buyin county warrants together—and he says 'sure' to a loan every time your pa gets another itch about more machinery he thinks he needs, that if they ever got called, no mine in this whole damn place has got enough gold on hand to pay them off."

Even though he didn't know where it was going, Tony thought he'd help it along. "That's a fairly strong statement, Celina. Jackson County mines are assumed to be worth quite a bit, aren't they?"

"That don't help if somebody tells a miner one night to get the money up next mornin! You people here are so damn dumb." She shook her head, and in spite of his dislike of her, Tony couldn't help but admire the cascade of her hair as she shook her head in disgust at the blindness of our locals. "You all keep forgettin that you can't eat chunks of quartz. Gold ain't money until it's been dug out of the ground."

Sam said, "I didn't know he was signin notes. I thought it was a partnership all the way."

"You'd better be knowin it. Mr. Witham puts his share up in cash, and for his share, Mr. Hume don't leave that bank one time without his John Hancock on another of them papers that's stacked in the middle drawer of the desk back there in the vault."

Tony, considering that enough profit had been reaped from the evening, put in, "Celina, of course Sam appreciates your concern, but it seems to be a rather painful subject for him and—"

"Butt out, Tony," Sam said. "How far's this thing gone, Seelie?"

It was hard to read whether the quick flash in her eyes was wariness or triumph. "I'm truly sorry if I riled you up, Sammy, but you can't blame me for worryin about what happens to you."

"Never mind that. Witham's fixin to push Pa over the edge?"

His quiet tones told her she must have gone on a shade too long. "I didn't say that. All I said was he was signin everything put in front of him and there ain't no businessman anywhere, let alone Mr. Witham, that'll keep forkin out money without someday callin it in and. . . ." The rest of her explanation was never delivered. Sam stood up and said, "Tony, you take care of Celina. He's home now and I'm goin to talk to him." He paused, thinking about the coming scene with his father. "Not that he'll listen but I owe it to him to say somethin before that weasel quits flickin the dice. Tony'll take you home, Seelie, and I probably won't be around tonight. Maybe tomorrow." The fondness came back as he added, "I know it wasn't easy for somebody as decent as you to be talkin about your boss that way and I'm obliged." He bent over, intending to kiss her cheek, but she turned to him and their lips met in what began as a farewell but ended in something much more.

When he'd gone, she turned back to Tony and said, "I hope he don't take it wrong what I told him."

"He won't. He's grateful that you thought enough of him to offer the caution."

She looked briefly down at the table and then back across it. "Sam takes too much for granted. All I was doin was what I'd a done for anybody I liked. I wanted him to know that maybe he could keep his pa out of trouble. That's all. But Sam probably thinks this means that him and me are, well, you know."

"Know what? I'm afraid you've lost me."

"Well, you know. Sam's always wantin it to be more serious than it is between us. You see the way he acts. And when I make one mistake and let somethin slip out like I did, then he's surer'n ever that I'm his girl. And I'm really not, Tony." Her big eyes were opened as far as they'd go as she looked up. "I just think he's one of the nicest boys I ever met. Honest. But he ain't exactly what I'd want all my life." She lowered her glance as she added, "If I ever do fall real hard for a man, he'd be somebody like you who's been somewhere else besides this pokey town."

Evidently she felt it was precisely the right chord because she continued, "I been in cities before. San Francisco, for instance. And I know what all the good things are but I'm only gonna share them with somebody else that knows it, too."

"Someone like me?" Tony asked, not quite believing that her approach could be this bald.

"Oh, no," she laughed. "How could I ever be goin with Sam's best friend, which is what you are. Right?"

"I suppose so."

"Ain't you sure?"

"Celina, I'm not certain of anything. Just before this I would have sworn that you and Sam were more in love than any two people I've ever met."

"Oh, I like him," she repeated. "Don't get me wrong. It's just that he wants it to be more, but there's a whole world I got to see before I settle down, and Sam gets so serious right away. You know what I mean, don't you?"

At that point, Tony didn't. She had intended exactly the effect on Sam that had been produced. The possibility had been established that her ties to the banker weren't so emotional that they couldn't be broken, and now she was probing to find out how far Sam's best friend could be trusted in whatever came next. *Or, perhaps more simply,* he thought, *her vanity requires setting friends against each other for her favors.* But, since he wasn't sure that her need for admiration wasn't the only thing on her mind, he said aloud, "No one would blame you for wanting to see more of the world than Jacksonville but, on the other hand, there's—"

"On the other hand, my foot!" She stood up and then, surprisingly, giggled at the effect of her rudeness. "Come on, English boy, you're supposed to be takin me home, not keepin me up all night gassin about what I should and shouldn't be blamed for."

As Tony rose in response, Tommy came over to the table and asked him, "Sam all right?"

"Certainly. Mr. Hume left to tend to a few family affairs. You restaurant people do fret whenever your guests leave suddenly, don't you?"

Their eyes met long enough for Tommy to catch that something quite different was being told him, so he bowed ever so slightly while saying, "I hope dinna was good to taste," meaning that he'd wait for the details.

She said as they went out through the door, "That Chinee boy gives me a bad feelin. I'm goin to tell Mr. Witham he'd really be better off with a closer watch on him."

"That might be a sound idea," answered Tony, wondering at her capacity to forget that within the last half hour she'd mentioned having already delivered this warning and, more, it had been conveyed to a man whom, a few minutes later, she'd described as a source of danger to her joint interests with Sam.

"There's something very sneaky about him," she continued.

"I've felt it, too," he agreed.

"I wouldn't put it past him to be havin all kinds of ideas. You know," she went on, modestly lowering her voice, "I heard in town that he's brought some Chink women here that he, well, uses for immortal purposes."

Immortal?

"And Tony, I wouldn't be surprised if he gets ideas about white women, too. Did you notice him lookin at me?"

"If I had," Tony said, "I'd certainly have put him in his place."

"That Chinee better ought not look at me that way when Sam is around."

"I'll bet he wouldn't. He'd try that only when a cripple like myself is with you."

"Tony," she said, taking his hand as they walked, "you're better lookin with one arm than just about any other man around here with two. You're just set on bein hard on yourself. Sam tells me that all the time."

"Do you really feel that way?"

"I sure do." She squeezed his palm ever so gently, and neither said anything further until they had reached the house she and her mother rented off California Street. Once there and before Tony could say good night, she whispered, "Wait here."

Less than a minute later she was back out again and still whispering. "Ma's asleep. If you're real quiet, she won't hear a thing." When he drew back, she added in normal tones, "Don't worry. She sleeps like a damn log."

He'd been wrong to accept that anyone, even one as brassy as Celina Sewell, wouldn't be satisfied with so much headway in a single night. "Are you insane?" he asked.

She giggled at his inability to believe his great good luck. To reassure him, she put out her hand again to take his, but he stepped away. "Celina, I'm afraid not."

A satisfactory explanation occurred to her almost immediately. "What are you afraid of? Sam?"

"Not really."

Thrusting her face toward his, studying him, she said, "I'm a son of a bitch. You don't like girls."

The contempt he'd been holding in check all night burst loose. "You wretched little tart. Isn't it just possible . . ."

At that point another voice came through the darkness. "Seelie, is that you, girl?"

"Oh God," she said, "it's him again."

Tony thought she meant Sam, but it was Jabez Witham lurching along the pathway from the street, tripping over bushes, and so drunk that Tony thought the man was desperately sick until he got a whiff of the smell of raw whiskey that enveloped him like a cloud. Not paying a bit of attention to Tony's presence, he said, while holding on to the doorpost for support, "Seelie, girl, I've been thinking about you all night and looking for you everywhere and where you been, because I really need you, girl."

"You could a saved your trouble," she said. And then contempt as sharp as Tony's had been a few moments ago came into her voice, "You goddamn drunk old billygoat, I told you to quit pawin after me!"

"Aw, now, Seelie."

"Seelie nothin! You don't leave me be, you can be gettin somebody else to tend to your business. I'm warnin you, Jabez, I'm goin to tell your wife, you see if I don't!"

Now she was raging mad. Tony backed into the shadows, wanting to get away from the two of them as quickly as possible. Seeing this, she screamed at him, "Shittin English nelly! Wouldn't know what to do with a woman if she put it in his face! You ain't too good to go after Sam's girl and you know why? Cause you're in love with *him*, that's why!"

He'd have smashed his fist into her mouth, but that was the moment Witham chose to throw up the rotgut he'd been drinking. Bent over by the retching spasms that seized him, trousers fouled with spew, he then pitched forward, face first, into his own vomit.

"You help him, nelly. Maybe he'll let you kiss him," she said and walked into her house, slamming the door shut behind her.

35

IF YOU'VE EVER WATCHED a Chinese businessman do sums on an abacus, his fingers are a blur of motion and the click click of its beads sounds like a volley of remote infantry fire. As Tommy told it, that's pretty much how the thoughts and concerns were whirring through his head while he was on his way into town to make the required monthly tax payment to our county sheriff, Dutch Westheimer.

The recollection of Sam's troubles, revealed at the table last night, was smothered under the pile of problems gnawing away at him. His store was going along like sixty, but he was the one who stocked its shelves, kept the accounts straight, and made sure the restaurant had a reliable stream of supplies. His new mine was yielding more gold dust than he'd even admitted to us, let alone his partner, Jabez Witham, but the coolies working it were as helpless without direction as a flock of cackling hens. There were times when he remembered the shoe factory of his early San Francisco days as an easy place.

As for his taxes, he was scared silly that they were going to end up beggaring him. Oregon had enacted a levy of four dollars per month on every Chinese and Kanaka miner within its borders, and to Tommy, this loomed as a possible beginning of a series of state laws that could return him to the brutal uncertainty of a houseboy's lot. That was a prime worry. Given time and peace of mind, he felt that if he worked maybe twice as many hours each day, he'd get through the other concerns.

Naturally, this set him to thinking about a possible deal with the scoundrel who held the office of sheriff. *Maybe Westheimer, in exchange for a gross sum larger than the dollar a head that was his share of the state's levy, could be persuaded to count just every other Sojourner during his periodic visits.* The abacus in his brain began to whirr along even more rapidly. After adding the coolies forwarded by his San Francisco agents to the work force he'd brought with him from China, his employees numbered approximately 600, leaving him with a monthly tax bill of $2,400. Tempting Westheimer into cutting his census count in half in exchange for an additional $600 under the table for himself would leave Tommy with a few extra dollars to hide away against the day when the white officials decided to demand everything in sight.

But, after the last bead clicked in place, Tommy realized that there was no safe way to offer the bribe. Westheimer couldn't be trusted not to brag in the barrooms over how he'd raised his own salary or, even worse, mentioning the new arrangement to Banker Witham to pry another increase in whatever closing his eyes earned him from that quarter.

Since Tommy had never seen a daydream return a nickel's worth of profit, he turned his thinking to other channels. He wanted to make another trip to China, but Witham, no matter how often Tommy mentioned additional profits, didn't think it was indicated. "Stick to your knitting, son," the banker had told him. "A bird in the hand is worth two in the bush." Witham felt he had one hell of an original way with a phrase.

But he *wanted* to go to China! The first trip had yielded him something even greater than money; it had given the former Cantonese wharf rat a sense of prestige. Rentals from the plot of land he'd bought in his family's village had made him a landlord. Now he wanted to buy more land and, given a fair wind, the right wife.

He saw the future Mrs. Chung Lin as a girl of quality, teetering on small bound feet, submissive but cheerful, moral but receptive to the idea of adventures in bed, and, although she would work hard alongside him, she'd glow with an illusion of helplessness. He was convinced that such a woman existed on a farm somewhere near his village. Maybe I was wrong about the only thing inside his head being an abacus.

These were the thoughts (as he remembered them for me) that occupied him to the point that he was surprised when he discovered he'd walked himself right to the front of the sheriff's office. Even more surprising, his partner, Jabez Witham, came out through the door and, seeing him, went over to say, "Howdy, Lin," which was an unusual thing for him to do. Out of respect for public policy, they never nodded when they passed each other on the street.

"Good morning, sir," he answered, the sight of his partner's face, puffy in the morning sunlight, reminding him to question the houseboy hired by the banker's wife as to whether Witham was a secret drinker and if his hunger for Celina Sewell had ever been fed. This would be useful information in light of the enmity Tommy had read in her eyes last night in his restaurant.

"Chung," said the banker, "I've been thinking. Maybe we drove a mite too hard a bargain. Would it be any help if I raised you, well, say a couple more percent out of my share?"

Tommy bowed his head briefly at this unexpected display of generosity, brought on, he was sure, by the banker's awareness that the man who counts the receipts is the senior partner in any business. He'd just been issued a veiled threat that made him more certain than ever his decision not to offer Westheimer a bonus had been a wise one. Aloud, he said, "I much happy with my share. Now I have seven hundred dollar for old age." He considered this a safe amount to name because it represented the fraction of his earnings that he kept in the banker's vault.

"Well, Chung, I don't know. This miner tax must be hitting you pretty hard."

This told Tommy there might be something even more behind the offer. The banker knew as well as he did that the head tax, plus a healthy heaping of interest, was being passed on to all the coolies in their employ. "If," he answered, "I no play *fan tan*, I have all dollars I ever need. This is from Mr. Banker Witham and I have many thanks for Mr. Banker Witham."

Another fiction. It would have taken an earthquake to change Tommy from dealer to player. Although the risks at this game were fifty-fifty, players could lose and dealers couldn't, so long as they had a partner's wallet at their disposal.

"All right, boy, but whenever you get enough sense to quit gambling away your money, I'll be there to stand behind you."

Wondering where the root lay for this uncharacteristic offer, Tommy filed it alongside the others he'd put aside for future contemplation. "I much honored," he said.

After the banker left, he went inside to pay over the pouch of gold dust that lay hidden in the hollow belt wrapped around his waist and underneath the loose folds of his blouse. Hefting it in his hand, the sheriff asked, "What were you and old Witham chinnin about?"

"Mr. Banker Witham asked for China boy do laundry."

"Be goddamn if that old bastard ain't gettin to be rich enough to hire somebody to wipe his ass pretty soon."

"Ah-h-h," said Tommy, sucking in his breath to show appreciation for this display of wit.

"Your men are keepin pretty busy?" asked the sheriff with an elaborate display of disinterest in the answer.

"We work much, but dust thin. Soon, no more dust, no more work."

"Sure, not," said the sheriff. "I'll just bet you ain't taken in more'n a dime a day for yourself. Goddam heathens takin away money that belongs to white men."

"Ah-h-h," Tommy hissed again for the same reason.

"Ah, my ass. You better get the hell out of here and get to doin some diggin, yourself. I got a feelin next month you're liable to find the head tax goin up because of all the expenses in this here goddamn office."

This was Westheimer's invariable ending to their monthly conversations, so Tommy bowed and left, realizing again that this man's greed never could be satisfied, no matter how many pouches of dust were poured down its throat. Then, as he went about his remaining errands, the other worries came crowding back through the door opened by the sheriff's warning and the banker's puzzling offer. *Maybe he'd been unwittingly nourishing the town's belief that he was reaping a white man's profit!*

He remembered how foolishly he had paraded his ability to Witham shortly after their partnership in the mine had begun. Pointing out the time that would be lost by his laborers in traveling each day from their lodgings to the pit site, he'd figured out a deal to buy, for a few dollars, the buildings used by the miners who'd been working the claim. Witham had agreed and, after it worked out just the way he said it would, patted him on the back for his thrift and good business sense. Still too young to resist being told how smart he was, Tommy had found a dozen ways within the next few weeks to remind the banker of his acumen.

Incidentally, those pats would have been delivered with ten times the force if Witham had ever learned the real reason for Tommy's suggestion of the purchase. The very first night, before any of the coolies had been assigned a place for their sleeping mats, he had set the dullest-witted of them all, a man named Wong Back Fong, to the job of sweeping the top layer off the dirt floor. Tommy's guess had been absolutely on the mark that the former tenants had followed the nightly practice among white miners of clearing the day's diggings in a blower before the fire. Almost a thousand dollars in gold had been washed out of Wong's sweepings.

It was only the beginning of his profits. The mine they'd taken over was a deep hole in the level ground between a fork off the Little Applegate River and one of its creeks. Once the former owners had dug below creek level, the amount of water seeping into it discouraged them into quitting, and they'd figured that, for once, someone laid it on the banker's eye when he actually forked over a few good dollars for the worthless claim. This might have been an accurate verdict if it had been anyone but Tommy behind the purchase.

He didn't know too much about mining, but he always had the kind of common sense that steered him to where the dollars lay. I'm not saying white miners might not have reached the same answers that he did, but there were very few in those days who'd put out anywhere near the same amount of time and effort Tommy would to further his goal of being *someone*. He had one of his workmen build a rough wooden pump that, after a week's worth of starts and stops, actually did the job of sucking out just enough mud to let his coolies get down into the pit and fill their buckets. These pails of paydirt were hoisted by hand up to ground level and run through a once-broken and abandoned sluice that had been repaired by the same carpenter who'd built the pump.

"Ah-h-h!" He hissed out a deep despairing breath. The fear that was always waiting beneath the surface had just poked up its snout. If the news of his mine's fat profits ever got out, not even Mr. Witham could have kept the whites from using their guns to drive his coolies away from it. At that time, the law didn't offer the slightest bit of protection to the Chinese.

They were disliked because they were so different. Their color, almond-shaped eyes, pigtails, preference for opium over alcohol, and *fan tan* over faro added up to too much to digest. Worst of all, coolies were capable of extracting gold from ground that everyone else had discarded as worthless. This particular trait often caused dislike to boil up past hate and into the kind of violence that would have gotten the attention of any lawman who gave the slightest damn beyond collecting the monthly head tax that Orientals paid in exchange for being allowed to work. There may have been some officers like these in other camps but not in Jacksonville. Certainly not Dutch Westheimer. He just barely tolerated Tommy on the day he paid his taxes.

Mistreatment of the Chinese was as ordinary and acceptable a part of a western town's life as the backyard privy. The "Coolie Bank," for example, was a bad general joke that meant that whenever the need for drinking money got a bit too onerous for some oaf, he'd hide out on the hill where Judge Hanna later built his house and rob the first Sojourner who came down the lonely trail separating Chinatown from the rest of the place. Often, out of cussedness, the robber also beat the victim senseless, but no coolie ever had the nerve to file a complaint. Especially after the way the sheriff discharged his duty when Wah Lee was murdered.

It happened right after three of our locals left the saloon on an afternoon when they'd run out of money but not yet the capacity for what struck them as fun. The sport that occurred next to these drunks was cutting off a Chinaman's pigtail, and, unfortunately for Wah Lee, this was also the day he'd picked to mourn the death of his father. He'd just gotten the sad news from one of the men in Tommy's latest labor shipment, and, since there was no way he was going to be able to visit the grave, he picked a mound out toward the hills as a proper spot to hallow. While walking toward it, scattering the papers on which were written his prayers, he was caught by the three men.

Two held him while the third, roaring with laughter, hacked off his queue. Probably because of the mood he was in—he had loved and respected his father—Wah Lee submitted to the ordeal with somber dignity, and this, of course, diminished the fun of his tormentors. Who the hell was this Chink to behave with such reserve? They drew their guns and pantomimed that he'd better execute one of those comical Chinese dances. To add spirit to the performance, they started firing at his feet.

It added too much to his grief. Instead of capering away from the bullets kicking up spurts of dirt around him, he stood silently in front of his captors, eyes not on the ground, where a properly meek Oriental should have kept them, but staring gravely at each of them in turn. Because this wasn't the sport they'd been looking for, one of the men raised his gun and shot away half of Wah Lee's head.

A townswoman saw all this take place, and as soon as the murderers had gone off to find some more fun, she headed for the sheriff's office to report the crime. Trembling with indignation after Westheimer let her know he was just about as interested as if a stray dog had been run over by a wagon, she said then that she'd lodge a complaint the next time the circuit judge sat in Jacksonville. That was exactly what it took to lift him up out of his chair. When he found the three, he assessed them twenty-five dollars for "discharging firearms within the city limits," and the four of them, plus an onlooker who happened to have the ante, stopped at the nearest bar to drink up the amount of the fine.

The incident was still fresh in Tommy's mind, which was one more, and maybe the most important, reason why he was so worried that morning. If he couldn't protect his labor force, then it was going to be a matter of just a short while before he wouldn't be able to protect his profits.

That's when he thought of Sam Hume.

36

AFTER HE'D MADE his rounds of the mining kitchens, there wasn't much to occupy Sam while Celina was working, so he'd taken to looking me up after I'd finished whatever newspaper business I had scheduled. Generally, except for the days we went to press, that meant we were together more than we'd been in a long time, which was fine with me because I certainly wasn't finding it easy to visit with Tony or Elva. Although I was growing to like newspapering, there's just no way to keep at it all day long in a small town, even when the publisher is as bone lazy as Alben Hensley.

Besides, it was fun spending time with Sam again. Not that it was a case of misery loving company—unlike Tony, he confined his judgments to calling me a weasel and then we'd go on to something else.

He and I were sitting on the bench outside the barber shop the morning after he'd left Tommy's restaurant in order to warn his father about what Jabez Witham had in mind. "I kept on him, Collie," he told me, "and it wasn't easy because I was humblin myself and he knew it, too. He was just goin out of his way to be nasty. In fact, once he grumbled to Ma that he guessed that what really had me in a stew was my worry whether I was ever goin to get a share out of that mine.

"Even that didn't stop me, bad as it was for him to say it. I'd tell him that Witham was fixin to strip him clean, and he'd growl over to Ma that her sellin pies to the saloons wasn't right, that she ought to be ready to live like a lady."

"How did your mother take all this?" I asked.

"She just kept cluckin at both of us, so much anxiousness in her eyes that I hated seein it, although it didn't faze Pa one bit. He was just totally deaf, dumb, and blind to anything I'd offer or what Ma was tryin to tell him by the way she looked at him. When I finally gave up and walked out the door, I heard him say how funny it was when people waited until after he'd made his strike to worry about him. I was going to turn back and tell him what a horse's ass he was, but it would have hurt Ma and it wouldn't have made any difference to him."

"Well," I said after thinking it over, "at least you can't be faulted for not having tried. You did the right thing, no matter how it turned out."

He shook his head. "It just wasn't good enough. Deaf as a post. Maybe there's something else I ought to find that'd head him back to where he used to be."

"Like what? Going to Witham and telling him to please treat your pa with Christian charity?"

"I might sort of suggest that it'd be healthier if he'd back off."

"Come on, Sam. Do you think he ever forgot how you treated him? Nothing would make him happier than your doing that. He wouldn't wait five minutes to let it get out that you've threatened him again, and then he'd be over to Westheimer's to pay for some deputies to go up one side of you and down the other."

He laughed, but there wasn't any pleasure in it. "He's not man enough to try something like that out in the open. He knows damn well I'd be back to push his face in." He thought for a moment. "Maybe that's why he's goin after Pa."

"You're not thinking. Witham goes after anything or anyone where there's a dollar to be made. Your father's just one more pebble on the beach." And then, seeing Tommy crossing the street toward us, I called, "Hey, storekeeper. Out for some air?"

He waited until he reached where we sat, and when he stood before us he answered, "Day too nice for store."

We both knew there was as much chance of his promenading for his health as there was of our growing pigtails. "What's up, Tommy?" Sam asked.

"I have business."

"With us?"

"Yes." But I noticed he kept his eyes on Sam.

"Grab a seat," I suggested, sliding down to give him room.

He didn't bother to reply to this, although he bobbed his head to acknowledge the courtesy. "Maybe we go to my store." And then, so the town wouldn't see what might appear to be three friends out for a walk, he added, "For me, more errand," meaning we ought to go our separate ways to meet at his place.

Sam wasn't having any. "Come on, Tommy," he said, standing and draping his arm over the slender shoulder, "let's do it right now. Later on something important like bein asked to be governor of Oregon might come up, and then I wouldn't have the time to give you all the confabulation you need."

Tommy had made it clear that my presence wasn't a matter of life and death to this conference, but I figured we were close enough to be told to scat if I was in the way. "Let's go," I told them. "Studying you two weasels talk business at each other is the kind of education a growing boy like me needs."

In addition to his discomfort over being seen on the street with us, Tommy was in a hurry. We were no sooner seated in his restaurant and sipping at our thimblefuls of tea than he took a chair across the table from us and announced, "Plenty problems," which we took seriously because the way he said it left no room for teasing, and it was unlike him to sit unbidden with us even in his own restaurant. "Anything we can do, Tommy?" I asked.

"Yes," he answered, which was another mark that something was plaguing him. He generally beat around the bush for quite a while before letting anyone know what was on his mind.

"Spill it," said Sam.

"You know how Wah Lee was murder?"

"Sure. Everybody does." Sam's answer was delivered in a way that left me squirming because it was intended to remind me of one of my adolescent attempts at editorial humor. Among other gems, I'd written a paragraph that went something like, "John Chinaman no likee Yreka, Marysville, or Auburn. He likee Oregon where Melican Man no catchee Celestials. So John Chinaman tell fliends come here chop chop."

I hadn't signed it, but there were few in town who didn't recognize its author, and I realized how mean it was after a few citizens had congratulated me on its effectiveness. To compound the felony, Alben Hensley refused to print the angry description of Wah Lee's death that I also turned in that week. "No use offending advertisers," he told me, "by looking like we're out to criticize our sheriff and a few high-spirited boys."

I cleared my throat and said, "Tommy, I'm really sorry about that editorial."

"Not read," he answered, but I knew damned well that if he hadn't, then someone else had spelled it out for him. He couldn't have been anything but hurt by my thoughtlessness.

"It was dumb of me and . . ."

"It sure as hell was," Sam broke in, "but if Tommy don't know by now that you run off in every which way you point your head, then he's even dumber than you're claimin to be, which is something I doubt on both sides."

I searched Tommy's face and was glad to find a flicker that told me he agreed with Sam. Then he shrugged in a way that said he had more important things to discuss. "My people here scared with Sheriff Westheimer."

"He already proved they ought to be," Sam agreed.

"It will be again," said Tommy, gravely. "Unpunish Wah Lee murder, more murders happen to us."

Since this couldn't be disputed, we waited until he asked me, "Mr. Doctor Gibbs be judge?"

"It looks that way. The only one running against him is old man Lohmeyer, and the people who don't drink in his saloon care about as much for him as the people who do."

Sam put in, "That ought to make you feel easier. Your people can depend on the Doc to keep Dutch straight."

"We do," he answered. "But is only beginning after Mister Doctor is judge if Mr. Judge got no work."

I thought he was pointing out that no judge could do anything to anyone until Westheimer hauled him into court, which was a correct guess because next he added, "Maybe get deputy come to work?"

"A deputy for Westheimer who'd enforce the law?" I asked. "Even if it makes sense, which it probably does, I know for a fact that there's no money in the town's budget for another law officer. And it'll be a cold day in hell before you catch old Dutch splitting his take with anyone else."

"You right." Tommy nodded in satisfaction that I'd finally shown some intelligence. "I pay deputy."

Trying not to grin, Sam asked, "Tommy, you don't mean you want to hire on your own armed guard for Chinatown?"

Tommy had the grace to look uneasy but not enough to take him away from the idea. "We need, maybe not honest-God deputy, but some man who do what Mr. Sheriff Westheimer don't. Good strong man stops bad people from doing murders and stealing or maybe carries them to Mr. Judge Gibbs. Maybe this man only walk down the street and bad people stop thinking bad things."

"That fellow would get himself shot his first day on the job," I said. "And if he were anywhere near as tough as you think he ought to be, then it'd be his back that was dosed with lead. But, front or back, he'd be dead long before he drew his first paycheck."

Tommy's face didn't lose the lugubrious expression. "Seventy-five dollar," he said.

"A week?" The size of the amount impressed Sam enough that he quit fighting the smile.

"Sure. If a month, only get loafers. If a week, get a strong man like you."

The gleam of hope in Tommy's eyes was doused by Sam's next words. "It wouldn't be for me. I'm not the littlest bit afraid of some weasel takin a shot my way, but, for one thing, I can't see old Witham carryin me on his payroll, and the other thing is I might not be around at nights when you'd need me most." Because the only answer to this was the look on Tommy's face, he went on, "You know I'd do it. There's nobody in town that scares me, least of all Westheimer. Hell, he might even like to see me workin as a vigilante. The less trouble there is, the more he likes his job. But I just can't take it on. Even for that kind of money."

Tommy, determined to push him to the wall, answered, "So?" which was enough to keep Sam defending himself.

"Witham wouldn't worry me. I know you'd set it up so all he'd see is that nothin was gettin in the way of the profits comin in. You could get a sore-headed dog to be your sheriff of Chinatown and he'd be for it so long as it didn't cut a hole in his claim. And it sure wouldn't bother me none seeing you snocker him into forkin over some of what he's fixin to rob Pa out of."

Tommy never paid half as much attention to what a man said as he did to the way he said it, and Sam's tones told him that it was no longer of any use to push his idea. It was just as obvious to him as it was to me that the real reason behind Sam's rare unwillingness to help a friend was that no one could offer anything that stacked up against what Celina Sewell was giving him these nights. Sucking in his breath, he asked, "More tea?"

Seeing this, Sam felt worse than ever about turning his back on a friend. "How about," he asked, "if I took a day shift? I could let it be known that I'm around here all day, and if there's any problem at night, the ones causin it could count on me bein after them next morning."

I dropped the objection that the only bonus a Chinatown deputy could expect was a bullet because another way to go had just occurred to me. "I might have something to add to that," I said.

Both of them looked at me without too much hope, expecting, I guess, one of my patented plans guaranteed to blow up in everyone's face.

"There's a perfect solution walking up the street right now." I pointed through the small window that was the only way that Chinatown or anything else could be seen from the restaurant and which now framed Tony picking his way through a path that the early morning April rain had turned into a muddy trail.

Luckily for the point I was going to make, as we watched him approach, another man, carrying a full load of rotgut, was staggering toward him with absolutely no awareness that Tony was in the same county let alone with him on the path. Tony acted just as oblivious, but, right before the drunk bumped into him, he canted his rifle butt and pushed it through the other's legs. Leaving the drunk sprawling in the mud, he came on into the restaurant as casually as if nothing had happened.

"The case for the next sheriff of Chinatown rests," I told them.

"Is this the annual meeting of the clan?" Tony asked as he walked over to the table, still just as calm, even though he must have wondered what was so all-fired funny that even Tommy had joined in our laughter.

"We're plottin against you," said Sam and went on to explain the conversation so far, ending with, "You keep tellin me how sick you are of the meat business, so here's your chance for a new job. Son, there's a world full of opportunity out there waitin for you."

Then, before Tony could trot out a dozen or so offhand objections, he played his trump against the other's sole speck of vanity. "Everybody knows you're the best man with a gun in these parts, so you can do it even if I wasn't goin to be right there beside you in case trouble comes up that you're not big enough to handle."

I pitched in by elaborating on the idea that this really would be a two-man force. Anyone who went after Tony was sure to be sobered up by the recollection that he'd also be taking on Sam Hume. "And," I concluded, "if they get you both, they'll still have me to contend with." I expected them to smile at that, and I'm glad they didn't because I meant it.

"Then why don't you take on the post?" Tony asked. "Jacksonville cries for a sheriff of your stamp." We could see he was beginning to find that the idea of this job wasn't all that unappealing.

"Because you want it so much. You're bored stiff by what you've been doing and just think of what it's going to add to your lies about the West once you get back home. Anyway, right now there isn't one issue of the paper that comes out that doesn't leave at least three people waiting to take a whip to me. That's trouble enough for someone with my delicate nature."

By now, the four of us were absolutely loving the idea of Sheriff Tony. Him, most of all.

"Horseshit, Gibbs," said Sam. And then, turning to Tommy, he asked, "How does this hit you, little heathen?"

In response, Tommy executed a very Occidental gesture. He stuck his hand out for Tony to shake it.

"Hold on," Tony said, "I haven't agreed to anything as yet."

"Horseshit, Tony," said Sam.

"You've quite a vocabulary there, my friend."

I saw Tony's stab of pleasure at Sam's answering grin.

Can you guess what went through Tony's mind in the next moment? He told me what it was long afterward when he could speak about these things without strain: *My God, could there have been any truth in that Sewell tart's accusation?*

He'd been feeling good, but this thought was like a dash of ice cold water in his face. "I've really some rather serious doubts about this," he said aloud, and then another fear hit him that he could no more stifle than he could the recollection of the girl's ugly words. *If you go away from this, you'll have that question haunting you for the rest of your life!* And its truth was so undeniable that he found himself slowly adding, "However, I'll have a go," and shook Tommy's still outstretched hand.

I was delighted. We all were together again! "You haven't heard the best part yet, Tony. The job pays seventy-five dollars a week!"

Now he was back on firm ground. "It's really not all that grand, is it? Especially after sharing it with a partner with no other visible means of support."

"You don't have to split nothin with me," said Sam. "I wouldn't take your damned charity."

"It isn't charity. If I don't halve it with you, then you won't be there when needed. A laborer is only as good as his hire," he finished virtuously.

"I'll tell you what," I said, appreciating this opportunity to arrange things for everyone, "Tony, you have the toughest shift, so you take fifty and give Sam the rest for laying around on his butt all night."

"That's fair," said Sam.

"I suppose it is," Tony agreed. "When shall we start, little heathen?"

Father's election as town judge turned out to be as lopsided a victory as everyone had predicted. If it hadn't been for the fact that he was my father, I would have been as optimistic as the rest, because the only place on God's earth where anyone paid attention to Lohmeyer was in his own saloon. So, in spite of my initial disbelief, we were there along with the rest of the town at the bonfire pitched that night in honor of the only magistrate Jacksonville ever had who was all its own.

At the beginning of the evening, I thought the fuss was way out of proportion to the importance of an event that would have been commonplace anywhere else, and then I realized that this was far from an average occasion—this was our first city activity that truly meant something. When Frank Sizemore had been picked to be mayor, that was only a popularity contest because some of the merchants felt they needed a legally appointed Sheriff, and naming Westheimer was about the last of Frank's official duties. If there had been any more, he'd have quit because he was out working one claim or another every day that the weather wasn't bad enough to keep him in town.

But a judge! That, with all due respects to Father, was a horse of another color. The election of a real one of our own guaranteed that everything that went on in town, like deeds, titles, and transfers, that had been generally ignored by the circuit judges sent here were now matters of record up in the territorial capital instead of being scrawled somewhere in Town Hall.

So far we'd been able to get away with quite a few dodges on the state and federal officials. We'd taken our own sweet time to establish and document things like whether Jacksonville actually lay in southern Oregon or northern California. The advantage to this was that whenever the tax collectors showed up, everyone claimed citizenship in the state the collector didn't represent. A few of the lighter heads got together on another occasion to proclaim the place as the independent country of Jacksonville, which, of course, lasted only until some of the more responsible people pulled together to keep the joke from interfering with federal benefits.

But now that we had our legally elected and duly constituted judge, the horseplay was over, and, as far as the citizenry was concerned, a long first step had been taken toward assuming our rightful place as the Queen City of the Northwest.

I'd argued Tony away from his new Chinatown duties on the ground that our yellow brothers would never know another night as safe as this one, since every bum in the area was at the celebration. That's why he felt free to walk around with me, watching the bonfire grow higher and higher as the celebrants added the loose boards, broken furniture, and benches they scrounged from all over the place. Of course we didn't have anything so fancy as a formal band, but quite a few men dug up musical instruments from wherever their wives had squirreled them, so this was the birth of the Jacksonville German Band, an aggregation that still exists.

Tony asked me, "What on earth is possessing these people? They act like lunatics!"

I was going to put my hand on Tony's shoulder to restrain him from drifting away, but just then the speechifying started, and, once it had begun, you couldn't have chased him away with a shotgun. For openers, the city fathers had gotten the mayor sober enough to be popped up on our bandstand to introduce Father, and he promptly surprised everyone by metaphorically soaring and swooping all over the place.

Sizemore told them that tonight's festivities wasn't the merest patch on what the future held in store for Jacksonville. He assured the crowd that their descendants were all going to be rich as kings because they, the founders of these potentially noble houses, had had the good sense to settle in a community that God obviously favored over everywhere else. Pausing to take another swig at his jug, he forgot what he was going to say next and began leveling a blast at Appler & Kenny for overcharging him on the shovel he'd just bought. Because he seemed prepared to go on, piece by piece, through their whole inventory, someone pulled him away and he went down backwards with a bang loud enough to say he was through for the night.

No one else up there seemed to know what came next, so Father walked over to the center of the rickety rostrum and waited until the crowd quieted down.

Another riproaring speech about the coming glories of the town was expected, but that wasn't what Father had in mind. He told them that the job of growing up still stood in front of them and that Jacksonville would be only as big and as prosperous a place as they were willing to work toward. It wasn't going to be easy, he said, but a metropolis might be a possibility so long as they held on to the spirit they were showing this night. Then he sat down.

It wasn't a very successful speech, but they cheered him anyway and then forgot him right afterward, as soon as the band struck up the first of the two songs in their repertoire which was, of course, "There'll Be a Hot Time in the Old Town Tonight."

The rest of the speakers were more enthusiastic. Just about every one of them dealt with the great destiny that was just around the corner, and no listener had a minute's worth of doubt that the promise would be kept. After all, they'd managed to get here after a long hard journey from the East, hadn't they? And didn't that make them infinitely more capable than all the people still sitting back there at home praying for something good to happen to them?

As we walked away, Tony said, "They really believe they are here for the ages, don't they?"

"Why not," I answered. "Do people think any differently where you come from?"

37

IT GOT TO BE unmercifully hot that summer. Our rainy season stopped abruptly in the late spring, and from then on we saw few days that offered the slightest puff of clouds. If it weren't for the snowpacks remaining on the mountains around our valley and reminding us of greener seasons, it would have been a coin toss to decide whether a man should bet more money on a career selling gold or peddling water.

One of those nights, while in a saloon, I heard an old prospector say that droughts weren't usual here, but, when they did come, they could last for as long as three years. At the time I put this down as a pile of mumbo jumbo Indian lore, but after we'd exhausted the mountain run-offs, there were many moments when I found myself wondering if he hadn't understated his weather report.

As we got into August, we began to figure how fast our water table was dropping by the number of wells that ran dry each week. Water is a serious thing in the West because the lack of it can turn an Eden into a place you'd just as soon avoid. Some of the more responsible people began to worry if the arid spell wasn't going to end by turning the fussing between farmers and miners into something more violent than the disputes that were brought before Father to settle.

The bad feelings grew. Farmers desperately needed the available water supply to irrigate their fields, but no mining company would ever consider locating here unless there was enough water available to generate the eighty-six pounds of pressure per square inch that tore the dirt out of a hill and sent it streaming through a series of sluice boxes. A one- or two-man mining operation is small potatoes compared to what a mining company adds to a community's wealth.

That was the fight: There was enough water for farming and there was enough for mining but, especially in a drought, nowhere near enough for both, and the time was coming when the people of Jacksonville had to agree on which one meant more to the place where they wanted to make homes for their children.

And all of this leads squarely to why I was enjoying the journalist's

life more than anything I'd ever come across. By damn, I was important!
Of course, Alben Hensley, as editor, was the most courted by the two
factions, but there was enough of an overflow to nourish my conceit to
the point where I began to feel insulted if I didn't get respectful attention
every time I cleared my throat in a bar. I guess that's why newspapermen
ruin their livers with cheap whiskey and can never spare a nickel to buy
their wives a new dress. Most jobs that pay decent wages seldom deliver
half the pleasure of hearing people discuss a story you've written and
then acting as though they were sure that if they were nice enough to
you, you'd tell them the rest you hadn't been allowed to print.

It was as heady as whiskey when a visiting territorial politician asked
for my opinion of the town's temper or when some merchant who could
buy and sell me ten ways to Tuesday buttered me up in the hope of
gleaning some advance tip that could swell his receipts. I confess that
these first kudos resulted in a hunger that's never stopped spurring me.

Tony was amused by my newly found profundity but, every so often,
I caught Sam and Tommy paying attention to my diagnoses of the way
things were. Elva was just about the only one who tried to bring me
down to earth. Once, while bragging that the important judge who was
also my father had wanted to know my opinion of which way the people
would vote if it ever came down to miners versus farmers, she asked,
"Collie, are you sure you know all that much about who's right?"

I had enough grace left to answer, "Maybe not, my girl, but what
counts is that people think I do."

"But, supposin you're wrong," she persisted, "mightn't you end up
by hurtin somebody?"

I knew she didn't mean this as a reproach because that wouldn't have
been her way. As a matter of fact, once when I tried to explain the
remorse I felt at her father's death, she had shut it off by saying, "Collie,
you wasn't any more than bein a handy way for it to happen. If it warn't
Richard Mulligan with that gun, it'd been somebody else, cause that's
the way God wanted it. What you don't want to see on account of you're
so busy blamin yourself, is that Pa didn't give a darn about livin ever
since Ma and the other children got killed. His life was over that day,
and the only reason he was hangin on was me. I've studied out that it
was blessed that he died when he did. All he had in front of him was to
get sourer as he got older."

Her conviction laid some of my devils to rest. There had to be truth
in her conclusion that Henri Boudreau was totally different in Jacksonville than the man described by those who knew him at Fort Laramie.

His fatal lunge at Mulligan was recalled by those closest to the bar that night as having been that of a man in a frenzy, far beyond the actions of a saloonkeeper wanting only to keep order in his place. After Elva pulled the curtain away for me, I recognized that this hadn't been the first brandishing of a gun in the Bella Union.

She'd given me absolution. A lesser girl might have gone to her grave before speaking to me again, but not Elva.

So, instead of patronizing her the way I would have anyone else with a question about whether I really knew anything about the equities in the miner-farmer squabble, I said, "Elva, in another year or so or whenever you're ready, if you'd consider marrying me I'd promise to walk in the paths of righteousness for the rest of my life."

"Pooh," she answered, "then you wouldn't be Collie Gibbs."

"Sure I would. I'd still be smart and good looking and . . ."

"And I wouldn't be able to stand you. The thing everybody likes about you is that you're fun."

"The hell with that."

"Don't swear," she said with that mock-solemn expression that, tall as she was, made her appear like a little girl in a spotless white dress. "I don't know why a boy of your education ever has to stoop to usin profanity."

"Elva," I said, "hell and damn and bastard."

"And son of a bitch," she added. "Don't forget son of a bitch."

"I didn't forget it. I thought it might be a touch hard for your dainty little ears."

She whooped at this with the hearty laugh that if more girls had, there'd be fewer old maids. "Collie Gibbs, you're the only person in the world that lies enough to call me dainty. How about these clodhoppers?" she said, extending a foot. "Wouldn't you say they's also as dainty as they could be?"

I shook my head. "Even I can't go that far. You've got the biggest feet anyone ever saw." We looked at each other, and although the smile was still on my lips, we both knew I was about to be serious. "Elva, isn't there some way . . ."

The solemnity came back to her face, but this time it was real. "I wish there was, Collie. I honestly wish so hard there was."

I shouldn't have brought it up. The fun fell away whenever I did, and although her hurt over Sam's affliction with Celina wasn't on her face anymore, it never left the back of her mind. "Well, the hell with you," I said. "If you don't want me, there's certainly those who do."

"Like, for instance, Charity Witham?"

"Among others," I admitted with a fine show of modesty.

"She's a very nice person, Collie. I mean it, too. You know she's real sweet on you and she's really a extra nice person."

I took out the notepad I carried since becoming a reporter. Flipping through it and consulting its blank pages, I said, "Hmm," what do you know—here's an open date next April. I'm going to write in right now to see her on April 10. I respect your judgment, Miss Boudreau, and I just wish I had an open date before then."

"I'm glad for her. Truly. I'm only worryin whether she's gonna be able to hold still that long."

I always felt both better and worse after seeing Elva. This time the worse predominated. Walking away from the corner where we'd been chatting, I was mortally convinced (now I was thinking along the lines that led Tony to describe me so often as a bloody idiot) that if I didn't do something about winning her away from Sam Hume, there just wasn't any chance at all for me to ever know happiness.

But, of course, I thought, *she does have a point there about Charity Witham.*

So far in my young life, Charity represented the sole introduction to sex, and, in light of her continued refusals to go bouncing with me again in her father's barn, every so often I considered making both of our fathers happy by marrying her. This was an especially persuasive alternative during my moments of greatest need, and it probably doesn't come as a surprise that my moments of greatest need used to have the habit of following each other in awfully close order.

Elva wasn't aware of it, but in those days, she filled the role for me of Lady Fair. Whenever the memory of Charity's pink and white young thighs set my groin to aching, an event that occurred at least fourteen times a week, I'd close my eyes and hold on to the vision of sweet Elva and the need to prove someday that I'd always been worthy of her. Sometimes, I admit, Elva lost.

At any rate, the glow of talking so easily with Elva again faded and was gradually replaced, as I walked away, by the vision of Charity's rosy buttocks. A few minutes later, I turned off the path that led to the print shack and headed for the schoolhouse where a few youngsters had their Rs drummed into them by Miss Witham.

The more I thought about her contributions to education, the more I hurried in order to arrive before school let out and she'd be gone, and although I met my schedule, her greeting didn't contain anywhere near the warmth that was so vital to the further tutorings I had in mind. "Well," she said, "the important Mr. Gibbs."

"The very same," I agreed, "full of the cares of the world but never too busy to put them aside for the prettiest little gal in the valley."

"Some other time, Collie," she said, walking on.

I caught up with her. "Charity, there's no need to be so mean."

"There certainly is, Collie Gibbs! You think you can come waltzing around whenever it strikes your fancy in between all the times you spend in those saloons?" She spoke a little too sharply, because two of the kids on the path overheard her, and when they giggled, she blushed, which added even more happiness to their little lives.

My calculation of the time left to me before her embarrassment outweighed her curiosity about what I might say next called for the heaviest dose of sincerity I could muster. "Honest, Charity, I've been working like a beaver. I *have* to go into the saloons because more of the things in this town gets talked about there than anyplace else. I swear that's the truth, Charity."

"My father doesn't think so," she said, proving that I'd won a stay by glaring at the children hard enough to scatter them ahead of us on the path. "You wouldn't catch my father wasting his time and money listening to a bunch of loafers."

"He doesn't have to. Besides, what's he doing owning the saloon if he's so all-fired holy?"

"That's business. Something you wouldn't know anything about."

I was pleased to note that she wasn't hurrying any longer but had adjusted her pace to mine. "I'm going to tell you something, Charity Witham, that I've never told to another single soul."

I stopped and looked around long enough for her to understand I was checking for eavesdroppers. Then, packing as much throb as I could into my voice, I said, "Maybe this isn't the proper time or place." I knit my brows to let her know of the struggle going on inside of me and added, "Well, maybe it's the right time, even if this isn't the place."

"For what?" The harsh tones were gone. So far, so good.

"Well, you know."

"No, I don't. Tell me!"

"Not out in the open like this. Those darn kids can hear a pin drop when it's none of their business. Let's go somewhere we can be alone."

I saw the cloud of suspicion creeping back into her mind. "What place do you have in mind where they can't hear us?"

"Oh, I don't know. Anywhere. I guess one place would be as good as another."

"Like my father's barn?"

I frowned while considering the suggestion. "Well, maybe that'd be a good idea. Nobody could bother us while I was telling you the things I want to say."

Her laugh was nowhere near as attractive as Elva's. "Collis Gibbs, you and I both know very well what you're after, so why don't you just come right on out and say it?"

I was shocked by this base thought. "Charity, I swear I had no such thing in mind!" That sounded too lame, even to me, so I tried again. "You think whatever you want, but all I had in mind was to tell you how much I like you."

After a long pause: "Do you really, Collie?"

After staring at each other for a few moments, I put an end to it by asking, "Now are you satisfied?"

"Sure," she answered sadly. "You like me and not in a million years would you ever get serious about me."

This was it and I couldn't bring myself to do a damn thing about it. All I had to do was say, "I love you," but I knew I'd stutter over the words. I just couldn't get them out no matter how badly I wanted her skirts up, which, I suppose, is about as much honesty as I could claim in those days.

"You're wrong about one thing, Charity Witham. I don't think a bit less of you." I eyed her earnestly, thinking that she had an appealing face in spite of her being a little on the buxom side, and went on, "And, another thing for sure; you're one of the prettiest girls in town and maybe one of the prettiest girls I've ever met."

"Even in Philadelphia?"

"Even in Philadelphia," I replied emphatically. "And the fellow who ends up getting you is going to be one of the luckiest around."

How could I do this? Talking like a fool and acting like a polecat, and then, for all my lust, I suddenly didn't feel like going on with it. "Charity," I said, meaning my words for the first time, "I want to tell you the God's honest truth; I just don't know. You're pushing me to be serious, and it's something I'm not ready for. I like you a whole lot, and that time with you in the barn was one of the best times in my whole life, but if you want to say we can't ever do it again unless we say we're getting married—I just can't. If I went along but didn't mean it, you'd know it right away. And you don't want me to lie, either, Charity Witham, if I'm right about you."

Sweet are the uses of Charity! Blessed is the honest man! Katie, bar the door! "Collis," she answered, literally melting in place, "you're an awful fine boy. If you want to go to the barn, I'll go with you."

I walked home whistling afterward, so pleased with myself that I could hardly keep from strutting. I didn't feel a shred of guilt because, if anything, Charity had enjoyed the tumbling at least as much as I had. And, although I did make the mistake of whispering "I love you" while resting before having another go, I'm not certain she heard me, and, if she did, I was convinced she knew as well as I that it didn't count.

I was aware of being quite well disposed toward the girl. Not a bad sort at all. Even though she wasn't a patch on Elva, and—oh, yes!—then I remembered once briefly seeing Elva's face when things had been at their most hectic, but I shied away from that and went back to remembering generous Charity, overflowing with milk and honey.

Nice girl, Charity. Once I quieted her disposition to turn all this fun into grim marriage, I'd have a very good thing going, indeed. I found myself seriously doubting that anyone else in Jacksonville was as fortunate.

Fine girl, Charity. So anxious for me to be pleased with her. A vulnerable girl, really. I shouldn't have bragged to Tony about my first conquest over her. It hadn't been the decent thing to do, and if it weren't that I was feeling so much like the head rooster, I might have felt more ashamed of myself for bandying her name about.

Tony.

What a marvelous idea!

I'd share her with him. Lord knows he was lonely and morose enough to welcome such a gift, and, after all, what were friends for? Besides, if she had the two of us on her hands, she might not be quite so intense over landing me as a husband. Especially if the other beau was someone as superior as Tony. As I thought this over, I became even more certain that I was doing everyone a favor.

This was the day's last untroubled thought. When I reached our cabin, Tony wasn't there waiting to be told of his incredible good luck, but Father and Edward Hume were, and, from the looks of them, the conversation they'd been having was miles out of tune with the way I'd been feeling.

"Excuse me," I said after I walked in on them, "if it's a private talk, I'll come back later." Actually, I thought that maybe Sam's father was there for physical matters that wouldn't keep until next morning's office hours. Father had taken to dividing his time equally between his medical and judicial practices, so it was difficult to recognize the reason for the sober air with which he greeted me.

"Not at all, Collis," he said. This is your home and I'm quite certain Mr. Hume will not care in the least if you are present. And, it might be, that you can contribute in some way." He looked over to Hume for confirmation and, accepting the surly answering nod, turned back to me. "Mr. Hume is having a bit of a problem with his partner, Mr. Witham, and the question seems to be whether a court trial can be avoided."

"What's it all about?" I asked. "Did Witham lower the boom?"

"He thinks he did," said Hume. "He thinks he's got me over a barrel." He cleared his throat, sounding like a barn door opening on rusty hinges, and went on, "He says he's got to have the cash for the notes I signed. He says it's not his fault, it's not him that wants the cash but the Wells Fargo people down in San Francisco that he sold them to. The skunk says he needs money to buy more Jackson County warrants, but they won't give to him if he don't shut me down."

"Can't you go to them yourself?" I asked. "You could prove to them how good your mine is and that you'll have enough pulled out by the end of the summer to pay whatever you owe."

Hume glowered at me by way of answer. After a moment, Father said, "It isn't quite that simple, Collis. They are already convinced that it's a good mine, but they feel it's overextended because of all the loans still outstanding for the machinery he's purchased. They told Mr. Witham that in light of recent bad experiences with Oregon gold mines, they'd rather be made whole."

"That's what the skunk says they said," Hume muttered.

"Without further evidence," Father answered, "a court would have to believe him."

I said, "Excuse me, Mr. Hume, for putting in my two cents, but it seems to me that, next to you, the one who knows most about this mine is Mr. Witham. They ought to be willing to take his word that they'll get everything owing them."

"He says he already tried it."

"Then work out another loan with Witham's bank to cover the Wells Fargo amount. It couldn't take more than a couple of months to have everything back in shape."

Hume simply shook his head and stared down at the floor. After it became obvious he didn't have anything else to contribute, Father told him softly, "Edward, I can't do anything. If you sue him in my court,

I'd have to decide in his favor right after you admit that it's your signature on the notes. And whatever territorial court you might next take it to will have to decide in the same way."

"What the hell do you know about the law?" Hume said. "You're nothing but a doctor. A piss poor damn quack at that!" With this, he rose and left the cabin, not slamming the door behind him but leaving it swinging open in his wake.

Father looked at me with real sorrow in his eyes. "What could I have done, Collis? Could I have said anything more?"

"I don't see how. Even if you decided in his favor, the first court Witham appealed to would uphold his case."

"If only I could have lent him the money he needs."

"Why don't you? It just takes a letter back to Philadelphia."

"It's gone," he said. "I dreaded having to tell you. The investment went bad."

"Oh, great." I suppose it would have been normal if I'd gotten angry about this, because it was a family inheritance. My grandparents had certainly intended that some part of it would descend to me, but Father was so obviously suffering from the guilt of losing it that, even if the money mattered all that much, I wouldn't have said anything more than I did.

"If I still had it," Father said almost to himself, "would I have given it to him?"

"You know you would. But it's gone, so there's no point thinking about it."

His face brightened because my answer was reassurance that I didn't hold his bad financial judgment against him, but that lasted just for a second. Hume's predicament weighed too heavily. He sighed, "Poor Edward."

"Maybe you can still work something, Father. Maybe if you went to Witham and told him that he'd be losing money in the long run because who, least of all the people in his church, would ever forgive him for taking the Sweetwater mine away from Mr. Hume? You could do it! You could convince him that no one will want to do business with his bank after the news of this gets out."

It was the peg he needed. "Collis, a fine idea! I'll do it the first thing in the morning."

"Why wait?" I asked.

"It's better to let Jabez sleep on it—he might arrive at this decision by himself. He's not a bad person, you know, just a hard businessman.

I'll just bet he'll have reached this conclusion by himself tonight and it won't be necessary for me to appear as if I'm favoring one man over another and—"

"But," I interrupted because I didn't want his notion of judicial fairness to keep him from helping Sam's father, "so far it isn't a court case and—"

"And, Collis, if he fails to arrive at the proper conduct by himself, tonight, then I'm certain I will only have to hint at it tomorrow!"

"I hope you're right, Father. I truly hope Mr. Witham finds his own way to doing the right thing. But, just in case he doesn't, let's go over the reasons again. That way, when you see him tomorrow morning, you'll be able to go right down the line with all the arguments for changing his mind."

"Fine. Exactly the thing to do. Let's rehearse the list right after dinner."

"Let's start the meal now and get it out of the way."

"Certainly. Shall we set a place for Tony?"

"I doubt that he'll be home. You never know which meal he'll skip."

Father frowned because he still wasn't sure that Tony working as a vigilante was a good idea. "I hope," he said, "that Anthony will find more suitable employment after a new sheriff is appointed."

"When that day rolls around, he'll be just as glad as you. And Chung Lin will be happier than any of us."

"Dr. Gibbs! Please sir, you'd better come with me!" It was Sam calling through the open door.

"Why, certainly, Samuel," said my father. "Is anything wrong?"

"It's Pa," said Sam. "He just shot himself."

Edward Hume died just a few minutes after we reached his cabin. His last words, delivered in mild tones, were, "I'm awful sorry, Ned. I should of done better."

Mrs. Hume, dry-eyed, looked at us and explained, "He never got over Ned's death. He always felt it wouldn't have had to happen if he'd taken off the boy's leg in a better way."

38

AFTER WE RETURNED from the cemetery and Tony had gone to his post at Tommy's restaurant, Sam and I sat on a log out at the back of their house near the vegetable garden. I had suggested we go there to get away from the crowd of people in the place because their condolences were making him more uncomfortable by the minute.

"It's real good seeing how many friends your father had," I told him.

"They're not his. Ma's. Everybody likes her, but that's all right."

"He'd be pleased, anyway."

"Not him. Not the way he's been."

"Sam, I heard what he said about Ned at the end. Was he always on your father's mind?"

"I don't know. I really wish I did. If that's what it was, it'd explain why Pa turned out so different once we got here. I'd hate to be thinkin from now on that he was always that crazy. I wouldn't ever want to get used to the idea of my pa killin himself because of lousy money."

This wasn't the kind of talk calculated to produce a lifting of spirits, so I started off in the direction of another subject. "Well, it doesn't make much difference now, I guess."

"The hell it don't!" He picked up and studied a handful of gravel. "I got his blood in me, and sometimes I take on in ways that make me wonder if I got any more sense than he had. I'm all messed up, Collie."

It was the first time he'd even hinted that his feelings for Celina Sewell—I knew that's what he meant—troubled him as much as it did his friends. For once I had the sense not to rush in with my own opinions.

"I act like such a damn fool, sometimes," he went on, "that right now, honest to God, I envy Pa laying out there. His problems are done and he's better off for it. I just about believe that most of the time he was just plain torturing himself."

"If he was, that certainly doesn't mean you'd be better off lying alongside him."

"Of course not. I don't know what the hell I mean. I'm all mixed up and I'm talkin in circles."

255

"You sure are, if you're talking about being cursed by bad blood. That's the dumbest thing I ever heard you say."

"Is it?" He threw the handful of gravel back to the ground. "You don't know half the things that go on in my head. We all said he had the Sweetwater Fever because of the way he acted about his claim and wanting to get rich as old man Witham. Well, how about me sittin out here, and Pa not even cold yet, and wantin to leave Ma and everybody and go see Celina? I mean right now, tonight!"

I said, "You're just out to punish yourself as hard as you can, probably because of that fight you two had. What you really want, maybe need the most, is somebody to put their arms around you and tell you that everything is going to be all right, big as you are. I'm surprised you don't see that. I do."

"Do you, honest, Collie? You don't think I'm low down for the way my mind works, sometimes?"

It hurt to hear him talking like this. I preferred him tough and keeping his feelings buried, because that's who Sam Hume was. "You're taking on too much. Anybody's mind can get twisted when they've had as bad a knock as what happened to your father." I stood up because I wanted to shut this off. "Tell you what, let's go back in and you sit with your ma for a while. She needs you pretty bad right now, and if you keep her company until she gets to sleep—my father said he was going to give her some laudanum to take—then maybe you ought to go on out to Celina's. It'd be a natural thing to do and you'd feel better. Then, in the morning, when you're thinking straight, take a good long look at whether you want to claim bad blood as an excuse for doing everything you're going to do anyway."

It was a long speech and the closest I'd ever come to a lecture where he was concerned. But it took. He stood up with the first bit of expression on his face since he'd appeared at our door to tell us about his father. "Collie," he said, "for a weasel sometimes you talk sense," and he put his arm around my shoulder as we walked inside.

That was the last any of us saw of Sam Hume for quite a while.

As for Tony, he was doing all right once he got over the latest letter from his brother Charles. It was short, but it was enough to set him to boil. There wasn't any family news in it, just a request that, for estate purposes, their solicitors would appreciate an accounting of what he'd done with the money sent him so far. They wanted to list it as an expense against whatever investments might be made in America.

Surprisingly, though, the anger didn't last nearly as long as it might have, say a year ago. After the latest evidence of his brother's stupidity quit stinging at him, he actually began to wonder if an American identity might not fit more comfortably than anything else. Here, people saw and thought of you as a person, and even if they ran over you, there was never a doubt in their mind that they were trampling a human being. Within a day or so of receiving the letter, he was able to laugh at it.

Of course, quite a bit of this new self-confidence was based on the savings he'd been accumulating. His living expenses were nominal—in fact, he'd have moved to a cabin of his own, but he didn't want to seem ungrateful to my father. His offer to raise his own rent by a healthy chunk was refused, so that left him living with us and sharing his bunk with the swelling stack of gold coins that were the wages paid him for his services as a lawman.

Finally, despite the discomfort involved in facing Celina Sewell, he was forced to move his hoard to Jabez Witham's vault. He had no choice. He felt he couldn't ask Sam or me to do his depositing; we'd have been sure to call him a damned fool. Keeping his savings underneath his mattress put him at the mercy of any wandering, larceny-bent stranger.

This morning was one of those when it no longer made sense to delay going to the bank. He found he had a little over $300 in his poke, and losing that kind of money would be even more awkward than standing across the counter from her cold, indifferent face. But, this trip, there was something else he couldn't quite read in her eyes when he pushed his deposit across the counter to her. He thought it might have to do with the fact that no one had seen Sam for the past week.

He was on his way toward the door with the receipt she gave him, when he heard "Anthony! Anthony Johnstone!" being called out, and, turning, he saw Jabez Witham smiling and beckoning to him. It wasn't a summons, it was more like a gesture to an unexpected but hoped-for guest. Wondering if the banker's warmth wasn't the cause of Sewell's attitude, Tony went over to where the banker was waiting to usher him into the office he kept in the back.

"Glad to see you, son!" Witham said. "Come on in. There's somebody here that wants so bad to meet you that I was just about to send Seelie out to hunt you down."

As he went in, a man seated at the side of Witham's desk rose and put out his hand. "I'm John Chaddock," he said. "It's a real pleasure to make your acquaintance, Mr. Johnstone."

"Mr. Chaddock is from the Wells Fargo company down in San Francisco," Witham explained, "and he's been telling me some mighty interesting things about you. Says your brother back in England is some kind of a duke."

"He is," Tony admitted, "but that has very little to do with me."

"Well," said Mr. Chaddock, "as a matter of fact I'm here specifically because of his inquiry concerning you."

I suppose I was the only one in Jacksonville who knew of the position of Tony's family, and that was only because I'd seen a reference to it once when he had left some of his papers scattered on his bed. When I'd faced him with it, I thought he was going to have a fit. In fact, he took on so that I finally agreed never to tell anyone else about it—a promise I kept since I didn't particularly fancy having one of his guns pointed in my direction. Believe me, that's not too much over the line of hyperbole. I've never seen him as furious as the day I told him I'd discovered what his family did for a living.

So, when this prosperous-appearing visitor led off by mentioning his brother, Tony knew he hadn't been called in for an idle chat. "May I sit down?" he asked.

"Certainly," the banker boomed, heartily enough to have Tony immediately recall his violent vomiting that night on Celina Sewell's doorstep. He wondered if Witham remembered his being there, but then he supposed not, because even the most professional actor couldn't have done that good a job of covering chagrin or of equaling the pleasure the little man showed as he bustled out to bring back one of the chairs from the front room. "Here, Anthony," he urged, "make yourself comfortable while we have ourselves a little chin chin about some of the things that brings Mr. Chaddock to our fair city."

Tony's feeling of being courted was reinforced by his chair being a bit higher than the other two. "Very well," he said, "now what's all this about Charles wanting to know the state of my health?"

"Well, I must say that his letter wasn't specifically about you," and Tony noted that Mr. Chaddock was being genially evasive. "It had more to do with our suggestions concerning investment opportunities in this part of the country. He mentioned that you were here in Jacksonville and that, although your family's original idea was to wait for your recommendations about the place . . ."

That's why Charles wanted to know how much I've spent so far, Tony thought. *He wants to close out the books, the silly bastard!*

". . . he's come to the conclusion that it might be a sound move to get the advantage of some independent thinking. Expert advice, you might call it, in light of our company's knowledge of what the West Coast offers to venture capital."

"You mean that Charles informed you of how little faith he has in my judgment?"

"Not at all! If anything, much to the contrary. As a matter of fact, your brother commented on the initiative you've shown since arriving here, but he seems to be wondering if you've gotten to care so much for the Rogue Valley that it might be you've become, well, a mite too optimistic."

Tony was aware that the man, for all his fine clothes and silky manner, was lying in his teeth. The flattery also convinced him that Chaddock was exactly what he'd been introduced as—a banker on the prowl. Privately, he went on to guess that the letter Charles had sent to this man's company was confined to a curt statement that never mind that he had a brother here, did they know of any absolutely safe places to put his money where it could be tripled or more within a short period of time. Charles was a stranger to any of the graceful ways of downplaying another's abilities, since anything more than *you're an ass* was beyond him.

"I'm glad to hear that Charles thinks so well of me," he said aloud. "I understand that the estate has done quite well under his management."

"That's the way we've read it," said Chaddock. "And that's exactly why I'm here to see you. We know of one or two situations that might be of interest to your brother, and our idea was that, perhaps, if you'd like to, well, sort of look them over, your favorable opinion might just add to the interest of your brother. . . ."

Every little bit adds to the load, thought Tony, *and this oily bookmaker doesn't neglect a pebble.*

". . . Of course we want to pay you your time and travel costs and whatever other expenses you might incur . . ."

A bribe. How splendid!

". . . to either of the places we have in mind, and you could stay as long as it takes you to become absolutely familiar with everything that you or your brother would like to know."

Tony found it difficult to keep the smile off his lips. There wasn't a better way of ruining whatever deal this man had in mind than his endorsing it to Charles. "This is very generous of you," he assured Chaddock, "and I'm quite certain that Charles will admire your conscientious approach. But other commitments would make it terribly difficult for me to leave Jacksonville at the moment."

"You mean working out there for Chung Lin?" Witham interrupted.

"Don't worry about it, son. I'll take care of the matter, get Lin some other guards, maybe three or four. He won't miss you a bit. Besides," he added, "the job just might probably be over soon, anyway."

Tony waited but when he saw that Witham wasn't going to offer a further hint about this possible new twist to Tommy's career, he refused again by saying, "Mr. Chaddock, I'm so pleased by the news you bring of my brother's reliance on my judgment. I do wish that I might accept your proposal, but I'm afraid it's simply not possible."

"It's your family's business, isn't it?" asked Chaddock.

"Not actually. I'm certain you are aware that, under English law, the eldest son is the sole inheritor. When Charles marries, everything will again descend to his first boy. The only likelihood of my ever being concerned with the estate would be if Charles were to die sans male issue, and, I believe, that's a rather remote possibility. Please forgive a further mention of family affairs, but our mother has written that he and one of our cousins have arranged their nuptials. Knowing Charles, it won't be too terribly long before a troop of children follow that event."

Chaddock said to Witham, "Looks like I made a trip for nothing."

"Could be," said the other, "but you don't ever want to lock yourself out a hundred percent. Maybe Anthony, here, will change his mind one of these days about going to work for you."

The San Franciscan wasn't a man to waste time in amenities when there was no immediate business in view. Pulling a thin gold watch from his vest pocket, consulting it while saying, "Jabez, if I get over to the hotel and pack now . . ." and not taking more time than to pump Tony's hand twice in a brisk farewell, he left the room.

After he'd gone, to Tony's surprise, Witham turned to him and executed a very large and deliberate wink. "He bit. Mark my words, he'll be back next week with twice the offer."

"I thought I handled myself rather well," Tony said.

"You sure as tarnation did. Son, how about if you come over to supper tonight where we can do some private chin chinning? Besides, Charity keeps asking about you, and it wouldn't hurt you young folks to get to know each other."

In addition to being mystified by what it was that Chaddock had bit, Tony felt that the offer of a daughter was a trifle quick, even for a banker who'd learned the extent of the Johnstone family's assets just that morning.

39

A S I SAID, Sam had dropped out of sight. The one most likely to know where he'd gone the night of his father's funeral was Celina Sewell, but she not only denied having seen him for the past week, she got huffy when I asked her about the way he might have acted when he visited her after his mother and Elva went to sleep.

"Collie Gibbs," she said loudly enough to interest the men standing behind me in line at the bank's counter, "that ain't a thing that concerns me in the least. If you want to know what Sam Hume is up to, you press him yourself the next time you see him!"

It didn't leave a feeling that she was hungry to chat with me, so I was surprised next morning when she pulled her rig over to the corner of California and Oregon Streets while I was standing there and passing the time of day with Frank Sizemore. "Whoa," we heard her call to her horse. "Hold! This darn cart'll be up on the sidewalk less'n you hold." Most girls in that situation would have seemed flustered and awkward, but not Celina. She looked more like a sweetly dressed porcelain doll who happened to be out of place on a mining camp street.

Our mayor, pulling off his battered campaign hat, observed, "There's a law against it, Miss Sewell, but if you want to go wheeling in and out of the buildings, I'll make an exception in your case."

"You don't have to," she called, laying the whip across the horse's flanks. "Once this darn thing quits twitchin and shyin, I'll be just as lawful as anybody else."

"Celina," I offered, "one way to get an animal to stand still is to stop sawing at its reins."

"If you can do better, then you try it." She held out the reins, inviting me to climb aboard.

I said to the mayor, "This looks like the train I've been waiting on, Frank, so if you'll excuse me . . ." and jumped up on the seat beside her. "Where to?" I asked. "Portland? San Francisco? How about London? I hear it's beautiful this time of the year."

"You don't have a lick of sense, do you, Collie Gibbs?" Her laugh told me that yesterday's petulance was no longer on tap.

"Not when I'm around a beautiful girl off from work."

"I wish I was. But I'm doin errands, is what. Right now Mr. Witham has got three separate things for me to do over to Medford."

Medford wasn't its official name then, but that's what it was called because it was where a feed and hardware store, a part-time saloon, and a gunsmith had clustered together around the middle fork in the trail from Jacksonville. "Mr. Witham figuring on opening a branch of his bank out there?" I asked.

"He's just about to. Till then, I got to fetch the deposits."

"Old Jabez certainly puts his trust in you. I can't picture him allowing anyone else to handle his money."

"I earn it," she said. "I work day and night for that skinflint, but you can just bet I won't keep on forever to make him richer'n he already is."

Anything that lessened Witham made me happy. But then I had a stab of fear that this might mean that she and Sam had reached a marriage agreement. "That sounds like you don't count on making a career out of your job."

"If you got about a week to spare, I'll tell you about it."

"Hensley would skin me if I took a week off. How about giving me just the first part of it this morning?"

"How about if you ride over to Medford with me? You ain't doin nothin important that I can see."

"I am so," I said, tugging at the reins to head the horse east over the Medford trail. "I just signed on as driver to the prettiest girl in the whole country."

"You talk so nice."

"Better than Sam?"

"Never mind about him. That big thing thinks he can boss me around and tell me what to do even worse than old Witham. Now quit it, Collie," she added to head me off. "The last time I seen him was about a week ago, and I don't know what he's been up to, and I don't care even the littlest bit."

Her tones warned me not to push so, for the next hundred yards, I concentrated on keeping the horse between the two ruts that passed for the Medford road. And, to be truthful, the day and the setting were too nice to be ignored. The sun was shining, the air was soft, and the girl sitting beside me was easily the loveliest I'd ever seen. My concern for Sam began blurring around the edges.

After we had ridden another short distance in silence, she sent me further along to treachery by leaning back and stretching her marvelous young body. I looked over and saw a mischievous awareness of the effect she produced. "It'd be just the right day for a picnic if I didn't have to work," she said.

"It sure would. All we need is food and maybe some beer. I already have the rest with me."

"Like what?"

"Like the desire to have a picnic. What did you think I meant?"

Her throaty laugh was filled with more promise than humor. "How would you like it if I said I'm not about to eat both the sandwiches Ma packed for me for lunch? She's always sayin I need more meat on my bones, and I keep tellin her that it's a sin the way I always have to throw out at least half what she puts up for me every morning."

"I'd like that fine. Just first class. Your mother's food wouldn't be wasted, and, no matter what she says, you've got enough meat to suit the Prince of Wales."

"You sure got enough talk on your own bones."

"Whatever that means."

"It means that I never did see a boy like you before. It's a wonder there's a girl left in town who you haven't been gettin next to." The smile was still on her lips, but I was conscious of being measured. "But you probably got a steady girl. Maybe that Charity Witham, right?"

"Wrong," I said. "Charity's nice but she's like a sister to me."

"Some people could get locked up for what they do to their sister."

"Not me. I respect womanhood."

"Sure you do. And how about that Elva Boudreau? I heard about her, too."

"You didn't hear anything." I tried to say this in a way that shut off any more mention of Elva but still wasn't stern enough to keep us from wherever we were going.

Fortunately, Elva didn't interest her as much as Charity. "And also a little bird told me that it won't be too surprisin if Miss Witham got her name changed one of these days to Mrs. Collis Gibbs."

"Was that little bird named Jabez Witham? If that's who it was, it wasn't a little bird, it was a bald buzzard who never gives up hope."

"That's the way he is," she agreed. "He's been hoppin after me ever since I came to town." She thought for a moment and then said, "Ugh!" in a way that made it clear she was picturing his skinny little body in bed.

"I've heard some things, too."

"Like what?"

"Like you and Witham have some kind of an understanding."

"Wouldn't he ever love that! Look what he gave me for my birthday." She twisted around searching for a package out of the cart behind us, and again I was conscious of a delicious young breast straining against a shirtwaist.

"How about this," she demanded, holding up a bag and pulling a bottle out of it. "Three of them in here—with love from old Jabez Witham! He says they came clear from France and they was rare and precious and just right for me and that I should save them for a celebration, and you know what he had in mind." This time the huskiness in her laugh was contempt, not promise. "The tinhorn probably got them off some peddler for next to nothin instead of givin me a watch or a pin or somethin else than what somebody ought to be doing for a pretty girl."

I've never bitten into a piece of pastry only to find my teeth crunching on an iron nail, but I'm sure the sensation would be close to the way I suddenly felt on that balmy summer morning. There was a purpose behind every thing she said and did. Celina Sewell wasn't idly bad-mouthing her employer, nor, probably, did we just accidentally happen to meet and find ourselves on the way to Medford.

"Let me look at that," I said, reaching for the bottle.

"Do you know French?"

"Speak it like a native." Of course, the only thing I understood from the label was that it was wrapped around a claret. "It's a very good year," I pronounced, handing it back. Mr. Witham's taste in wine is as good as his taste in bank tellers."

"Let's drink it. Let's use them all up for our picnic. That'll show him."

"Oh, I couldn't do that," I protested, wondering whether this series of happy coincidences included a corkscrew. "They're your gifts and you ought to be holding on to them for a very special occasion."

"Like now?"

"Like now. How do we get the damned cork out?"

"I'll show you. Pull over there by that big tree and we'll have our picnic right on the grass."

I surveyed the spot and shook my head. "And everybody else that comes riding along will be hurt because he wasn't invited to our party."

"Not that tree, the one over yonder in there." She pointed somewhere past the rejected spot, and although I didn't see the site she had in mind, there didn't seem to be any question that it lay behind a row of bushes tall enough to screen us from the notice of a riderby.

By this time, I couldn't have given less of a damn if finding this particular place was part of a plan or just another lucky accident. I headed our rig in and between the trees and tethered the beast where there was enough grass to keep it from bothering us. When I walked back to the tree she had picked out, the horse blanket stored in the back of the cart had been spread, and she was unpacking the sandwiches a mother had designed for a job her daughter proved didn't need doing each time she bent over to set them down.

"You haven't answered my question," I said.

"Like what?"

"Like how do we get the bottles open."

"Fiddle! You never been among 'em, have you?" Taking one of the bottles by its base, she broke off its neck by swinging it against the tree. Then she swished out the top few inches of wine, presumably discarding any shards of glass that might have fallen inside. "Some man I used to know showed me how to do this, and never in all the time I seen him do it did he ever cut himself inside or out."

"How long did you watch him?"

"Maybe over a year."

"And what happened to him?"

"I don't know. I finally got enough of him bein so mean to me."

"It might have been different if he ever came across a regular bottle opener."

"It might be different," she said, handing the bottle over, "if you'd take a drink once in a while."

I don't believe she intended getting me totally drunk, but it was clear from the way she kept urging more drinks for us both that she wanted me in an agreeable frame of mind. Unfortunately for her purposes, she underestimated my capacity and overestimated her own. By the time we were halfway into the second bottle, her words were slurred and her grammar even worse than normal.

"Collie," she said at one point, "you're the only man in this damn town that I honestly believed if I was in bed with and told you to get the hell out, all'd you do is go whistlin on out the door. Real down deep, you just purely don't give a hoot, do you?"

"I wouldn't say that," I answered, still not too touched by the wine we had taken aboard. "I certainly care about you."

"And you care about fat Charity Witham and . . ."

"And quite a few others. Sure. But most of all, you."

"How pretty do you think I am?"

"Do I have to tell you that?" The sunlight was glistening in her hair, and the ivory skin had taken on the glow that turned her into a figurine.

"Sure. I'm too skinny."

"You'll do." I answered, watching her smooth her skirt down over her hips.

Her giggle informed me that she knew the exact size of the lump in my throat. "Wish I could get you to talk pretty. I like it when boys talk pretty." She reached over me to get the bottle. "Let me have another drink of that."

"Careful you don't cut yourself," I said, leaning back to let her get it.

"A hell of a lot you'd mind!" The giggle disappeared without leaving a trace. "The only thing that'd bother you is if it kept you from getting any poon tang. Right?"

"Right!" What else was I going to say? I realized I was almost home and wondering what I was going to do after I got there.

"You're all the same. Sweet talk everybody, swear to do everything in the world, just let me do this little thing to you, but as soon as it comes down to doin somethin for somebody else, it's a different story."

The only way to keep from traveling down a spur that wouldn't lead to anywhere good was to shake my head in a sympathetic manner. So that's what I did, but she was already at the place where no agreement was enough. "You take that big gawk of yours, Sam Hume; you think for a minute he'd be willin to give somethin back for all he was gettin?"

"I guess he pretty much likes his own way," I answered, not feeling a bit disloyal.

"You're damn tootin! That Witham drives his very own father to shoot hisself, and when somebody gives him a chance to get even, all he does is get sore and badmouth them and go away to nobody knows where."

This was it. I was conscious of a moment of total clarity that can happen when you walk down a path and suddenly find a coiled rattlesnake facing you. Before you either run or bash its head in with a rock, there is that split second of fear and fascination. "Let me have the bottle, I want a drink," I said.

"Here."

I took the bottle, drank, and returned it. She lifted it back to her mouth, so intent on what was in her own mind that it was an automatic gesture. "You'd think somebody as big as him had guts," she said, "but he's as yellow as they come. I give him the chance to get his hands on more money than he ever knew was around, and all he does is call me names and walk out, leavin me layin there like some sow that's been serviced and is waitin for somebody to load her into a barrow and get pushed back to some damn farm!''

She was yelling. The anger unleashed by the wine and the memory of Sam's refusal to go along with whatever it was she wanted him to do caused flecks of foam to appear on her lips. Despite that Dresden doll image of hers, she was a very unstable girl. For a moment, I thought she was heading for the edge. But she wasn't.

Her story was coherent even though she raved and spittled as it came out, and it was simple enough to make me wonder if Jacksonville wasn't peopled exclusively by fools, myself chief among them. None of us had guessed the reason why a girl as merchantable as this one had chosen to bury herself in our backwater.

She and her mother were thieves. Her mother wasn't her mother—she was someone Celina had picked up in San Francisco to add a facade of respectability. Her loyalty was insured by the promise of a generous split of the gold Celina Sewell had begun planning to steal from Jabez Witham right after a Wells Fargo employee had bragged to her of the money they were making out of this spectacularly profitable two-bit bank up in Jacksonville. She'd come here, succeeded in playing on an older man's dread of impotence, and entangled a strong young recruit to load a cart up some midnight with the heavy bags looted from a vault to which she'd been given the key.

Midstream in the tirade, I saw the frustration that had touched this all off. It went: *How could the plan fail? Sam was sick with wanting her, he hated the banker for what he had done to his family, and why would he turn his nose up at all the money they could make? He was low enough to take money to guard Chinamen, wasn't he? Sure, you can expect something like that from an English nelly, but a man brought up as proper as Sam Hume ought to have enough respect not to take Chink money! But he did and then he drew the line at taking from an old polecat like Witham. So it had to be that Sam Hume was sick in his head, that's what. There was no way it could be her that was wrong!*

Her words also told me why Sam had disappeared. He'd gone too deep into self-disgust. The guilt he carried into her bed that night after we had come home from Edward Hume's funeral had been misread by her as proof that he was ripe to listen to an offer to become a thief. I was willing to bet anything that after he'd heard her out, he'd gone off into the woods to try and work the poison from his system. As his mother observed, he always wanted to be alone when he hurt.

But what about me? I had no score to settle with Witham—the man

actually wanted me as a son-in-law—and I certainly hadn't had the opportunity to prove I was ready for anything that would get me into her
bed. No matter how drunk and frustrated she was, spilling her plans
this way didn't make sense.

Unless, of course, I was the candidate to take up Sam's slack, which,
as it turned out, I was. Collis Gibbs was the next well-bred young romantic who'd stay in love long enough for the loot to be stashed away
somewhere safe—not like any of the town oafs who could be relied on
only to beat her silly after the robbery and make off with the whole
bundle.

"Sam's not as good as you, Collie," she said after having yelled herself
out. "You're not the kind that has to go around tellin everybody how
tough you are because, deep down, you're tougher'n anybody."

This time, my pull at the bottle was an earnest one. *How in hell do
I handle all this?* After this scene, I certainly wouldn't have put violence
beyond her if she sobered up without having enlisted me as some sort
of an accomplice. Of course she was vain enough to believe there wasn't
a man around who wouldn't do whatever she asked if she went about it
the right way. Whatever it was, I was going to agree and get the hell
back to Jacksonville as quickly as possible.

"Collie," she said, "we could do it together. It ain't such a big job.
What-all do you have to do but load the cart? I already got a key and
we could do it maybe three or four in the morning, and if anybody'd
see us, they'd only be a couple of drunks who wouldn't know what we
was up to, anyway. And then we ride out."

She was growing more excited again by the minute, and although
she still slurred her words, the wine was now telling her to say things
like, "I don't know why it never struck me before, but you'd be the
most right person to do it with. It ain't such a big job. What do I need
that big grumpy Sam Hume for—just to load a cart? Then what?"

Then he'd be the one the drunks saw loading the cart, I thought.

"What could I be doin with Sam Hume in San Francisco, lookin at
the sights? But you, you already seen the elephant. You're a gentleman.
You're good lookin and you know what to do to show a girl a good time.
There ain't a girl I know in San Francisco that won't be jealous.

"Oh, Collie, all the money we'd ever need and we'd be livin like a
real king and queen, not like you chasin after merchants around here
with your hat in your hand. We'd have cards and spades over everybody.
What do you think, Collie, wouldn't we be livin the life, though?"

For the first time since I had met her, she wasn't the young siren.

Now her eyes seemed to be bulging, instead of big. Vehemence and drink put coarse red patches on that flawless complexion, and although we had been leaning back on the grass, there was no grace in her body. There was nothing fragile left.

I drained the remains of the bottle and laid it on the ground between us. "Celina," I said with as much conviction as I could muster, "you're hitting me with too much all at once. I've just got to think about it for a while—not that there's one thing wrong with the idea I can see just yet. It'll work, that's for sure."

"Of course it will!" She narrowed her eyes. "You wouldn't be holdin off because of you and Charity, would you? If you're meanin to marry . . ." (she punctuated this with a contemptuous snort) ". . . hell, that'd be the dumbest thing I ever heard of. Once you get her old man's money, what do you need a fat thing like her for?"

I carefully knocked off the neck of the third bottle and said, "Girl, you haven't come up with one thing I can quarrel with. All I've got to do is figure out the other end of this situation. You know I'll be leaving my father here to face everyone after we've gone, and that's something that takes a lot of thought."

"Sure, I can understand that." She knit her brows, pretending to help me think through this dilemma, but it was as transparent as glass that I had said the words that fitted perfectly into her private plan. "I think I got the idea, Collie! I got a wonderful idea!

"Suppose we load the cart as soon as we pick the right night, and then you go home and I ride out, maybe over here to Medford with it, where any of them dumb farmers'll put me up for a couple of days without askin no questions. Then, after the smoke clears away and everybody is sayin that awful Celina Sewell must a done it because she ain't nowhere to be seen, then you just politely say you got some business in San Francisco, maybe drum up a newspaper reason for it, which is something you could talk that old rummy you work for into so long as it doesn't cost him nothin, and then you come over to Medford for me, and then we'll go get one of them coast steamers down to San Francisco. How's that, Collie, for somebody else havin some bright ideas once in a while?"

"It's just perfect!" I said, matching her enthusiasm. "The only thing is, Celina, please, I beg you, let me think for a few minutes. This is my first time for doing something like this, you know."

"Would it be your first time for somethin else?" she asked, not getting that husky promise just right in her voice.

She was ready to seal the deal right then, but something told me to stall long enough to see if her excitement was, as I hoped, the last brief flare of the candle before it went out. She had accounted for most of the two bottles of wine we had emptied and was well ahead of me on the third. I lifted the remaining soldier to my lips and handed it over, saying, "No, it won't be the first time for me, but I know damned right well it's going to be the best time."

Celina Sewell was never going to doubt anyone who told her how desirable she was. She giggled while drinking, and some of the wine ran down her chin.

Before she could offer me another turn at the bottle, I said, "You hold on to that for a minute, pretty girl, I've got to go pee. I don't know how you can take so much aboard without needing to, but I guess you're a better man than me," and I stood and walked off beyond the trees that surrounded us and waited for ten or fifteen minutes.

It was enough. She was asleep and bubbling her breath by the time I came back. The noonday sun and the wine must have worked on her like a gandy dancer because she'd only half undressed before going off, leaving her skirt in a crumpled heap just a foot or so away from her hip. And, as had been abundantly clear all morning, she didn't have that much underwear on, either. She may have arched her back a bit as I pulled off her drawers, but it certainly wasn't conscious cooperation.

I stood up then and looked at her, and I've got to admit that drunk, sleeping, and snoring, she was still a marvelous girl. Her thighs were a touch heavier than I had imagined, but, even so, that girl had a body beautiful enough to erase the last question in my mind, which was whether it mattered being hung for a sheep as well as a goat.

Then I stripped off my own pants and bent over her. It wasn't easy going, but it didn't bother me even when she muttered, "Not now, Sam, can't you wait?"

Afterward, I dressed and came back to where she still lay, not having so much as shifted her outstretched legs. I wondered if I could be scoundrel enough to leave with her horse and cart and drive back to Jacksonville, but I finally decided that it might not be the gentlemanly thing to do. After all, she set such store by gentlemen.

So I walked the two miles to town, guessing for a while what she'd do to get even with me. Then I found out I really didn't give a damn. I didn't even bother trying to make myself believe that I sure had squared things for my friend Sam.

The good feeling and the wine didn't wear off until I passed Witham's bank, when it struck me that I was probably going to need more protection than all of Tommy's coolies put together. She was a mighty tough girl.

Also pretty. I found myself trying to think of a way to convince her that I'd been so drunk I didn't know what I was doing and all that my final enlistment required was a touch more persuasion.

40

FOR THE NEXT few days I walked around town waiting for the lightning bolt to hit a sinner but, after a while, my worry came down to a more practical level. God might not be out to get me for the way I'd behaved toward a woman, but the odds were fairly long that the idea occurred to Celina Sewell. There was no way for her to think of me except as a bomb waiting to blow her plans for Witham's bank sky-high.

It was up to me to do something until the right plan to draw her teeth could be worked out. But what? Even if Sam were around, I certainly couldn't go to him for help, not for a while, anyway, since that meant comparing a set of notes I'd just as soon not have him know were in my possession. Talking to Tony involved another problem. I doubted how fast he'd get past his disapproval of my behavior, no matter how much he disliked Sewell. To tell the truth, I was queasy at the thought of describing to him what I'd done at the picnic. The way he'd looked at me after the march of the Petticoat Army was still too fresh in my mind.

As for Tommy, I couldn't reasonably expect him to talk to Witham or Witham to listen to him where Celina was concerned.

I was left with warning the banker about the trouble facing him, but a moment's thought told me I was dead wrong about thinking it an option. The girl hadn't robbed anything as yet, so it would end up as my word against what she was offering him. And suppose she caught me going into a private meeting with the old man? If she wasn't already entertaining the idea, it would be the final straw that within the next twenty clock ticks would send her out to charm one of the hard cases around town into helping her clear up the problem I represented.

That last thought grew and, in no time at all, turned Jacksonville into another place. After it occurred, whenever I stepped into a saloon, I couldn't help but wonder if Celina had already primed one of the loafers around the bar to pick the final fight with me. The woods as a hiding place weren't any help because there were too many who knew them better than I did. Worst of all, I hated the feeling of walking anywhere, even into our cabin, tensing against the possibility of a bullet winging into my back.

And that's why I settled on the only path open to me. I had to face her, talk it out, try to convince her that I'd been so drunk I didn't know what I was doing or remember anything she'd said. Some way, I had to sell her on the idea that she needn't fear I intended taking the story to old Witham.

But do I try seeing her during business hours? Not on a bet! Then I thought of waiting outside the bank until she finished work. She wouldn't want to create a scene on the street, and maybe I could talk fast enough to let me walk her home as I explained my side of the story. No good, either. She'd be the last person to balk at a scene and, even more, would turn it around to where the onlookers would be convinced that all that was happening was I'd taken aboard a few drinks before getting fresh with her. She'd be believed because enough of them probably had the same idea at one time or another.

This left me with going to her house in the evening, hoping that after she'd done with cursing me out, there would be a few minutes or even seconds to start whatever story seemed to have a chance of working. At the very least, I'd be alone with her long enough to know how much time I had left before she tried settling my score.

And all of this is why I was at her door at nine o'clock that night.

I knocked once, then again. No answer. Although it seemed that someone ought to be stirring because there were slits of light around the drawn oilcloth curtains, I didn't attempt a third knock and was about to go away when the door opened.

It was Celina, hair disheveled, wearing a shapeless robe, and scowling out into the darkness, but, oh Lord, was she ever lovely with the kerosene lamp's soft light behind her turning into a halo around her head.

At first, she didn't make me out, but after squinting and almost pushing her face into mine, she said, "Why Collis Gibbs, what a pleasant surprise!"

I'd been prepared for yelling, having things thrown, or even a shotgun nosed toward me, but not this. All I could do was stutter, "Celina."

She answered, "Yes," as if a chat on her doorstep with me was one of the nicest things about the night.

I repeated, "Celina," trying not to sound the complete fool she'd turned me into by looking so beautiful and then hitting me amidships this way, "about the other morning. I mean, our picnic."

She said, "What on earth are you talkin about, Collie? We had a real nice time and you're a real nice boy and you do your Pa real proud."

My wind caught up with me. "Do you mind if I come in?"

"I'd like that fine, Collie. I really would. But right now isn't a very good time."

Of course. Someone was in there with her. Not her mother because she wouldn't have bothered keeping the lid on for that fraud. Was Sam back? If he was, she was shrewd enough to realize there couldn't be a better place or time for us to compare notes than with her ready to call either one of us a liar because we each wanted her. Further, if she screamed loudly enough to draw a neighbor, being in her nightgown she'd have barefoot proof that the two of us had ganged up on her.

My mind just wouldn't work because, I guess, deep within I'd been dreading facing her. All I could do was stare—and be damned if she didn't smile back in return. She was figuring a step ahead of me every inch of the way and waiting until I caught up. "I'm sorry it's so late," I said, "but I wanted to talk things over with you."

"What things?" The smile on her face dared me to go on. She might not have been on the best of terms with grammar, nor able to hold her drink as well as she thought, but, sober, when it came to dealing with men, that girl was as keen as a Damascus bayonet.

Then I heard the thump-thump behind her of someone putting his boots on.

"It's not important," I said. "Not to someone as pretty as you. It just took me so long to work myself up to where I could ask you to go riding with me someday that I was in a fret to do it while I still had the nerve. I'm awfully sorry to have bothered you, Miss Celina."

I turned to leave, but this wasn't what she had in mind. Stepping back so that the door pushed open behind her, I found myself looking at Jabez Witham buttoning his jacket. Before I could either say hello or get away fast enough to pretend I hadn't seen him, she called, "Jabez, we got a visitor and guess who it is!" But her eyes didn't stop boring into mine with the loud and clear dare: *Go ahead. Go blabbing to him and see if he'll believe anything you say, now that we done it.*

Witham didn't want to see me any more than I did him, but he put a face on it. "Howdy, Collis," he said, "why don't you come on in? We're just about finished with the month's accounts."

"They really keep you in the traces, don't they?" was the way I tried to tell him that I believed they'd been working, and only working, this late.

"Certainly do. No matter how much time we put in down at the bank, there's never enough hours to get it all done. Things go on this way much longer, we're going to have to get another clerk to help out. Right, Seelie?"

"Right," she said, walking away and heading for the bed in the corner of the room. While she was bending over and pulling the covers out of a tangled mess, there was in Witham's look at me the pride of a bantam cock struggling with the fear that I'd tumbled on to something he desperately didn't want out. Pride won and turned into pure vanity that one of the town's young bucks had seen him conquer a prize as rare as this.

We stood there until she finished making her point about what had been going on, neatening up the sheets, patting the pillow, and seeing that the blanket was tucked in just so. Then I realized I was being waited out. She'd already gotten her message over to me, and Witham was too cautious to leave before he knew what she was going to say about all this. Especially why her mother was so noticeably absent. Since it wasn't reasonable to expect a suggestion that I stay around for a chat, I made my excuses and left.

I walked very rapidly away, my mind whirling. She had me. Now that she'd given in to the little banker, she didn't have one damn thing to worry about until every one of her ducks was in a perfect row. With Sam gone and an accident about to happen to me, she held all the trump.

The hell with worrying about that frozen English look of disapproval! I needed help, so I headed for Tony's post at Chung Lin's restaurant. Within another hour, I found that Tommy needed help as much as I did.

There were those who would do something about an unprotected man riding around with a bag of money in his buckboard, so Witham never went to Tommy's store for his split of their weekly profits. Instead, he had Tommy divide the funds between two deposit bags, tag both with his name, and bring them in to Celina Sewell who then stored the larger one in the corner of the vault where the banker kept his own property. The charade was intended to pass for just another merchant making his regular deposit.

On this day, after he'd handed his bags over to her, she said, "Don't go runnin right off, you're wanted in the back office," which Tommy immediately recognized as involving a problem. Witham seldom called him in when things were going well.

He was right. He was no sooner through the door before Witham looked up from his ledger sheets and announced, "Lin, it's not working."

Tommy stood quietly, waiting to see how big a calamity this was going to be.

"It's no good," the banker continued. "I know that neither the Wah Lee thing nor the bad feelings coming out into the open between those two Chinese societies is your fault, but it's getting mean enough to set folks to talking, and no matter which way I add it up, my bank is going to be hurt by me being known as your partner. I heard just yesterday that the sheriff and some of his boys were making jokes about it in the saloons. There's just too much ill will here against your people."

Tommy saw that it wouldn't be of the slightest use to point out that the Cantonese and the Hong Kongs had always been at each others' throats and that Wah Lee's death couldn't be laid at any door but that of the three white ruffians who had murdered him. His partner's mind was made up. His case had already been dismissed by the court of last appeal.

"The fair thing to do, Lin, is divide up our interests. Of course, you'll always be able to count on me for help so long as it doesn't aggravate the situation, but we have to separate. Legally as well as practically because I wouldn't ever want anybody to point a finger and say that under the table we're still partners. I've got to be able to show there's nothing between us."

"Shu," said Tommy, relapsing into coolie English. It wasn't an occasion where he could concentrate on locution. Right now, his mind was racing frantically toward the slightest opening that might keep Banker Witham from a division that equaled their individual standing in the community.

He was so preoccupied with this need to save any part of the identity he'd worked so hard to attain, that he scarcely heard the banker continue, "The way it looks to me, there's only one divvy open to us. You can't keep working the mine because that's where all the hard feelings come from, so I'll take that and hire some white miners to run it, and you get outright title to your store and restaurant." He leaned back to give Tommy the time to digest his large-heartedness.

Naturally, Tommy didn't point out that a Chinese restaurant or store wasn't worth very much in a town where there were no employed Chinese workers, because the banker knew it as well as he did. Instead, he said, "Mr. Witham one fair man. I do what you say and be glad for what you give. You always be one fair man."

"Fine," boomed Witham in that deep voice he always used when he was being genial. "I'm glad, boy, that you see it the way it is. You're a crackerjack businessman and we'll be getting together again someday after the feelings die down, you mark my words!" Then, calling out to Miss Sewell, he told her to bring in the documents they had prepared.

Tommy didn't miss the note of triumph in her eyes when she arrived with the releases that took away his ownership in a gold mine. Nor did he sign them with anything but the "X" Witham suggested as his mark, although he was perfectly capable of writing his name in English. When he pushed the papers back across the desk, Celina collected them, saying the first words she ever addressed him as a human being. She said, "There ain't many men who'd a been as generous to a Chinee boy."

Before I could ask Tony's whereabouts after I reached the restaurant, Tommy held up his hands and said, "First, must be different banker," and went into the back room to turn the *fan tan* game over to one of his employees while I slouched at one of the three small tables in front. When he returned, he sat down opposite me in a way that said he had something on his mind, too. So, instead of asking right off for Tony, I decided to wait until he showed up.

To make conversation while Tommy marshaled whatever was bothering him, I said, "I hear some talk that the bad blood is churning up again between the Hong Kongs and the Cantonese."

"Is some problems," he admitted.

"Way I heard it, there's more than just a few problems going on. Some blacksmith was in the Bella Union and said that one of your boys, he wasn't sure which side he was on, was at his forge to ask how much it cost to get a dagger made."

"Only Sojourners play act, is all. Maybe I get Chinese actors here from San Francisco for real show."

I studied him. "Tommy, are you worried I'm going to put something in the paper about a fight that might break out?"

"Yes. Sometime you put in wrong things."

"Then I won't."

He knew this was a promise and that I'd keep it. "What else you hear?" he asked.

There was a real depth to the rift between the two factions in Chinatown. In fact, there was so much bad blood that the hatred could easily end in an open battle, and that would be all the excuse our rougher element needed to drive the area's Chinese away to another camp. No

wonder he looked worried. "You probably know this better than me,"
I said, "but the guess in the bars is that there might be a full-scale tong
war one of these days. In fact, some of the boys talk about chipping in
for weapons for one side or the other and then getting some bets down."

He sucked in his breath. He didn't expect that all the talk of bad
blood could be kept down, but this was the first he'd heard that it had
gone as far as becoming a gambling matter in the Jacksonville saloons.
I didn't realize it for a few more minutes, but my news represented
something he had to add to the plan he was working out in his mind to
get back with Witham.

"Got to chop weed even if root remains," he said. "Hong Kongs and
Cantons always fight, but if they make money, they wait to go home
before they make war."

That puzzled me. "I thought that's the way it was. Has anything
changed?"

"Yes-s-s," he answered, fairly hissing it out as he expelled his breath.
"Sojourners soon hear no more work. Mr. Banker Witham takes gold
mine away from me today. Is going to use white coolies. Be soon in other
mines too. Not too much work for all—so only white coolies be hired,
like Mr. Witham do. Soon be no more Sojourners."

"Oh, my God, Tommy! When did this happen?"

"Is happen today. Mr. Banker Witham and lady clerk tell me this
morning."

That must have been the last item required to push Witham into her
bed, because it would have taken something big like being given Tommy's share in the mine. I wondered how long it would take her to figure
out that if she played Witham just right, there'd be no point to risking
recruiting someone to help burgle the bank.

Tommy and I were now in the same box, so I told him the whole
story of the picnic, including its finale and the way she had neutralized
me an hour ago. He didn't seem surprised by any of this, nor did he
comment after I added, "She doesn't even have to go to the trouble of
denying anything, because she hasn't done anything. All she has to do
is keep her legs around old Witham."

He thought in silence for a while and then nodded, which I took to
mean he saw as well as I did that everything was going her way. I had
one forlorn hope left. "Maybe if we tell Witham's wife, she'd scare some
sense into him."

"Is no good," he said. "Wife has enough own bad things. She give
Mr. Sheriff same as joy-girl give Mr. Banker."

After I had digested this, he said, "Maybe one more plan is possible."

I waited until his study of me became unbearable. "Don't just sit there like Buddha, spill it!"

"Only thing Mr. Witham likes more than joy-girl is money."

"If there's enough of it But it'd have to amount to an awfully big pile before it beat out her hand. Right now, anyway. And I don't know how soon before she'll come down on Sam and me and squash what's left of you. And what pile's bigger than a gold mine? Goddamn that Sam, what a time he picked to disappear!"

Again he waited, this time to make sure my outburst of frustration was all spent. He wanted me to listen very carefully. Somewhere along the line, Tommy had gotten the idea that I was apt to go off half-cocked. Then he said, "Is much more money to be made. Banker Witham will like and so will joy-girl because now they want same things. Now they be happy to even use my coolies again if they make money together. Later, maybe not."

He looked so positive about it that, without knowing anything more, I felt as if he'd lifted a hundred pounds off my shoulders. "Tommy, for God's sake, tell me about it. If I fit into it, let's get started."

"You very necessary. In beginning, you do most of work."

"Meaning?"

"Farmers need water like miners. We get maybe year more drought, then Jacksonville not ever be a big city. Be no city at all."

Although I didn't have the foggiest idea of where this led, I'd long known that he was the smartest of any of us. I said, "You've got my vote. Go on," and shut up.

"Farmers make much talk of dry ground. So we get water. We dig ditch to bring water from Applegate River, go through Sterlingville, and end here to make farmers and miners more happy to stay."

When I saw that was as far as he was going for a while, I whistled softly, "Tommy, that's at least twenty miles. Do you have any idea what it could cost to dig that long an irrigation ditch?"

"Much thousands. I know. Too much for one man."

"It's the kind of a thing that only a big company could handle."

He shrugged, because now I was on the trail. "Stock like big mining companies have must be sold. I hear man who sells stock makes much money."

"Oh, Lordy," I said, "that's where Witham comes in."

"Shu."

"He's got the connections to get it going!"

Tommy sat back, expecting me to go the rest of the way by myself.

"And he's got the Wells Fargo people in on anything he wants to do. If they prime the pump, there won't be a man here hesitating two shakes before digging into his sock to round up as many shares as he can get. And that skinny polecat will collect a commission on every share. But you figured that, didn't you, you precious marvelous heathen. He'd go ahead with the idea even if it rains tomorrow. He'd talk himself hoarse reminding everybody that next summer was coming, too."

"Shu," said Tommy.

"But where in hell would they ever get enough men to dig a ditch that wide and that long—oh my God . . ." I said again because Tommy was turning me into a true believer, ". . . your coolies! And if you don't have enough of them, Witham'll fight to send you back to China for more."

"Is possible," he admitted. "But plenty Sojourners already here."

"And now you want me to go spring the idea on him, right?"

"No."

"Why not, goddammit! I'm the logical one. I'm the one he wants for a son in law."

"Not you. He wants Tony."

"Tony! Are you crazy?"

"Yes. Same houseboy catch Mrs. Witham, hear Mr. Witham tell daughter Tony be best for her."

"For the first time, you're wrong. That old buzzard would never believe for a minute that someone like Tony could ever get serious about a daughter of his."

"If Tony will help, makes no matter. Is only important if Tony will make like he thinks marriage to Missy Witham not bad."

"I'm afraid of that. It's not the kind of an idea they'd expect Tony to come up with. It would still be better coming from me."

"Is no good. Your idea, and Missy Joy-Girl shows Mr. Witham everything wrong. The way you tell me, you say day and she say night."

He was right. She'd be bound to sniff away at anything I suggested and then point out to him which was the part most likely to go bad. Besides, I was getting superstitious about doubting anything Tommy said. "Fine, then it's Tony with the bright idea. It's probably even better than that. Witham thinks Tony's brother would come in on any investment that he thought up."

Tommy looked thoughtful. He was still working out the details. "Maybe Tony waits until you write story in paper. You write that big citizens do this some other place where it work just fine. Then Tony gets big idea. Then Tony tells how good is idea to Mr. Banker Witham."

Flooded with happiness, I yelled loud enough to stop, but just for a moment, the noise in the back room. "It works, Tommy. She won't do a blessed thing to any of us until the two of them collect all those commissions. We've got the time, bless you. I know damned right well you've figured out how it's going to put you back into Witham's pocket . . ."

"And Sojourners make money," he pointed out.

". . . and it works out for me because no matter what Sewell says, Witham will go out of his way to keep on the good side of Father until his great new company is rolling. And she sure as hell isn't going to do anything that might make Sam upset the applecart if and when the simple bastard ever gets back, and . . ."

". . . and all you do is go home now and write how big citizens make big money with irrigation ditch," said Tommy. "Then you, not me, tell Tony of his big idea."

41

NEXT DAY, Tony was back from his latest search. For the past week he'd been scouring the forests and fields surrounding Jacksonville and not finding the slightest track of Sam Hume. "Either something nasty has happened," he told me while we were sitting in the Bella Union, "or the scoundrel insists on lying doggo."

"If 'doggo' means he's hiding out until he's sure that being made a fool of by that joy-girl isn't the end of the world, then that's the one I'd pick," I said.

"Joy-girl? Really, Collis."

That's when I told him the whole story; everything that happened at the picnic (staring away at one of the tables on the other side of the room while I hurried through the last part of it), how Celina had undoubtedly teased Witham into giving her Tommy's share in the mine, and ending with all of last night's events. When the smile stayed on his face, I added, "And now that you have this brilliant big idea about a canal coming down from the Applegate, you've got to wangle another bid for supper, yes, supper, limey, at the Withams."

"Dear boy," he said, "you're rushing your fences. As I understand it, I wait until you've printed the news of this remarkable canal coup in that journal of yours, do I not?"

"You do. But I want you to be ready. I'm not sure you don't require at least a month to rehearse what you're supposed to say."

"Ass. Tell me more of this blow for justice that you've struck. The feeling is strong among the troops that you may have omitted a detail here and there."

His words were light, but the way he said them gave me a glimmering of the depth of his dislike for that girl. I went through the story again, but this time he didn't laugh. Something was still festering because it cost him noticeable effort to go back to talking about the ditch scheme. "And I'm to fob this off as my idea, is this correct?"

"No, you idiot, you haven't been listening to anything but the dirty parts. Do you want me to start from the beginning again, or do you just want another description of her marvelous buttocks?"

"Try to forget them, will you? Simply tell again how I happen to be so intimately aware of ditch-digging techniques at my forthcoming—forgive me, Mother—supper at that charming Witham home."

"It's *me* that writes the story. It's *you* that sees where it works for Jacksonville. *You* don't go blurting out your opinion the first time you bump into the old goat, you wait until he invites you over again, which he will certainly do since he likes you and your brother so much. Then, over a sociable glass of tanglefoot, you two old friends discuss the money the canal can bring to the Rogue Valley, and then you allow as how Charles is going to be so anxious to rush over here with a fistful of pounds that he won't even wait to change them into the dollars he needs to buy the Applegate & Sterling Company's bonds. Do you think you can remember that much?"

"It was you who named it, of course."

"Of course. Sounds impressive, doesn't it?"

He thought for a moment. "Yes, loverly. I'd expect no less. But I'm not quite certain that you should appear as having quite this much to do with the project. Especially the name. As a matter of fact, it may be that I broach the entire thing, including the grand company title, in a way that will make it seem as if it were all his idea. A bit tidier, don't you think?"

"Much tidier," I said. "Loverly."

Tony didn't have to wait forever for Jabez Witham's invitation. The banker was out looking for him the very day my story reported the enormous gains an irrigation ditch had produced for an area with even more severe water problems than ours. The mythical source for this account of how prosperity had been snatched from the jaws of ruin was an engineer who had been directed by a huge eastern company to visit here and remain incognito while he determined whether we of western Oregon wanted wealth badly enough to do something about it.

My story soared on from there, detailing the immediate love the engineer had felt for our blessed area and his chagrin that the oath of secrecy extracted from him by his company kept him from sharing the solution while he was still among us. I ended the story with what I emphasized was an exact quote of the words that fell from his lips:

> By thunder, it isn't fair to keep your good people here in the dark about forming the Applegate & Sterling Ditch Company [I just couldn't keep this part of my promise to Tony—I couldn't risk that name being ignored].
> Although there's nothing I can do to convince my superiors to put their money up, because there's no thought being given here to a ditch just

yet, there's nothing to prevent me from coming back some day as soon as I retire and starting one myself. It's going to make me a millionaire, you wait and see!

Tony thought the story a bit overblown, but he was the only one who did. When Witham came scurrying after him as he walked along California Street the day the paper came out, he had already passed several knots of men excitedly discussing the engineer's dream. "Morning, Anthony," Witham called even before he'd finished crossing the street. "I been hoping to bump into you."

Summoning a pleasant smile, Tony answered, "Mr. Witham! I was just thinking of you."

"Were you now?" Witham returned the smile with more interest than he'd ever paid over his counter. "That's fine. That's real fine."

They stood facing each other for a moment, until Tony couldn't resist any longer. "What do we do now," he asked, "shake hands?"

The banker didn't hear him or, if he did, paid no attention. He was on the track of a deal. "Mrs. Witham was asking me no later than this morning if I'd seen you lately. She's really got her heart set on you coming over one of these nights for supper."

Tony frowned as if he were consulting an internal appointment calendar and then, as if struck by a happy thought, asked, "Perhaps this evening? I'm not much for hunting trips these days and that leaves tonight absolutely free, doesn't it?"

"It certainly does!" He boomed this as if Tony's freedom were the best news he'd heard in a month. "When I go home to dinner at noon, I'll tell Mrs. Witham to fix you whatever you like most. What's your preference?"

I'd prefer you knew dinner was the evening meal, you ass. "I'm quite certain that anything prepared by your wife will be delicious," Tony said aloud. "And I must say that I appreciate the invitation no end."

"Yes, sir," the banker never wound up a deal without stressing its benefits, "I'll bet it's been a long time since you had a good home-cooked meal."

"Yes, sir," echoed Tony, smiling just as toothily as the other.

When he reported this conversation to me, I warned, "The man isn't a total damned fool, Tony. You'll exercise that warped sense of humor of yours for just so long before he catches on."

"He's a grasping damned fool," was his answer, "and they are the very worst sort. There are none so blind as those who will not see."

"Oh, kiss my ass," I groaned. Tony turned insufferable whenever he rode one of his rare high moods, and this one was so marked, I was afraid it might boot the whole thing. "Just follow the plan. Don't improvise." Actually, I was as delighted as he and couldn't wait to hear the rest of it.

So, for the second time since coming to Jacksonville, Tony found himself at dinner in the home of Jabez Witham. This time, however, it wasn't nearly as festive an occasion as it had been that first Christmas. The feeling stayed forced and dismal as they sat at the table, although Witham saluted each dish with gusto, smacking his lips while eating it and grunting appreciatively when its remains were removed by the Chinese houseboy.

Tony did his best to match his host's pleasure in the burnt vegetables and barely cooked pork, but his efforts were ringing hollow in the face of Charity's uneasiness and Mrs. Witham's withdrawn, stiff-necked manner. It was obvious she didn't get the same amount of pleasure her husband found in his visit. She didn't seem to hear half the remarks he addressed to her and went totally deaf whenever Witham spoke, which was often, and in every pause in the conversation.

Charity, seldom speaking and darting occasional looks at her mother and father, evidently also found the meal an ordeal. And Tony thought he saw a hint of tears in her sidelong glances at him.

None of this bothered the banker. As Mrs. Witham and her daughter cleared away the last of the meal (Tony found it interesting that they didn't leave this to the houseboy), he sat back in his chair and said, "Hard to beat a home-cooked meal, hey Anthony?"

"A lovely treat," Tony agreed, wondering how long their civility demanded a guest remain after a meal.

"How about a good cigar?"

"Thank you, no. It's a habit I've never acquired."

"Good boy." Witham nodded approvingly. "Me neither. Waste of time and money, and the good Lord never sends us too much of those commodities." He reached inside a vest pocket, brought out an enormous watch, and, after consulting it, announced with a frown, "Almost seven o'clock and I'm supposed to be over to Mayor Sizemore's house in an hour, and we haven't even had the chance to talk about anything important."

At this, his wife placed the cleaned dishes in the huge teakwood sideboard kept in the corner of the dining room and turned and left. Tony heard her walking up the stairs. As if she'd never been there,

Witham continued, "It's too draughty in the parlor. Let's set here a spell."

But I'll bet Charity is still lurking about, Tony guessed, and, abandoning his hopes for an early escape, sat back to wait for whatever his host had in mind that would yoke Charles to the Applegate & Sterling Ditch Company.

It wasn't long in coming. "You know, that report about the engineer in today's paper had some horse sense to it."

"Yes, it did. Rather a bit."

"Sure made sense. I cut it out of a half dozen copies, and one of them will be on the next freight wagon to San Francisco. I've got a hunch that the Wells Fargo could be mighty interested in this kind of a proposition."

It flashed through Tony's mind, *Tommy was so right! He'll do our job for us.*

"There's lots of money to be made in a deal this smart. Could be a chartered company with bonds and shares. That's what I'm going to talk to the mayor about."

Liar! If Sizemore wasn't drunk and incomprehensible by eight in the evening, it would have been only if all the saloons had burned down. That left Sewell's cabin as his destination, and, for the first time that evening, Tony doubted that it was he who had inspired Mrs. Witham's hostility. *Of course she knows. How many secrets are there in a village?*

He said aloud, "It certainly seems as if it has possibilities. That engineer may have been a bit optimistic, but the principle is quite sound. Of course, I wonder about the work force required to dig a canal uphill and down for that distance."

"You've a good head on your shoulders, son," he said, "but it's not as up and down as you might think. I've been all through that territory and I know what I've been looking at. It's all downways coming from the Little Applegate. Wherever there's a rise, there's enough head of water built up to force it over. Be no problem at all."

Since the conversation was swimming along so well, Tony saw no reason not to push on beyond the limits he and I had set for the night. "Save for the digging," he offered as another objection to be overcome, "it's not the kind of a task that would seem to engage much interest among field workers, is it?"

"I thought of that, too!" The banker relished proving that he was a man who considered all sides of a problem. "No question but all we'd get to sign up for a job like this are loafers who'd quit after a day's drinking money was in their pockets. But did it ever occur to you that there's more Chinese around here than you can shake a stick at? They're being used to build railroads in other places, you know. And mostly they're digging through hills to get the job done."

"What a first-rate idea!" Tony could hardly contain his enthusiasm. Then he shook his head, again in doubt. "I'm afraid it will take an awfully long time to import as many as will be needed for a project like this. I don't suppose the coolies with us now will be willing to leave their work at the mines." He thought for a moment. "Unless, of course, they were offered a sizable increase in their wages. Do you think a company such as you contemplate can afford to pay premium wages?"

"We'll see if we have to," he said, leaving Tony with no doubt that Witham had already assembled what he considered to be a mighty tight package. He was so greedily traveling the exact route Tommy had planned for him that he overlooked the possibility that Tony had already heard his post as lawman didn't have long to go.

"Would you mind terribly," Tony asked, "if I wrote home to Charles about this? He'd be enormously interested in reading the article by—the article. You know how he feels at the prospect of an investment in the Rogue Valley."

Tony read the answering smile as meaning Witham's last doubt of the canal's worth had been resolved. If it came about, well and good. If for some reason it was never completed or even officially begun, there were still all those commissions to be made selling shares in the company after it became known that a genuine English duke was putting up good money to buy as many as he could get into his hands.

Leaning forward, the banker said, "Anthony, I'm going to tell you something that I'd just as leave be kept between ourselves."

Tony leaned an equal distance forward.

"I've been putting together a block of mining and farming interests here that's big enough to interest a man like your brother," Witham said, referring to the properties he had taken away from Chung Lin and Edward Hume among others, as well as the farms he'd foreclosed, "and someday Jacksonville is going to be bigger than Sacramento, mark my words. Whoever owns the land around here is going to make millions. The dollars will be dropping down on him like pears falling out of the trees. Mark my words, son, there isn't a better place for your brother's money!"

"It may well be," said Tony, "but doesn't everyone feel that way? After all, there are quite a few Jacksonvilles sprinkled throughout the West, aren't there?"

"None with something like this going on," he said, dropping his voice in intensity. "The opportunity of a lifetime is coming about here. The key to the whole thing is that whoever gets control of the water company is the party who can buy and sell whatever he wants. If you want to pick up a farm at a reasonable price, you just don't sell that farmer any irrigation. It's as simple as waiting until they come to you with their hats in their hands begging you to buy their property because there's nothing else they can do with it!"

"What an amazing plan!" said Tony, the amazement really directed at himself for his ability to get a smile of approval on his face instead of a reflection of the dislike welling up inside of him. "My brother must hear about this. I shall write him of it this very night." Then, feeling that he'd had his quota of this man's company for one night, he stood up.

Witham looked surprised at this abrupt move and then rose, too. In the pleasure of unrolling his scheme, he'd almost forgotten about Celina. But not quite. "I've got to run, Anthony," he said, ignoring that it was Tony who was trying to close out the night. "I don't want to keep the mayor waiting, so we'll have to talk this through again. And maybe you'd better let me make sure of the Wells Fargo money before we go to your brother. Be time enough then to talk to him after there's a big company showing that they're willing to put up their dollars and cents. Then you move with all the gumption you've got."

"Absolutely right," Tony agreed, thinking of how cold hell would have to get before he would ever lend himself to furthering the plans of someone like this. "But, as you say, this *is* the opportunity of a lifetime, isn't it?"

"You bet!" he answered, raising his voice from the conspiratorial level to which it had sunk while entrusting Tony with perhaps one-third of the things he actually had in mind. "And you're a crackerjack businessman for having seen it as fast as you did. I don't mind admitting being surprised by the way you know how many cents there are in a dollar." He consulted his watch, now torn between getting to the cabin where Sewell waited and the need to complete the other item he had scheduled for the evening. The schedule won. He dropped his voice back to its former confidential level and added, "Anthony, I wonder if you'd mind doing me a little favor."

"Of course."

"It's late and I don't have the time to do it myself, so I have to have Charity take care of an errand for me. It's not real important, except to him, but I promised Stoney Flora down at the stables that I'd drop this off for him tonight," he said, taking a golden half eagle from the other pocket in his vest, "because he's got to pay for a load of feed tomorrow morning before the bank opens. I don't like Charity going out after dark, but I'm a man of my word and if you'd just walk her over there and back, you'd be doing me a good turn."

He asked this in a way that said that, after all, he'd done so much for Tony there couldn't be any question of this small service being rendered. Not waiting for Tony's half-hearted murmur of agreement, he walked out of the room to the foot of the staircase. "Charity," he boomed, "will you come down here for a minute, girl?"

She would and did. Nor did she point out that so long as Tony was leaving, it wouldn't be that much trouble to him if he dropped off the five dollars on his way home. All she said, after Witham left them was, "Let's be going," and this was more to the door than Tony. "The sooner we get there, the sooner we'll be back."

Tony heard her sigh once or twice on their way to the stables, but, other than that, her answers to his attempts at polite conversation consisted of nods and a few not very intelligible mutters of agreement. Once, when he mentioned me, she answered, "Collis is a very nice boy, but he's so crazy . . ." and her voice trailed off.

Flora had already retired to his bed in the stable's loft, and it took a full five minutes of pounding at the door before it opened and he stood there, yawning and scratching. But once the purpose of the obviously unexpected visit percolated through his head, he grabbed at the coin and stowed it in the pocket of the pants he wore night and day.

The absurd chore had accomplished its purpose. They walked no more than ten paces on the path back, when she stopped, faced Tony, and giggled, "That man thinks it's the easiest money he ever made, but Pa will have six ways to get it back before tomorrow night."

"I would have expected no less," said Tony.

"That's Pa," she said as they resumed their walk. "Once he gets something in his mind, he'll be forcing it to happen before you can say boo."

"And what is he forcing now?"

"You on me. Or, more like it, me on you. He's had his heart set on getting us together ever since he heard your brother was a duke. That's true, isn't it?"

"An earl, actually."

They walked on in silence until she asked, "Does it mean a lot?"

"It does to my brother. It means quite a bit to him."

"But not you?"

"Well, of course it does. It's really rather pleasant. But, Charles is the earl and has the estate. I'm Anthony Johnstone, who won't have a shilling if he doesn't earn it."

"Oh," she said quite seriously, "I know that much. I read up on all about it after Pa told me. What I was talking about was whether it all didn't seem so silly to you to be here. Your family being royalty and all."

"Not royalty. Aristocracy. The peerage. And those are just words."

She considered him carefully and said, "I like you, Tony. I was afraid to go along with you tonight because I was sure you'd make me feel small."

"Why should I do that?" When she didn't reply, he added, "Oh, I see. My family being royalty and all."

"Now you *are* laughing at me," she said, but not timidly. "You don't understand. It's *you* that scares me."

"Really?" He found himself liking this open, friendly girl and wondering how'd she come by those qualities with that set of parents.

"Sure. It wouldn't hurt you to smile once in a while. You sat at the supper table tonight like you smelled something bad but were too polite to say anything about it."

"Oh, Lord," he said, "did I give that impression? It's almost exactly what your mother seemed to feel about me."

The dullness crept back into her voice. "It wasn't you. I don't think she even knew you were there more than once or twice."

"Then what was it? I've attended happier funerals."

"Oh, nothing," and she sighed again.

Tony had no taste for any family situation, let alone the Withams'. In an attempt to back away, he said, "Your father and I had quite an interesting chat and—"

"I don't want to talk about Pa."

They walked again in silence until he saw the tears coursing down her cheeks. It was the fastest way anyone would ever melt Tony. "What is it, Charity," he asked. Does it upset you that your father and I discussed business?"

The tears became racking sobs, and when he turned to her, she impulsively buried her head against his chest. "It's just so awful," she cried. "Everybody knows about him and that Sewell lady and it's driving Ma crazy, and I can't even face people when I go out because I know they're laughing at me."

He stood and awkwardly patted her head until he thought of saying, "Don't take on so, Charity. I imagine this sort of thing happens whenever a man gets older and there's a pretty young girl waiting to send him up. But it passes. Of course it does. All that's required is patience."

"A lot you know," she said, looking up at him. "Nobody'd dare laugh at you, so how would you understand?"

Celina's derision briefly crossed his mind. "Charity, if you don't stop crying, when we get home your mother will swear I've beaten you. Then she will have even more reason to dislike me."

"Oh, gosh! I can't let her see me like this. If Ma thought I had any idea what's going on, it would just plague her worse than ever. I'm so worried about her! Sometimes I think she'll go out of her mind and do something to herself if Pa don't quit it."

Again, he didn't have the right words. They walked in silence until they reached her door, where she turned and said to him, fresh tears brimming in her eyes, "I just can't go in. Please don't make me go in just yet."

"I shan't make you do anything. Of course not."

"You go on home," she told him. "I'll stand here until I get a hold of myself. I'll wash my face at the pump and she won't know. Go ahead, you go. You've been nicer and sweeter than any boy could be."

"I'll wait. We'll talk of other things."

"She'll hear us. I'd be real glad if you want to stay a while, but we can't stand here. She'll be out in a shake, soon as she hears I'm back. She always worries about me."

"Shall we continue our walk?"

"Sure. Please. But not back into town."

"Then where? There on that bench near the barn?"

"Oh no!" she said and drew away. "Did Collis tell you about him and me?" she asked.

The question made no sense to Tony until my description of what had gone on in the Witham barn came flooding back to him. "Well, yes, actually. He did."

"What did he say?"

"He said that the two of you had made love and that he thought a great deal of you."

She shook her head sadly. "Is that why you want us to go to the barn?"

"If you must know, I hadn't thought of it."

"Honest?"

"Really."

She searched his face earnestly and then said, "Most boys wouldn't have owned up that they knew. You're a very good person, Tony."

"And so, Charity, are you."

She thought, drew in her breath, and said, "If you want to go to the barn, it's all right with me."

"If it's all the same, I'd rather not." Then, fearing he might have delivered a hurt he hadn't intended, he added, "I'm sorry. That wasn't meant the way it must have sounded."

"I know it wasn't. You wouldn't do that." Her eyes filled up again, this time with sentiment. "Come on," she said. "I just want to talk and be with you for a while. You don't mind, do you?"

He said that he didn't, and although he had meant it seriously, within a few minutes of their entry to the loft, they were locked together. He never remembered which was the one who kissed the other first, but he never forgot the hunger of those kisses. What followed was an almost effortless preparation, and there was never then or later another question of Anthony Johnstone's manhood.

It was altogether wonderfully fine, and it wasn't until they had lain back that he remembered his fears. His feeling crested into—he used the term *gratitude* for her womanliness.

Nothing alloyed the moment. When she reached for his hand, forgetting that his only arm lay on the side away from her, he was able to say, "You don't have much choice, do you?" and he leaned over to put that arm around her.

She said in his ear, "You're my one-armed sweetie, that's what you are."

"Does it bother you?"

"It used to. Oh, not the way you think. I mean, you looked so fierce and dashing with your sleeve pinned up. Whenever I'd see you walking in town, it was always the most romantic thing I've ever seen, even though you scared me half to death."

He smiled into her hair. "I thought I was quite civil."

"You were not! Your eyes were always fierce as an eagle's, no matter what else you were saying."

The exultation remained with Tony. What a delight it was after he'd left and had walked all the way back to our cabin to find that he wanted her again.

42

"**S**AM'S BACK! Collie, do you hear me? Sam's back!"

It was Elva, yelling to me from the other side of the street. I crossed over through the first gap in the stream of horses and carts heading for the mining fields—this damn town was getting bigger than San Francisco—and went over to where she was beaming with so much happiness that she couldn't wait until I reached her side. "We got him back last night!" she called again. "Can you imagine, he's been sick out there by hisself all this time!"

"Whoa, start at the beginning." She was still shouting, even though I was now standing alongside her. As a matter of fact, she was babbling on so that I wasn't able to see it all in detail until later when I had patched her account into the version that Sam Hume let drop in dribs and drabs over the next week.

He had gotten unmercifully drunk the night Celina Sewell had asked him to go in on the bank robbery. She wouldn't let him interrupt, and instead of slapping or cursing her when she'd finished, he got out of bed, dressed, and left, understanding for the first time what she'd been doing to him.

He'd gone home, headed for the keg of whiskey his father had kept in their shed, and began ladling the stuff into himself. Elva, awakened by the noise of his soft, steady swearing, came out to see what was bothering him, and, by that time, he was drunk enough to start pawing at her. It was that damned drive of his—any girl would have served because he was trying to find a way to shut off his mind.

She'd wanted Sam ever since she'd been old enough to understand the stirrings inside her. This certainly wasn't the way it had been in her dreams, but his torment was so plain that she would have let him do anything he wanted that could help. That is, up until he muttered in the middle of one slobbering kiss, "Seelie," and she pushed him away so hard that it brought back a smattering of sense.

He gasped, "Oh my God, Elva," but it was too much and too late. Hauling back, she slapped him as hard as she could across his face and

293

ran out of the shed to a nearby field, where she stood crying in misery and loneliness.

When the memory of the agony in his face became stronger than her misery, she returned to the house, but he had disappeared. As Tony had guessed, his goal was the forest and one of their hunting camps, but he never reached it. The whiskey and the violence of the anger he had vented on Elva because he couldn't express it to Celina combined into overwhelming fatigue, and, not having the wits left to find shelter under a tree, he sank to the ground in a sleep that wasn't interrupted by the driving rainstorm that hit the mountain that night.

When he opened his eyes late next morning, he'd already been claimed by a severe chill. Rolling out of the water-filled gully where he lay, he got to his feet with just enough sense in him to know that he couldn't face going to Jacksonville. He was never able to remember how he accomplished it, but he thought maybe it was some instinct that sent him over the trail that led to the Table Rock Mountains. All through that trek, he kept fixed on the idea that if he could reach the Indian tribe in camp there, Billy Tell or some of his family might let him stay on until he felt better.

The fog clouding his mind didn't lift even after he reached the campground. One of the Indian boys, seeing him stumble through the brush that led to their clearing, ran to fetch Billy Tell, and he and another brave carried Sam, burning up with fever, to his tipi. None of the Indians knew the medical name, but they all recognized the symptoms of pneumonia, because that was the disease that killed more red men than all the tribal wars put together.

At Billy's behest, the tribe's squaws tended to Sam in shifts throughout that night and the two that followed. Some of the elders attempted to dose him with herbs and bark tea, but he vomited up everything they gave him, and, after a while, the squaws shooed away the medicine men and sat by him day and night, cooling his forehead with rags dipped in water and making certain that he stayed covered by the blankets in which they wrapped him.

The fever broke on the third day, and, for the first time, Sam was able to keep down a few bits of the stew they brought him. Billy waited another day to make sure he'd come through the siege and then left that night for Jacksonville and Elva.

Naturally, Mrs. Hume wanted to go right out to her son, but Billy wouldn't let her. It was a hard trail under the best of circumstances—the clusters of brush driven into it by the fall winds now made it impassable for all but the most surefooted. And he didn't want to wait until the morning for Tony or me, so that's why Billy and Elva made the trip back alone.

When he looked up and saw her, tears came to Sam's eyes before he said the thing that sealed her to him for the rest of her life. Weak as he was, he told her in tones that were just as reasonable as if he were mentioning the sun had come up, "I saw your face in front of me all that time."

It could have gone on from there into something dramatic, but that would have made Elva uncomfortable, so she just nodded and humphed, "Well, you weasel, it took you long enough to understand it," and she bent down, going about tucking the fur skin blanket underneath him wherever it had come out.

Three more days passed before enough strength returned for him to make the trip home. During that time, no squaw but Elva tended to his wants, which was all right with them because they understood. When it came time to say goodbye, it was Elva who thanked Billy and the tribe while Sam stood alongside. He neither smiled nor shook hands but looked at each of the Indians in turn, and they read in his stare all the gratitude they needed. It was only with Billy Tell that he showed emotion by gripping him by the shoulder before leaving with Elva.

His mother, of course, was nowhere near so stoic. Her clucking filled in all the words left unsaid by the two of them as they had traced their way back through the forest. As Elva told me, "It was so treacherous on that trail that we saved his strength by not talkin of anything besides, 'watch out for that hole,' or, 'it don't look like that log will support us both, so let's go one at a time over that gully'."

After he was undressed and in bed, his mother got a bowlful of strong beef soup into him, and, because the return trek had been so hard, he fell asleep and stayed that way for a day and a night. When he awoke the following morning, he wanted to get up, but the two women raised so much of a fuss that he agreed and lay back in his bed. He was too weak to move much, anyway.

Not once during any of this did a word pass between him and Elva about the cause of it all. He'd said enough when she had first appeared at the Indian campground. She had answered *I forgive you* by everything she had done for him and by never once asking why it had happened.

"Don't press him about anything," she said to me as we walked back that morning to the cabin. "It'll be enough for you to be there. You know him—when he's ready to talk, he lets out everything that's in his mind."

So, as I went into his bedroom, I said nothing more than, "Howdy, Sam. Been away?"

He grinned weakly. "You damn weasel, how come you're not working?"

"I am. I'm going to do a big story for our front page on how dangerous it is for greenhorns to go wandering in the woods."

"That's about the size of it."

"Then you admit you're an idiot?"

"I do," he said. "And I don't need no more proof than I'm layin here listenin to you." The half smile went away as he added, "I'm sorry, Collie."

"For what?"

"I did you a wrong. I didn't say nothin, but in my heart I was holdin it against you about what your father told mine about his claim. When Pa came back here and said Dr. Gibbs was in cahoots with that polecat, Witham, I believed him."

"I can't hold that against you. He was your father."

"You should of. I've been doin an awful lot of dumb things, but that was the dumbest—one of them, anyway. Even if your pa had been siding with Witham, which I know he wasn't, there was no call to hold it against you."

I was surprised that Sam took a thing like this so seriously, but then I realized that the actions of neither of our fathers was the point—he was simply and desperately struggling to clean out the evils that had beset him since Celina Sewell had come to Jacksonville. The plea in his face told me it was a much tougher battle than I could imagine. To try and help him through it, I said, "Well, you don't have a corner on badness. I've pulled a dirty trick or two on you, too."

"Like what?"

"Like never mind. You'll go to your grave not knowing. But just remember that, from now on, every time you catch me looking at you, I'm laughing inside."

"Collie, the first thing I do after I get out of bed will be to break your neck. Just on general principles."

From the doorway, Elva said, "Now both of you quit it. I swear, Collis Gibbs, you're supposed to have more brains than to be raggin a sick man. As for you, you big ninny, you just lay there and save up your strength, and never mind tellin one of the best friends you'll ever have that you're gonna fart thunder and lightning as soon as you get your hands around his neck!"

"Elva Boudreau, what a thing to say!" called Mrs. Hume from the kitchen. "I don't know where on earth you learned that kind of language."

"From your son," said Elva. "He's got the worst mouth I've ever heard on a man." She turned back and observed, quite seriously, "Now you've gone and shocked your ma," and both of us broke into laughter.

"You get out of here, Collis Gibbs," she told me. "You don't know how sick he's been. Right now he oughtn't to be sayin another word, let alone horsin around with you."

It was a sensible command. If, on our way over to the cabin, she hadn't described how close Sam had come to death, I'd have seen it in his face.

"Give me one more minute, Elva," Sam said. "I need a little time alone with Collie. There's something I got to say to him."

I suppose she could have done the feminine thing of insisting that no matter was so important it couldn't wait another day or two, but that wouldn't have been Elva's style. As she went out the door, Sam called, "Close it, will you?" and even that didn't produce anything beyond acceptance.

When she had gone, Sam said, "Come over closer, Collie. I wouldn't put it past that weasel to be listenin at the door, even if she does do what she's told, sometimes."

"When it suits her," I answered, not enjoying the prospect of a confession.

I should have known better. It wasn't a confession, it was an announcement. Straining up to a sitting position, he said, "I'm gonna get rich, Collie. Poor people don't have a chance. The hell with tuggin at your cap out of respect when money goes by. That ain't for Elva and me. Somehow I'm gonna get everything good for her and Ma."

"Nothing wrong with that," I agreed.

"You're damned right." He studied my face and then lay back, satisfied because he saw I believed in his regret for all that had happened. "Go ahead, now. I'd better be gettin some sleep."

I went out and, as I closed the door behind me, Elva came from the kitchen to meet me. "How did he seem to you?" she asked, using the corner of her apron to rub flour from her hands.

"All right, now, I think. Much better than he's been for a long time." She thought I meant since Celina came to town, so I went on. "He's different than he's been—than he's ever been. Being as sick as he was seems to have turned him over into thinking beyond the next hour. Weak as he is, he's got a grip on himself."

"Maybe. I pray that's it and not just the weakness. This morning, before I brought you back over, he started right out tellin me that his mind is set on bein somebody and that he's gonna make it up to his ma and me."

"That's close to what he told me, too," I admitted, "and I think he's going to make it stick. The best thing for him would be a good job and staying with it long enough to clear away the monkeyshines."

"He ain't thinkin of a job. He's got some big ideas."

"A mine? No, he wouldn't do that. Don't tell me he's thinking of becoming a farmer or a merchant."

"You're close. What he's figurin on is land. He says that the best money here is gonna be in land, and he's fixin to do somethin about it. He wants to file a donation land claim as soon as he's up and around."

"Sam Hume a land speculator?"

"It mightn't be all that bad. It might even be good. He knows just about as much as anybody about where houses could be built and where there's water underneath. Oh, Collie, it's all too good to be true!"

"If it stays that way," I answered.

Tony reacted almost the same way I had after his visit to Sam. He also saw the change in our friend, but his happiness was even richer than mine because he'd been delivered from Celina's malicious charge. Sam was one of the closest friends he'd have have—but that was all.

Tony was feeling good about just everything that fall. He no longer got that faraway look in his eyes that meant *what am I doing here?* that used to come to him every so often—*here* was where he'd proved himself as a hunter and a man. He'd taken to Charity more than I would have thought possible. And it didn't matter that I'd had the first experience with her. Indeed, once, when I started off on some explanation designed to make him feel better about the matter, he cut it short by saying, "Really, Collis, it's the girl who matters to me, and I couldn't care less about anything that went before."

I grinned. "Thank you, Lord, for the European mind. An American would be waiting to climb all over me, or else he'd pretend I no longer exist."

"You don't," he said. "I'm surprised you haven't heard."

"She's good medicine for you," I answered seriously.

She was, too. Now that the canal was being seriously talked about, Tommy wouldn't let him leave his nightly Chinatown post, but almost every afternoon he met her at the schoolhouse so they could walk home together. And, most of the time, that's all they did. Oh I suspected that on an occasional Sunday when her parents were at church they paid a visit to the barn, but since he'd never shown half the interest that Sam or I had in sex, that must have been just nature taking its course.

Naturally, it was too tender a subject for me to tease him about, but on one occasion he brought it up himself. "I *like* being with Charity," he said. "She's actually quite perceptive, good company—laughs easily whenever she isn't being chivvied by her parents, quite a sense of humor, and, indisputably *my* girl—the first I've ever had. No matter what may happen, she'll always occupy a very special place, won't she?"

"She won't," I disagreed.

"Why on earth not?"

"Because you're fickle. Fickle and venal." I liked the way that sounded, so I repeated it, "Fickle & Venal, Hardware Merchants to the Crown."

"Fickle, certainly. But venal? Why venal?"

"Aren't you after her father's money?"

"Oh, but of course. I'd almost forgotten it, even if he hasn't."

Her father positively beamed whenever he saw them together and devised more opportunities for them to see each other. Tony believed that most of this was due to the banker's hope of an introduction to the Johnstone family funds, but I'm not sure it was so open and shut. Witham was infatuated with Sewell and he was afraid of his wife, but if there were an honest soft spot in his heart, it certainly belonged to Charity. I saw him look at Tony one day and, as clearly as if it were written on his forehead, he was thinking, *He's only got one arm and he's no duke, but, danged, he makes Charity happy!*

The old man went out of his way to engage Tony in conversation. He'd talk about everything from banking (which Tony found only slightly more intelligible than Chinese), his own shrewdness (most often), a few veiled references to his wife's many attacks of "the nerves," and always ending with a catalogue of Charity's virtues.

Just once did Tony find Jabez Witham to be more than the sum of avarice, provincialism, and boredom. After walking Charity home from her teaching chores, he was surprised to find that the old man hadn't yet left for the bank after his noonday "dinner."

"It was a full hour later than his normal departure," Tony told me, "and, as we arrived, he was sitting on the front porch, staring off into the hills. It startled Charity into a hasty goodbye to me and no more than a very quick, 'hello Father,' as she hurried past the rocker in which he sat and into the house. Since I had no taste for an unneeded conversation with him, I waved as soon as she had gone through the door and started back for town.

"But he stopped me.Calling, 'Anthony, don't be in a hurry, son,' he left the porch and came down the path to where I stood. 'I'm waiting a spell before I go back,' he said. 'Can't go just yet. Mind keeping me company for a bit?'

"Of course a polite refusal wasn't available to me since, by now, he's aware that my duty begins in the evening. So we began a walk that circled perhaps a hundred yards or so about his home.

"I had expected another of his eternal probes into our family affairs, but no. As a matter of fact, for at least five minutes he said nothing at all; he simply walked beside me and every so often stared at his home in a way that if I didn't know the emotion to be foreign to him, I might say was mournful. Then, with a sigh that was quite deep, almost convulsive, he told me, 'She's off again.'

"I said, 'Oh?' not knowing what else was expected, but, evidently, a response wasn't required. It was as if I hadn't been there. The reference had been to his wife. And then came an utter torrent of words.

"Collis, I was simply overwhelmed. He spoke of Mrs. Witham as if she were some unimaginable disaster that never left him. Evidently, the woman is daft or at least on its thin edge. He described her as always having been a shrew, but since she entered her middle years, she's become his nightmare. He doesn't dare permit her to be alone, leaves the house only when Charity is on hand because she's attempted to take her own life several times.

"When she isn't morose or withdrawn, she seems to be capable of screeching tirades that leave him weak and trembling. According to him, from the time they were married she punished his slightest transgression by withholding herself from his touch for months at a time—which probably explains his eagerness to believe that a tart like Sewell can find him bearable. She's run away from their home more than once, and each time he found her, it was with a man from the lowest of stations.

"He told me of other matters so personal that, at first, not only did I not want to hear, I found I could not look at him while he went on. Once, I did. Although his voice had continued stable, he was crying as he spoke. What could I do? I walked with him until we'd traversed the circle for at least the fifth time, and all during that time he never quit pouring out his personal torment.

"And when at last his emotions were spent, he left my side and walked into the house without a word of farewell. A shattering experience, really."

"Poor bastard!" I said.

"I'm afraid so," Tony agreed. "It wasn't a man shifting blame for his own iniquities, it was rather a man who had to say these things aloud before he snapped."

"He'll never feel easy with you again."

"I'm not certain. It may be that he'll no longer feel the need to recite those bloody dull stories of his business successes. Throughout our walk, he punctuated his distress by speaking of his love for Charity, that she was the only thing that mattered in his life, and that, in some curious way, the fact that I have an affection for her has knit us together."

"Suppose he had to choose between Charity and the bank?"

Tony laughed. "We'd have to think about that, wouldn't we?"

43

MANY OF OUR FARMERS had gotten their land through the territory's east donation land laws. When mining became too onerous or when a man was too lazy to make a go of a farm somewhere else, all he had to do was file a claim and the government would give him 320 acres. If he had a wife, she was entitled to the same amount of land.

They were liberal with Oregon land in those days. At first, the donation law said that a settler had to be in the territory before December 1, 1850, but that was soon amended to include those who settled here before 1853. Later on the politicians stretched this to 1855, and it probably would have gone on beyond that if there hadn't been so much rumbling from those who already had their land and didn't want anyone else aboard the train. But while the land rush fever was raging, especially after the news got out of the Applegate & Sterling Ditch Company being organized by all the big money, it sometimes seemed as if we were attracting as many land speculators and lawyers as we were farmers and miners.

It became so bad that some men hitched themselves to anything in skirts in order to double the free property they could get to sell off to new arrivals, and for some the results were just godawful. You'd see some lout walking down the street with a child young enough to be his daughter, and he wouldn't have the grace not to introduce her as his wife. I remember one Sunday when I joined Tony in attending church with the Withams, there was this man, at least forty years old, sitting in the row ahead of us. He'd been staring solemnly ahead throughout the service, and the only indication that he was moved by anything the minister said occurred when he nudged his wife to stress how much he agreed with the sermon.

After the services ended, as she followed her husband down the aisle, only the infant clutched in her arms kept her from seeming like a sleepwalker. I've seen the same expression on the faces of those stupefied by too much opium, so I supposed she'd probably pulled too hard on the

302

laudanum bottle before leaving for church that morning. That opiate was the primary ingredient in many of the patent medicines settler women swigged to get them through their days. But, as we walked out of the church into the chilly sunlight and I saw her thin little flanks outlined under the calico dress, I realized that the vacant look wasn't from a bottle, it was the accumulated brutality of a marriage entered into before her body was ready for it.

Land speculation sounds terrible, doesn't it?

Well, it was. But since it's the business Sam Hume turned to as soon as he felt well enough to be up and around, I must explain that, away from girls, he was the most pragmatic man I've ever met. This wasn't a flaw—when a friend needed help, it was one of the qualities that made him such a tower of strength. Some of the things he did during the days he dealt in Rogue Valley land weren't especially wholesome, but we had learned that he was a complicated package for all his single-mindedness, and if you wanted his friendship, you accepted everything that went with it.

His first deal was fairly uncomplicated, and it took place right after the door had been shut on the donation land claim law. He filed on a plot of land along Pair-O-Dice Ranch Road on the side away from the Jackson Creek mining claim, and, because it was an easy walk into town from there, it wasn't too long before a new farming family determined that it was where they wanted to build their homestead. Even though he hadn't yet put in a nickel's worth of improvements, they paid the seven dollars an acre he asked for it.

When he told me about it, I said, "You stole the money, you weasel! For something that didn't cost you a cent, you got damned near a thousand dollars clear and—"

"Not near a thousand. It was $2,240. And I didn't steal the money, neither. They got a good buy because they'll be right off the ditch comin down from the Little Applegate. While everybody else is whistlin for water in drought times, his fields are goin to be green. That farmer is no sucker, he's a darn smart man."

"He must be shrewd," I agreed. "It's a wonder he didn't get your pants, too, while he was taking such advantage of you."

He answered with that slow grin. "Collis, this is the business to be into. How about coming in with me?"

"Well, I've got about nine dollars. We'll both have a lot if we pool our money together."

"I don't give a damn about what you put in. We'll use my profits for starters, go on from there, and you can pay me back as soon as we get rollin. We can be partners every inch of the way."

Ordinarily, I'd have jumped at the offer because it was new and promised to be interesting, but I didn't. The drawback was that although I've never minded dealing with rascals, I've always been too repelled by land and livestock traders to want to have anything to do with them if it can be helped. As Tony says, I'm a romantic.

Traders literally flooded our way during those days. Too much of the land claimed through the donation acts ended up in the hands of those who never did a lick of work beyond scratching out the legal papers that wrung profits out of the back of some poor farmer. These weren't rascals, they were parasites. They were all riding high on claim trading, and when they filed themselves, it was for the purpose of being bought out by an adjoining owner who wanted a properly operating place but couldn't get it going because the speculator had purposely laid out some kind of an odd section that ruined the worth of the normally proportioned tracts around it. None of them ever intended to manage the lands given away by the government—they just wanted to hold onto it long enough to make a profit.

So, right after the donation law ran out, they began selling to each other, using their acres as pawns in a get-rich game. The ones who worked out the nuisance claims or manipulated their chunks into substantial holdings made big money selling off pieces at unholy prices to real farmers and ranchers hungry to exchange their lifetime's savings for a piece of ground where their families could live and grow in peace.

Sam could stomach people like that, but I couldn't. "I guess you'd better count me out," I told him. "It doesn't sound like my kind of fun. I'd rather throw my cash over some bar instead of staying up all night to count if any of it's missing."

He shrugged, and that was about as much of a judgment as I expected. "Suit yourself, but don't be lookin to me to borrow from one of these days."

"I'd prefer Witham to you any day of the week."

This time there was no grin. "Might be the same thing. Who knows?"

I studied him closely and then whistled. "My God, Sam, don't tell me you'd think of ever coming closer than a hundred miles to that shark?"

"His dollars are no better or worse than anybody's else. They sure as hell don't have his name on them. If I get into a big enough jackpot and the profits look right, he'll go along, and all I'll need to do is to watch out for my back."

I couldn't keep from saying, "But your father—"

"My father's dead. Now it's up to me to take care of Ma and Elva, and this is the fastest way I see of gettin the money to do it. Once I got enough, then maybe I can try something else."

"Would they want you putting in with Witham?"

"Can't see where it's any of their business." He eyed me carefully and added, "That's why havin you with me would be so good, Collie. Even Witham can't talk fast enough to get by you. I'm not saying we'd go to him tomorrow, but if the chance came up to get a hell of a lot of really prime land, he's the only one in town with enough cash to swing it. If it was you workin out the deal with him along with me, then we'd be on the high ground."

I shook my head and said, "Sam Hume, I'd take my hat off to you if I wore one. I still can't see myself into land trading, but I'll sure keep you company if it ever comes to working up a deal with that man. And you won't have to give me any part of what you make, either. I'd pay my own money to watch what happens if and when the two of you get together."

For quite a while Sam had enough cash to bankroll his deals by himself. They were small, but every one earned a profit, and Phoebe Hume began feeling as proud as Punch over the way her son was turning into a solid businessman. One afternoon, while I was there for some pie and milk and she and Elva were sitting in the kitchen with me, I said, "Mrs. Hume, that boy of yours is going to end up owning half of Jacksonville one of these days."

"He's a right smart go-getter," she admitted.

"He is, for sure," Elva chimed in. "But somehow or another, him bein so busy buyin and sellin land makes it hard to think that it's Sam."

"Any man with the kind of steam he puts into things is bound to be a big success," I said, "once he's on the right trail, and, from what I can see, Sam is on the best in the valley. He's going to be a rich man, and you'll both be proud of him."

I wished it sounded as good to me as it did to them. The truth of a remark Mrs. Hume had made about Sam having another version of the Sweetwater fever became more pronounced with every sale or swap he made. He was buying and selling creekside properties and making money at every turn. Many of the other traders fell by the wayside because their capital was all on paper, and when they guessed wrong on a piece of land, they couldn't hold on until a buyer came along with as much capacity as they had to fool themselves.

But Sam didn't stumble once. He never bought a piece that wasn't

capable of being turned over whenever it suited him. Within a few
months he'd earned a name for being willing to pay a few dollars more
than the going market for any prime property and, as a result, got the
first cut at most of the good propositions. Of course, none of this just
dropped into his lap. He was out day and night in all kinds of weather
checking things like water access, road possiblities, and whether drainage
patterns left logical places on which to build a cabin. Before long he was
enough of a land expert that other traders sought him out for the advice
he didn't mind giving since it led quite a few times to deals he took for
himself. We saw very little of him during that period.

As a matter of fact, none of us saw too much of each other until the
winter was almost spent. Alben Hensley was leaving more and more of
the *Sentinel*'s work to me, and Tony was taking quite a bit of pride in
his ability to keep order in Chinatown, so, when he wasn't sleeping
daytimes, he was off somewhere with Charity. As for Tommy, he kept
hopping faster than any of us. Another horde of coolies had been im-
ported, and, because the winter had been mild enough for double shifts
on the ditch, he was making better progress with it than anyone had
expected.

It was quite a time for four fellows barely into their twenties, but in
those days and places, people tended to perform as maturely as their
natures allowed. Frontier life offered two choices; either you acted like
a man and met your obligations, or you stayed footloose and followed
the promise of fun from camp to camp. I tended to drift toward this
latter group since I certainly had neither the taste nor need to assume
responsibilities, but I found myself becoming just as steady as any of
those who hadn't left to see the elephant.

It became my job to put out the paper, and this brought me just
short of the point where I was either going to offer Hensley a few dollars
to buy him out or else start up a new one in competition. I liked newspapering, and more than once I surprised myself by turning down a
chance to lark with some of the other young bucks because I found I'd
rather spend my time getting the next issue together. I even rigged a
bunk in our little office shack so I could work right through on the day
before publication.

That's where I was when Sam came along with the big deal he'd been
heading toward ever since getting into the land speculation business.
Barging in one morning and ignoring the pile of galleys on my desk, he
asked, "You busy?"

"No. I always hunch over a table this way when I haven't anything to do." In spite of my words and the fact that there was a story that had to be finished, I was glad to see him. It had been a while.

"Glad to hear it. I'd hate to be botherin a man who had something on his mind."

I put down my pencil and sighed to the wall, "Lord, wouldn't it be nice to be a rich and greasy land trader with no need to slave away for wages?"

"You'll never know," he said, "unless you come in with me. The deal's still open for a couple of things I got my eye on."

"I recognize you now. You're Satan. You're here to tempt me."

"Almost. It's time to talk to Witham."

"You don't need me. You haven't been doing anything else since late fall but learning how to deal. If anybody needs help, it's more likely to be our friendly banker."

"Sure he does. Maybe you ought to drop him a hint about how he needs somebody like you to protect him."

"I'm serious, Sam. You still see yourself as a boy going up against a tough old man—"

"That's not it."

"Sure it is," I insisted.

He sat down on the rickety stool we kept around to discourage visitors from overstaying and leaned back against the wall. "It's complicated, Collie. I know somethin I'm not supposed to. Witham'll jump at doin a deal with me, but how fast he jumps depends on how green he thinks I am." He looked at me as if he expected a decision based on this skimpy observation.

I pushed the galleys aside. "Sam, you know I'll tag along with you if you want me to, but it'd be better if I knew what's in your mind. Right now all I've heard is that Witham wants to give you money and you don't know how to take it, but I'll bet our flatbed press that there's no truth in either item. Just for fun, why don't you start at the beginning?"

"I was fixin to if you ever got done yammerin long enough for me to get my thoughts together."

That was another of Sam's ways—keep circling around a situation until you got the idea that he wasn't sure he knew what he was doing and then move directly in. So long as it suited his purpose, it didn't bother him to give the impression of being not much more than a big country boy. I repeated, "It's time to tell me what it's all about."

"The railroad's comin to Jacksonville."

"So?"

"There's only one way to run the line in here. It's got to come over some parts of the Clinton Trail." Then he stopped to study something on the wall about a foot above my head.

"That's nice." I felt like I was pulling teeth.

"It sure is. I can buy damn near all that land down there for less than a dollar an acre."

After some rapid thinking, I said, "Then I don't know what you need Witham for. There can't be more than a thousand or so acres on a straight line along the trail."

"You're as dumb as the rest of them. What kind of a man would just buy the track route? It's the land on either side of it that's gonna make the money. Nobody ever gets rich just sellin line routes to the railroad because they go another way if you want too much, or else they get the government to take that land away from you for a song. Hell, I'd give them the land they put their tracks on. Just let me have what's on either side and there'll be people shovelin dollars at me to get their hands on it."

I finally saw where he'd been driving. No doubt Witham was also aware of the railroad coming in over the Clinton route, but if he thought Sam knew it too, he'd gobble up all that property for himself before Sam got the stake together for a bid.

My figuring was interrupted by Sam's short laugh that didn't contain a drop of amusement. "Maybe you're right," he said. "If you can't see what I'm talkin about, then I'd be better off without you."

I didn't bother answering the charge. Instead, I told him, "What worries me about this deal is that maybe it's you that's missed something. You're not the only one with the brains to map the way the railroad will get here. What makes you think that Witham isn't already two steps ahead of you?"

"Because I know he's not."

"How so? You two been getting together to compare notes?"

"Better'n that. He had the railroad people over to his house the other night and they talked out a timetable that gives him plenty of room before he has to tie up his money. Charity heard them."

"And Charity told it to Tony?"

"And Charity told it to Tony, who told it to me."

"You're going to make a million dollars," I said. "The railroad doesn't care who they get their land from. You want to stall Witham by convincing him you need money for something else—but you're going to buy along the Clinton Trail."

"Goddamn right. And you're gonna help me, so let's get started."

If anything, the meeting in Witham's back office went better than we had hoped. A few times Celina made it her business to bring in papers for the banker to sign, but she couldn't have derailed it, even if she had tried, which she didn't. Her attitude toward Sam and me was as polite as if we were two doctors trying to settle on a new place to locate our vegetable compound factory.

Oh, there was one thing. On her second or third visit, she couldn't resist looking soulfully at Sam while Witham was facing the other way, but that was only to test the water. She'd have cut him dead if he had responded, but he was just as good at acting as if they'd never even shaken hands. As for me, I blushed at her first appearance, but, since no one noticed it, I figured the hell with it and set about being just as professional as everyone else.

Witham was the best of us all. He neither frowned nor crowed when Sam told him the reason why we'd wanted to meet privately with him, and, while we sat at his desk, his manner said as plain as print, "I'm a businessman. If it's a good deal, I'll make it."

That's where I came in. After Sam described the fictitious plot of land he wanted to acquire out along the Rogue River near Gold Hill, I pulled my oar by saying, "There's probably going to be a city there in the near future, Mr Witham. Most of the inquiries our paper gets from other places always end by asking that if there are no more mining claims available, how about some rich river land. Sam's right—that's where the new town is going to be and—"

He interrupted the glowing description of Gold Hill's prospects I was about to paint by nodding his head vigorously. "Collis, I have a great deal of respect for your vision, and I certainly have no reason to doubt Samuel's judgment when it comes to property. That's why you don't have to go any further about how good the land is that you want to buy. I take your word for it. But there's no way I'd risk my dollars on something that might *probably* happen. My advice to you, Samuel, is if you're so sold on the property, then you ought to trade off the pieces you're holding now and use the proceeds to go there and get it before the prices go up."

We knew he'd loan us the money, but, like all bankers, it was his second nature to argue first—which is what we wanted. We had to convince him that we were so set on the idea that there wasn't room in our minds for anything else.

I introduced the next tack. "Mr. Witham, the property we own (Sam and I had agreed to present ourselves as partners since there had to be a reason for my attendance) is undervalued right now. The loss we'll take if we sell it off would be big enough to wipe out our profits from Gold Hill. How about, instead, if you go into the deal with us? You take care of the down payment, and we'll make every payment after that."

He answered quite sensibly according to his lights, "Then what do I need you for? If I make the down payment, then I don't need partners."

"It'd be easier for you," I insisted, "if you let us worry about carrying the mortgage."

He thought for a moment, cleared his throat, and then said in a mild voice, "Maybe I can do better than that. Samuel, there's been some differences between us. I know you put a thumping lot of the blame on my shoulders for what happened to your father, and even though I think that's wrongful because he was past twenty-one and should have known that business is business, I can't help but feel that I might do something to help out you and your ma. So I'm willing to stretch a point. I'm going to lend you all you need for that Gold Hill proposition. Yes sir, that's what I'll do. And you don't have to make me a partner, neither."

Sam and I kept from exchanging the glance that wondered whether the other saw where the hook was buried, but the thought certainly occurred to us because we each then sat back and waited for the next step in the dance that this polecat was about to perform.

He didn't disappoint us. "All you have to do in return," he said, as casually as if this were the least important part of the conversation, "is to sign some notes and put up the land you hold now for collateral. I don't care if your acreage doesn't amount to halfway near the value of whatever loan you want. It'll be enough to show your good faith and keep anybody from criticizing me if they look at my books."

Witham didn't think we had a prayer because we were in his back-yard. And, after he called Celina in to help with drawing the papers, we weren't the least bothered by the look that slipped away from her before she could collar it. We knew the two of them were going to be a mite premature when they set about congratulating each other after we left.

44

J ACKSONVILLE was riding and growing on a crest of prosperity. New roads branched almost weekly off California and Oregon Streets, and, by December 1855, we had eight dry goods and grocery stores, three blacksmith shops, two livery stables, one hotel and several boarding houses, a brewery, a stove and tin shop, a few boot and millinery emporiums, two more physicians, and God knows how many more lawyers.

Of course, none of it seeped down to the Chinese who made so much of it possible. No one bothered taking a census of the Orientals on hand, and the first reference to any Asian I've ever been able to find in the official county records was that, in 1873, a woman named Polly Yung Ty was jailed in Medford for running a house of prostitution.

Of course, the coolies didn't care about this lack of official attention. They worked too all-fired hard to concern themselves about such matters. They'd been recruited by Hong Kong and Cantonese agents in the street beating drums and waving banners bearing slogans like *Be Rich! Go to the Land of the Golden Mountain*, and all of them were lies, although of course, wealth is always a matter for personal identification. Throw a penny into a beggar's bowl and he considers himself a man of means.

Sure, some of them saved up enough after the costs of their passage and employment contract money were deducted to go back to their villages as substantial men, but all of them worked long and hard for whatever pittance came their way. Few of them ever had the luxury of a moment's rest beyond their New Year's celebration or an occasional night at the *fan tan* table, but their dreams of dignity and freedom vanished as soon as they returned to their brutish work. They were lonely, sexually frustrated, and had no family life, so it wasn't any wonder that they channeled their disappointments into the rivalry between the two factions that dominated Jacksonville's Chinatown.

Many of them were ex-convicts and Manchu rebels who'd escaped prison by signing up with the labor recruiters, and they brought their hostilities with them on the trip to America. It was easy for them to infect the others in camp because there certainly wasn't anything else around to engage interest.

Infection became passionate conviction. Almost every coolie joined either the antiemperor elements or the Manchu loyalists. Even the ones who didn't want anything to do with politics found that it made sense to join the tong of the people from their own province because both sides regarded an independent as an enemy. In China, a *tong* means "a hall"— the place where members of a community meet to discuss interests and grievances. Here, in America, the term came to describe a group who'd banded together for mutual protection. There were very few Occidentals in Jacksonville with ears sharp enough to hear the drums on which the tongs had begun to beat.

But the beats sounded loud to Tommy. As an entrepreneur, he couldn't afford to affiliate with either side, so he secretly assured the leadership of each group that he was with them. That left him in the position of a man trotting along the blade edge of a very big knife. He needed help and support and hadn't the slightest clue where to find it so, naturally, he turned to Sam Hume.

He held his problem in check until Sam showed up one day at his restaurant. After he'd eaten the meal Tommy brought him, he asked, "Has Tony been around? I know he's not due here till tonight, but I can't find him anywhere else in town."

"Must be with Missy Witham."

"Nope. She's the first one I went to, but she didn't know, neither. I need him to step off some land with me."

"Forest? He walks much in the forest."

"That might be it. Guess I'll have to wait for the weasel. How's it goin with you, Tommy?"

It was the opening Tommy had been looking for. He described to Sam how tight the tensions were drawing between the tongs, his concern about what his work force might do after the ditch was completed, and his belief that Banker Witham was again going to sacrifice him to the city's anti-Chinese mood immediately afterward.

Sam shook his head. "For a smart fella, Tommy, you're readin it all wrong. As fast as you can get that ditch finished, there's gonna be another big job come up for your coolies."

Tommy didn't answer, but he felt his heart leap at the possibility Sam saw some other factor that could give him enough time to consolidate his gains in this white world. He knew Sam seldom said anything designed solely to make someone feel better, so he sucked in his breath and sat quietly until his friend had his ideas in exactly the order he wanted to bring them out.

"You see, Tommy, there's a railroad comin here, up either from San

Francisco or Sacramento. They're gonna need men to lay the tracks, and you'll be the one with all the coolies to get the job done. Everything I got is bet on it."

"I hear of what you buy to the south."

"And you didn't figure out why?"

"Too much for me to think."

"Bullshit."

Tommy shook his head sadly at his own limitations. "I hear railroad might come. I hear land you buy is Clinton Trail. But much worry keep me from putting together."

"Stop worryin, will you?" He thought for a moment and then went on, "Listen, it's only a matter of time before everybody starts addin two and two, but I think I'm all right.I got enough money from Witham to get options on just about every piece I want down there."

"You no need to go Mr. Banker."

"You mean borrow it from you? It crossed my mind, but I had to have a hell of a lot, and, besides, it'll be sweeter than anything else when Witham finds out he's made me a rich man."

"Then you deal with him?"

"As far as I can take him."

It was Tommy's turn to think before he spoke. Very hesitantly, he asked, "Is hard for you to deal with Missy Clerk?"

"Not as bad as it was at first. Now I see her for what she is, so it don't bother me. Hell, we're both doin the same thing—diddlin the old man."

"Missy worries me," Tommy warned. "Mr. Witham much bad if she be by his side. She never let him be fair to you, to me."

"She won't be able to help it if you get your contract done right. Just build that damn ditch as quick as you can, and the old polecat could stand on his head and the railroad people won't let him do a thing to you. Neither will the town. You put your people to work layin tracks and nobody'll care because it's a job no white man wants. They need you, Tommy, and, as lopsided as it sounds, they're gonna have more use for you than they do Witham."

Sam's summary was logical and should have made Tommy feel better, but it didn't. "So much good hope," he said, "but so much walls."

"What walls? Goddammit, you cry with a loaf of bread under your arm."

"Walls my Sojourners build. They are two tongs. Maybe they soon fight. Railroad soon bring workers with no tongs."

Sam had enough sense not to try and discount this problem. He knew it was a real danger because he was instinctively able to place himself in Tommy's position. He sat just as quietly as the other for a while, and then that slow grin broke through. "I think I might just have an idea, Tommy."

Tommy couldn't keep from saying, as if it were a prayer, "May it be so."

"Why don't you handle it like it was a help instead of a problem? Don't try to patch over the trouble between the two sides—bring it out in the open. Divide the work in half. Put the tongs against each other, only the way they fight it out is to see what side gets their part of the work done first. Offer a decent enough money prize to the side that wins, and I'll bet you get your ditch dug and done before next summer is over. Think about it, Tommy. If you go about it proper, they'll be fightin out their feud in a way that'd make any railroad boss slobber over the chance to get them workin for him."

Tommy had further doubts. Shaking his head slowly, he said, "Maybe not so easy. Sojourners more like argue in winter than work."

"Goddammit, Tommy!" said Sam, exasperated by the other's worrisome nature. "You know as well as I do that if there's enough money in it, you could get a ditch dug through hell! All you do, you cheap bastard, is push their wages up another fifty cents or so a day. Make the purse at the end of the job amount to something big, like a thousand dollars. Then they won't be fussin about cold or Indians nor anything else. All they'll be thinkin about is beatin each other to get at that much money."

As reluctant as Tommy was to part with the additional dollars this involved, he recognized that if he didn't pass them out in the way Sam suggested, he'd lose it all. He shook his head again, this time in agreement. "I do. I do what you say. All is left is Missy Clerk and—"

"Don't worry about her."

"I worry about everything," said Tommy.

45

THE *Sentinel* had begun to get under Father's skin. "Don't you see, Collis," he asked one night as we were turning in, "how improper it is for Mr. Hensley to keep hammering away in favor of slavery?"

"Of course. But he's a dedicated southerner, so there's not a thing I can do about it."

"I thought you were all but in control of the newspaper?"

"I write most of it, sell most of the advertising, and I've learned to set type—but when it comes to slavery, Alben's never gotten so deep into the whiskey barrel that he'd let me have my own say. Besides, what difference does it make? There aren't any slaves here."

"We have no guarantee that it will remain that way," said Father. "Even so, if he continues to agitate the pro-South element in Jacksonville, we will find ourselves as badly divided as the rest of the country."

"Honestly, I really can't see where it's our problem."

"Anything is our problem, Collis, if it creates barriers between this city and the future it deserves. We have it in our grasp to become one of the great ornaments of the Northwest. We cannot permit our progress to be slowed by the spleen of one man against the Negroes."

Father spoke that way at times. There wasn't a straw fluttering in the wind that he didn't jump on as evidence of the great and glorious times before us. When Witham and a few merchants had our legislature designate Jacksonville as the seat of some future territorial university, he didn't foresee that politicians, like God, operate on the theory of self-help and that there was as much chance of getting the $100,000 they left it to us to raise as there was of my election to Pope.

A few small donations came in, but that was about all. When one derelict old miner roused himself from a stupor in the Bella Union and volunteered to contribute the rest, everyone laughed but Father. He said, "The man's heart is in the right place, and if his spirit could spread . . ."

It was the same with the ditch. Even Witham wasn't more zealous than Father when it came to persuading our citizens to buy shares in the Applegate & Sterling Ditch Company. Well, maybe it wasn't quite the same. Unlike the university, the canal promised a fat profit, so raising the cash wasn't a bit of trouble. We had a man named Waterhouse come up from Yreka, where they had done the same kind of a project, and, after he examined the route and declared it practical, it wasn't more than another week that the $45,000 came in that Witham said was needed to complete the job.

It was all local money, too. Once Witham saw that he didn't require Wells Fargo's investment, he neither offered them the shares nor waited any longer for an answer from Tony's brother. It was just as well that he didn't because the letter Charles sent Tony wondered why in bloody hell all these Americans were bothering him, and that he, Charles, had simply sent Wells Fargo the same letter of inquiry he'd written to a dozen other places in this country, and so far he hadn't received one answer from anyone that persuaded him he could trust a single shilling to the thieves who were evidently in charge of this outlandish place.

Tony never mentioned the reply, and since Witham was busy printing up and issuing stock certificates, he didn't ask about it more than three or four times. Everyone seemed to be making money in Jacksonville. Many days that winter were warm enough for the miners to be out at their claims, and Tony and his coolies were going such great guns on the ditch that the optimists among us were predicting it would be done before the coming summer was over, and that, too, wasn't a prospect that brought any particular pain to Jabez Witham.

He kept urging Tommy to import more coolies, saying the quicker the canal was dug, the quicker he could scout around for more mines to serve as a basis for their new partnership—a statement Tommy recognized as pure moonshine. He knew that after the ditch was finished, a few hundred unemployed coolies would scrape no skin off the banker's nose, and if anything happened to the railroad, he'd be just another long-gone Chinaman. So he didn't do anything to expand his crews, although he told Witham that they'd been augmented by another contingent from down in the Yreka area.

Witham really had nothing to bother him these days. Even when it became generally known that the railroad was coming here and that Sam Hume had been bright enough to sew up big chunks of land along the Clinton Trail, all he did was chuckle and tell whoever it was that came to him with the story, "Be danged if the lad didn't put one over on me. You just mark my words, he'll yet turn out to be one of the real rich men in these parts!"

I couldn't help hearing about the way Witham had taken this news because people all over the place were repeating it as an example of how good a citizen as well as a banker he was. It prompted me to ask Tony, "Isn't it marvelous how much brotherhood gets generated by profits on their way in?"

Instead of smiling, Tony said soberly, "Tell that to Tommy."

"What's happened to the little heathen? I thought Witham was watching the sun rise and set in his asshole these days."

"Not by half. He hasn't left off chivvying Tommy since they began digging the canal. If it isn't the problem of securing rights of way over existing claims, it's saying he's afraid he must cut his contract price because it's costing his infernal company so dearly to buy the land needed for a bypass."

"Those aren't Tommy's problems."

"Witham makes them so by hinting that some of these complications may turn out to have no solution, and that just might cause the company to call a halt to his operations."

"And Tommy believes him?"

"Of course not. But that doesn't keep his innards from churning whenever Witham feels it's time to tweak him again."

"There's another problem," he said. "Mrs. Witham."

"Celina Sewell again?"

"Still Celina Sewell. Charity tells me her mother is at wit's ends for fear that Jabez may leave home over that girl. The woman rarely leaves her room these days, and the only food she takes is when she picks at the trays Charity brings to her. A good part of the time she simply stares out the window and cries. Once Charity overheard her mutter, 'It's God's will. He is punishing me.' You know the reference, of course."

"Sure, Sam. But I'll be damned if I thought he was the only gun in town. There's Westheimer and whoever else puts her on tap by coming along."

"Evidently she's seized on the affair with our friend as the sin of her life. Pitiful. Charity hasn't actually said it, but I know she thinks her mother is going crackers."

"Another one for Sewell. Right?"

"Right. Tommy feels that Witham's breath wouldn't be quite so hot on his neck if it weren't for her prodding."

"Someone's going to have to do something about her, aren't they Tony?"

"I'm afraid so."

The hunch that Celina was the most powerful kind of bad medicine became bedrock belief in my mind the day I went along with Sam to the bank. We were still passing ourselves off as partners, but I was coming to the conclusion that it was no longer important at this stage of the game whether Witham believed us or cared about it. His only concern seemed to be that Sam didn't skip paying any of his loan installments. That puzzled me. He had to know that there had once been something between Sam and Celina, yet it didn't worry him a bit to have set up a situation where the two of them did business with each other.

I asked Sam about it as we walked over to the bank one morning. He answered, "It beat me, too, up until the last time I was in. He wasn't there and, for a change, there was nobody waitin in line, so I pressed her just a tad around the edges. I said somethin like that it was a little strange for there to be a counter between us, and she said, like it was the most normal thing in the world, 'Oh, I've told Mr. Witham about us and he told me he didn't mind no ways because he knew it was all over and how he admired me for bein so honest with him about it.' "

After thinking this over, I said, "Something stinks like a real dead fish."

"I smell it, too," he answered. "But I'll be damned if I can figure out where it's stashed."

"Maybe she's got him so fuddled, she can tell him anything."

"I wouldn't put it past her."

At that time in my life, I was still unfamiliar with some of the forms sexual attraction can take, but even then I suspected that Witham might be getting some perverse pleasure by the way he had arranged Sam and Celina's new relationship. Her confession to the old man must have stopped short of explaining all of her plans for Sam and the bank, but Witham probably had that figured, too. As we approached the bank, I said, "If she told him about you two, the old buzzard's got her where she doesn't dare go off the tracks. No wonder she's out to take him away from his wife as soon as she can manage it."

"Shut up," said Sam as we went through the door. "I don't need you explainin to her what she's up to," which sounded as if he had sense enough to stay on guard, but I'll be damned if it seemed that way while we stood at the counter in front of her.

Her attitude as she counted the money he shoved over was, well, pleasant and charming and all the other things that indicated respect for the man who had tied up so much valuable property in these parts. As for him the best word is "uncertain," which was as if he were saying, *I know you're tough, but, what the hell, you're not all that bad.*

I swear that's the impression I gleaned from watching the two of them. To tell the truth, it was awfully hard for me, too, to reconcile this neat and trim and awfully well-built little girl with the sloppy drunken thing I'd used in the fields on the way to Medford. They weren't the same person at all.

When she'd finished counting and signed his receipt, she said to him, "Thank you very much for your business, Mr. Hume," and, at that, both of them burst into laughter. It was such a godawful lopsided statement in light of what they'd done together and to each other, that there was no way she couldn't have scored by saying it, and, after it came out, there was appreciation in Sam's eyes for her nerve. It probably came out funnier than she had intended, but, damn her, it made her look cuter than ever.

The woman was just about unbeatable. I knew it then because I would have jumped at the chance to take her on another picnic, and I knew it for sure a few days later when I saw Elva Boudreau on the street. When I asked her why she was looking so glum, she blurted out, "Sam ain't home much. I think he's gettin with that Sewell again."

46

TONY ALSO FELT that Sam was near the edge again with Celina Sewell. Unlike me, the girl held no attraction for him, so he understood long before I did that someone as hungry for success as Sam was apt to make excuses for quite a few flaws in anyone who could help get him there. To Tony, this boiled down to keeping an eye on our big friend, and that involved traveling with him on some of his land investigations. Sam had no intention of resting, even after he'd acquired the property he wanted out of the Clinton Trail area. He was too strapped for other investments, but he kept busy listing other ground he wanted to acquire as soon as his profit from the railroad came through.

On one of their expeditions, Tony asked why he drove himself so hard, and he answered, "It's all here, that's why. And it's damn near a torment to me. Once the ditch and the railroad comes in, this valley is goin to be like nothin you ever seen, and I'm gettin my share of it, even if it means lettin Witham end up with some of the Clinton acreage."

"Perhaps you shouldn't wait until then," Tony told him. "Charity mentioned that the other night at their table he said he thought you were one of the most capable—"

"I already heard that," said Sam. "Witham's told it to others, me included. Don't worry, I got a raft of other places to go before I have to end up with him. As far as I can see, nobody but old Jabez has ever made a thing out of the partnerships he puts together. He ain't a man, he's a hog."

"Then why are you with him in so many transactions?"

"It's just the one. That Clinton Trail property. And Celina says if she was me, she'd pay it off as quick as possible so it's all locked up and safe."

"You seem to be believing in her again."

"Not one inch of the way. You think I'd ever forget how she tried to do me the first time around?"

"I'd hope not."

"Stop hopin, cause I don't. But she's smart as a whip when it comes to business. Even Witham thinks so—look at all he trusts her with. She does me favors because she wants me beholden to her and she don't know when I'd be of use to her in something I can stomach. I'm takin all the advantage of that I can until after I unload the Clinton deal."

"Do you really mean it, Sam?"

"I just said it, didn't I?"

"Well then, there's no problem, is there?"

"Course," he added after they'd ridden in silence for another mile, "I got to be honest with myself. There's something about Celina that draws me. I'm pretty sure I'm not lyin about it's just business because right now I want to be a success as bad as anything. But that damn girl . . ."

As his voice trailed away, Tony looked over, realizing that in spite of the strength he radiated, Sam would always privately flounder in the gap between what he was and what he thought he should be. Twisting another loop around his hand, Tony said, "This bloody horse has a mind of its own."

"That's not what you're thinkin, is it?"

"Of course it is. Why should I be concerned with your need to master every situation?"

"I'm that bad, huh?"

"Come off it, Sam. We've been down this path before, haven't we?"

"Well," he said slowly, "there ain't a hell of a lot I can do about it. Sometimes I think you're right and my bein able to talk to Celina without wantin to knock her ass over tin cups is only because it's goin to stick in my throat that she's thinkin she's licked me. And maybe it's more true when it comes to business. I got something to prove there, too."

"And maybe she's just too damned attractive and so is being rich and all that plagues you is the need to flog yourself."

"Why indeed?" answered Sam in what he thought was a reasonable copy of the other's accent, and nothing else arose to cloud the pleasant spring morning as they spurred their horses and rode the rest of the way to Darrell Kabat's farm on the outskirts of the cluster that was coming to be known as Medford.

For all his reuben airs, Kabat was as shrewd a trader as Sam. He was a tall, heavy man, and, as they talked, his rough clothes began appearing more of a costume than a working man's outfit. Sensing that the two wouldn't have ridden this far without a specific purpose, he stalled getting down to business by offering them lunch, and, during it, spoke of his crops, his animals, and all the valley news including the digging of the canal. "How's that ditch comin along?" he asked after circling about it for at least five minutes.

"Right fine," answered Sam, matching him hayseed for hayseed.

" 'Pears like the folks who's in on that Applegate Company stock might make theirselves a dollar or two."

Sam looked puzzled. "I heard you were in on it."

The other sighed. "Just about every penny I got is tied up in my place here and a couple of other little pieces I took on for my boys against the day they was old enough to farm for theirselves."

Sam was aware that Kabat owned enormous tracts of land all through the area, but his face brightened at the idea that apparently had just hit him. "Might be you could snipe off a few acres to tide you through these hard times. You might even to get a little extra for the day another plum like the Applegate Company comes along."

The brightness wasn't contagious. Kabat's face became even more mournful as he admitted, "Well, I was able to pick up a share or two that my neighbor give me in exchange for some hay I loaned him, but it ain't so much that I'd set down and cry if it never panned out."

"It will," Tony put in to preserve the fiction that he was part of this conversation. "The coolies were able to accomplish quite a bit through the warm winter."

Kabat sighed again, which was evidently his method of expressing doubt. "May be, but don't you forget if there ain't no snowpack, there ain't gonna be enough water in the Little Applegate to damp down any ditch. Only my opinion, of course."

There was a measure of truth in Kabat's words, but their real purpose was to downgrade the value of Jacksonville property in case Sam had it in mind to swap him some of it for any part of his property. "Worse comes to worse," Sam said, "and the mines give out and the ditch ain't helpful, Jacksonville's still gonna be the county seat and the best place for a way station on the trail goin north and south. Be hard for farmers to find a better . . ."

His plumping up of the property he was about to dangle was halted by the appearance of Kabat's daughter carrying another pot of coffee to the table on the porch where the men sat. Because this was her second interruption, her father said impatiently, "Put it yonder and leave us be." And although she kept her eyes on him as she obeyed, Tony had the pronounced feeling that an overture had just been made to Sam. It was as if she had said aloud, *I'm here and worth dickerin for, too.* The impression was reinforced when Kabat called after her, "Now you quit pesterin and leave us be for a while. You got enough work to be keepin you busy."

Sam's expressionless stare at Tony left no doubt that, in that moment, he had smelled availability. *Sam, you ass*, thought Tony, *you'll be back here discussing deals until you tumble that girl.*

"Another thing frettin me about J'ville," said Kabat, "is them dinged Chinese. I hear they split into two sides and both of them are brewin bad blood at each other."

"Nothin to it," said Sam. "Ever see a Chinese that cared about anybody but hisself?"

"Never seen but one Chinee in my life," said Kabat, "and that was enough. Sneaky lookin little feller."

They went on from there and into the haggle over the land Sam wanted, and although no deal was struck, it was evident to Tony that a trade could be made for whatever Jacksonville piece that the farmer finally allowed he might be interested in. The main issue left unsettled was Sam's insistence that every acre of his ground was worth at least ten of Medford property, but Tony knew this was just a bargaining point. Sam had told him on the ride over that he'd be satisfied with a swap of five for one.

As they saddled up to leave, Kabat proved the accuracy of Sam's estimate that a deal could be made by saying, "I ain't gonna push you, but don't be too long in thinkin over our swap. You ain't the only one comin over here after some of my property."

I was glad to see them riding back into town. "It's time you showed up," I told them after they'd dismounted in front of Flora's stables.

"What's up, Collie?" Sam asked.

I'd been waiting anxiously for them, but now they were here I wasn't quite sure how to go about describing the worry that had kept me up all night. As a matter of fact, in the light of day, I began to wonder if I weren't starting something that, when it simmered down, would be one more mark against me as a damn fool.

"You've seen the ghost, haven't you?" Tony's tones were light, but he seemed to understand that I was honestly upset.

There was no way to edge into this thing. "I think maybe Elva is headed for trouble, and it's tied into just about everything!"

Sam said nothing, but Tony asked, "A real problem?"

Facing him, but really speaking to Sam, I answered, "I think so. Witham came to our cabin last night. He said that the coolies might quit work on the ditch unless the town does something to keep the Indians away from them."

"What's this got to do with Elva?" Sam asked.

I didn't know how to tell him short of blurting it out, so I went on, "Witham told Father that the way he's been hearing it, no one in town doubts that the redskins aren't crazy about all the new people the canal's going to draw here, so they're fixing to do everything they can to stop work on it."

"I'll ask you once more," said Sam quietly. "What's all this got to do with Elva?"

"I'm trying to tell you, goddammit!" The concern I could no longer handle sent my voice up about an octave. "The bigmouths are starting to claim that since Elva's a half-breed and she's always been a friend to Billy Tell, it's pretty damned sure she's been letting him and the braves know which way the canal's being dug and how long it's going to take to reach someplace that's right for an ambush. Once the coolies hear what's in the works for them, they're bound to throw down their shovels and quit!"

"That doesn't make the slightest bit of sense," Tony put in. "Why on earth would Elva . . ."

"Don't ask me," I told him. "Ask Witham. He had my father shaking like a three-dollar horse last night—I don't know where you were, Tony . . ."

"At the camp."

"That's what Tommy thought."

Sam asked, "You was there, too?"

"Sure. I went everywhere looking for you. Especially after Tommy agreed that a couple of his people really had started asking him about protection while they dig."

"He's never said anything about it to me," Tony said.

"He wasn't that bothered by it until I told him about Witham saying that the Indians might be back here and that General Lane isn't going to do anything because he thinks we're secure. Then he saw it could be a problem, not only about Indians, but everything, especially Elva."

I no longer cared what Sam might do if he went off half-cocked down to the bank. "Sam," I told him, "Witham kept harping that Elva is the one who's going to hurt the ditch out of her friendship with Billy Tell, and Father didn't put up the slightest argument—he's gotten to where he thinks he discovered Jacksonville and takes it personally when anything bad looks like it's about to happen. If the town gets steamed up about Elva, it's going to be my father in the lead."

Tony repeated, "It simply doesn't make sense!"

"That's not the point. He's past good sense when it comes to Elva. He was ready to be scraped off the ceiling right after Witham started on her. I would have walked out after five minutes of it, but I thought I'd better stick around just in case something was said that I could nail down. They just kept saying awful things . . ." And then, because I knew what this would do to Sam, I caught myself and softened it. "Father has never liked Elva. Doesn't like her at all. Both of them agreed that the town'd be better off if she went somewhere else—which is something Witham put into Father's head."

After a while, Sam said, almost to himself, "That wasn't Witham talking."

I was relieved. "Sam, I didn't want you jumping down my throat, but that's where it had to come from. I know it. Celina. Witham didn't mention her name once, but it had her stamp every inch of the way. No man could put such a vicious face on damned near everything!"

Tony said nothing, busying himself with making sure the horses were hitched properly to the stable post, but his face was dark with thunderclouds.

There was no reason to hold anything back now that he'd understood where the poison was coming from. "Sam," I said, "he was twisting it around to where it was Elva who convinced you to quit working for your father and that's the real reason he killed himself. He had the two of you living in sin in your house, with your mother looking on and not able to say anything for fear of losing you altogether. And, according to him, when her father was running the Bella Union, it was Elva the men were coming in after—he said he noticed the drop in business as soon as he took over the place."

Tony finally burst out, "The bloody son of a bitch! Why didn't you call him on all this filth?"

"I tried, but my father took whatever I said as proof she had her hooks into me, too. He actually used those words! I felt like cursing him out for being so damn blind and stubborn, so that's when I left, looking for you two. I haven't been home since. I slept at the hotel last night."

Sam shook his head as if he were trying to clear it of a bad dream. "It just don't add up. I can't see where neither of them," meaning Celina and Witham, "has a thing to gain by hurtin the girl."

"Neither do I. All I know is that's what they're trying to do, and, through Father, they're going to have the town's help."

Tony said, "We'll have to do something about Sewell, won't we?"

Sam shook his head in deliberate agreement. At last he'd made up his mind.

47

THE ARRIVAL of the first regularly scheduled stagecoach between us and Sacramento caused so much excitement, you might have thought the Pilgrims had just landed at Plymouth Rock. This, plus the news that the telegraph line had been brought through from Yreka helped smother almost all the talk about the redskins gathering again.

I say "almost" because Elva's friendship with Billy Tell was still a threat to enough of our people to earn her very few cordial greetings along California Street. It hurt her pie business, too, so we didn't doubt that Witham and Celina were still fanning the flames. They had accomplished what they'd set out to do with my father, which was to raise his doubts into real suspicions that, in turn, became common knowledge after he'd mentioned them to a few others. Remember, everyone respected the man who was both physician and judge.

I hoped that all the good news of our progress would water down the bad feelings toward her, but that wasn't the case. Not a bit. I knew it for sure the day she visited me at the print shack. She came storming in and was at it before I took my pen off the paper. "Collie," she said, "it's bad enough when some damn drunk of a miner comes huntin me up because he's heard whatever it is that half-breeds, and me in particular, are willin to do, but it don't end there and I got to stop it, and I'm goin to do it too, even if it means—"

"Hold on!" I said, pretending ignorance and hating to see that the evil had finally come out in the open and touched her. "Who's been saying what to you?"

"It's me'n Billy Tell they're talkin about. I heard it more'n once. They say I'm an Indian's girl and all somebody's got to do is give me a dollar and I'm all theirs. And that's probably why Sam is doin other things . . ."

"No, he's not. Elva, he doesn't have a thing to do with Celina Sewell that isn't all business."

"He's *my* business, dammit! I ain't afraid to fight that girl for him,

326

no matter what you or anybody else thinks. I swear I'm goin to take a whip to her if she don't leave him be!"

"You've got it all mixed up. Honestly. Now, just simmer down and listen to me. First of all, you can believe it when I say there's nothing between the two of them. I'm sure of it. There's no way Tony or I could miss seeing if it started up again . . ."

"That's fine," she said with a bitterness that didn't belong in her. "It ain't happened yet. Ain't that just great? And when it does, do you promise to send me a letter about it?"

"It isn't going to happen! You're forgetting what he said out at Table Rock. It's you he thought of, and it's you he wants once he gets all his land deals squared away."

"I ain't waitin. I'm goin to take a whip to that girl."

"What good would that do? It will only make Sam mad, and it sure won't stop the talk about you and Billy Tell. Honey, please don't be hurt when I say this, but if you were to go searching for her with a whip, everybody would say it's no more than they expected from a breed."

She looked as if I'd just struck her, and, for a moment, I thought she might cry. "Oh, Collie," she said, as the storm she'd come in with gave way to vulnerability, "what will I do? He's gonna believe them about me bein another cheap Indian girl."

"Are you crazy? How can you be this dumb?" For the first time in two days I was about to laugh, but she stopped me. Cold.

"I already let him do it," she said, and her voice was almost inaudible because she was looking down at the floor.

At first I didn't understand her meaning and waited for her to go on, but after realization flooded over me, I couldn't respond with anything more than, "Oh, Elva."

She took in a deep breath and raised her eyes to mine. "I don't care. If that's the way he wanted to do, then it's what I wanted, too."

Strange. My first reaction was a prayer that he hadn't taken her as casually as he had so many of the other girls who had been drawn to him. And then I realized it couldn't have been that way. Not Sam where Elva was concerned. Bittersweet as the knowledge was, I knew he had as much feeling for her as she for him but was just too damned stubborn to face it.

Then I really did laugh, forcing it just a bit. "All right. You've sinned. If you wait a minute I'll get some scarlet paint and put a letter on your forehead."

She didn't understand the allusion, but she felt better after she saw my reaction. "Don't you dare laugh at me, you simple seed," she said.

"You know," I told her, "after he gets some sense in his head and you two get married, I'm going to tell him—"

"You say a word, Collie Gibbs, and I'll take a whip to you, too! You swear to God right now and cross your heart that you're never gonna say nothin!"

"The hell with you, sis. You don't think a minute that I'd let him get away with this, do you?"

She smiled then, but briefly. "He'll never marry up with me. If that woman don't get him, he'll always have it in mind that there was somethin between me'n Billy because of us bein Indians."

"You aren't an Indian, Elva. You're starting to believe what the town wants you to. You're a girl with some Indian blood and some very fine French ancestors. That red hair of yours, if—"

"No," she said, sadly shaking her head, "he'll remember the talk and won't be able to help thinkin maybe there was somethin to it because I let him do it to me."

God damn that Celina Sewell!

"Tony," I said after telling him of Elva's visit and our talk but of course skipping over her confession, "she's in a bad way. Celina isn't going to quit trying to hurt her because right now she's got everything on her side. There doesn't even have to be anything solid for her to go on because the people around here are willing to believe anything where breeds are concerned. Elva's out there all by herself!"

It worried him, but not as much as me. "That's drawing it a bit strong, isn't it?"

"Maybe. And maybe not. For some reason, Witham wants to keep this town on edge—and that's what he and Celina are doing, using Elva as a lightning rod to get it done. And they're going to keep at it until whatever it is they want is settled."

"Don't you think it might have something to do with Sam?"

"No. I don't know why, but I don't."

He thought for a moment and said, "I suppose we must talk with Sam about it."

"What good would it do? He'll think we're just watching out for Elva and call us a couple of worry warts." I was tempted, but I just couldn't go into the other things she told me. "Of course, that's all we're doing, anyway."

"Not really." Tony's face seemed to be getting more frozen by the minute. "I wouldn't feel as if I'd lost something precious if Sewell were to move elsewhere." He stared ahead and then added, "And, of course, Tommy. She's taken by a ferocious dislike of him. She'll hurt the boy even more after she's trapped Witham."

Tony was no longer considering if there was a need for action. His mind was made up, and he was ready to move. "I rather think Sam must be brought into it," he said.

"All right, then. Let's go hunt him up."

"I think not. Don't be offended, Collis, but I'm not quite certain that you ought to be present. He'll be put off by the slightest trace of the enthusiasm that comes so naturally to you when you've set about convincing someone. Long before you've finished, his heels will be dug into the ground. Let me talk with him."

"You're heading for thin ice, Tony."

"I'm afraid I'm aware of it."

Maybe even then nothing would have happened if we had been given the time to get Sam on the tracks or if we'd had a few more days to think through a proper plan, but we didn't get them. As always, Celina Sewell didn't know when to quit. The venom in her spilled out again with a vengeance, and, unfortunately, it was Elva who triggered it because of her own uncomplicated nature.

As we learned later, she had in fact talked with Billy Tell during that time she had gone to Table Rock to get Sam. She had told him about the plan of an irrigation ditch leading from the Applegate to Jacksonville, and he'd answered, "This is why, some day, we will drive the white man from here."

When she pushed him for the reason he believed he and the braves could accomplish what Chief John had failed to do, he said, "Because they are stupid men."

He was referring to the irrigation ditch. One of the facts of life among his tribe was that the Applegate River dried to a trickle during any hot dry summer that followed a winter without snow. No flow in the Applegate meant no water in the ditch, and if Indians laughed, that's what he would have been doing while telling Elva that the settlers here were so greedy that they failed to see what the earth was ready to show anyone who took the trouble to look.

Elva had chalked this up to Billy's wishful thinking and didn't recall it until it became general gossip how much our miners and farmers were depending on the canal. Then she felt it was her duty to repeat Billy's scornful appraisal to whoever could best warn the people around here that perhaps they ought to hold off a bit before swapping their nest eggs for shares in the Applegate & Sterling. Naturally, this included warning Jabez Witham—and, just as naturally, from that day on the banker and his lady clerk began to devote quite a bit of thought to discrediting her.

She told me all this later. At the time, there was no way she could have understood that Witham's first reaction was to find a way to keep her quiet. This earnest girl was about to tip over the applecart he'd taken such unholy pains to build and was now just about to wheel to the cider mill. He must have been shaking inside with the need to gag her until he had the time to sell off his stock in the company to either Wells Fargo or any of the outside investors who'd heard we were the new El Dorado. He didn't have the luxury of waiting to see if Billy Tell knew what he was talking about when he told Elva that there was a fiasco in store for us.

Working on her innocence, Witham had agreed to take proper steps but asked her, in order to avoid a panic, if she'd say nothing further about the situation to anyone, including her friends, until he could figure out a fair way of getting the investors' money back to them. She agreed because she felt it wasn't up to her to question the judgment of an important banker, and she certainly didn't want to be the one who touched off a panic.

He'd been elaborately appreciative of her public spiritedness as he showed her out the door, but I doubt that ten minutes more passed before he and Sewell had hatched the scheme to make her look so bad that no one would take her word she was wet while she stood in the middle of a rainstorm. It happened the afternoon of the night he'd hotfooted it over to our cabin to retail the story to Father.

It was dumb of Elva not to have mentioned it to any of us, even though she'd given her word to Witham that she'd stay mum. But she was being pushed off balance by her worry that Sam was taking up with Celina again, and that drove everything else out of her mind.

It was Kim Lee who put us on the road.

Kim was the Chinese cook at the Hawkins & Emory mining camp, and on his weekly trip into Jacksonville, he always tied up his mule at Stoney Flora's stable while he shopped for the flour, salt, coffee, and other items he needed to prepare daily meals for thirty men. Meat and fish were supplied by the company hunter, so, on this day, after he'd bought his staples, he had nothing left on his list but to get the load of goods from Mrs. Hume and Elva's bake shop. The company's miners went along with most of the meals he prepared, but they drew the line at his campfire pies. As a result, Kim had set up an arrangement with Elva where she'd meet him at the stables with a big basket of pies and sweet rolls to be stacked on top of the provision sacks already on the mule's back.

This week, Kim finished his list earlier than usual. Since there wasn't any place in town where he felt particularly welcome, he went back to the stable, intending to nap where he wouldn't be bothered until Elva showed up.

For a change, the place wasn't comfortably empty.

On the platform of the stairs leading to the loft, he saw Stoney Flora seated with a woman he recognized as the clerk who came with Banker Witham when he visited the Hawkins & Emory camp to arrange the amount of the Saturday payroll and estimate the value of the gold that had been mined the previous week. He didn't know the clerk's name, but it didn't seem right to him that a woman of her position could be a stablekeeper's intimate, especially a ruffian like Flora. In spite of being just a camp cook, Kim wasn't a stupid man, so he turned to leave.

But he'd been seen. "Goddamn you!" Flora roared. "Git the hell out a here, you goddamn slant-eye!" And as Kim obeyed, the stablekeeper added, "Ye'll git yore goddamn mule later. Don't be back a fore a couple of hours if there's any goddamned idea in your head of stayin in one piece!"

As I mentioned, Kim wasn't stupid, so he didn't pause to remind them that the young missy from the bake shop was due in shortly. He headed directly for the *fan tan* table at Chung Lin's restaurant because he'd been given an acceptable reason for returning late to camp.

That might have been the end of the episode if Tommy's well-being didn't depend so totally on being aware of any changes in the routine around him. It wasn't right that Kim Lee show up on a weekday afternoon. Kim was due at his place only on the Sunday he was given off once a month as a vacation.

He questioned Kim who answered truthfully that the unexpected gift of free time had been bestowed by the man who owned the stables and agreed to by no less a person than the missy clerk of the remote and powerful town banker. The one additional detail he could supply was that the two of them were drinking whiskey together on the steps to the loft.

After Kim left to gamble in the back room, Tommy sat down at the window table in his restaurant and tried to fit this piece of news into all that was going on. It wasn't unexpected that a woman like Sewell would offer herself to anyone, even a groomer of horses, but certainly Flora must have know that Elva would be in with her baked goods before anything so involved as a coupling could be accomplished. Sewell wanted something of Flora, and this accounted for the whiskey. Therefore, it had to be a discussion, not a tryst. And, since it preceded Elva's visit, only a foolish man would close his eyes to the possibility of a thread between the appearances of the two women in Flora's stables.

He stood up, went into the back room, delegated dealership of the game to one of the players he halfway trusted, and left—heading into town to find Tony and me.

48

TOMMY DIDN'T GET PAST his second sentence before the message was loud and strong enough for us to hear. He hadn't finished describing what he hoped wasn't happening before Tony and I had swung off and were running toward Flora's stables. Nor did he hesitate before following us—and none of it was a moment too soon.

The big barn doors were blocked from the inside, but there was so much loose siding on the place that it was no trouble to push aside a few of the boards. What we saw was everything we feared. Elva was cornered and crouching in one of the stalls, her face bruised and her dress torn almost off, not crying but staring at Flora the way a bird looks at a snake.

Flora's pants were down to his knees, and, since he had the equipment of one of his horses, his erection looked like a big, ugly branch of a tree that had just been peeled. He hadn't gotten to her yet but was just about to when we broke in. He rose, slewed toward Tony, who was racing at him, and drew back one of those fists of his that looked like massive hams. He hobbled a step forward, but Tony ducked and lashed a smashing kick into his groin.

Flora hunched and fell, and, before anyone saw or cared whether all the fight was drained out of him, I delivered another kick, the toe of my boot catching him flush on the temple. At this he jerked straight off, stiff, his eyes went white and then closed, and he didn't move again.

I didn't know whether we had killed him and certainly didn't care. Neither Tony nor I looked back at him as we went to Elva. He put his one arm around her to help her struggle to her feet while I gathered together the shreds of her dress as if, by doing that, I could hide the hurt away from her.

She didn't cry, even then. She said, "Oh that awful animal, that rotten rotten pig."

"Did he, Elva?" I asked, almost whispering it as a prayer that nothing had happened to her.

"He tried," she answered, her voice steady, "but all he did was beat me up. That what he was gonna do—keep beatin on me until I couldn't fight no more. But I was nowhere near there yet."

In tones more gentle than I had ever heard him use, Tony said, "Dearest, are you all right? Are you certain?" and this broke through the aftermath of the ordeal that still held her in its grip.

When the tears came, both of us pressed close to her, trying to say with the nearness of our bodies that she was safe and it was over. Tommy, who loved her as much as we did, circled around, occasionally reaching out to smooth down her disheveled hair with little caressing pats.

When her sobbing became less convulsive, Tony turned to me and said, "Take her home, Collie. See that Mrs. Hume gets her into bed. She'll want to know what has happened, but put the best face upon it that you can." Reading my look toward Flora, who hadn't twitched a muscle since I'd caught him in the head, he added, "Then get back here. I'll wait for this bastard to come around."

"He might be dead," I said.

"Then I won't have to wait long, will I?"

"How about Tommy?" I asked, because I was aware that he hadn't the slightest intention of leaving although it wouldn't have gone very well for him if someone walked in while he and Tony stood watch over Flora.

Flora was awake by the time I returned, but it wouldn't be correct to describe him as conscious. After they had trussed him to one of the center poles in the stable, he had slid down to its base, the inarticulate noise of a just-cut bull calf welling up from his throat as I walked in. "It took several more kicks in the ballocks," Tony explained as if he were talking about a walk in the woods, "and then he was quite willing to volunteer how he arrived at the idea."

"Sewell?"

"Certainly. But first, Elva; is she all right?"

"As good as you'd expect. She's a tough girl."

"Poor slip," said Tony, and although that might have been considered an odd description for someone so big and strapping, it didn't sound amiss.

"Mrs. Hume was marvelous. Took one look and told me to brew some tea with whiskey in it from old Ed's barrel while she was getting her into bed. When I brought it back, she'd already washed Elva's face and put some salve on the bruises—that son of a bitch really gave her a beating—and had her into a nightgown. Elva was asleep before she drank half of it.

"Then I told Mrs. Hume that we'd stopped it in time, but I didn't say who it was or what the circumstances were and, bless her, she didn't ask a single question. All she said was, 'I'm sure the Lord will forgive anything you've done to the man who's responsible.' That's the whole story. Now, what do we do with that skunk?"

Tony said, "We can't hale him into court before your father, can we?"

"Of course not. I thought that one through on the way back over here. The best Elva'd get out of it is that most people would hold on to the suspicion that, maybe, she led him on. So, the hell with that. I want to hear what you got out of the skunk."

"It's what the whiskey and the chummy talk were all about. Everyone knows that Elva delivers the baked goods here for the mining camps, so Sewell thought Flora need only wait until she walked in. She convinced Flora that it would have the same result as when any squaw is raped by a miner—a few dollars after it's concluded, and there's no hard feelings. She gave him a half eagle to boot. He showed it to us."

"He told you all that?"

"The bloody louse would have told us his mother was a bitch spaniel to keep from another kick in the jewels. I believe him and so does Tommy. He showed us that gold piece as if it were a splinter of the True Cross."

"What do you think, Tommy?" I asked.

"Nothing to think. If he do it, people say Elva another half-breed. He tells men in bar she need only be argued."

"Then what do we do?"

"Stable man?" Tommy jerked his head toward Flora. "Let him lay. Somebody soon untie him. But too much shame for him to tell what happened."

"I didn't mean him. Sewell. We can't let her get away with this."

Tony said, "Tommy and I chatted about that, too. We've already agreed."

"On what?"

"He has a plan. He wants you and me to deliver her to him tonight."

The pinched look on Tony's face should have discouraged me from wanting to know what the plan involved, but it didn't. I was too much a part of this not to ask, "What are you going to do with her, Tommy?" although I wasn't really sure I wanted to hear the answer.

"She will go away. My coolie boss take her on Gold Springs Mountain Trail. She's go out over that trail . . ." It had never occurred to me to speculate about it but, of course, long ago, Tommy would have chosen a quiet route to bring in his crews, both male and female—one that was secluded enough to keep from calling attention to his business. I didn't require being told a destination, so I asked, "How about Sam? He's capable of killing Flora and maybe her, too, as soon as he hears about this."

That final question had been directed to Tony, but it was Chung Lin who answered with a firmness that fit nowhere into the boy I knew as Tommy, "Sam know *after*. Him too soft. Be no chance for him to interfere."

Tony and I waited until midnight before traveling over to Celina's cabin. We knew there was a danger that Witham might be with her, but we were resolved to go ahead anyway. If he were there, we agreed on enough patience for a brief explanation, but nothing more than that. It was worth trying, because what Celina had put Flora up to was not good business, and, if he was anything, he was a good businessman. And no matter how much it was to his advantage to have Elva discredited in the eyes of the town, he was still, according to his lights, a God-fearing man. There would have been no way he could have reconciled himself to the benefits of a rape. Besides, we knew about it.

We needn't have worried. He wasn't there, and, as we expected, the woman fobbed off as Celina's mother had already taken aboard her nightly load of tanglefoot. She'd passed out so deeply that I doubt if a gun going off by her ear would have stirred her.

Celina didn't put up much of a fight, either.

After forcing the front door, we walked quietly over to her bed in the corner of the room. Tony and I hadn't put together much of a plan beyond wrapping her in a blanket, tying it, and dumping her in back of the cart we'd borrowed, but the abduction went off as well as if we'd been rehearsing it for a month. The only thing that neither of us counted on was that as she slept, in the dim light she looked like a pretty little girl who needed only a doll cradled in her arms to make the picture complete. It caused me to pause and, I guess, draw back, but that lasted only until I glanced over at Tony and saw him glaring like an angry hawk. That did it.

He leaned over, pressing his hand over her mouth to stifle an outcry, while I shoved the blankets underneath. Swathing her in them as if she were a moth wrapped into a cocoon, the two of us lifted her and moved so quickly that we were halfway back out through the room before she was awake enough to twist against our grip.

Once outside, we dumped her into the back of the cart. When we took the blanket away from her face to tie strips of cloth around her mouth, she let out a strangled "Goddamn you! . . ." but we had them fixed in place before she could add to it. Tony pinned her down while I arranged the blanket more securely, lashing it about her so there wouldn't be any way for her to move an arm or leg, and the only words said between us was Tony's warning, "Make sure she can breathe," and my answer, "I'm trying to do it so she can't yell."

We drove in silence toward Chinatown. I don't know what Tony was thinking because he kept staring straight ahead, but a million fears and doubts were certainly whirling through my own mind.

This wasn't a lark; this was a violent and unlawful thing. No matter how vicious she had been, she was still just one girl against a group of men, and that didn't make me feel at all that I was mixed up in anything of which I could be proud. She had looked too small and defenseless in the bed when we took her.

Tony's attitude kept me from saying any of this aloud, so the short ride to where we had agreed to meet Tommy seemed endless. It didn't help, either, to hear her thrashing around in the back. The noises she made were churning my own turmoil up into something that might have come close to hysteria, but, thankfully, Tony turned around once and whacked the spot he judged to be her backside and, after that, she lay quietly enough.

Tommy was waiting for us when we reached the clearing outside the Chinatown camp. And so was Sam Hume.

"Oh, bloody shit," said Tony when he saw him, "he wasn't supposed to know until it was over!"

To tell the truth, now I was scared. Sam's face didn't offer the slightest hint of the way he might move.

But Tony wasn't about to be daunted. He swung down off the cart and started for Sam. "Do you have any idea of stopping this?" he asked.

"No," Sam answered. "But it's my show, too."

"How did you know about it?" I was so relieved he wasn't going to fight us that I didn't know what else to say to him.

"I saw Elva when I was home," he said, not taking his eyes off the squirming bundle in the back of the cart, "and I come out here to find Johnstone. Tommy, here, brought me up on the rest."

"And?"

"And nothin." He seemed unable to move from where he stood. "She's a rattler."

"Sam," said Tony, "this is not easy for you. Why don't you go home? Tommy has promised that she'll come to no harm. He plans to ship her far enough away so that it will be quite a while before she can return. Please go."

"I can't, Tony," he answered. "I wouldn't be a man if I ducked out on this."

"Then you'll have to stay, won't you?" Tony told him. "Come on, Collis, let's unwrap the package."

Tommy spoke up for the first time. "Not so. Be easier, you leave her as she is."

"Can't do it," said Tony. "Wouldn't be proper. The woman's a horror, but she's owed being told that she really ought not to return."

Since there wasn't anything else said, I climbed aboard the cart, picked up the bundle that was Celina, and handed her down to Tony. Tommy helped him, but Sam didn't move, still standing in place, his face dark and unreadable.

After she'd been slid down onto the ground, Tony gave up picking at the knots that had become tighter because of her straining against them and cut the bonds with his knife so that the blanket fell away. I jumped down to help her to her feet, but she pulled away with a growl that sounded positively alien coming from that small throat.

It has to be admitted—there, in her nightgown, in the moonlight, rubbing at the places on her arms where the rope had chafed her, she looked damned delectable. Maybe the words for that small figure standing in front of us were, well, exciting, feminine—and more of the same.

But not her eyes. They were wild and fierce, and there was no question after looking into them that this wasn't a luscious little mannequin but a very dangerous person who wouldn't have thought twice about shooting any or all of us the first time she got her hands on a gun. "You sons of bitches," she said in that low, husky voice. "You filthy goddamn pimpin whore-mongerin bastards." And it was the best thing she could have done for us because the oaths snuffed out our last feelings of guilt.

She must have sensed this. Then her eyes darted left and right as if she were looking for a place to run, but she wasn't that far out of her mind with anger that she didn't understand it would have been the wrong and futile thing to do. So she used the weapon she'd always had. "Sam," she said, turning toward him, "please don't let them do me this way."

He didn't stir for another moment, and then, slowly shaking his head as if this might clear it, he told her, "Seelie, it's got to be. This Flora thing. You been doin too much harm. I'm not goin to let anybody hurt you, but there's no way you can stay around here."

His words were unyielding, but his face certainly wasn't. It lost that expressionless cast, and, as he answered, it was almost as if he were bending toward her. That must have seemed to her as a possible way out. She went over, put her hands on his shoulders, and, looking up at him as if they were alone, she said, "Sam, I always been on your side. You don't believe that because I was so mad when you turned me down, but after I thought about it, I knew you was right, that it was a crazy notion, and all the time after that I ain't thought of nothin but how to get back with you."

I looked over at Tony, but he shook his head sharply at me as a signal not to interfere. It was plain he wanted her to have her say, and whatever happened after that would be something else again.

Sam continued to stare down at her as if he were putting away a prize, and she took this as evidence that a case could still be made. "I swear I been on your side. I can prove it."

He found his voice. "How?" It sounded like a prayer for her to convince him.

"I made Witham promise not to let you get hurt. You ask him. I told him if he didn't get you out of the Clinton Trail before they find out the railroad ain't comin to Jacksonville but is goin instead to Medford, I'd never let him come near me again. Ask him! I ain't foolin, just ask him! He'll tell you what I made him promise."

Sam had been a fool where this girl was concerned, but it didn't extend this far. "Seelie, I don't give a damn if that's true or not. Don't you see what you done to Elva was just short of tryin to kill her?"

Before she could deliver her excuse for even this, Tony saw it had gone far enough. He said, "Sam . . ."

"Leave her be," he answered. "She's got a right to explain."

There was a silence in which we all stood frozen until Tony reached under his coat and took out his revolver. The noise of the gun being cocked sounded in the night air like an old sluice gate creaking open. "Sam," he said, "I'll use this against you if you force me to it. I won't have you permitting this creature back where she can hurt Elva or anyone else. None of us will."

When Sam didn't reply, I moved over beside Tony, and although Tommy didn't shift position, there was no question where he stood.

Sam said in a puzzled voice, "No, you won't use that gun, but what the hell is wrong with me? I wouldn't trade any part of her for Elva's little finger, and that's what it comes down to." And without a word of farewell or go ahead or go to hell, he turned and walked off on the path to Jacksonville.

After he disappeared into the darkness, Celina found her voice. "Sam Hume, you big son of a bitch, I'll get you if it's the last thing I do!" she screamed after him, and when the dark woods remained silent, Tony turned and said, "She's yours, Tommy."

He and I got back up on the cart, and, as we drove away, we heard her shriek again, this time in a high pitch that couldn't be understood.

49

YEARS LATER, I wrote to Tommy asking if he'd ever known what happened to Celina Sewell after that night. In reply I received the following letter from Chung Po Fong who was Tommy's nephew as well as his bookkeeper:

Esteemed Sir,

Even in punishment, dissension was handmaiden to Miss Sewell. It began when the two burly coolies whom my uncle, Chung Lin, detailed as guards against her escape from the shack where she had been placed that night, began their argument over which of them was to be her first visitor and continued until morning among the men who thereafter stood in line for the same purpose in front of her cabin.

Chung Lin had seen the possibility of quarrels between the men of Hong Kong and Canton if placed in proximity for so intimate a purpose, and yet he was convinced it was a risk he should take. A coarse fellowship is sometimes engendered under these circumstances, and it was his hope that the rivalry that lately had caused the two factions to eat, sleep, and live in separate groups would somehow be dissolved in this enterprise.

Then, too, it was necessary to break the woman's will. Unlike his friends, my uncle had no illusions that matters could be arranged in such order that her subsequent return to Jacksonville would not again disturb them. He was convinced that this woman would never lack for the desire nor the means to create trouble. He could not know whether the winds would keep his friends forever in this place, but he believed it was where he intended to remain. The task of understanding boundary lines would be too difficult to begin again in another city, and so it was necessary to his interests that she be left without intent ever to return here.

Her spirit had to be crushed before such an unlikely emotion could be introduced, and this was the reason for the lines of coolies waiting before the cabin in which she lay and where, after her first six visitors, she possessed neither the sensibility nor the will to leave, even though her guards, wearying of their duty, had gone elsewhere.

The breach of his word to yourself and Mr. Johnstone that she would come to no harm was seen by Chung Lin as an unwelcome necessity. He felt that his manner of creating an insurance against her return would never disturb you because it was unlikely to receive your attention. My uncle considered this course to be in the best interests of his friends.

It is immaterial to describe the treatment received by Miss Sewell from the coolies who visited her. Each man, in his turn, did that which brought him satisfaction, and the cumulative weight of these visits was such that she was ever after left with but a dull recollection of that night or probably any of the remaining days of her life.

The opium pipe offered her the following morning by the turtle woman who saw to the interests of Chung Lin among his joy-girls, eased much of Miss Sewell's pain, and she clung to her drugged dreams in such a fashion that she was only dimly aware of being carried out of the enclave and over the trail to Brookings. There, she was dressed in the rough clothing of a laborer and placed unnoticed among the other returning coolies in the hold of a ship bound for San Francisco. The old woman who accompanied her saw to her needs during those moments when clarity returned and, upon docking, delivered her as arranged into the care of Miss Mary Soo Ling.

Miss Sewell quickly became a favorite of the patrons of the House of Many Pleasures, but, after a year, she disappeared, and no one whom I questioned could tell me what had become of her.

With respect,
Chung Po Fong, for Chung Lin

50

TONY AND I didn't have much to say to each other on the way back to town. He sat beside me like a graven image, and, to keep myself from thinking of what we had just done to that girl, I considered him and what he'd become and found myself disbelieving that he could ever return to the role of younger son of an English house, letting the past rule him and agreeing that the future wasn't his to control.

What was he now, twenty-two? Yes, a year older than me. But the set of his face belonged to a much older man. "Man," because that's what he was in everything meant by the term. That diffident English boy I'd met almost six years ago in a makeshift San Francisco hospital had turned out as good and strong as any on the frontier. How many of them out here could have held a gun on a best friend to make sure he did the right thing? I knew Tony had done that more for Sam's benefit than anything else. And, unlike Sam, I felt he could have pulled the trigger. If he had, he'd have been a friend in the way only a real man could.

When we reached our cabin, he said, "Let's not go in just yet. I'd like to see how well Elva is ticking along."

He didn't say he wanted to see how Sam had taken his dismissal from the drama that had just been played out, but that's what he meant, and, because it concerned me, too, spoken agreement wasn't required to turn us toward the Hume cabin.

Elva and Mrs. Hume were up, but Sam was nowhere to be seen. They were sitting in front of the fireplace, talking, when we came in. Elva seemed as if she'd already put the afternoon into a place in her mind where it wouldn't bother again, and you couldn't have told from the manner of Sam's mother that this wasn't just another of our visits. I said, "Thought we'd stop by and see how you ladies are and maybe chin with Sam for a while."

His mother shook her head. "I swear, I thought he was with you. He put his head in here not more than fifteen minutes ago and all he said was that he'd be back, that he was going over to your house."

"Did something happen, Collie?" Elva wanted to know. "His face looked closed in as a thundercloud, and it was like he only wanted to be sure we were all right, and then he walked out."

I was about to add to their worries by saying we had just come from our cabin and hadn't seen him when Tony intervened. "If I know your son," he told Mrs. Hume, "he's wandered off to plan another of his land schemes."

"Ain't it the truth," said Elva, relieved by this explanation. "It's a wonder his head don't bust with all the figurin he does in there."

Accepting Tony's lead, I chimed in, "He's going to end up by owning . . ." when the door opened and Sam came in. He didn't waste any time beyond nodding in our direction and then, turning to the women, said, "Ma, Elva, you get your clothes on. We got to get over to Judge Gibbs's house."

The two exchanged a questioning look, but there was something in Sam's manner that didn't admit of discussion, so they rose and went into the back room. We didn't hear much talk coming from there, either.

Then he said to me, "Collie, I been to your house seein your pa."

"We were just there, but we didn't notice you coming or going."

"I know. I seen you, though, and I waited till you made up your minds to head back here."

"Did you really speak with Dr. Gibbs?" asked Tony.

"I did. He's waitin for us now."

"What on earth for?" It was hard for me to accept that Sam intended to lodge an official complaint for the actions of Flora, Celina, and, maybe, Witham.

"Don't ask so damn many questions. Just you two come along."

That's what we did. The four of us trooped along, following Sam on the path toward my home, and, since none of us had answers for the others, we walked in silence. It was an unsettling trip, quieting even Phoebe Hume who normally filled the gaps in any situation with a stream of talk.

Father was waiting for us when we arrived, if anything more grim-faced than Sam. The expression wasn't new to me because it was the one he assumed every time his sense of duty made it necessary for him to do something he didn't relish. But I was totally unfamiliar with the sight of him holding a Bible.

"Are you certain of this?" he asked Sam.

"Go ahead, sir. It's what we're here for." He turned to Elva and said, "Honey, I arranged for us to get married up, and Judge Gibbs here is about to do it. You got any thoughts about holdin back?"

Tony said, "I'm a bloody son of a bitch," but I doubt if Elva heard him. She was staring full in Sam Hume's face and radiating neither surprise nor jubilation but simply an acceptance that this was meant to happen in her life. Well, maybe there was a speck of relief in her look, and just a smidgeon of wonder that he felt it necessary to ask—but there definitely weren't any questions.

Sam's mother made the sound that broke the moment. She wailed, "Oh, children!" and broke into tears.

I put my arm around her and said, "It's what you've wanted, isn't it?"

"More than anything since I prayed for Ned not to be taken from me," she answered. I tightened my arm to still the shuddering of her bony little shoulders.

I looked back at the others. Sam's face was still set, but now there was a slight loosening around the edges; Elva was serene and smiling; and there was a small, tight grin on Tony's lips. The only one who didn't share in the happiness that suddenly enveloped that room was my father, but that didn't matter. "Go ahead, Father," I told him. "We're all here: bride, groom, in-laws, the best men, and even this . . ." forcing from my little finger the ring he had given me for my twelfth birthday.

Then, it broke through to him, too. The look in his eyes as I passed the ring to Sam was one of recognition of what all of us before him in that room felt for each other. I knew him. He no longer thought it was a mistake for these two to be together.

After he had finished, if there was anything held back in him, it went away forever as he looked on when Sam took Elva in his arms and said, "Girl, there's nothin that'll ever hurt you again. I love you."

She would never have told me about the sex part. Not in a million years. But she was so proud of the rest of it that she would have burst if she hadn't told someone, and, since I was her best friend, within a week I knew most of what there was to know about Sam Hume's wedding night.

They had made love in a way that had brought happiness to both of them and, promptly afterward, Sam fell asleep. But she remained awake, sitting up, arms clasped about her knees, looking long and gravely at her husband. After quite a few minutes of this, she leaned over and hit him on the head.

He awoke with a start, his first reaction to lunge at whoever had done this, but when her face became clear and familiar in the dim light, he said, "Now what in hell did you do that for?"

The sober expression on her face didn't change a bit. "Cause you had it comin."

"What does that mean?" Rubbing the back of his head, he added, "You'd better quit foolin around, Elva."

"I ain't foolin. I been thinkin it over. I made a big mistake marryin you."

"Did you now?" His face was as grave as hers. "What are you goin to do about it?"

"Keep hittin you. Every time you go to sleep, I'm goin to hit you."

"Are you crazy?"

"I got to keep remindin you how bad you are. You got a mean temper, and you chase after girls, and you can't say nothin gentle to people, even your own wife, without bein afraid it makes you less'n a big tough man and . . ."

"And I married a crazy girl. Come here, you," and he grabbed at her.

She twisted away. "Go get Celina or anybody else handy."

He got a grip on her shoulders and wrestled her beneath him. "I don't want nobody else."

"Never?"

He thought for a moment. "Well, never is a long time."

She giggled. "I catch you with anybody else and I won't wait till you start snorin before I whack you."

He looked down at her in a way that told her that there never could ever be anyone else again for him.

"Say it out loud," she demanded.

"Say what?"

It was her turn to stare at him, and, finally, he dropped his eyes and looked away as he said softly, "I love you, Elva. I truly do. I love you with all my heart."

"Look at me when you say it!"

He grinned, but she saw the moisture shining in his eyes. "You're my wife, Mrs. Elva Hume."

"And?"

"And kiss my ass!" He bent, kissed her, and they made love again.

Neither of them was familiar with the word, but when she told me about it, I knew they had performed a sacrament.

51

THE DISSENSION that Celina Sewell brought to Jacksonville stayed with us after she was shipped out. Some of it flared up again the night the coolies lined up in front of the cabin Tommy had put her in before sending her on to San Francisco.

In his eagerness, one of the Hong Kongs jostled a man from Canton, and this led to a pushing and elbowing for position that one of the guards quieted, but it stayed bitter enough to keep the two sides glaring at each other for quite a while. After about an hour of this, one of the Hong Kongs announced he wasn't going to stand in any queue that contained Cantonese worms, so he and the others of his province split off into a line of their own. For quite a few more hours, Celina's cabin was fed by two alternating groups.

Ordinarily, next morning there'd have been a truce to the name-calling and bad feelings when the crews went off to work, but, since Tommy had been ordered by Witham to quit the digging, there wasn't any work to go to. Witham wasn't about to fork out any more salaries for the project. He had his hands full returning money to the investors who'd started a run on his bank after they'd heard that the Applegate & Sterling Ditch Company might not yield much more than a trickle in a severe drought. He redeemed the investments with a good face because he knew damned right well that something would happen to him if he didn't.

The only item the two sides agreed on was in blaming Tommy for their unemployment. He tried a few times to tell them that a railroad was on its way here and that meant jobs and better pay for everyone, but no one believed him. He didn't believe it himself. If Celina had been right and the tracks were scheduled to lead to Medford, then that's where the coolies would go, and whether or not he ever got his cut from the salaries they earned, it would be future money that was no good for present bills.

So, idleness opened the door to increased bad feelings. There were very few Sojourners that morning who concerned themselves with their customary breakfast of a bowl of rice and a few scraps of fish. Instead, they passed around their globes of rice-distilled tiger whiskey.

Everyone knew that a battle was brewing in earnest. The members of the two tongs spent the rest of the day tossing insults at each other, many of which dealt with the conduct of those who'd visited Celina's cabin. There were a few shouting matches, quite a few sleeves rolled up, some spitting and cursing of ancestors, but no blows were struck.

The real violence didn't begin until that night. A group of Hong Kongs, belonging to the tong *Sam Yap* stormed Tommy's restaurant, beat him severely, and smashed up the *fan tan* table. That was the night Tommy learned that success didn't always go to the man who ran the fastest and that no one ever gets the last inch out of any deal. It was a hard last step in growing up.

The Sam Yaps were led by a man known as Charlie Yung. Because the Cantonese tong had twice as many members, Charlie pulled his men out of the restaurant right after they'd accomplished what they'd come to do. By now, Chinatown was no longer one enclave. It had physically split into two camps, and Charlie took his men back to the one they had established, and that's where they hunkered down, waiting for the response.

It wasn't long in coming. The men of the *Yan Wo*, who were the Cantonese, had prepared themselves by hiring a professional killer named Hi Long Chang as their leader. This man and a few of his lieutenants walked over to the outskirts of the Hong Kong's camp and began shouting a long stream of filthy threats. When a Hong Kong appeared to answer with what he hoped would be an equal tirade, Hi Long Chang drew a muzzle-loader horse pistol from beneath his blouse and killed him with a single bullet through the heart.

That was the opening shot of the infamous "Coolie War" that stained Jacksonville for so many years.

To avenge their loss of face, the Cantons responded by taking up the weapons they had been accumulating and storing ever since it had become obvious to the most stupid man on either side that the argument between people like the Cantonese, who supported the emperor of China, and those, the Hong Kongs among them, who wanted to bring down the throne had to erupt eventually into bloodshed even in this little town that was so many thousands of miles away from the Celestial Empire.

A word about these weapons: During the past few months, while the will to battle was gathering strength, Jacksonville blacksmiths had been kept busy making weapons for the members of both tongs. Charlie Yung had ordered from Tom Carr's forge fifty iron shields and twenty-five spearheads to be attached to fifteen-foot pike poles. He'd also brought with him, for Tom to duplicate, a picture of the *Kwan Doo*, the enormous sword of the war god Kwan Kung. Tom had filled the order even though he'd been warned against it by Sheriff Westheimer.

When Hi Long Chang heard of this addition to the enemy's arsenal, he paid his visit to Carr's forge to double the order the other side had given him. He also described one more weapon he wanted; it was similar to a salmon-fishing spear but a lot deadlier since its middle tine measured fourteen inches, two inches longer than the two outside tines. The points of each of these three prongs were to be filed needle-sharp.

This arms' bill was the one that settled the matter for Dutch Westheimer. He didn't give a damn about any Chinaman being killed, but he'd certainly miss the tax they paid. Disregarding the white miners who wanted to see a fight and who told him to quit butting in, he made one last trip to Tom Carr's place to say that if he delivered the weapons to Hi Long Chang, he'd be fined $500 for breaching the peace. Carr laughed at him. "Fine and be damned," he told Dutch. "I'll triple that as soon as the Chinks pick up their order."

We all know that no arsenal is ever allowed to get rusty, and the Coolie War wasn't an exception. The morning after Hi Long Chang fired that fatal shot, both armies began military drill in the streets of the town, chanting, playing strange musical instruments, and hurling insults. Hop Sing, the Canton with the loudest voice, called the Hong Kongs pigs, dogs, and worms. Not to be outdone, the Hong Kongs shouted back awful descriptions of the other side's ancestors, and, after this, a couple of the nastier-minded yelled that the woman bank clerk had said that Cantonese men made love like monkeys and begged that they didn't send in any more from their line. As I understand it, one of the worst things you can do to an Oriental man is to impugn his sexual prowess.

The drills continued for two more days, the Hong Kongs taking the upper end of California Street and the Cantons the lower. The saloons lining each side of the street had never sold more whiskey, because miners and farmers from all over the countryside were flooding in to witness the spectacle. Wagering reached a fever pitch among the whites, and more than one miner with a dab of military training volunteered to help instruct the army on which he'd placed his bets. All these offers were refused, except the one that resulted in a final victory.

Tommy was caught squarely between the two. His loyalty was with the Cantonese—not because he'd been born in that province but because they had the most men. But he couldn't overlook that the Hong Kongs

were famous for their fighting spirit and were apt to be more reasonable
in victory. It was a bad time for him, so he couldn't be faulted for
contributing weapon money to each faction. If he'd failed to do so, he
ran the risk of one side or the other considering him the traitor who'd
cost them the fight. It tore quite a hole in his savings—in fact, it cost him
almost every penny of it—but he didn't see that he had an option.

Jacksonville was at fever pitch by the end of the second day. Most
of our citizens stayed awake all night. Some camped on the high ground
above town, and the roofs of store buildings lining the street became so
crowded that it's a wonder they all didn't cave in. More bets were placed,
and pretty soon the odds were two to one in favor of the Cantons. This
shifted right before daybreak, when the rumor spread that Charlie Yung
of the Hong Kongs had made a secret deal for outside help. From there
on, the wagering bounced up and down, depending on who'd heard the
latest rumor.

That morning, the Hong Kongs were the first arrivals on Oregon
Street, which, by common assent, had been set aside as the arena. They
all wore red turbans to distinguish themselves from their enemy, and,
blowing horns and beating gongs, they lined up at the far end of the
street.

The Cantons, in black turbans, appeared next, looking really sinister
with their long spears, swords, and flags. At their head was Hi Long
Chang, holding onto an ungodly sized saber, a hatchet tucked into his
waistband. He had two men flanking him, one carrying the Dragon Flag
of the Imperial Army.

Westheimer made one last attempt to stop it. Riding his horse among
the onlookers, he tried to round up some help but was only jeered for
his pains. "Go to hell," one man told him. "I came for a fight, and that's
what I'm damned well going to see." Another man yelled, "Go home,
Dutch. You keep ridin through here and you're gonna get a sharp pole
up your ass!" A third man said, "Don't spoil it, Dutch. I laid out twenty
ounces of gold on them Canton fellas, and if you keep your nose clean,
I'll bet the same for you on your next election."

The last statement was the one that quieted down our sheriff. This
was one of the most popular spectacles that ever had come to Jacksonville,
and he saw where interfering with it could easily cost him his job. His
falling back was the signal the combatants needed to begin their battle
maneuvers.

They marched and countermarched over the street, singing, tooting
horns, clashing gongs, and screaming curses. They kept at this for almost

two hours before the spectators, impatient to see the blood flow, joined in the cursing.

It didn't bother Charlie Yung. He had no intention of committing his troops until the time was ready. He waited until he had led his men to a position where one flank of his column was protected by the hill that rises to the top of the Jacksonville cemetery and then, suddenly, the battle was on.

Shouting "Kill! Kill!" the Cantons attacked the other and unprotected flank of the Hong Kongs, but, to the surprise of everyone, a group of whites—I saw Sam among them—rushed in the same direction, followed by hundreds of spectators who thought this was the way to get a better view of the fight.

Afraid of hurting these Occidentals, Hi Long Chang ordered his men to attack from the other direction, but, to his frustration, the group of whites moved in with him again, blocking the way. In the heat of battle, he couldn't have noticed that this interfering group was being led by the Chinatown lawman, Tony Johnstone.

Nor did he see or care that another white man, a Swede, standing among a knot of people off to one side of the street was firing his pistol indiscriminately into the massed Chinese, shouting, "Fight, damn you! Let's see some blood!" Before he'd emptied his pistol, the man behind him, angered by what he probably thought was handicapping the side he had bet on, drew his own gun and shot the Swede in the head. In the excitement, few noticed the dead man lying at their feet. They pushed around him, some stepping on the body instead of over it in their anxiety not to miss any of the action.

Out on the battlefield, the Hong Kongs had moved into a position to attack the Canton rear guard. This was the strategy that Charlie Yung had decided on, and the blocking move of the white group following Tony Johnstone was all that was needed to launch it. Taken by surprise, the Cantons dropped their weapons and ran, the men with the red turbans chasing and hacking away at them with their long swords. Those who hadn't been able to get a sword or pistol, lit their fire balls—rags on the ends of sticks dipped in kerosene—and threw them at the retreating Cantonese.

One of these torches hit the roof of a nearby wooden shack, which went up in flames before spreading to the next cabin. My father died trying to rescue the infant lying on a cot in this building. This is a memory that I cannot dwell upon, even now.

It wasn't long after that the battle ended. There were nineteen dead

Cantonese and three Hong Kongs left in the street as well as the trampled body of John Malberg, the impatient Swede who wanted to spur the action on. His corpse was collected by a few of the men who drank with him, and, since they were already at the foot of the cemetery, they carried it up there and dropped it in the first empty hole they saw. None of them bothered with the customary last words because they were drunk, excited by the sight of a battle and anxious to collect their winning bets.

Tony was nowhere to be seen. He'd filled his promise to Tommy to help on the side of the Hong Kongs, because they were the ones Tommy expected to give him the least trouble after the fight was over. He'd done it by leading the group who didn't realize they were being herded by him and Sam Hume in a way that blocked the Cantons from attacking the unprotected flank of the men in the red turbans. Why did Sam and Tony go this far toward helping Tommy? The answer was that the world he'd built was coming down around him, and he had nowhere else to turn.

The two of them left to bring Tommy the news so that he could start preparations for a Hong Kong victory banquet, and it was lucky for him that they didn't wait for anything else. As a matter of fact, it was not until much later that they heard about my father.

When they approached the Chung Lin Restaurant, they saw Tommy being held by two men still wearing their Cantonese black war turbans. A third was Hi Long Chang, the professional killer. Although neither or them understood anything more than a smattering of Chinese, it was clear that the angry words of Tommy's captors were building up to some very bad things. Hi Long Chang already had his hatchet out, and, as soon as he'd screwed his temper tight enough, he was ready to swing it through Tommy's head.

They were cursing Tommy so loudly for betraying his Cantonese blood that no one heard Sam and Tony burst through the open door. Tony threw himself at the body of the hatchet man while Sam pulled Tommy out of the grip of the other two. Then Sam grabbed these two Chinese by their throats and pushed them against the wall. Tony had Hi Long Chang pinned to the floor, a knee on each shoulder, and when he saw that the resistance was over, he called, "What do we do with them, Sam?"

"How the hell do I know?"

They turned to Tommy who answered the question by stepping forward and, as he translated later for them, asking the killer whether being allowed to keep his life was enough payment to guarantee that he'd never come back here again. After the other answered in tones that had anger, contempt, and, finally, resignation in them, Tommy said, "Let them go. They no more make trouble."

The trio of assassins didn't wait, although the last one through the door stopped long enough to look at Tommy with a threat that was too easy to read.

After they'd gone, Sam said, "They'll be back, won't they?"

"Not maybe them," answered Tommy, not adding that Hi Long Chang had promised him that since he'd lost face in being bested by a man with one arm, there'd be others here to kill him for the bounty the Cantons would place on his head.

"But someone else will?" Tony prompted him.

"Shu," Tommy admitted.

"How did they find out?"

"Mr. Blacksmith Carr. Pay him much money, but he talk much. Cantons hear."

Sam shook his head in disgust. "Goddammit, everybody in your camp is gonna know. From now on, every time you turn around, somebody'll be comin after you."

"Is business," said Tommy. He shrugged. No matter where he went or what he did from then on, he was a man who'd never forget that everyone's life hung by a hair. "No more you, no more anybody can do. You go along home to wife."

"I'm a son of a bitch," said Sam with his first smile of the day. "I sure got one at home, don't I?"

52

THE BURIAL of the Chinese who died during the Coolie War started out as another exciting spectacle, but when it went on too long, the town's interest turned to indifference and then anger. It was just too damned exotic, and it stressed the idea in the minds of most of our citizens that we had swallowed an indigestible mass.

Death among frontier whites was a part of every day, and the burial ceremonies that followed were fairly customary: A person died; he was laid out; words were said and tears were shed; and, after the body was placed in the ground, people went about their business. But this wasn't remotely the way the fatalities of the Coolie War were interred.

Since there weren't any priests in the work force, a few Sojourners put on white robes that flapped and tripped them as they paced somewhere between a glide and a jog trot among the bodies lying in plain pine boxes before the shack they used as a joss house. A temporary canopy and three tables had been put up before the row of coffins, and on each table was a whole roasted pig, bowls of rice, and enough food and drink to feed a regiment. Burning punk, paper prayers, and fluttering banners and ornaments of all colors completed the decorations.

In a circle around this were the Sojourners and, of course, the priests busy at performing the ceremonies that went with the ritual. Every one of the hundreds of coolies there took turns bowing on mats, sometimes singly, sometimes in pairs, and, every so often, there were three together, all of them repeating the performance at both sides of each table. While this went on, a group of musicians sitting in a nearby cart maintained a constant clatter. When the rituals ended, they were followed by a procession that struck most of the watching whites as the funniest thing they'd ever seen.

It took almost an hour of running backward and forward, wrangling and chattering before the various elements of the pageant were properly lined up and ready to march. The difficulty seemed to lie in placing the two white-robed musician-priests, who were evidently the most important factor in the display. Each bore across his shoulder a long pole with a gong suspended from the front end and a banner hanging from the rear. They beat these gongs at what appeared to be haphazard intervals.

After the cortege moved out, they were led by two coolies on mules who could neither keep abreast of each other nor track a straight course down the street. Following them were carts pressed into service as hearses and a few other wagons piled high with the belongings of the dead men. Then came the mourners on foot, and these included just about every coolie in the valley. I don't know if Tommy was among them because I couldn't pick him out in that straggling mass, but I suppose he was there. I imagine if anyone had been watching this from somewhere above, maybe a spot like Marguey's High, the impression would have been that a giant wounded caterpillar was inching up the hill toward the Jacksonville cemetery.

The town had agreed to let them use a plot to the east of the 100 F section of the cemetery because, as Tommy had long ago explained through Witham, this was to be only a temporary resting place for the bones of the deceased. As soon as their families or friends saved enough for the fares, the remains were going to be dug up and shipped back to China.

Well, once they got there and had the dead Sojourners underground, they held another ceremony consisting mainly of wailing and sprinkling on the graves the tea and rice wine and most of the rest of the food that had been on the tables before the coffins. They brought the roast pork back to their compound, leaving the dead with what one of the English-speaking coolies told me was called the Tempt Aroma. I stayed there until the end because it seemed to me as good a place as any to mourn Father.

There wasn't any way the people of the town could reconcile themselves to this kind of pageantry, so the nastiness began a day or two after everyone had done with laughing about it. Then it became the target for the frustration over the way the canal had petered out and the thinning of the gold scrapings in the hills.

More than a few people were ready to believe that the now highly visible coolies were the source of our bad luck. Some began convincing each other that there would be enough water for the rest of us once the Chinks quit hogging it. You've got to remember that, by this time, our Chinatown numbered several thousand residents while our miner population was dwindling in direct proportion to the number of rumors reaching us of the new gold fields opening up in eastern Oregon and over in Idaho.

The only thing left to feed our town's bloodstream was the coming of the railroad, but that was still in the talking stage. Even that slowed down to a trickle after we heard that Medford was going to replace Jacksonville as the county seat. The official reason for this was that we lay too close to the hills that offered so many advantages to hostile Indians. Mayor Sizemore said he'd been told that the official records would be safer in the flatlands, but there were very few who weren't convinced that the real reason for our civic demotion was that we were awash with Chinamen.

Anyway.

I'd spent the day after the Coolie War alone in our cabin. My friends must have understood what I was feeling, because none of them came over. After I packed all of Father's things in a big box—I didn't sort them out, knowing it was a job for a time when it wouldn't hurt so much—I sat down on his bed, and in a while the tears came that I needed so badly, although I wasn't sure whether they were for him or for me.

The following morning, Sam and Tony came back and said some of the right words to me, and when Tommy walked in, it wasn't necessary for him to add much beyond, "Mr. Dr. Gibbs, a good man. He make man out of alley rat you find in San Francisco."

53

THERE WASN'T MUCH left to hold us in Jacksonville after that. Tommy saw no point in waiting for a visit from one of the *Boo Hao Doy*, the professional hatchet men whom either the Cantons or Hong Kongs were sure to hire after any of them reached San Francisco. Tony's ties were less than Sam's and certainly, now, mine.

It's true that Sam's mother was a strong link for him to the place, but there were so many bad memories here that it took only a small reassurance from Mrs. Hume before he agreed that he and Elva would go along with us to eastern Oregon. "Only one thing I got to do first," he said. "There's some business that needs finishin up."

I looked over at Elva. She and Sam had taken the large bedroom after their marriage, and, although his mother was in the other, tidying it up, the whole place was still too small for a private conversation. Elva nodded back to me as a way of saying that Mrs. Hume wasn't privy to whatever it was her son wanted to do before leaving.

Sam added, "Maybe Tony's got some things to wind up, too."

"Not really," said Tony. He'd already told Charity of our decision and invited her to come along, but, as much as she was tempted by the offer, she couldn't bring herself to leave her mother who was on the verge of a collapse or worse.

Sam was busy roping up clothes boxes, so, after a pause, Elva said, "I know Collie can do anything he sets his mind to when we get there—whether it's startin another paper or whatever. But Tony, how about you?"

Tony shrugged. "I can hunt or fish or even do a bit of carpentry. But I've thought it through, and if you and Sam still intend the offer, I'd like very much to join you in the horse ranch." That was Sam's idea for the future. He was sure that he'd be able to get some good strings of horses from the Nez Percés, who, from all reports, were great traders.

When Sam tied the last knot, Tony asked him, "Sam, perhaps I should trot along with you. There are, after all, one or two things I'd like to see completed."

357

"Sure. How about you, Collie?"

I knew where they were going and what their business was but didn't have much heart for it. "I'll stay here with Elva," I said. "Maybe I've got one last chance to change her mind."

"You do," Sam said. "I been tellin her since were married how big a mistake she made when she picked me. But I just as soon you come with us Collie. It's owin to you."

"All right," I agreed.

Elva said, "Let me go with you, Sam."

"Nope. Wouldn't make sense. Tell you what; you and Tommy go on up to Marguey's High. We'll meet you there for a last look around."

Our meeting with Jabez Witham was easily enough arranged since his bank conducted so little business these days. Most of the departing miners and farmers had pulled out their money before they left, no longer having all that faith in the proprietor of the Applegate & Sterling Ditch Company. Even so, he was in a surprisingly good mood when we walked in.

"Glad to see you boys," he boomed, smiling in approval of God knows what. "Good to know there's some left who aren't scared of a little setback now and then."

"Like to talk to you a bit, Mr. Witham," Sam said.

"Sure thing, Samuel. What's on your mind? Tell you what, there's nobody about to bother us, so let's go into my office and set." Not waiting for an answer to the invitation, he turned and walked into the back room, and, after a moment, we followed.

He seated himself behind his desk and motioned us to move our chairs into comfortable range. Evidently, in his unaccustomed idleness, Witham relished the prospect of any commercial conversation. "Now, what can I do for you lads?"

"Maybe it's the other way around," Sam answered. "We come over to see about gettin something done for you."

"That's real nice. Real thoughtful. But I shouldn't be surprised. You've all proved there's enough of the right stuff in you."

"You, too," I assured him, remembering how scarce he'd been during the Coolie War and all through these days when people had begun to face the fact that Jacksonville's bright future was crumbling as fast as any of the frontier settlements that turned, almost overnight, into ghost towns.

Sam said, "Glad to hear you hold that kind of feelin for us, Mr. Witham."

"Shouldn't be a question of it in your mind." He cleared his throat and took on his brisk, businesslike face. "But, if you're here with a proposal, I'm afraid there's not much to be done. Truthfully, I've been wondering if it's going to pay me to keep my bank open."

"Well," said Sam, "maybe you could start in someplace else."

"I've thought about it," he admitted.

"Like Medford?"

"Oh, I'm not all that certain of Medford's future." The voice was still booming but now in a more tentative register.

"Way I heard it, Mr. Witham," Sam persisted, "you got a lot of property out that way. I been over again to see that farmer, Kabat, and he told me the offer you made him for the lands he was savin for his sons was so good, he just couldn't afford to turn you down."

Witham took an unnecessarily long time to clear his throat once more. "Well," he admitted, "I've got property all over this country. That's just another—"

"Why don't you cut out the horseshit, Mr. Witham?" Sam asked. "You already been told exactly where the railroad is comin through the valley."

It had just become clear that ignorant goodwill wasn't the reason for this visit, so Witham didn't add anything more.

Getting up and walking over to the single small window in the office, Sam said, as if he were speaking to someone on the other side of it, "I been thinkin about you buyin my Clinton Trail property."

The banker glanced at Tony and then at me, as if wondering whether we were partners in this attempt at extortion. When we made no gesture except a noncommittal return of his stare, he said, to Sam's back, "Now, you know there's no way that would be good business. I'll admit it's going to be prime property some day, but right now it's worth about half of what you paid for it."

"That's about all it was worth when I bought it." Sam turned and walked back to Witham's desk, laid his hands flat on it, and leaned forward. "You knew it when you loaned me the money in the first place." He stood erect, taking his hands from the desk, which relieved Witham somewhat since they had been so near him. "All the time you knew the railroad was goin to Medford. I wasn't the only one you sold out—you did it to the people here in town, too. Pumpin 'em up with the big future waitin for everybody."

Witham, misreading the conversational tones said, "Well, now Samuel, there isn't anyone who can swear I told them we had the railroad for sure. It was their business if . . ."

"Business is pretty much all you got in place of blood, isn't it?"

The banker saw his mistake. Sam's voice was flatter than ever, but now it told him that he'd been wrong in believing there was no threat. He sat back, eyeing Sam with great care. "Now, Sam, I'm truly sorry you feel this way over what was just a transaction. I truly am. And, no matter what you think, what I'll do to prove that I had as much faith in that deal as you is to write off the four hundred dollars you still owe me. Yes sir, I'll take my licking right along with you, and there isn't a man who's ever known me that wouldn't say they don't need any more proof than that of my good faith."

"Couldn't let you do that," Sam said. "It wouldn't be good business."

There was another silence that we allowed to continue while Sam reached into his back pocket and brought out a small leather poke. "There's just about enough dust in here to square our balance," he told the banker as he placed it on the corner of the desk in front of him. "And I'm goin to hand it over to clean up my account."

Another silence. Witham filled it this time by staring at the pouch as if it were a rattlesnake coiled there. It seemed to me I ought to say something in the event he thought Tony and I were there as moderating influences. "I wouldn't reach for that just yet, if I were you," I told him.

I don't believe he heard me. The man finally understood the menace in the room and was frightened enough to chatter over the last of his words, "Sam, I swear I don't want your money. Our accounts are paid up—"

"Only from me to you, but not the other way around. I ain't blamin you for what that stableman tried to do to Elva, and, besides, I was as dumb as you when it came to Celina. And I don't hold it all against you for what you did to Tommy or even Pa's shooting hisself. I've studied that last one through, and he died from a fever, not a shotgun. But there ain't any question in my mind that you're the worst two-legged skunk I ever met and you foul whatever comes near you, so . . ."

"Are you going to kill me?" The question fairly burst from Witham. It was as if in his panic he wanted to run toward the violence and that would put an end to it.

"Oh, shit, no," said Sam. Turning, he said to Tony, "Did you hear me offer to do somethin bad to Mr. Witham?"

"Not a word. As a matter of fact, you've been quite forbearing. If it were me, I might place Sewell at his door. He did put her in motion, didn't he?"

"Got to be fair," said Sam. "He didn't do all that good with her, neither." He addressed the banker again. "But you got an idea what I'm disposed to do to you, don't you?"

The banker wasn't going to gamble. His stare at Sam told us how certain he was that he was in for a bad beating.

Sam went on. "Reason I'm sayin all this is because I'd like you to remember it don't bother me to do anything—anything at all—when there's somethin important to be saved. That's why I'm here."

The banker saw this as a narrow ray of hope. "Samuel, tell me what it is. Anything I can do! I'll—"

"Shut up, Witham. I'll pull your chain when I'm ready to hear you talk, and that ain't today. Just listen. I got so much faith in your respect for your own skin, that I'm appointin you in charge of my property while I'm gone." He took some papers from the pocket that had contained the poke of gold and tossed them on the table. "These are the land contracts to the Clinton Trail property. Just like you say, that land is gonna go up. When it goes to the right price, and nobody's better'n recognizing what that'll be than you, then you sell it and give the money to my Ma."

Then I realized the reason for the cat-and-mouse game, although Witham's mind was still too clouded by fear to see what the papers on his desk meant.

While he looked at them without comprehension, Sam added, "If you got any problem in studyin out what I just said, take your time over it. I won't be around to press you none because I'm leavin here today. All you got to worry you is when I might be back, so, durin that time, I'd sure appreciate if she didn't lack for nothin."

The message was finally seeping through to Witham, but, to make certain, Sam underlined it in a way that told all of us how seriously he intended the threat. "Anything happens to her, Witham, it's your fault. And if I ain't able to come back for you, Tony or Collie will."

I said, "I'd enjoy it."

"You understand me, Witham?" Sam repeated. "I know you're figurin on movin your bank to Medford, but that ain't Ma's problem. It's yours. Cause I'll kill you, you son of a bitch."

He turned to us, saying, "Come on. We're done," and, lifting one boot, he placed it against the edge of the desk, straightened his leg, and shoved hard enough to topple it over on the banker as he crashed to the floor beneath it.

As we walked through the front door, I told him, "I'd forgotten about that Clinton Trail thing."

"I don't give a real cuss about it," he answered. "And neither does

Ma. I just wish I still didn't feel so damned wrong about diddlin his wife."

Elva and Tommy were sitting on a rock underneath the big madrone tree on Marguey's High when we came up. We joined them, and, after looking down at the valley for a while, I said, "Damn sleepy-looking little place."